LIZZIE HUXLEY-JONES
Reality Check

SIMON & SCHUSTER

London · New York · Amsterdam/Antwerp · Sydney/Melbourne · Toronto · New Delhi

First published in Great Britain by Simon & Schuster UK Ltd, 2026

Copyright © Lizzie Huxley-Jones, 2026

The right of Lizzie Huxley-Jones to be identified as author of this work has been asserted in accordance with the Copyright, Designs and Patents Act, 1988.

1 3 5 7 9 10 8 6 4 2

Simon & Schuster UK Ltd, 1st Floor,
222 Gray's Inn Road, London WC1X 8HB

For more than 100 years, Simon & Schuster has championed authors and the stories they create. By respecting the copyright of an author's intellectual property, you enable Simon & Schuster and the author to continue publishing exceptional books for years to come. We thank you for supporting the author's copyright by purchasing an authorised edition of this book.

No amount of this book may be reproduced or stored in any format, nor may it be uploaded to any website, database, language-learning model, or other repository, retrieval, or artificial intelligence system without express permission. All rights reserved. Enquiries may be directed to Simon & Schuster, 222 Gray's Inn Road, London WC1X 8HB or RightsMailbox@simonandschuster.co.uk

Simon & Schuster Australia, Sydney
Simon & Schuster India, New Delhi

www.simonandschuster.co.uk
www.simonandschuster.com.au
www.simonandschuster.co.in

The authorised representative in the EEA is Simon & Schuster Netherlands BV, Herculesplein 96, 3584 AA Utrecht, Netherlands. info@simonandschuster.nl

Simon & Schuster strongly believes in freedom of expression and stands against censorship in all its forms. For more information, visit BooksBelong.com

A CIP catalogue record for this book is available from the British Library

Paperback ISBN: 978-1-3985-3613-5
eBook ISBN: 978-1-3985-3614-2
Audio ISBN: 978-1-3985-3615-9

This book is a work of fiction. Names, characters, places and incidents are either a product of the author's imagination or are used fictitiously. Any resemblance to actual people, living or dead, events or locales is entirely coincidental.

Typeset in Bembo by M Rules
Printed and Bound in the UK using 100% Renewable Electricity at CPI Group (UK) Ltd

Praise for Reality Check

'Laden with drama, tension and explosive twists
underscored with so much heart ... Healing, gratifying
and hilarious – all with the perfect dash of spice'
Bea Fitzgerald

'Huxley-Jones writes brilliantly on the modern
mechanisms of romance, but with a timeless sapphic
love story at its heart. Sweet, soaring and splendid'
Elle McNicoll

'*Reality Check* is a tender, authentic love story full of wit
and warmth about out how to find the courage to truly
be yourself. It made me laugh, cry and swoon!'
Rowan Coleman

'*Reality Check* is a whirlwind of joy, drama and romance!
Huxley-Jones writes with such warmth and humour, and exactly
the kind of representation that makes you feel truly seen!'
Beth Reekles

'*Reality Check* is a tender, gratifying romance filled
to the brim with hope, humour and heart'
Hannah Bonam-Young

'Lizzie Huxley-Jones has created a world that is so immersive and
brilliant that I hated to leave. Sexy, inclusive and totally compelling'
Laura Wood

'*Reality Check* is perfect for fans of *Love is Blind*,
Love Island and *Married at First Sight*'
Jodi McAlister

'It was the kind of full-hearted disability representation that
dreams are made of – bursting with compassion, warmth
and wit. Deeply nuanced yet light and sparkling'
Talia Samuels

'Twists! Turns! Drama! Laughs! Romance! *Reality Check* packs just about every possible emotion into every single one of its pages and is endlessly entertaining'
Justin Myers

'*Reality Check* allows its queer, disabled and neurodiverse characters to be messy, flawed and fully human, while crafting an expertly observed satire of reality television that captures both its allure and its emotional cost'
Zac Hammett

'It brought me so much joy. I roared laughing and I also felt the whole broad spectrum of human emotions. I will be thinking about Carys and Dolly for a long time to come'
Lucy Vine

'Lizzie Huxley-Jones created the perfect balance between sweet, spicy, funny and tender, and gave me the emotional punch I crave in a book. An absolute swoonworthy read!'
Dana Hawkins

'A gorgeously written refreshing take beyond the mainstream, with beautifully drawn and endearing diverse characters you can't help but root for right away'
Eva Verde

'*Reality Check* is an absolute dream! Actual tears formed; I was laughing so much. Huxley-Jones is an auto-buy author for me now'
Rebecca Ryan

'Lizzie Huxley-Jones once again gifts us with a delightful romcom full of queer joy and endless fun. *Reality Check* is a warm-hearted hug of a book and I adored every word!'
Catherine Walsh

'A gorgeous exploration of queerness, disability and reality TV all folded into a heart-stopping love story. This is a must read!'
Elle Everhart

'A delicious slice of pure escapism! Funny and sweet, Huxley-Jones has crafted a gorgeous story with refreshingly diverse characters that jump off the page. I loved it!'
Elizabeth Drummond

'Perfect for fans of *Love is Blind* and *Married at First Sight*, this is the smart and funny sapphic slow-burn of your dreams ... it feels like you're binging a real series on streaming'
Chloe Timms

'A queer love story with the kind of representation that made me want to cheer'
Anita Kelly

'An addictive, swoony romcom bursting with drama, warmth and queer joy. *Reality Check* delivers on all fronts and does so with a vibrant inclusive love story'
Anika Hussain

'*Reality Check* is sizzling with empathy, humour and warmth. A gorgeous masquerade of a love story. Dolly and Carys are utterly believable and charming'
Sarvat Hasin

'A joyfully queer and tantalisingly spicy romcom that combines passionate sapphic yearning with a deeper examination of identity and the reality TV industry'
Morgan Owen

Lizzie Huxley-Jones is an autistic author and editor based in London. They are the author of the queer holiday romcoms *Make You Mine This Christmas* and *Under the Mistletoe with You*, the young adult summer romance *Hits Different* co-written with Tasha Ghouri, and the Waterstones Children's Book Prize shortlisted fantasy series *Vivi Conway and the Sword of Legend*. *Reality Check* is their third adult romance novel. They write joyful stories that centre queerness and disability. You can visit them at lizziehuxleyjones.com and follow them on Instagram and X @littlehux.

Also by Lizzie Huxley-Jones

Under the Mistletoe with You
Make You Mine This Christmas

Also by Lizzie Huxley-Jones and Tasha Ghouri

Hits Different

To all the autistic authors who came before and helped me find the words, and to all my autistic readers still searching for their own.

Also, this one's for me too.
Well done, kid.

CONTENT WARNINGS

While *Reality Check* is a romcom at heart, there are a number of sensitive topics within the pages that might be difficult for some people to engage with.

These include the psychological and physiological costs of autistic masking, meltdowns and overstimulation; the threat of being outed as LGBTQ+; homophobia; the difficult dynamics of being a carer and cared for; emotional manipulation by a partner.

There are also references to ableism, racism and fatphobia, though none are on-page experiences.

For Immediate Release:

***WEDDED BLISS* FINALLY SAYS I DO TO THE UK**

Today Sunset Motions Productions have announced that *Wedded Bliss*, the romantic reality TV show taking the world by storm, is headed to the UK & Ireland.

Twenty lovestruck hopefuls enter the warehouse, with multiple compatibility options, but will they find love? And how will they like their matches once they can see each other? Once engaged, couples will compete against each other for cash, venues, caterers and much more for their dream wedding.

The public will have the final say on which couple most exemplifies the core themes of *Wedded Bliss* – Communication, Cooperation and Compatibility – bagging the chosen newly-weds a grand prize nest egg of £100,000 so they can start their lives together.

The show's US hosts and aspirationally loved-up couple Karina and Lucas Nguyen will return to present the new season.

The UK & Ireland season of *Wedded Bliss* is set to air on Watchie this autumn.

[continues below]

Production Schedule for Cast (Strictly Confidential)

Please take note of the outlined production schedule below. You will be required to be present for filming on all days. If at any stage you have no mutual matches, you will be asked to leave.

Days 1–8	WAREHOUSE
Days 7–8	PROPOSALS
Days 9–11	HONEYMOON, LOCATION TBA
Days 12–17	APARTMENT PHASE
Days 18–20	WEDDINGS

Please recall, as per your contract, that the hours of filming are whatever the production team deem necessary.

Sunset Motions reserve the right to use footage captured from any part of the experiment, including those from hidden cameras, interviews and, if relevant, security footage.

If you have any concerns, please speak to your chaperones.

Chapter One

Carys

Carys Cadwallader, 27, London

Should I start talking now? Haha, this is so weird, isn't it? Sorry, I'll start now. Um. Hi, I'm Carys. I'm twenty-seven, and I'm from London. Well, I'm not from there, I'm from Wales, but I live there. I'm on Wedded Bliss *to find love . . . isn't everyone? I guess I like men who are nice and nice looking and kind. That's what I want. Someone who is kind. And likes animals! After all, I work on a city farm and sometimes have to bring home a baby lamb to bottle-feed so they've got to like animals. Does that sound alright? I don't want to sound too silly.*

In three weeks, I'll be married to the love of my life.

Well. Provided I actually *meet* him. I hope I will.

If I'm honest, I never thought I'd fall in love on television. Though, I suppose most people don't expect that, but on *Wedded Bliss* the matchmakers do all the hard work of finding men who are perfectly compatible with me, which cuts out most of the hard work.

Maybe it's a drastic way to find a soulmate, but when all else fails, what you need is courage, and the intervention of a successful reality television show.

It feels old school, kind of romantic. There's no swiping

left … Or is it right? I can never remember. And this way I don't have to *see* quite so many men holding fish. Not that I can *see* if they're holding fish for the first few dates.

Oh God, what if he's some kind of fish-holder?

That's not a thing, is it? I'm spiralling.

I try to push this out of my brain, and focus on who he will be. Or who he *is*? Presumably he already exists and they aren't just cooking up a bunch of people in the lab when we get there.

I take a deep breath. I don't have time to worry about whether the dating show I'm going on is an elaborate cover for a covert human cloning operation.

I would probably calm down if we could just get out of this traffic jam.

I had naively thought being driven around in a fancy car sent by the production company would be relaxing.

'We'll be there in about five minutes, pet,' says my driver, Victor. He must sense the barely suppressed panic radiating off me.

Hopefully he can't smell it. I fake a cough and dip my head down to surreptitiously sniff for anxiety-armpit. Not that I can smell anything over the aggressively pine-scented air freshener hanging from his rearview mirror. When I glance up at the offending item, I meet his unexpectedly kind eyes. 'Roads always gets bunged up this time of day.'

I hope he didn't just catch me sniffing my armpit.

A car horn honks violently, and I let out a long rush of air to try to steady my nerves. I very much dislike getting stuck in transit and losing control. You can't *will* a halted tube to move; trust me, I've tried. There's nothing I can do about the gridlock. And even if I accept it, surrendering to the lack of control, I still get sweaty and panicky like now. There's no winning.

I know it could be worse; I could be one of the people stuck on a toilet-less Lizzie Line train for hours who had to designate one corner a makeshift loo.

I suspect Victor is still watching me, so I force a smile that I'm not convinced wasn't a Cheshire Cat-like grimace. Oh well. I tried.

Victor cranks up the air con and fresh cool air rushes across my hot face. I block out the traffic and try to focus on what matters. Falling in love and getting married is what every little girl dreams of. I might be about to feel the spark, those fireworks that tell you that man is The One and you're on track for a beautiful wedding, family, life. The whole shebang.

Congestion is temporary; true love is forever. That's probably on a pillow somewhere.

It still counts as true love, no matter how you find it, right? Not all of us can Disney princess it. If I lose a shoe in London, that's gone forever and I'm barefoot. Even if I did find a Prince Philip (Disney version, not the deceased royal family member), the idea of having hundreds of women try on *my* shoe is ... well, gross.

I think I'm spiralling again.

I need something to do with my hands that isn't picking at bits of my skin, so I smooth out the wide skirt of my dress, hoping the tucks and pleats still lie where they are supposed to, and that the bum isn't too wrinkled.

I try to tune into the London skyline and work out how far we might be from the city farm I work at, or my house share. There's no clear starry sky here, so navigation is all by buildings and landmarks. But try as I might, I can't orient myself.

A driver behind us beeps their horn in a staccato beat, and each honk makes me jump. My heart beats wildly out of control.

I tap on my sternum in a steady rhythm to try to ground myself.

Don't lose it, Carys.

I'm supposed to practise self-compassion when I'm finding things hard – that's what my therapist used to say. I give it a go. Yes, I'm nervous but it's *normal* to be nervous before big life changes. This is a pretty big life change. Not just the romance but the prospect of sharing part of a window-less East London warehouse with nine other women I'll meet for the first time today. That might be the scariest part of all.

'As we're stuck here, why don't you tell me about this show you're going on?' Victor's voice is a beacon, calling me back to safety.

I'm so grateful for the distraction. I know most people think autistic people hate small talk, but I live for it. I think that's why I've done so well on the farm, where I'm constantly meeting new people, reeling out animal facts and pleasantries so we share a tiny moment of joy before they go back to their lives. Those kinds of fleeting moments are much easier than building something bigger. There's no pressure.

'It's a dating show. *Wedded Bliss*, have you heard of it?' I say, hearing the rasp in my throat.

He shakes his head. 'No, I haven't. Is it like *Love Island*? Are they going to jet you off to a nice hotel?' Victor glances again at the SatNav. 'Poplar isn't their usual sunny destination.'

I can't help but laugh at that. 'Basically, I'm going to find my husband.'

I've practised this conversation plenty of times, long before I told my family or my colleagues, who up until my last day at work thought I was off backpacking and had gifted me more DEET and factor 50 than I might ever need. Luckily, the global success of the US seasons meant that most of them knew where I was going.

Turns out my sisters, Del and Ang, are big fans, deep in the gossip. I told them I didn't want to know much; I want to go in without any preconceptions. The only thing they told me is that before the UK, Sunset Motions did a season in Australia that was a total disaster with only one wedding, and that couple broke up at the altar. Awful.

Despite their requests, obviously I didn't ask any of the production team interviewing me for behind-the-scenes info. I don't want to be a bother.

Anyway, I must say enough that something clicks for Victor. 'Oh! Is that the one with the screens that go down every few dates so you end up seeing them and kissing before you get engaged? I think my Shreya watches that.'

'That's the one,' I say, my knee bouncing with nerves. At first, I'd thought falling in love through voice alone was romantic, and now I'm just worried about everything hinging on me not saying the wrong thing.

'Best thing I ever did was get married.' He raises his hand from the steering wheel to show off a burnished gold band on his ring finger. 'Forty years, four kids, a few grandkids on the way. Luckiest man alive, I am.'

Wow. That's the kind of life I dream of. A family of your own built together. A whole life of *lives*.

'Any advice for me?'

'On life in general or marriage in particular?'

'I don't think we have enough time for you to fix my life,' I laugh.

What do I want to know? You'd think I'd have talked to my parents about this. They met as teenagers and are about to hit their fortieth wedding anniversary, but when I told them I was going on the show, we got distracted with Del and Ang explaining what it was. Plus, the extent of their interest in my dating life is asking how the revolving door of men I see once is going.

'What should I be looking for in someone that might mean they make a good partner?'

Victor nods slowly as he ponders my question. 'Some people

think it's about liking the same things, that kind of hobby matching, but I don't agree.'

This throws me. 'Really?' Wasn't compatibility partly about liking the same things?

'Oh yeah. Shreya has her Pilates and brunches with her friends and I like going to watch the cricket. We've done those things together before, but she hates sitting around in the stands and I am more of a jogging in the morning man. It's not that we don't like spending time together, but we have our own things separate from our relationship.'

I'm not sure I'm entirely following him, but I nod along eagerly so he doesn't stop.

'We have our separate lives as individuals, but we've *made* a life together. And to do that, you need someone you can collaborate with. That's what a relationship is: a collaboration,' he explains, and that part makes sense to me. A shared life is like a group project you're both invested in, I think. 'For some people that's a partner who challenges them or complements their own personality, but at the end of the day, they've got to be someone who always has your back and isn't afraid to tell you when you're wrong.'

All this sounds right and very smart in terms of the big picture stuff, but if you don't like the same things, that seems like a day-to-day problem. You can't have one without the other, surely? What would you even do for dates? Maybe Shreya and Victor are just obscenely lucky people who don't worry about things like this. Couldn't be me.

'Thank you, Victor. I'll keep that in mind,' I say, deciding to politely disregard the hobbies part. After all, you still have to talk about what you like in your daily life. I could end up with a fish botherer *and* have to hear about it.

'Carys,' Victor says, catching my eyes in the mirror. I know he means it nicely, because some people love eye contact, but

I feel like he's peering into my soul when he says, 'I hope you find a nice man.'

I'm about to say *me too* when both my thoughts and mouth are interrupted by a very loud, long beep of a car horn that jolts my body like an electric shock.

Victor winds down his window, and leans out. 'There's some commotion up ahead. Maybe there's been an accident?'

I crane my neck but can't see any blue lights, or hear sirens. 'I hope they're okay,' I offer, because that's the sort of thing you're supposed to say rather than wonder how much longer it'll take.

I try to ignore the hot fizzing in my hands. I hate being late. My phone's clock confirms it. It might just be by a few minutes, but still. I don't want to get in trouble or let anyone down. Is it premature to call someone yet?

It's going to be weird without my phone. I'm not massively one for social media, but having an audiobook on the go while I'm mucking out or fixing fences keeps my brain happy. Today I'll hand in my phone, and I'll get it back when I'm engaged or leaving matchless.

At the top of my screen are previews of messages sent to my family WhatsApp, 24 Penrhos, named after our address, which seems like bad personal security.

I don't want to interrupt their chat about Dai the butcher's impassioned affair with Phyllis from the chemist from the town over, but this is probably my last chance to say goodbye.

Carys

> Hiya, I'm nearly at the warehouse. I'll text you in a few weeks, if not before. Remember you can call Rebecca Wallbank my chaperone if there's an emergency. Love you all.

None of them questioned why I was going on *Wedded Bliss*, which was probably the biggest confirmation of my tragic status. The only thing that spurred a reaction out of Mum was when I told her the show didn't pay for makeup and wardrobe. Luckily, I've been working on my extensive vintage dress collection for years, and being dolled up every day will be a nice change from fleeces and leggings.

Del

> Traa babs. Don't come home with a dickhead.

Ang

> Or the villain!! No Nasty Nicks or Adam Collards!

Del

> How will she know who the villain is? Isn't that all in the editing?

Mum

> don't get Carys'd away, have a good time, love you muchly.

I wince. My parents used to say that to me when I was a sometimes-too-impulsive kid with my head in the stars. Given I'm on my way to film a dating show where I marry someone, the horse might have bolted already.

Ang

Look for the red flags, Caz!!!

Del

Ask about his credit score.

Carys

I'll try! Wish me luck.

Mum

Find a nice boy, like a doctor or a dentist, love you lots.

Del

Really? Someone who looks in people's holes all day? Caz you can do better than that.

Ang

Caz looks at animal holes all day. Match made in heaven.

Carys

I really don't look in that many holes.

Mum

girls please stop saying holes

It's not the first time they've told me to ask about financial stuff, but given I live off my overdraft and spend most of my day working with sheep, I'd feel hypocritical ruling someone out for their job. Unless they work for some kind of evil political party. We all have limits.

Before I can put my phone away, my group chat with just my sisters, affectionately called CadWallies, lights up.

Del

And don't forget to ask for reasonable adjustments if you need them.

Del

I know you won't but still.

Del

You should.

Ang

What she said, also don't kiss frogs x

Del

Stay on message! >:(

Ang

I am!!!

Ang

That's important too!!!!

They know me too well, because obviously I'm not going to do that. And yes, maybe I did lie to my sisters just a *tiny* bit by insinuating that production know I'm autistic, which they do not. But in my defence, I didn't want them to worry. This way is better and I didn't *technically* lie.

Carys

I will be okay! I have a chaperone to support me :)

Truth is, I'm not going to ask for anything special. Everyone gets access to therapists if we need them, as well as a dedicated member of the production team to look after us. I'm sure that will be enough. My chaperone Reb seems nice enough.

I'm not ashamed of being autistic. I just didn't want to risk being knocked out of the audition process. Or worse, risking the show positioning me as some kind of inspirational poster child for autistic adults finding love – *The Undateables* part two. Barf. If that little omission means my scenes aren't scored by cutesy, kid-show music about how adorable and sweet hearted it is that a disabled person can find love, then good. I'll go stealth. If I need help with something, I'll just talk about it on an individual issue level like 'I'm overwhelmed' or 'I have a migraine'. Stuff that neurotypical people can understand easier than 'I am upset because I don't have my usual cup'.

The warehouse stage is only eight real days, even if they call it two weeks on the show. It'll be *fine*.

I doubt I'll get found out. It's not like neurotypical people know what autistic people are like anyway. I did the psychological assessment that all the contestants have to do, to make sure we're safe to go on the show, and I made sure to answer the opposite way to the truth on a few things, just to be safe. There was no follow up, so I guess I did a good job of masking.

I just get read as slightly kooky. That's what people have been saying about me since I was a kid. *She's a character. She's unique. Oh, isn't she like Jess from New Girl.* I can live in those awkward, eccentric girl stereotypes if it gets me what I want.

A final message comes through to the family group chat.

Dad

Bye.

Effusive as ever.

Five minutes pass, then ten. The back of my thighs are sweating so much that I'm sticking to the seat, and yet the air con is so high I'm in danger of arriving at the warehouse looking like I have two of the Eryri peaks in my bra. I'm back to tapping on my chest, wondering why people honk when it just makes everyone so upset.

Suddenly everyone is beeping in a cacophony so body-rattling that I almost vomit all over my sundress. That or meltdown, and I'm not sure which is worse. Vomit is easier to explain away, but then it's everyone else's problem.

God, I can't deal with this. I curl up in my seat and shove my fingers in my ears, keeping my eye on the silent, slow clouds above.

My strange position means I see her face, framed in the window. She steps out of the car next to us, I think. Her icy blonde hair is cut into a sheer bob, her mouth a mirrored red lipsticked slash.

I sit up, and see the slinky scarlet dress wrapped around her curves. She glows, I swear she does. It's not *just* my overstimulated brain warping the colours; she is a Goddess of Wrath.

I can't keep my eyes off her, spinning round up onto my knees to watch her through the back window as she storms over to the perma-honking car behind ours, and slams her fist down on the bonnet. 'Can youse shut the *fuck* up?!'

Woah.

The driver holds up his hands in apology and quite a lot of terror, mouthing *SORRY* over and over.

Imagine being that brave. It must be easier to be brave when you're tall.

There's a chorus of cheering around us.

Even Victor applauds. 'Now *that* is a woman.'

'Are blondes your type?' I ask, then regret it. You can't just ask someone that. I'm not on *Wedded Bliss* yet.

But he laughs. 'Any woman who puts a dickhead in her place is the kind I want to go home to. Having someone set you straight when you're out of line?' He makes a noise that would confound any spelling bee participant. 'A beautiful woman who can see right through your bullshit? *That* is my type, Miss Carys. Mind you, I'm about twenty years too old for her.'

I smile at him. 'Is that what Shreya is like?'

'Oh, you bet. I was a total mess when we met – what twenty-year-old man isn't? But she said this is how it is and how it's gonna be, and if you want that you gotta be this way.' He laughs and shakes his head. 'Boy, did I get in line quickly!'

'I can't imagine you being that much of a mischief.'

He laughs, but it drops off quickly. 'Oh now, where is she going?'

I follow his gaze, as our blonde saviour storms through the rows of stationary cars.

Her driver gets out his car, waving his arms furiously.

Victor whistles. 'Hey! Mike!'

'Vic! What is this business?' Mike yells, and I wonder if all car drivers in London know each other. 'Come back please, Miss! I can't leave the car!'

Victor sucks his teeth. I guess he can't either.

Maybe I should go after her? I can't see where she's gone. My hands still shake with adrenaline, and it's not got quieter outside. I peer through the front window, trying to see where she is.

And that's when I see a plastic iced coffee cup tumbling out of the car in front of me onto the grassy verge, lid still attached. Perfect bait for a small animal to get stuck in.

Something in me snaps. You don't work on a city farm without developing some strong feelings about littering.

I can do this. I am a champion of nature!

I barely hear Victor's protests as I get out the car, nor register how numb my legs are. Channelling the blonde Goddess, I strut up to the metal barrier at the roadside and lean down to pick up the cup with my fingertips.

The barely-older-than-teenagers react with horror to my knock on the window. They panic bicker for a moment, and I knock again so they know I'm not leaving.

The passenger window rolls down very slowly, releasing Billie Eilish's husky vocals into the air like perfume.

I hold out the clear cup spattered with iced coffee, and with a deranged smile I say, 'You dropped this?'

They stare at me, open mouthed. What, like they've never seen an angry girl in a tea dress berate them for littering?

The passenger gulps and takes it from me, setting it back in the empty cupholder, which is even *more* infuriating – why litter when you had space?!

'Thanks,' he mumbles. 'I mean, sorry!'

'Don't litter! It's bad for the environment,' I say in my best teacher voice. 'And Billie Eilish protested for the climate with Greta Thunberg. You can't like "Birds of a Feather" and litter at the same time.'

'He won't do it again!' says the panicked driver, leaning across the handbrake towards me, as though I might somehow have a direct line to Billie herself. 'I didn't even know he did it!'

'Dean, shut *up*,' the passenger hisses.

'You're the one who littered!' Dean grumbles.

I let them argue for a bit before clearing my throat to get their attention. 'Just don't do it again.'

And with that, I walk away. God, that felt *good*.

I strut round to Victor's rolled-down window. 'Did your dream woman come back?'

'Hey now, my dream woman is back home,' he says, as though I'm going to tell Shreya. 'Mike's charge is still missing.'

I'm still hopped up on adrenaline from the thrill of scuppering a mild environmental crime, so I say, 'I'll go find out what's going on.'

Victor catches my wrist. 'Please, Carys, just get back in the car. We just need to wait it out. I don't want you to get hurt on my watch.'

'I'm a first aider and someone could be injured,' I insist. 'I'll come back at the first sign of danger, I promise.'

He sighs. 'Alright, just be careful.'

I swear I hear Mike mutter *what is up with the women today* but I choose to ignore it as I walk ahead.

The problem becomes pretty apparent as I reach the front of the traffic jam. One car is jack-knifed across both lanes, wedged close enough to the barriers that no cars can pass.

My emergency first response training kicks in. There's no sign of collision or fire. The car isn't damaged, in fact.

I'm relieved not to hear any screams of pain, but instead, on the other side of the car, are two women, one on a Lime bike, arguing very loudly. I can't believe I couldn't hear them from the car.

And watching the whole scene is the golden Goddess herself.

I take a deep breath and walk up to her. 'Is anyone hurt?'

She turns her head, and adjusts her gaze right down to me. Even in my heels, I'm nearly a foot shorter than her. The Goddess thumbs at the yelling women. 'Are they yours?'

'Them? No, I was in the car next to you and wanted to make sure . . .' *That you're okay? Is that weird to say?* 'I mean, I'm a qualified first aider. I came to help.'

'Oh.' When she shakes her head, her icy hair flicks about like the tip of a flame. 'Not physically.'

'Oh? Good. I think?'

'A lotta hurt feelings, though.'

'What?' I say, just as I hear the one on the bike yell, 'I just want my cat back and for you to fuck off out of my LIFE.'

My ears prick up. I take animal welfare very seriously.

As if for emphasis, she rips off her helmet and flings it down on the concrete, where it bounces dully. So dully that I think it's probably not a very good helmet.

'You agreed we could share custody,' whines the Car Woman, pressing her hands to her forehead. 'What happened to an amicable breakup? What happened to doing the best for Leonard?'

'That was before you *fucked* my ex!'

The blonde Goddess beside me sharply takes in air. 'Sheesh.'

I realise that I'm watching some kind of interpersonal drama unfold. 'I think we should intervene,' I say, my voice in steady emergency mode. I've always been good at managing Situations, probably because my life is just a constant stream of Situations. 'Before things escalate further.'

The Goddess's gaze on me is like being stripped bare. I've never been one for eye contact, but I can't look away from her. It's like she's seeing through the layers of me. I don't know how to describe it in a way that makes sense or sounds *good*.

'Dolly,' she says, and I realise this must be her name. I must admit this isn't what I was expecting. Freyja, Eris or Athena feel more appropriate.

Dolly sticks her hand out, and for a second I wonder whether to shake it or kiss the back of it, like I'm swearing fealty. Luckily, I remember to be normal. I hope it wasn't too sweaty a handshake.

'Carys. Shall we?'

'After you,' she says, and we walk over to the yelling women.

They're still so deep in the argument that neither of them seem to notice our arrival.

'You *know* that Lily and I have always had a connection. That is all before I even met you!' wails the Car Woman.

I can't quite tell if they're arguing about the ex or the cat. 'Excuse—' I begin, but they barrel through.

'Oh, and you can't change how you act towards a person because you want to protect someone else's feelings?'

'You didn't protect mine!'

Inexplicably, they both burst into loud wailing tears.

Dolly strides forward to stand between the crying women. It's impressive scene management. Perhaps she's done first aid training too. 'Okay, ladies. This has gone on long enough. Are either of you hurt?'

'Only in my *soul*,' yells the Bike Woman between sobs.

'That must be dreadful. But I meant physically so Cherry over here can check you over.'

I get a flutter in my stomach as she nods over to me. 'It's Carys,' I say but I don't think anyone hears.

Car Woman holds up a purplish hand sadly. 'I caught my finger in the door when I was slamming it for emphasis.'

'Do you have a first aid kit in the back of your car?' I ask, and she shakes her head. What kind of irresponsible person doesn't have a first aid kit to hand at all times? I suppose, the kind of person who'd stop their car across traffic to have an argument in the street.

'I do,' shouts a man leaning out of his car window behind me. The boot pops open automatically, and I'm grateful to see a new, in-date first aid kit awaiting me. This is the kind of man I'm looking for. Someone organised, who pays attention to things.

'Ow,' whimpers Car Woman, and I suddenly remember I'm supposed to be helping her, not mentally listing criteria for my future husband.

There's a crash as the Lime bike falls to the floor. 'Sorry, it was just really heavy,' wails the Bike Woman.

'I'll take Car Woman,' I say to Dolly, keeping my voice low. 'You take Bike Woman.'

Dolly snorts. 'Not cyclist and motorist?'

'That would make more sense, yes.'

'But be less linguistically fun.' She flashes me a smile. 'Bike Woman it is.'

Car Woman leans against her car, sniffling and pink-cheeked. Her light brown hair is pulled back into an Ariana Grande-style ponytail that pulls her eyebrows into a surprised angle. I worry for her hairline.

'Can I check over your hand?' I ask.

She nods sulkily but doesn't speak. Her finger, while purple, doesn't seem to be broken. I check over her whole hand for good measure.

'Nothing serious. Just a bit dented, but you've broken the skin, so I'm going to wrap it up,' I explain to her, as I flick through the kit for wipes and bandages.

A few tears land on the tarmac between us, and I feel the urge to hug this beautiful screaming lady. Sure, she's made poor choices, including but not limited to sleeping with someone she shouldn't and holding a cat hostage, but she seems so sad and small.

She winces as I clean her punctured skin. 'Thank you,' she says finally, as I tape up the bandage to protect the cut from dirt.

'I'm sorry about your cat situation,' I say, even though I'm not sure she's the wronged party. Perhaps neither of them are. I should apologise to the cat.

'Leonard deserves the world and we've not been very good parents to him,' Car Woman sobs. 'I didn't mean to cause a scene. But I saw her cycling, and I had to talk to her – she's blocked me everywhere. How are we supposed to co-parent under those conditions?'

I nod sagely, as though I have any understanding of the complexities of long-term relationships. 'It sounds like she's quite upset over you and her ex too?' I accidentally say as I'm zipping up the first aid kit. Sometimes, words just fall out of my mouth before I can think them through, especially if I'm distracted.

She doesn't seem to take it too badly. 'If we all avoided everyone's exes, lesbians would die out everywhere. We'd all have to become nuns. Though they probably were lesbians too.' She pauses and looks at me. 'Maybe I should become a nun?'

I'm not sure if she's truly asking for my advice but I think, as a straight girl, this is outside my remit. Maybe being a nun is a normal thing lesbians do. It's not like I know many lesbians. I mean, I probably *do* but it's not like I go around asking, especially not at work where it would be inappropriate. Though, one of the weekend girls has a flag badge that I *think* is a gay one. Not that I'm very good at country flags either. For all I know, it could be Croatia.

And my main non-work friends are girls I met in first term at university, all now married to men they were dating then. If I'm honest, four weddings in a row might have had a teensy influence on me applying to *Wedded Bliss*. My sisters date men too.

I try to be a good ally. I'll always sign a petition, and I donate regularly to the Switchboard hotline. I've never been to Pride, but I've been invited once by Ollie who works in the farm café, so that's quite good, I think.

'I know you didn't technically crash, but I'm just going to do a quick neurological exam just to be safe.'

'Is this because I jackknifed my car and talked about being a nun?'

I can't help but laugh. 'No, no. Just being safe. Follow my finger with your eyes,' I tell her. 'What's your name?'

'Miri,' she says. 'And that's Sara.'

'Okay, Miri, I'm Carys.'

'Not Cherry?'

'I think she misheard.' I glance back at where Dolly awkwardly pats Sara on the shoulder as she bawls. 'Did you break up recently?'

Miri releases a fresh barrage of tears that splatter all over her crop top. 'A month ago. And it was amicable. Well ... I thought so. Sara thinks I don't want to settle down.'

I position her along the road's centre line. 'Walk along this towards me.' Miri complies and thankfully walks evenly. Neuro exam clear. Just an obvious case of heartbreak, and battered finger.

'And I know sleeping with Lily was stupid. I only want to be with Sara and Leonard. I'm just ... frightened.' She shakes her head and her ponytail flicks like an angry cat's tail. 'I guess that's why ... I did all this. It's not just the cat.'

I'm not sure how to politely suggest not resuming the screaming. 'You stopped traffic to talk to her. So, go talk to her. Be honest and tell her what you told me.'

She sniffs, and the tip of her nose wiggles. 'Do you think she'll want me back?'

'You won't know until you ask.'

'Okay.' Miri shakes out her shoulders. 'Will you come with me?'

We reconvene between car and bike. Despite the traffic jam, Miri and Sara need privacy, I think.

I return the first aid kit to the helpful man's car, and Dolly follows me. 'Do you think they'll be okay?' I ask, as the boot closes slowly.

'I've seen worse.'

'Worse than causing a major traffic incident?'

She tilts her head. 'It's really more a minor incident.'

It's such a funny thing to say. Perhaps she's some kind of couples counsellor, or hostage negotiator.

'Queer girls can be vicious,' Dolly laughs, and I'm not sure if I'm allowed to laugh in agreement, even if I don't know if I do agree.

'Oh,' I say uselessly. 'This is all new to me.'

'Lesbians or public fights?'

'Both.' We both laugh then. 'I guess I'm just a homebody.'

'A homebody first aider in a killer dress,' she says, and I feel heat rush to my cheeks.

Before I can reply, cheers sound around us. Between car and bike stand Miri and Sara kissing, a kiss of apologies and wishes and hopes and wants.

I really hope they can make it work.

'Me too,' says Dolly, and I realise I've said it out loud.

I know I shouldn't stare, but I am captivated by their kiss. When they break apart to clear the road, their arms outstretch so their fingertips touch until the last minute.

Like they never really want to let go of each other again.

That's the kind of love I want.

We dash back to our respective cars, as the traffic starts moving quickly.

'Oh, *finally*,' says Mike. 'Victor and I were worried the show was going to have our necks.'

The show?

Dolly's red lips flicker into a smirk. 'Off to a warehouse you definitely didn't have to sign an NDA about, Cherry?'

It all makes sense now. The dress, the hair, the general Goddess demeanour. Dolly is so beautiful, she was made for television.

I nod my head a little too enthusiastically, like a toy dog on a car dashboard.

'Well,' she says flatly. Something has changed, but I can't read her; autistic occupational hazard.

Is she worried about us knowing each other? Production did background checks, and I can imagine making sure we didn't know each other was part of it. If they found out about this, maybe they'd make one of us leave? That would be unfair. Especially when we're just helping.

I step a little closer to her. 'Let's keep this between us.'

It's her turn to nod, though she does it slowly, considering. I catch a lovely scent, maybe her shampoo or perfume. 'We'll be perfect strangers. Just to be safe.'

'Just in case.'

The traffic has started moving, so we get into our cars.

Everything that just happened hits me at once – the new situation, the new people, Dolly, the hum of the traffic. I practise my breathing, my tapping, and feel the rush in my blood ebb. When I glance out the window, I'm pretty sure that Victor has been driving us in circles to buy me time.

Despite that, when we finally do pull up in front of a redbrick warehouse, I'm still not ready to be a person.

It's busy outside. Furniture is being unloaded from vans, and crates of water bottles are stacked high, passed by people shouting into walkie talkies.

Someone waves Victor into a parking spot, and once in, he looks back at me through the mirror. 'Need a moment?'

I nod silently.

And so, Victor makes a very slow million-point turn, manoeuvring the car 180 degrees into the space.

It's just enough time to get a hold of myself. Yes, I'm late but I'm here, actually *here*, where I'm going to find a husband.

'You can do this,' Victor says softly to me, and I believe him.

'I think you're my guardian angel,' I say, and he winks. I'm going to miss him. Perhaps the only reasonable adjustment I'd be brave enough to request is having an emotional-support Victor on set.

'I think you were an angel for someone else today. You've a good heart, Carys. I'll be watching for you!'

My door opens, revealing a very tall woman whose hair is scraped up into a messy bun on the top of her head.

'Carys!' Reb cries, pulling me up and out the car. I've met my chaperone Reb before as it's her job to look after me while we film. 'Wow, you look gorgeous. Doesn't she look gorgeous?' She directs the second part to Victor, who has got out the car to open the boot.

'That she does.' He sounds so proud that I want to cry.

Reb glances at her phone, and growls.

'Everything alright?' I ask.

'Oh. Yeah. Don't worry about the growling and scowling. It's just work, isn't it.' She laughs heartily, and I try to work out where her accent is from. Midlands, I think? Reb slips her phone into the back pocket of her light denim jeans, and takes the suitcases from Victor.

'Give 'em hell, Carys,' Victor says, gently placing a hand

on my shoulder. I pull him into a hug. Maybe it's not socially acceptable, but I want to say goodbye. I hope I get to see him again.

He drives away, and I look up at the warehouse, trying to take in every brick, every blacked-out window. When you're about to start the rest of your life you want to remember every detail. We pass crew members who wave politely at me, and I make a note to try to learn all their names when we get going.

'Need anything before we go in?' Reb asks, gently dragging me from my thoughts.

I shake my head, and hold out my phone for her to take. 'I'm ready.'

Reb pockets my phone, holds open the great glass door for me, and I slip through into the dark.

Time to go find my future husband.

Time to start my life.

Chapter Two

Dolly

Dolly Doherty, 28, Liverpool

Three interesting things about me? I'm a professionally trained chef, so you'll never go hungry with me. I have – hopefully now – over a million followers on Instagram and TikTok where I share lifestyle content, including recipes. And I might have a cutesy-sounding name, but like Ms Parton herself, I'm no pushover.

Why did I come on Wedded Bliss? *To find a partner, of course. I'm very career driven, and I either want to find someone who will match that energy, or be happy to support me in that, you know, a cute little house husband with his own hobbies? I'm mostly attracted to personality and drive, so no, I'm not afraid of forming connections without seeing them first.*

Do I think my ambition might scare some people off? Boys, maybe? But I'm looking for a man.

Today is *not* the vibe.

Mediating in a traffic jam-causing cat fight between exes was not really how I expected to begin my first day of *Wedded Bliss*, but when did my life ever go to plan?

I feel sweaty. According to the mirror in my compact, my makeup is intact but I look rattled. I was going for the effortless, in-control look celebrities wear on the red carpet. In the great words of Paris Hilton, this is not hot.

God, I wish I could call my mum, even if all we'd do is argue about the show again. Our last conversation was about me making it to London. Not unloving, just a little terse because I know she's just worried about me.

Come the fuck on, Dolly. Get your head in the game. You already triple-checked that the bills are paid. Auntie Carol is going to look after Mum. No one is going to find out you're a lesbian.

That little internal pep talk does nothing. My head is *not* in the game. I am, quite seriously, wigged out. And I'm not the kind of person to be bothered – I pride myself on keeping calm. Usually.

Times like this, I wish I still had some proper friends to call.

I need to get it together. You're on your own kid, and all that.

My driver's phone loudly announces in a twangy accent the next directions, and it throws me for such a loop that I snap out of my funk.

'Mike, what made you pick Australian?'

'For what?' He eyes me in the mirror with suspicion, like I'm about to jump out the car again to assist more women in distress. We didn't get off to the best start.

I point at the phone. 'Your phone. Are you Australian? You don't seem Australian.'

'It's aspirational, isn't it?'

'To be ... Australian?'

He looks at me like this is the most obvious fucking thing in the world.

'Well, good for you.' I can hardly yuck his yum considering the state of my life choices.

Though it is a little ironic, considering my main current

touchpoint for Australia is the failed season of *Wedded Bliss* that ended up with only a single wedding out of a possible ten, during which the bride dumped the groom mid-vows. The show wasn't renewed there.

With luck, I can help ensure the UK series is a success. That's why I'm here.

If I can get my shit in order. Breaking up that fight, then the kiss and make up ... It feels like the universe is sending a very pointed reminder of who I *really* am.

And I'm shutting that Dolly back in the closet, over a decade since I came out of it ...

This will all be worth it. Focus on Mum. If I find the right man, our lives will be radically different.

I can do this.

The cute little redhead I'm going to be living with for the next few weeks could be a problem.

Hopefully she didn't clock me. Straight girls rarely do. And I'm probably overthinking this. After all, why would she care what I'm up to when she's got ten men lined up for her?

I'd forgotten how stressful living in stealth is; I had chalked much of it up to teenage hormone surges making everything feel more dramatic.

But then, I'm not out on my socials. That started as a privacy thing, really. And, if I'm honest, I know that playing the tradwife straight men yearn for helps my views. Bit of cake, bit of tit? I could be their not-quite-Nigella in the kitchen, mildly supporting their careers and not talking back to any of their rancid political opinions. That's part of the fantasy of it all. Everyone reads me as politically engaged, community focused. Presumed-Straight Dolly.

I know how to be her, I've been playing her a long time. And I can be her on television, full time.

I can do this.

I'm just terrified of production clocking that I'm perhaps not as heterosexual as I've claimed to be, because if they find out I'm a lesbian, I'm out (in more ways than one). I know production take pains to cast people who aren't just there for the money. I've fooled them so far.

There's no failsafe there. I don't think claiming bisexuality (a different kind of lie) would play well either, because let's be real, reality TV likes queer people as gimmicks and not much else.

I cannot afford to be edited down. I'm here to be a beloved main character. I'm here to start something.

My cousin Jas has tried to coach me on the ways of the heterosexuals. It's not like I've not been surrounded by straight people culture my whole life, but I've not had to actively *pretend* to be one either. Well, not since I was about fourteen, though I'm pretty sure everyone saw through that, what with my scholarly interest in the work of Kristen Stewart.

Anyway, what I've gleaned from Jas is that many straight relationships sound abjectly miserable. 'Me and this one, we've had our ups and downs.' Never mind the toxic masculinity of bill etiquette, I'm pretty sure many men don't even like their partners. Misogyny and patriarchy have a lot to answer for. Too bad those kinds of men are reality TV bread and butter. I can only imagine some of the absolute ding-dongs I'm about to meet.

I can see from the map on Mike's Australian phone that we're nearly at the 'undisclosed warehouse location'.

My head is still in need of a good wobble. I go to wind down the windows for the breeze, and this time Mike really does lock the back doors.

'Oh, come on,' I groan. 'I just wanted some fresh air.'

The door *thunks* with the sound of unlocking. 'You won't find that in East London.'

I quickly realise he's not wrong, but then we're pulling up.

The warehouse reminds me of the Albert Docks, regenerated industrial buildings for flats or trendy art spaces for the hip and middle class. Though here, the windows are blocked out to make it easier to film. That and it stops us tracking the time of day. Production are in control of *everything*. All the power is in their hands. It might not be *Big Brother*, but they're always watching, or whatever the slogan was.

The door is flung open by my cheerily plummy handler, Louise (not Lou). I slide out with all the elegance I can muster, which is quite tricky when you're in a body-hugging dress, are pushing six foot in heels and are categorically not built like a waify starlet.

'Darling, hello!' She welcomes me with a hug and a kiss on each cheek. Very European, very Chelsea. 'How *are* you?'

And finally, I find myself again. On-Camera Dolly is all charm, and a bad bitch. I slip into her like an old coat.

'Excited to meet my man,' I say, flashing a smile. I will be the Nation's goddamn Sweetheart, and everyone will believe I am desperately in love.

'I bet you are,' Louise laughs, throwing back her flowy, horse-mane hair. 'Let's get this party started, shall we?'

Mike unceremoniously dumps my things on the ground, and drives away in his Australian car.

'Charming,' Louise says.

I reach for my bags, which Louise whisks away from me. 'Allow me. Let's not ruck up that killer dress, darling.'

'Thanks. How are you?'

'Positively wired, I've had three espressos!' She extends her perfectly manicured hand. 'Now, let's not make this more painful than it has to be.' She wants my phone.

'Can I just shoot my mum a last text?'

'Naturally, sweets.' Louise, after all, knows about my home life, and will be checking in with my family for me.

Dolly

> Just arrived at the warehouse. Chat in two weeks. Don't forget your meds. Love you xxxx

It's still early so chances are she's asleep, but I wish I knew she was okay. I'm not used to leaving her for long. I'm glad Auntie Carol and Jas have her.

'Let's take a selfie to document the first day?' I suggest, and Louise gleefully agrees. We both know behind-the-scenes content always does well; I've seen Ariana's many, *many* Instagram carousels of *Wicked* photos.

No reply from Mum, so I hand my phone over to Louise, who puts it into her back pocket. 'Rather you than me, babe.'

After cultivating a whole career online, it feels very weird to be sans phone. My work phone is locked up at home because, frankly, I didn't feel comfortable handing over my whole career, even to someone as seemingly reliable as Louise.

There's not much on my personal phone beyond the possibly AI generated, heavily pixelated pictures overlaid with 'great quotes' Auntie Carol downloads from Facebook to send to Jas and me, and all my texts from Mum.

'You're the first girl going in,' Louise tells me as we walk towards the front doors. 'Slight change of plan: no filming today. We'll reshoot arrivals tomorrow. Gives you a chance to settle in.'

That's a bit of a relief, because the nice dress I'd worn for *just in case* is looking a little less nice now I've sweated and stomped and sat in the back of a cab in it.

'Let's go, I can stake out the best spots,' I say with a winning smile.

After one last look at the sky, I follow Louise into the warehouse, and even though I have seen every publicly available series of *Wedded Bliss*, and read every article interviewing production, it's still a little eerie to see the set replicated here.

We pass the famous long corridor with its many doors, behind which are the date rooms. I hold in a squeak of recognition when I spy the setup for post-date interviews, with its strange fake set backdrop. All these key spaces, little clusters of activity just waiting to happen. I was right about the blacked-out windows and can feel my body craving vitamin D already. After a kitchen area and some utility rooms, we turn to one last door.

The sign on it says *Female Contestant Dormitory*.

This is where I'm going to live for the next two weeks. Or well, two show weeks, which equates to about eight or nine days' filming.

I can do this. It's just another job, even if this job is being fake-married to someone for the next twelve months, or until six months after the show has officially aired (whichever is longer), as set out in the contracts that all of us signed. This is simply business.

I can do anything for twelve months, even marry a man.

For Mum.

'Ta-daaa,' Louise sings as she pushes open the door.

For a window-less space I need to share with nine other women, it's nice in here. It very much looks like the ideal of a converted warehouse loft, with exposed brick walls and lots of negative space and good lighting. As expected, there's not a single clock.

There's a kitchen with a big island to sit at, another separate dining table, a living room made up of a few long velvet couches arranged like a seventies-style conversation pit, and around all that there are lots of little nooks to sit in with enough seats for two or three women, perfect for quieter conversations. Right above it, is a camera nestled into the wall.

Louise leads me to the shiny kitchen and opens a very full

fridge. 'We're well stocked with all the essentials, and if there's anything in particular you'd like, we can get it in for you.'

There's lots of fresh fruit, packs of fresh herbs, bits to put in sandwiches, about five kinds of milk. I realise that in all this planning, there was one thing I hadn't checked. 'Am I allowed to cook?'

Louise hesitates. 'We have caterers for that, darling. You just need to focus on your dates.'

Ah. I had hoped to show off some skills for the brands, establish myself on camera as a cook you want to watch from home. How to spin this? 'What if I want to cook for my dates? Perhaps as a gift?'

She instantly brightens. 'Oh well, obviously that would be allowed!'

Good enough.

Louise tells me about the illustrious soft furnishings company I vaguely recognise from posh girl TikTok they used for décor, while I try to scope out the cameras. The only two places they don't film in at this stage are the bedrooms and bathrooms.

Once you're engaged, all bets are off, because dating shows love nothing more than footage of couples surreptitiously shagging.

'You'll never find them all,' Louise says.

Ah. Bit too obvious. 'I just want to make sure they always get my good side,' I insist, and she seems to enjoy that.

'Shall I show you the bedrooms?' I notice a slight change here, a hesitation in her voice.

She stops in front of a door. On the other side, I see two twin beds. So, there's that budget cut.

'Due to constraints of the building, we have everyone sharing rooms in pairs.'

This is the first I've heard of this, of course. Ex-contestants from the first season did mention sharing a room, but I'd hoped that was left behind. Could be worse – at least it's not ten girls to one room.

'Oh, that's fine,' I say airily, determined to be the contestant who causes the least trouble. 'It'll be like Brownie camp.'

Louise looks instantly relieved. 'We've pre-assigned roommates just to make things easier, but if you girls want to swap later, just let me know. You never know who accidentally ends up as enemies or fighting over the same man.'

'Hopefully that won't happen!'

She laughs. 'Well, we *do* have a television show to make.'

'If you'd rather I designate someone as my mortal enemy, I'll do it for you.'

Louise honks. 'You always make me laugh.' Her walkie talkie buzzes something incoherent. 'Got to dash. If you need anything, you can just go back to the dormitory front door and knock. There'll always be someone outside, twenty-four-seven. We'll be in early tomorrow to mic you up, but until then you guys can focus on just getting to know each other. Any questions?'

'None right now.'

This is officially it. I can't leave.

'Perfect.' Her phone pings, and she frowns at it. 'Actually, there's been ... another last-minute change of plans,' she says with barely controlled annoyance. 'Our showrunner, Richard Lee Aldridge, wants to do some quick filming later today, once everyone has arrived. Likely after dinner, with a relaxed vibe, so dress comfy.'

I also take note of her vague timing. No numbers for us anymore.

'Girlie sleepover vibes! Sounds great.' I've got a bright red athleisure set that will be perfect for this.

Naturally, they want some early friendship footage. Or potential *before it went wrong* clips, in case we all end up hating each other.

'Good luck, Dolly.' Louise gives me another quick squeeze and disappears in a cloud of Jo Malone.

This is the last time I'll be alone for weeks, so I take a moment to savour it and go over the plan. Reject any saps here for love (some kind of misguided act of faith), and find men who, like me, know that the opportunity to be on a brand new series of a dating show on terrestrial, free-to-watch (as long as you don't mind the adverts) broadcast television a couple of nights a week for an entire summer is the kind of out-of-your-usual-audience-bubble exposure that no algorithm could ever deliver.

I am not leaving here without a husband.

~

Water, water everywhere and not a drop to drink. Except, instead of seawater, I'm surrounded by some of the most beautiful, brilliant straight women the UK has to offer.

I'll admit, I'm not the world's most *natural* extrovert. I like people, a lot, but I have the kind of charisma that can captivate you on screen, not corral a crowd of people. That is, unless I've got a job. So, I take up residence at the kitchen island pouring fresh prosecco or the non-alcoholic option into opaque bronze-coloured stemless ceramic cups. Smart, really: no continuity issues if you can't see how much liquid is in the cup.

Anyway, a job means I'm in control. It means I'm remembered as helpful.

I try to keep track of everyone's names, but it's hard, as a new contestant and her handler appear every few minutes.

Bridget, who arrived right after me, takes it upon herself to be an unofficial greeter in her sing-song South Wales accent. I wonder how many *I can't tell what she's saying* tweets there'll be about her. There's a reason I dropped my home accent before I got on camera – too many preconceptions too.

It's a smart play, though. Whoever controls the room,

controls the game. Befriending everyone early is a smart strategy. After all, who is going to compete with their bestie over a man? And later on, if they pit any couples against each other, well, you might not go quite so hard against your bestie. Perhaps Bridget is someone I need to keep an eye on.

I try not to watch the door. I swear there's a visible difference between being curious about who is walking in, and *knowing*. Even if we're not officially filming till later, it's possible the wall cameras are always on, just in case. Which is precisely why I can't be watching the door.

But I can't help but wonder where Cherry is. Her car was right behind me, so what's taking her so long? Did she quit?

Another girl enters the warehouse, and Bridget and most of the other arrivals gather round her. They flow together through the warehouse, a natural flock.

Except for one. As I fill an ice bucket from the ice dispenser in the fridge door, my first customer walks over. She has deep brown skin, and shiny chocolate-brown hair, piled up into a bun on her head. It's not quite messy bun aesthetic so much as an attempt at ballerina that got loose.

'What can I pour you?' I ask, setting the ice bucket down on the marble top.

'Whatever fizzes.' Her deep brown eyes flash with the possibility of mischief as she adds, 'And is alcoholic.'

'Good choice. I'll join you. Even if it is –' I mime checking a watch '– potentially still morning.'

'Who knows! Not us anymore.'

There are only a few bottles, presumably so we can't get hammered before filming, and split between ten of us, we'll be getting anaemic portions.

'I'm Dolly,' I say as I pass over the cup.

'Whit.' In a lowered voice, she says, 'And thank you for not assuming we all memorised everyone's names already.'

Unconsciously, I glance over to where Bridget is opining about the bathrooms. Apparently, so does Whit. When we catch each other, we share a smile.

Whit throws her head back and cackles in one big 'Ha!' It's a good laugh.

I pour myself a similarly measly spritz of bubbles. 'One of us has to remember who we all are.'

Whit taps the pads of her fingers against her cup. 'Yeah, that's not going to be me. I am the *worst* for names and faces.' I note the Northern accent. Perhaps my own natural ally.

'I'm sure you're no worse than me.'

'Well, whenever I see patients, I'm always pretending I'm in-depth reading through their chart before I say hello when really I'm checking their name.'

'Good job they're not filming right now or there'll be riots in the NHS.'

'God, I wouldn't count on that. The filming, not the riots.'

So it's not just me being paranoid then. After all, we've all seen the blurrier footage of contestants that 'suddenly appears' when someone has been a total dickhead.

'Luckily, I think my patients know to expect someone who is personally a bit scatty but professionally quite good.'

'What do you do?'

'I'm a surgeon.' She says it so casually that I almost choke on my prosecco. 'Well, training to be. I've got a way to go.'

'I suppose if you're not talking to them much, not knowing your patients' names isn't that important,' I muse. I'm more used to speaking to consultants I see once or twice who run tests, shrug, and send me away. Maybe surgeons are different.

She taps her temple. 'I'm using my big old brain to remember where all their important bits are.'

'I'm sure they're very reassured when you tell them about their *bits*.'

We share another laugh, and I think I could get used to hearing that barking bellow. 'Even more so when the nurses have to write *not this leg* on them in sharpie.'

'Horrifying. But that's very impressive,' I concede. 'The surgeon part.'

'Thank you. I like to think so. And, I've been doing it long enough that I barely even have to check the sharpie scrawls on their bodies.'

I almost choke on my bubbles again for laughing. Note to self, choking on bubbles probably looks horrendous on camera. Stop drinking while other people talk.

Whit hops up on one of the velvet and gold barstools. 'What about you?'

'Oh, the usual. Influencer. That sort of thing.'

'That sort of thing,' she says, with a raised eyebrow. 'Okay, keep your secrets.'

'I'm not being coy. I just know you're going to have the exact same job conversation with at least three other women here because it's such a reality TV show standard, and also I think you're interesting and cool enough that I don't want to bore you immediately.'

A smile curls at her glossy lips, and I notice the ghost of a piercing in her lip. A faded teenage rebellion perhaps? 'Come on, give me the TLDR.'

'Okay, fine. I'm a trained chef who pivoted out of the kitchen to making recipe and lifestyle content.' There's more to it than that, like how all my lifestyle stuff is filmed at Auntie Carol's nice house instead of our pokey little two up two down. Or why I had to leave the restaurant in the first place.

Whit's eyes light up. 'Oh, so like the girl who did like twelve days of potato recipes?'

'Yes, pretty much.'

'That spoke to my soul.'

'Then I promise to make you some really good potatoes.'

She clinks her cup against mine. 'We're going to be friends.'

There's a chorus of cheers as another new girl enters the warehouse with her handler. She's small and incredibly beautiful, with thick long black hair that *almost* makes me want to grow out my choppy little bob.

In fact, this might be the most hair I've ever seen in a single room. These girls could put Barbie or My Little Pony to shame.

Still no Cherry.

I turn my attention back to Whit, who has fished an ice cube out of her drink and is crunching down on it. 'Who are you sharing with?'

'The white girl in green. Brunette. I forgot her name already.'

'Niamh?' Even though I intone it as a question, I know I'm right. She's the only Irish girl among us. I never forget an Irish person because of Scouse–Irish solidarity. I was hoping to chat to her, but she's glommed onto Bridget. Celts unite, perhaps.

I should probably be strategic about alliances, but I like Whit, who could be someone I'd befriend outside. I know the classic *Love Island* line is 'I'm not here to make friends' but given I'm specifically *not* here to fall in love, maybe friends are allowed.

'Niamh! See, told you I was rubbish at names,' Whit says.

'I'm sure it doesn't help that we have a lot of thin white girls with the same tan and haircut,' I say. For a dating show purportedly not just about looks, the casting has still chosen similar flavours of beauty. You could mistake the line-up here for a Pretty Little Thing advert.

Not a lot of body diversity either; I think I might be the largest girl here. Not that that's unusual for me in most settings – being almost six foot and fat has me both towering over most women and out-sizing them. I knew coming on a show that hides what you physically look like as a plus-sized woman was going to be a gamble, but I'd forgotten just how slight the model-types can be.

'I don't think mine has arrived yet,' I say, turning my attention back to Whit. 'So, Manchester girl, are you?'

Whit nods and then, for some reason, squints her eyes in focus. 'I can't place you. Except maybe somewhere in the North? Did you go to private school? Or are you from York?'

Relief. The accent is working, even on someone fairly local.

Now, I'm not ashamed of who I am – Scouse and working class among many other things – but I do know this: the British are obsessed with two things: class and accents. Accent *implies* class, in some cases at least.

On-Camera Dolly exclusively uses what Mum calls my 'telephone voice'. Maybe it's a coincidence, but the minute I started making content without my normal accent, dialling my cadence up towards the posh London lifestyle girls, my followers and views rocketed up. I had tested it out, just to see if I was right that people want their aspirational life content from someone who sounds like they're off the BBC or went to Oxbridge. I leaned into it, and haven't looked back.

My family love to rip into me about my posh persona. You can't rely on the algorithm forever – hell, that's why I'm here – but so far, On-Camera Dolly's content has given us a stable enough income that means I can be at home with Mum and we're not quite so terrified of the harbinger of doom from my childhood, i.e. the brown envelope.

Coming on *Wedded Bliss* as On-Camera Dolly was a bit more controversial. Mum doesn't like the lying of it; she's never been good at hiding how she feels. I think she thinks I'm getting notions.

Jas made me practise at home so that I don't get caught out.

And yeah, obviously I don't have the connections of people with an actual silver spoon in their mouth, but I can sound right even if the rest isn't there. Fool them just enough to get a foot in the room.

I think this might make me a class traitor. I'm sure plenty of people have done worse for less good reasons, but I might need to get my moral code checked.

'Liverpool,' I manage to say, before there's a cheer as another woman enters the flat.

'And that makes ten,' says Whit.

I try very hard to hide any flicker of recognition as the little redhead walks in.

In this light, her red hair looks less phoenix feather and more ground cinnamon. Her smile is enormous and infectious. She's small and slight, like most of the women, but where some of the others are striking, she's cute. Pretty in a delicate way. Her patterned tea dress looks straight out of one of those size-inclusive faux vintage brands that always get advertised to me, because the algorithm knows I'm a fat woman.

I wonder what took her so long. I hope she's alright.

Bridget rushes over to her first, almost sending Cherry's bag-carrying chaperone flying. 'Hiya, babe! It's dead nice to meet you!'

Bridget wraps her up in a hug, and I swear I see a sparkle of terror in her eyes.

I'm truly thankful I walked into an empty warehouse. The poor girl is being accosted by nine of us at once.

When they break apart, Cherry waves to us all. 'Hello, I'm Carys.'

'OMG you're Welsh too!' cries Bridget huskily, clearly detecting something in her that the rest of us missed. They babble together in Welsh (I'm pretty sure) but then abruptly switch back to English.

As everyone greets her, this would be a great time for Whit and I to try to learn everyone's names, but I'm too distracted by Cherry.

No, *Carys*. You can't start giving girls nicknames, Dolly. You *know* how that goes.

Eventually, Bridget drags Carys over to Whit and me in a way that reminds me of a small enthusiastic child with a less-enthusiastic leashed puppy.

Her eyes lock with mine, just for a moment. She seems stiffer in here. And there's that nervous look again – the one I saw when she hugged Bridget, or rather, when Bridget hugged her.

'I'm Dolly,' I say, as though it's the first time.

'Carys.' Hesitation hangs heavy on her lips. It's plastered over with a smile, but I swear I can see the edges, where it's not quite real.

'Oh, you must be Dolly's roommate then,' Whit says.

Fuck. She's right.

I feel rather warm all over. 'Our room is this way,' I say, taking Carys's bag from her harried chaperone, who bids goodbye.

As I nudge open our bedroom door, Carys catches up to me. We pause on the threshold, and don't speak. A silent *hello again*.

It takes a certain something to leap out of your car to follow a stranger into God-knows-what, just in case someone needs help. And now we're stepping into another uncertain situation, still as strangers and allies. I just hope she doesn't put two and two together.

But maybe this will be fine. Maybe I'm worrying for no reason.

The only problem is that I've always had a thing for redheads.

Chapter Three

Carys

Bridget Evans, 26, Swansea

My dream man? Oh, he's got to be a bit buff, hasn't he, babe. I'm a gym bunny! I need someone who is going to keep up with me, and who knows a good protein pancake recipe. What good is a man who can't throw you around. [Bridget laughs dirtily.] *No, I know we don't get to see them at the start, but we do eventually, don't we? We do, right?*

I release a deep breath once we're safely in our shared bedroom. I tried really hard to pretend we were meeting for the first time. I hope I pulled it off. Mum always said I have the face for losing at poker.

It is very strange to see her here. The golden Goddess in my bedroom.

At least I'm not sharing with a total stranger. And I know she's the kind of woman who will run into traffic to help; that feels like a good character trait for a roommate. Not that I've ever shared a room with someone before.

The room is *really* small, and Reb didn't tell me I was sharing until we got here. No space to decompress. No escape from the mask.

Two steps into the warehouse, I had to beg Reb for a sit down and a cup of tea. I don't think she really had the time, but as I narrated my day so far, her eyes got progressively wider with horror. We sat in an empty crew area with steaming cups of sweet tea, which helped. A bit.

I had asked if we were allowed to be there, realising we were on the men's side of the warehouse, but Reb had just insisted I was doing her a favour, that she needed the break.

Luckily, I didn't have a meltdown, but the hot sticky edges of getting close enough gum up my thoughts. I feel like a melted candle; even though the flame was snuffed out quickly, I'm still soft.

Maybe my sisters were right; perhaps if I'd told production I was autistic they might have told me about the room-sharing situation.

Or they'd have dropped me from the show.

Dolly has already set her things at the end of one bed, so places my bag at the end of the other. 'This one okay for you?'

'Yes,' I say, hoping that my heart isn't beating so loudly that she can hear.

'Do you need a moment, Carys?' the Goddess asks me, and now, with the door closed, the bedroom feels very, very small. Not because of her body, but it's like the space shrinks from her presence.

She's clad in a matching set of scarlet red leggings and crop top, and it's like looking at the sun. It's a hard colour to pull off, but she wears it, rather than the other way round. Her icy hair and warm skin seem more vibrant against it, whereas I'd look pink as an early strawberry.

I think I'm intimidated by her. I feel a little thrill when she says my name.

I still haven't said anything in reply, and I only realise quite how long it must have been when Dolly perches on the end of her bed and, into the gap I left, says, 'I could do with one.'

'Yes,' I manage to say.

This morning should have been an inkling, but I get the sense that Dolly is very kind, very empathetic. I feel ... almost safe, protected by all that intimidating power.

My heart ceases its impression of a marching band, but I'm a sweaty mess. I sink onto my bed, and flop back to lying down, even though I'm wrinkling the back of my pretty sundress something horrid. The cartoon lobsters around the hem must be all distorted and squished, but I've run out of energy to care much about that.

To my relief, Dolly does the same. Flops back, not worrying about cartoon lobsters. I think.

The room is silent except for the sound of our breathing, and I try to match my breaths to hers.

Maybe this will be okay.

My mouth is dry and I regret not grabbing a glass of Prosecco on the way in here, though that would have catapulted my racing pulse. Fizzy always makes me dizzy, as the girls would say. Inhibitions fall away with a drink, but so does my mask, which is a whole other problem.

Like she knew, Dolly goes to our bathroom, and returns with a glass of water.

I drink it down hungrily. 'Thank you,' I gasp.

She refills it and sets it by my table. 'What a day, huh.'

I wonder how she reads me, this moment. Can she tell what I am? I feel the old urges kick in – to sit up straighter, smile more, still myself. But I am going to have to ration my energy for self-surveillance for the cameras. Unless—

'Are there cameras in here?' I whisper.

Dolly rolls her shoulders. 'No. Not at this stage.'

I can't help but notice the gap her words circle. Not at *this* stage. It's not easy for me to read non-autistic people, but I usually notice the holes, even if I can't see what's missing.

Still, at least this means I don't have to mask quite so hard in here. Dolly doesn't seem repulsed by my exhaustion, which is a low bar some don't clear.

'Have you not seen the show before?' she asks.

I pull a *Wallace and Gromit*-type grimace. 'No?'

'Wow. That's ...'

'Yeah.'

'Bold.'

'I don't know if that's the word for it.'

'It's certainly *one* of them,' Dolly laughs. 'Just so you know, this cohabiting isn't exactly normal either.'

'Oh', is all I can think to say.

'I would consider myself a little too much of an expert, but transferring to a new country always brings its own challenges. Like with Australia.'

'What happened in Australia?'

'I'm worried if I tell you I'll scare you off the show.'

I gulp. 'Okay, don't tell me then.'

'Well, Carys, as your literally resident expert, I'll be your guide.'

My cheeks feel hot. Maybe it was silly not to watch very much at all, but I had this idea that it might colour my choices, my behaviour, to know what I was walking into. For once.

'I need to get out of this dress,' I say and I swear I see Dolly's eyebrows shoot up into her hairline. Was that weird to say? I feel all flustered again. 'I mean, Reb ... my handler, she mentioned something about filming?'

'Yeah, later on. They want a kind of girlie sleepover vibe, I think.'

I kneel down and open my suitcase so I don't have to look at her when I'm red as a beetroot.

'This one's yours.' Dolly taps her nails on the wardrobe door. 'Here, let me help you hang things up.'

'No, it's okay. You chill out. You've been on pouring duty. A very, very important job.'

Dolly chuckles, and sits back down. 'It was very difficult. Those girls love a tiny weeny portion of Prosecco. At one point I ran out and had to hurriedly open a new bottle. I feared for my *life*.'

I laugh, though it's on its way to a snort. Not very delicate of me, Mum would say. Not very ladylike, Dad would add. Note to self: no snorting on camera.

The wardrobe is optimistically small given how many outfits they expected us to bring – one per warehouse filming day, plus a separate outfit for filming all our interviews for continuity. It doesn't help that most of my dresses have circle skirts, much more fabric per outfit than anything fitted. It's a squeeze.

Once everything is as squashed in as well as it'll go, I take my designated comfy clothes into the bathroom to change. I think all of us chose a 'looks like exercisewear but is actually loungewear' vibe. It's new, but I wore the outfit at home to test that I could stomach wearing it without fidgeting uncomfortably.

I'm a little too self-conscious to wear a crop top, so I slip into my oversized knitted cardigan with stars on the elbows. It's incredibly soft. Ages ago, when I was sad about leaving my sisters after a visit, Ang sprayed her sweet perfume on it, and the lovely scent seems to have bound to the fabric. The moment I slide it on, something in my brain switches off. I don't know how to describe it, but it's a kind of emptiness because my brain has stopped manually processing. I can never quite pinpoint what it is, even when it's taking up so much of my mental energy, but some clothes just give me that feeling. That deep breathing-out sensation.

Unfortunately, it seems to leave space for other worries. I get the horrible feeling that I've got her name wrong. I'm sure

Dolly is right. But, well, maybe I need to check? Or maybe that's rude?

She's sitting up cross-legged on the bed stretching, like she's gearing up to do some exercise.

'Just to check,' I say, still a little nervous of getting things wrong. 'It *is* Dolly, isn't it?'

'Yep,' she says, while twisting her torso round and revealing the long slope of her back. I wonder what it's like to be that tall; I'm forever having to ask people to reach things for me.

When she spins back round, she catches my eyes. I feel hot embarrassment rush through me, even though she smiles. I quickly return to my suitcase and zip it up just so I have something to do. I hope she doesn't think I was staring at her. I don't want to make her feel uncomfortable. She's so beautiful that she must get people looking at her all the time, but it's not the same in a tiny shared room. I don't want her to think I'm ogling her, for God's sake. I don't want to give her the wrong impression.

Seemingly oblivious to my internal panic, Dolly continues her stretches and says, 'When I was a kid, people used to think it was a fake name, like I chose it, but nope, it's my real name.'

I tuck the sleeves of my cardigan into my fist, and somehow that makes me feel more of a person again. 'After Dolly Parton?'

'No, but she is an icon. My mum was well into The Cranberries when she was pregnant with me, so I'm named after the lead singer Dolores, but she has literally never called me my government name in my life. Even when I was being a little shit.'

'I thought it might have been the blonde,' I say and then realise that's a very silly thing to say to someone who has very obviously bleached hair.

'Oh no, this is all the handiwork of Derek on Bold Street.'

She flicks her icy edges, sharp like a knife. Something about it reminds me of protective animal camouflage, like big scary eyes on butterfly wings to ward off predators.

'It suits you,' I blurt.

'Thanks. I agree.'

'And thank you, about confirming your name and not being, you know ... I just mean, I don't want to make a faux pas on my first day.'

She holds up her hands, presumably to make me stop word-vomiting. 'After today, I barely remember my own name.'

'I've heard it's Dolly.'

'Oh *yeah*, that's it.' She jokingly hits herself on the forehead, and we both laugh.

There's that calm again. I wish I could say I wasn't always like this, oscillating wildly between awkward and messy and comfortable and nervous. It's definitely more pronounced right now, because I want Dolly to like me. She's my roommate, and maybe a friend? I never really know about the latter until someone tells me, if I'm honest.

It feels strange to still be at square one after the Situation, but we didn't really get a chance to speak in that way. Maybe I should ask Dolly about herself now, so I panic a little less. If we're missed, I'm sure Bridget will come get us.

I sit down on my bed cross-legged the way I like to but shouldn't because my knees always get angry. 'So, where are you from?' I ask.

'Liverpool, born and bred.'

This throws me a little because her accent does not say Scouser to me. Maybe she's posh and went to private school? She sounds posh to my naive ears.

'I'm just over the border. But not the holidaying part of North Wales. I'm from Wrexham.'

She narrows her eyes at me, but there's a flicker of a smile on her red lips. 'By the 'holidaying part' do you mean Anglesey, or the caravan parks along the Rhyl seafront?'

She's got me there. I *did* mean Anglesey. The posher holidaymakers don't generally hit up the caravan parks and the rickety old fairgrounds (more fool them, I think). I know accent doesn't always mean everything, but for English people it does tell you a lot. Someone with an accent like hers usually has one of those second homes they're trying to triple-tax people into selling.

Did I read her that wrong? Dolly doesn't seem upset by my misjudgement.

'Auntie Carol took me and my cousin Jas to one of the caravan parks on the coast for a holiday when we were teenagers, but I think it was way further round than you. Shell Island it was called, and it was bizarrely not an island.'

'Many shells?'

'I mean, as many as you'd expect to find on a beach but not so much to name yourself after the fact.'

I snort-laugh again. Dolly seems able to summon them from me.

'Anyway, Carol had this notion we'd do a load of "wild swimming", but it was too cold to do more than stick a toe in.'

'We just call that swimming.'

Dolly barks with a laugh, and I feel proud. I want to make her do that again.

The group cheers from the living room, and we both glance at the door. My stomach sinks, because really I'd love to just stay here and talk to Dolly more. Sharing a room doesn't seem quite so scary anymore.

'Time to face the music?' I ask, and we both get up from our beds.

With one last glance in the mirror, I straighten my back and stand a little taller, welding a smile to my face. I've already made Dolly laugh; I can befriend the other eight women out there. Bridget seems friendly. Maybe we'll all fall in love with the men of our dreams (individually, with no competition), and there'll be no fights and it'll all be chill and nice and edited into a nice show ... Right?

I fling open the door with too much gusto and it clatters hard against the wall, making me flinch. The sound echoes through the warehouse like a struck drum.

There's no time to be nervous or scared of myself; I need to bury all that. It's time to be friendly, approachable, supportive Carys. A girl's girl.

When we stride into the living room, all the other women are curled up on the couches and stare right at me. It's unnerving but probably because I just slammed a door loudly. I can do this.

With all the false courage I can muster, I loudly announce, 'Let's get ready to find our men, girlies!'

To my relief, they all whoop and cheer.

Bridget jumps up, dislodging soft furnishings and almost several drinks. 'Yes, babe! Let's get this party started!'

I follow Bridget to the bar where she empties the end of the Prosecco into the last bronze cup for me. 'There's tiddly in there, babe, sorry.'

'For the best,' I say as I take it from her. 'Drinks-Carys can come out to play another night.'

Bridget laughs throatily. 'Oh, I can't wait to meet her.'

I'm so glad there's someone else Welsh here – we've got something to bond over.

With a hand on the small of my back, she leads me to the couches. I notice Dolly has perched herself on an arm next to the incredibly beautiful girl with the braids, and they're already chatting away. There's no space for me to sit there, so I squeeze in next to Bridget and an Irish girl who immediately introduces herself as Niamh. She tells us that Lina, the girl with long black hair, is Scottish, so we can all bond over how strange English people are. I smile and laugh, though obviously, I don't want to be bitchy because I am a girl's girl to all now.

I try to keep up with all the names as conversations slip and slide over each other around me.

Three near-identical tanned girls with long blonde hair sit together, and I glean they are somehow all called Hannah. There's a Hannah C., a Hannah P. and a Hannah S., though I'm not yet sure who is who. With Bridget, they look like a matching set.

'Sooooo,' says Niamh loudly, grabbing everyone's attention. 'What are we looking for in a man?'

'A man with nice teeth,' says one of the Hannahs with a clipped Southern accent, which causes a few people to burst into laughter. 'Look, I can handle anything but bad teeth!'

Whit leans forward to look right at her. 'Hang on, I thought the whole point is that we can't see what they look like?'

'Only for the first two dates, and then we get the face reveal.' Bridget gestures violently with her now emptied cup. 'Hannah C. is right – looks matter. We're just giving them a chance to flash their personality first. This isn't *Love Is Blind*, babes.'

'More like Love is Blurry,' says Dolly, and this time I manage a much more controlled, pretty and crucially snortless laugh. An on-camera laugh. A wifely laugh.

'Teeth matter!' insists Hannah C. 'They're like the windows to the soul.'

'More like to your mouth,' Whit counters.

'Isn't that the eyes?' Niamh asks.

Hannah C. gasps. 'Why would you put someone's eyes in your mouth?'

'Come on, you've got to be attracted to your partner,' insists Priya, a woman who radiates Grown-Up Adult vibes.

'We all want a wee ride to come home to,' agrees Niamh.

Whit nods. 'Yeah, I'm not getting engaged to someone I don't want to *engage* with, but I don't have any preconceptions about his looks.'

'So, what *are* you looking for?' Dolly asks.

Whit laughs awkwardly. 'I have no expectations of finding someone who wants to date *me*. Even if they like me, surgeons basically live at the hospital. Our hours can be nuts. It's why hospital staff date each other, but I don't want to shit where I eat.'

Dolly barks with laughter, as Priya coughs awkwardly.

'It would be cool to meet someone who likes me and isn't bothered by that being a big part of my life. I guess I'm on *Wedded Bliss* for a good time, if not a long time,' explains Whit, and my God, I wish I could be that relaxed about anything. Maybe when you're used to slicing people open, a reality television dating show feels like small fry.

'Well, I'm looking to get *married*,' another Hannah says a little haughtily, a Bristolian lilt to her *r*s.

I guess Whit's relaxed attitude didn't land well with everyone. Before anything can escalate, I say, 'I'm looking for stability, and someone who is good to me. I'm open to who they are as a person.'

This gets a few nods. Dolly gives me an approving wink.

'I don't think I know *what* I want. Dating is so hard. I never feel like we're on the same page,' says Lina. She has the softest voice I've ever heard in my life. I could curl up inside it. Earlier, I heard her mention she teaches Pilates and I have no idea how anyone stays awake in her classes.

'But you want to get married, right?' asks Bridget.

'Yes, of course. And I feel like I'm upfront with men about that, but then we get to date four, and I find out it's casual.'

Everyone in the room groans.

'Isn't it always,' sighs Dolly, shaking her head. I wonder what she's been through. And everyone else of course, but as my roommate, I want to be able to support her.

'Or they say they're being honest about what they want, but you don't find out the truth until you are six months in and falling for him,' Priya says.

Lina shivers like something crossed her grave.

'The number of men who've said they want kids when they don't,' whispers Bridget. She sounds so small and sad that I grab her hand and squeeze. She squeezes back.

'Basically, we're all looking for men, not boys,' says Dolly, and everyone cheers our empty bronze cups together.

This seems to snap Bridget back to herself. 'What's everyone's type?'

I knew this would come up eventually. Unfortunately, I truly do not know what my type is. My high school to university boyfriend Mikey was a sweet little blond guy with a-mouse-from-a-Pixar-film vibes. He's been my only relationship, and all the other men I've dated had little in common looks-wise. They were all nice, though! I'm not convinced not knowing my type is why I've yet to have a life-altering connection. Maybe looks aren't that important for me?

I'm surrounded by women professing variations on 'tall, dark and handsome' so I guess looks do matter. I can't fault their taste; I'm not immune to the charms of any Mr Darcy (and I sit firmly in the camp that both adaptations of *Pride and Prejudice* are good in their own ways). But does that mean my type is also a tall brunette white man? I don't really know.

'I love a tall man,' sighs Bridget. 'Six foot? Yes please.'

'Yeah, but is he actually fit, or just far away?' says Whit.

'Oh, babes,' Bridget says wistfully, her voice low and throaty. 'I've had a few just far aways in my time.'

Whit pokes Dolly in the leg. 'What about you?'

'I'm more attracted to personality,' she says.

I'm so relieved that someone feels the same as me that I hardly notice when everyone groans.

'That's a copout,' grumbles Bridget.

'It's not,' Dolly insists. 'And I'm not saying I'm a sapiosexual—'

The final Hannah gasps and looks at everyone nervously. 'Dolly, I don't think you can say that word.'

There's a moment of confusion while everyone reassures her that it's not a slur.

Bridget giggles. 'And I thought it meant you fancied chimpanzees.'

'King Kong's a bit much for me,' Dolly says and I resist the urge to point out he's actually the last of a species of gigantic gorilla-like apes. Mikey had a real thing for B-movies.

'Don't get me wrong,' Dolly continues. 'I want to feel that spark and snog their face off, but I think it's not always the only type of attraction for me. Like it could be charisma or charm or humour instead.'

No one else seems on her wavelength, so I find myself saying, 'I feel the same, Dolly.'

She gives me a big warm smile. 'See, Carys and I are just more enlightened than the rest of you,' she says jokingly, and everyone laughs. 'I am just teasing, I promise. Here's to hot husbands for us all.'

And at that, everyone gets up to cheer glasses again.

The unfamiliar sound of the front door closing rings through the room and we all turn in unison.

'Well, ladies, good to see you're all getting on well,' says Karina Nguyen. *The* Karina Nguyen. Ethereally beautiful, former model turned television presenter, and happily married mother of two. She's the woman we're all trying to be. Or at least, I am. She's been writing a newsletter for a few years about her experiences with growing her own food that I've been reading for ages. I would kill for that kind of smallholding life, I think. She makes it look perfect.

As she approaches, a few of the women check their makeup in the blurry bronze cup reflection.

'Don't worry, ladies. There's no cameras yet. Just me,' Karina says, perching on the arm of the couch next to me. I can't believe the real Karina Nguyen is sitting so close to me. Mum said that famous people always look like they smell good, and she *does*. 'The team still want to film after dinner, but I wanted to come in and get to know you first.'

We all introduce ourselves one after the other – which helps fill the gaps for me on which Hannah is which. We say what we do and where we're from as though we're practising for our dates tomorrow.

There are a few confused looks when I say I'm an educator on a city farm. Hannah C. narrows her eyes at me. 'Hang on, a *city* farm?'

I'm used to this confusion. 'Yeah, it's a farm, but in the city.'

'Why?' She tilts her head like a confused puppy.

'Why what?'

'Why is it there?'

This question feels more existential than I usually get. I glance over at Karina, and the approving look she gives me powers me on. 'Why any farm? We grow food and raise animals, but we also bring schools in to teach students about where their food comes from. There are mental health benefits – all that good green outside space – and we have gardening and craft classes too.'

'But . . . it's in the city?'

I really don't know how else to explain this without having a phone to hand to show her the beautiful photos on our website. The stables and animal enclosures backdropped by trees and plants, and then the gigantic tower blocks of the financial district of London. I guess it probably is a bit odd if you've never been to one.

'I'm sure Carys can explain in full later,' says Karina, gently but swiftly moving the conversation along. 'Tomorrow you'll get the show-scripted spiel but I wanted to remind you to have fun, and if you're not having fun make sure you talk to your chaperones. I've been on TV a long time. I know how the doubts can creep in.'

She looks down briefly, and I wonder how hard life in the public eye has been for her. I feel like I'm always being watched, but she *really* is.

'I got through all that thanks to the people around me. I know with a dating show, it can feel competitive, but the friendships you form here could last your lifetime. Stick together, support each other, and you will all have the most wonderful experience.'

I suddenly feel a lot of affection for the women around me. We're bonded by this weird and unique journey, and nothing will take that away. That feels special.

Even more so with Dolly.

'Right, ladies, I've got kids to feed and put to bed.' Karina rises with complete poise. 'I'll see you all tomorrow morning.'

As Karina waves goodbye, Dolly catches my eye and smiles. Does she feel it too? It's a wild thing to know that someone is going to be very important to you.

And I know that Dolly is going to be. I can feel it.

Script: Episode One intro

[Karina and Lucas Nguyen stand in a softly lit corridor, with doors visible down the side of one wall.]

KARINA Welcome to *Wedded Bliss*! Over the next two days, our twenty contestants will be matched up together to explore a voice-only connection.

LUCAS Here at *Wedded Bliss* we believe true love runs deep, so we think that the foundations to solid connections can be built off words alone. Don't worry, they do get to see each other, but let's see what sparks are lit when only conversation is on the table.

KARINA We've selected our ten men and ten women through an extensive, specialist matchmaking programme that ensures that each contestant has multiple possible matches based on wants, likes and type, but it's up to them to decide who is the one for them.

LUCAS For the first two days, every woman will date every man to see if any sparks fly.

KARINA After that, they will each decide if they'd like to see each other again. If it's a yes on both sides, they get a second date, their match still unseen. It's such a wonderful process, I'm so excited for everyone!

LUCAS And maybe at the end of the road they'll find Wedded Bliss, just like we have.

[Karina and Lucas kiss as the camera zooms out.]

Chapter Four

Carys

Whit Vempati, 29, Manchester

Look, you've all seen Grey's Anatomy. *Dating doctors is a bad idea. And all I really want is someone nice. I just want to feel like extreme happiness with someone, you know? Like, so happy that dopamine is shooting out of my arse! God, imagine if that was a medical condition. That reminds me, you wouldn't believe the things people put up there and then come to A&E to have removed.* [Whit leans closer to camera.] *Whatever it is needs to have a flared base and should be safe for going inside bodies, you hear me? Make good choices!*

Production wake us all up with a knock at our doors. It's the first day, and I feel strange, like my skin doesn't quite fit.

Finding change difficult is hard to explain to other people, because it's not just the new bed, or just not being home. The people are different, I've no idea what food there'll be, and then there's the smells – I don't mean anyone stinks, but there's perfume and scent diffusers and different clothing detergents, and it all combines in a complex bouquet that says *not home*. When I've tried to explain, people just told me to care less about it, but that fundamentally misunderstands the problem. It doesn't matter if I care; I can't ignore it. My senses are tuned up to Spidey-sense levels. All I can do is occasionally huff one of the solid perfumes I keep in my pocket for a blast of familiarity – my current favourite is cardamom coffee.

And so, waking up isn't just the nerves about today but the heavy weight of a new environment.

Luckily, I've always been an early riser. I like the time to myself – my housemates all work corporate jobs, so live on a different schedule to me. Plus, working on a farm quickly gets you used to very early starts. At least here my early start doesn't mean mucking out (so far).

I showered before bed last night, after dinner and filming of us all sitting round talking, so I dress as quickly and quietly as I can in my outfit for day one while Dolly occupies the bathroom. Somehow, she manages to look beautiful even when she's half asleep.

Only Whit (leaning against a kitchen counter sipping a coffee) and Lina (curled up on the couch) are up and in the shared space. We say polite little hellos, but thankfully they don't seem up for talking.

The breakfast buffet laid out on the kitchen island makes me think of fancy hotels. I never like to eat on a flippy stomach, but I should or I'll get not just hungry, but *hangry*. Whenever I get a little irritable at the farm, someone usually shoves a cereal bar in my direction, and it tends to clear everything up pretty quickly.

I don't want snappy, frustrated Carys to be my first impression. Queasy Carys is easier to suppress, especially if they can't see me.

I fill up a bowl with things I could probably eat – strawberries, a dollop of raspberry yogurt, a handful of honeyed granola on top, and then some slices of melon in its own bowl. I could kill for a massive sugary coffee and an egg sandwich, but that's farm-day food and even if my dates can't see me, the cameras will see egg yolk spilled down my front.

Even though Lina and Whit aren't talking to each other or me, I can't work out if I should sit purposefully away from them. What is the right amount of space to give someone? I wish I was the sort of person who just knew the answer to that. I perch on a stool at the island which is equidistant from either woman. It wobbles under me, which doesn't help the nausea.

I focus on trying to eat as more women pour in, raising the base level of sound.

One of the production team, Hellie, comes in and hands out show regulation notebooks for us to make notes about our dates in. The navy velvet cover feels itchy under my fingers, the sensation only broken up by the smooth gold capitals of my name on the front. When I set it back down, I see I've somehow left a splodge of raspberry yogurt on the cover. Shit. I never was good at taking care of things, Dad always used to tell me off for that, but this might be a world record. I rub at it with a cleaner finger, but it just disrupts the pile, leaving an angry circle of shame.

I force another bite of breakfast and try not to think. Not about all the men I'm going to meet or the imperfect notebook or the cameras in the walls. The juice goes down in one big gulp, and I try not to slam it down like a shot glass, but the rush of sugar on my battered nervous system feels as shocking as absinthe.

'God, this is a bit fucking bonkers, isn't it?' says Dolly, who appears right next to me so suddenly that I flail, punting the not-quite-empty glass onto the floor. Sticky orange pulp slops all over the carpet and all I can do is stare at it while my mind turns to TV static. The hot lick of *you're about to fuck it up* swirls around me.

Is this all too much? This might be too much. God, just get up and clean it, why are you so slow? Why can't you just react?

But then Dolly is on the floor, with a sheet of kitchen towel, and the juice is gone. It happens so fast, so easily. She didn't shout or tell me I'm clumsy or anything. She just cleaned it up and now it's gone and it's over?

The buzzing recedes and I take one long breath in.

'Sorry, that was my fault. I don't think any of us are in the state to be crept up on,' Dolly says as she drops the mess into the bin. She rejoins me at the counter, leaning against it.

My eyes are drawn to the bright red lipstick she's wearing. The kind of bold colour that says *I'm here*. It suits her, though I don't think she needs lipstick to announce her. She does that all by herself. It's admirable really, the way she seems so confident in any room.

I've been looking at her lipstick for too long. I swallow down the swarm of bees raging through my body. 'No. Sorry. Thank you,' I manage to say.

My brain lags, like I'm still reacting to the glass falling. Like it is, in fact, still falling. That's one part of autism that's hard to hide: my reactions. Too slow or too fast or too big or too upset or none at all. I can practise conversation until the cows come home, but a spot of yogurt and a spilled drink might be enough to reveal it all. Luckily, most people don't know what they're looking at.

Dolly seems, again, unaware of my internal crisis, and is instead investigating the stools. 'God, look at these fucking things. I could barely get one arse cheek on there. Stools should be banned.'

My giggle turns into wobbling so much that I have to grab onto the counter.

'See, even a slight thing like you can't sit on them, and you've got both arse cheeks on there. I mean, I presume.'

I flush and I'm not sure why, though I'm not particularly used to talking about bums with other girls outside of the nightmare *does my bum look big* questions my friends occasionally posit (I have learned, from trial and error, that the answer is never, ever *yes*). 'Can confirm. Both cheeks planted unsteadily. Perhaps it's a kind of low-level psychological torture for us?'

She tilts her head playfully. 'Go on.'

'Like, what if they shaved off the bottom of all the stools and table legs so everything wobbles a bit, just to upset us?'

'Unsteadiness in the mind *and* in the physical environment,' she nods admiringly, as though I haven't just uttered total horror. 'Carys, you might be an evil mastermind. You could have had an incredible career in reality television in the 2000s.'

'I'm not sure that should be a compliment,' I laugh awkwardly, but I still take it as one.

Now I'm not spiralling, I notice her outfit: a two-piece Bardot top and ankle-length skirt in black and white, creating a kind of curved yin yang shape that mirrors the curves of her hips. It looks incredible and somehow effortless on her. I hope I'm not staring. 'Are you feeling ready?' I ask instead.

'I think so?' She leans in a bit closer like we're sharing a secret. Her perfume is all spices and a hint of something light, maybe citrus, but underneath it is a deep heavy oud. The men won't get to enjoy it so I guess this is just for her. The last embers of panic-fire snuff out as I breathe her in. 'Actually, no. Not at all,' she admits.

'Me neither.' I push a loose strand of hair behind my ear.

Even if she is nervous, you wouldn't know from looking. Sometimes I wonder if I'll ever feel grown up, like one day it'll click into place. To me, Dolly is an end-point, a goal of who I'd like to be. I want to drink her in, learn everything about her. Perhaps that's a bit intense, but that's how it feels. I want to bridge that gap between us somehow.

'Ooh, here we go,' mumbles Dolly as a member of production walks in. 'That's Louise, my handler.'

'Morning, everyone,' calls Louise, raising her reusable

coffee cup in the air in a kind of cheers gesture. 'How are we today? Good? Nervous? Excited? Bit of both? Great!' She doesn't leave time for us to answer. 'I'm here to give you a rundown of how today will go.'

I take my notebook and try to make notes as she speaks, but it all rushes past me in a blur. Is she being serious? Five individual hour-long dates with a new man each time, and the same tomorrow? Five in *one* day? Ten men in two days? Apparently this is only news to me, because Dolly nods along like she's heard all this before.

Maybe this is why my sisters were worried. The social load is higher than I thought it would be. I'm already shaking like a shitting dog, and nothing has even happened yet!

I think about what they'd say. *Calm, Carys.*

There's no eye contact, no body language masking. It's just you in an empty room, and your voice. And the cameras, but you've spent your whole life finding ways to stim that are deemed 'more normal'.

I'm here now. Walking in ignorant was my choice. I have to live with it.

And hope that someone likes me.

Though, will they want me overstimulated? My snappiest, most frazzled, the part of me that feels animal-raw?

I try never to let anyone I'm casually dating see that version of me. I know that when I'm engaged or living with someone, they'll see *that* me. Eventually. What if they see me, and change their mind?

Louise's five-minute warning startles me out of my anxiety, and I watch as she disappears out the door we'll be walking through to start this whole process.

'Five is so many.' My words come out in a flat murmur.

'*So* many,' sighs Dolly. 'When's a girl gonna have time to eat? I noticed there was no mention of a lunch break.'

'Exactly, the priorities are all wrong. There'd better be good snacks.'

'*Really* good snacks.' Dolly stands up straight. 'I think this will be the most men I've spoken to in one day since I had to take my car to the garage. And I didn't want to talk to most of *them*.'

'Hopefully you'll be a bit more thrilled about today's men.'

'At least they're behind a wall, so if they utterly annoy me, I can roll my eyes as much as I like.'

'I imagine that did not go down well at the garage.'

'Oh no, I'm positive they charged me more, but fair enough. The dickhead tax got me.'

'The dickhead tax?' She has such funny sayings that I want to write them down.

'Yeah, you know, when someone ups the prices to factor in dealing with someone you'd rather push off a cliff. Or like if you're freelancing and you don't actually want to do whatever it is, so you charge three times as much to make up for not wanting to do it.' She glances at me sideways, then looks at the wall. 'Not that I've *ever* done that to any of my clients,' she adds in a theatrically honest voice.

I burst into giggles.

'Hey, come on,' she whispers with a smile. 'I'm trying to keep my clientele.'

'I don't really get that option on the farm. The pigs would revolt,' I sigh.

Dolly taps her fingers on the counter. 'Are they tight? I feel like pigs don't tip well. I've read *Animal Farm*. That's the plot, right?'

I laugh. 'I don't think so, no.'

'Also I imagine you can't go about pushing them off cliffs without the RSPCA getting a little narked.'

'Not many cliffs going in the East End of London.' I shake my head with faux disappointment.

'Also now I'm so confused about how your farm works. You're invoicing the individual animals for their care?'

I snort with laughter. Her jokes flush all the worries away. It's like she can turn down the volume on the world for me.

'How do you set your fees? A sliding scale based on how big the animal is? God, imagine if you had an elephant pop in, you'd be *rich*.'

'Stop,' I gasp, trying to catch my breath. 'I'm dying.'

'So are all these large mammals you're fleecing.'

I swipe at her with my hand, and she laughs in triumph. 'Alright, I'll stop. For now.'

I wish I could just stay here and be silly with Dolly. We've barely known each other a day, and she seems to understand when I'm being swallowed by my own nervous system better than some of my friends and family do. It's nice.

My cheeks ache from laughing. 'Thank you. And, I feel a lot better now, though I suspect my makeup might have run everywhere.'

'Nah, you're good. Beautiful as always,' she says, and I feel a hot flush on my cheeks.

Other women don't often call me beautiful. Cute, maybe. Adorable.

Beautiful feels special.

Before I can thank her, Louise summons us to the door. We naturally form a single-file queue in front of her. The invisible cloud of perfume and hairspray surrounding us makes my head swim.

One by one, microphone wires and sound packs are threaded down our backs, surprisingly cold against my hot skin.

'It's like a Britney mic,' I say excitedly, as a nice man hooks it behind my ear.

'Yeah,' he replies with the weariness of a man who hears that every time.

Once we're mic'd up, Louise leads us to a long corridor lined with doors. I still haven't learned everyone's names, but one smiley woman leads me to a door. At the end of the corridor, Reb rushes past giving me a flappy good luck wave. There's so much going on that everyone is on high alert today. Except Louise; she seems unflappable.

I wait in front of a door as all ten of us line up. Eventually, after what seems like a lifetime, Louise announces, 'Okay, ladies, good luck!'

Some women cheer, but my mouth is too dry.

This is it. Time for my first date with a stranger. And four more after that.

I stand a little straighter and hope my face won't ache from all the smiling I'm going to do.

I take the handle of the door and walk through.

~

For the room my life is supposed to begin in, it is quite unremarkable. It's just a softly lit, pink room, decorated very much like the warehouse with a big couch to sink into, layered with throw pillows and blankets. It's about the size of a stable. Hopefully the snacks in the mini-fridge are better than hay and a salt lick.

The only strange thing is the huge gold-edged mirror that must cover the partition between rooms. I wish it was a blurry screen or just a blank bit of wall. I don't want to look at myself the whole time ... though at least it means I can check I'm making the right expressions at the right time.

I wonder if I'll always be in this specific room, or if we move around?

Either way, I'm finally alone, so the buzzing in my head disappears. I feel a little bruised by everything this morning, but maybe with silent time now, I'll be alright.

I can't hear anyone on the other side yet. It's hard not to

think about the man who will be behind the curtain. Or mirror. It's all a bit Ozian, isn't it?

I'm dressed as if I'm ready to play Dorothy, which I'd like to say was unintentional. Baby-blue babydoll dress over a white blouse, and a big blue ribbon in my half-up, half-down hair. My ruby (yes, to match Judy instead of the silver ones in the book) slippers don't glitter, but they do have little patent leather hearts on the toe. They're not easy to walk in, but I'm sitting down all day.

I take a cold bottle of water out of the fridge so I will have something to do with my hands that's not digging my fingernails into my own skin. I set it down on the side table with my notebook and pen, and sit down carefully, spreading my skirt out so I won't wrinkle the back much. I sit ankles crossed and tucked away, like a princess.

Above the mirror, a light I didn't notice before shines yellow. Does that mean it's starting? Is he here?

'Hello?' I call out, like I'm speaking into a cave, expecting my own voice echoed back.

'Hello!' The echo is a *much* deeper voice than mine.

My hands go straight to my lips, smothering a nervous giggle. 'Hi! You're there! Wow.'

'I am! Hello!' His voice is happy, excited like my own. 'May I know who I'm speaking to?'

'Carys,' I say, trying to make my name clear. 'And you? What's your name?'

'Lovely to meet you, Carys. I'm Patrick.'

We break into nervous laughter at the exact same time.

'Gosh, it's a bit strange, isn't it,' Patrick says, in what I'm pretty sure is a Yorkshire accent, though I'm not sure I can narrow it down.

'It's very strange talking to my own reflection, and then hearing you reply.'

'I know, I can barely look at myself.' He laughs heartily. 'Oh dear, that probably doesn't sound particularly good, does it?'

'I'm sure you're lovely to look at, but I understand what you mean. I feel like I need to double-check there's nothing between my teeth.'

His next laugh is a scatter burst of joy. I really like his laugh. I wonder if it will sound the same in front of me as it does coming out of the hidden speakers.

'Hey, I wonder if you can hear me?' Scuffling sounds from the same direction as his voice, but then there's a knock on the wall right in front of me.

My reflection jumps in shock. 'It's you!' I spring up, and knock back, first cautiously on the mirror. The sound is tinny and thin, so I move to the wall next to it.

'I heard you!' I could swear I feel the rumble of his voice through my palm against the wall.

'Wow. You really are in there,' I whisper.

He knocks back in a tune.

'Shave and a haircut, two bits!' I sing the same tune back, with the answer added on. 'Oh no, now I'm thinking of the really scary bit in the bar in *Who Framed Roger Rabbit*.'

'No toon can resist!' His impression of the villain Judge Doom is uncanny.

I burst into nervous laughter. 'Oh God, please never do that again. I'll die!'

'I promise to keep my impersonations of vintage children's media villains under wraps.'

'You have more?'

'I had a very wasted youth.'

I giggle. This is going surprisingly well for a first date. I'm not sure I've ever laughed so much on one before. 'I know we're not supposed to know how each other looks, but I can't help picturing you with the top hat and a cape now.'

'Are you sure you can't see me?' he teases, and I hear him move around. 'Do you have spy-cameras in here, Carys?'

'I'd never,' I gasp flirtatiously. This is surprisingly fun. *He* is fun, and I feel fun with him.

'Okay, I trust you. You have a lovely singing voice, by the way.'

I realise that I've not actually moved from the mirror, so I sit back down on the couch as elegantly as possible. 'Thank you.' Like every wannabe manic pixie dream autistic, I had an open mic with a ukulele phase.

'Oh gosh, I thought you'd gone then.'

Oops, I must have left a big gap. 'Sorry, I forget you can't see me. I've never been the best at phone calls either. I always get distracted.'

'What distracts you?'

'Oh. Anything I guess. I've always got a few million thoughts going on at once. Though at work it's usually a goat with its head stuck in a fence or something.'

'A . . . goat? What do you do?'

I explain that I work on a city farm in London's East End, and I'm not just wrangling various animals from an office cubicle.

'Well, I wouldn't judge you if you were.'

I laugh, and I can feel the smile in the mirror stretching my cheeks. It's a real, real smile. I can just *tell* he's a good person. You just can't be a bad person when you sound like he does; he's sunshine, I think.

I'm trying to work out how to ask for his biography – I really think we should all come with a Wikipedia-type summary – when he says, 'Can I ask you a question, Carys?'

I nod and then remember he can't see me. 'Yes! Go ahead.'

'Okay. If we were hosting a dinner party and you could invite any one person, living or dead, who would you invite?'

Well. That's a different train of thought than I was expecting, but I'll go with it. I know it's probably the opener he asks everyone, but throwing a *we* in there from the off just feels special. I repeat the question back to him just to make sure I understood.

'I know my answer,' I say eventually. 'But it does make me sound like a bit of a nerd.'

'I'm sure I won't think that.'

'Okay.' I feel the excitement of talking about something I love ripple in me. 'I would invite Jane Austen because her novels are such interrogations of people, of how we act and love and who we are, and even if she was quiet at our dinner party, I know she would have thoughts that I'd be fascinated to hear.'

I feel my cheeks flush – I have a *lot* of feelings about Austen.

The thing I don't add is my opinion that her novels, particularly *Pride and Prejudice*, are about autistic people of the past. Her characters are people I know and understand (sometimes literally), even if they act completely bananas sometimes. It's like their DNA is familiar to me: the way Darcy restrains himself to the point of squashing; Lizzie's loud brilliance and opinionated nature; Lydia's impulsiveness. Even Mrs Bennet's *obsession* with propriety. I see them in me, and my family, all the time.

'Which is your favourite novel?' he asks, which is always a good sign because men usually seem to think she only wrote *Pride and Prejudice*. That's if they even know it's a book and not just a film or a TV show.

'It changes, but I love Lizzie and Darcy. Their spiky romance is my heart-story.'

'I'm more of a *Sense and Sensibility* man myself but I must admit that's because I love watching Alan Rickman as Colonel Brandon.' He says it so boldly that I know this is a truth. 'There's something so wonderful about him.'

That's when I know for sure that my first instincts are right; there's something special about Patrick. I've never met a man who would choose lovely dependable (and kind of old) rescuer Colonel Brandon as their favourite if they were trying to impress. They'd choose Fitzwilliam Darcy because they know he's rich and because Colin Firth walking out the lake is imprinted on so many women's minds. Or if they do know *Sense and Sensibility*, they choose Edward Ferrars because he's played by Hugh Grant.

I know Victor said that liking the same things isn't everything, but this feels important. This isn't just taste, this is like a literary horoscope. Brandon is *reliable*.

'I love Colonel Brandon,' I whisper. 'Are you a romantic too, Patrick?'

'I am. To a fault. I imagine all of us must be.'

I spin his question back to him.

'Oh, I'm afraid my answer is a bit boring but I'd pick David Attenborough. I think he'd just have lots of really good stories from his lifetime of adventures.'

'That's not boring. He's what my capybara is named after.'

'You have a capybara? On your city farm?'

'I have a cuddly one who lives on my bed,' I say, because it feels safe to tell him that. Poor David is still stuffed in my suitcase because I felt a little embarrassed about bringing him. Now I know her, I feel like Dolly wouldn't bat an eye at my emotional-support capybara.

'I look forward to meeting him. I mean, sorry! That's rather rude, isn't it? He just sounds like a nice chap. That's not me presuming I'll see your bed. I'm . . . I'm making it worse.' He's so spluttery and sweet that I can't stop laughing.

I know the show's matchmakers set it up so that there are multiple on-paper compatible matches for each of us. But . . . wow. Do I really need to speak to anyone else?

There's something about him: the way he talks, the way he asks me questions. I really want to see him again.

What if he's the one? What if in two weeks' time, he's the man I'm engaged to? What if we're married in a matter of weeks?

I think . . . I think I could see that.

I think Dolly would like him. He's funny and silly and awkward and he sounds like a good man.

Our time flies by as we chat. He tells me about his quiet childhood watching a lot of television with his family pets, while his parents were working, and how all this time with animals led him to become a veterinarian, instead of a GP like his parents. I can't believe we both work with animals. We both *love* animals, and, if we got married, I wouldn't have to explain about bringing babies home to feed. He's open to relocating, and wants children when the time is right. All box ticks for me.

My notebook is untouched, and I've only drunk when my mouth felt dry. I've been so excited speaking to him that I haven't had to find things to do with my hands.

What luck. How incredible that he was my first date. Does he want to see me again?

A jingle sounds through the speakers that apparently signals that it's time for us to say goodbye and make our way outside.

'I—' I begin just as he says, 'Oh really – sorry!'

'You go first!' I insist.

'No, you!'

We share a giggle.

He clears his throat. 'Maybe this will get easier with more dates?'

My heart catches. 'So you're already hoping for more dates?' I whisper, trying to steady my voice.

'Yes, I'd like to see you again, Carys. I've . . . I've got a good feeling about us.'

Me too, I think. 'I want to see you again too,' I say. 'Goodbye for now, Patrick.'

'Have a lovely day, Carys. I'll see you again soon.'

The light dims and his voice disappears.

Gosh, I can't believe I'm so lucky, to have maybe found my person on the first day. What are the chances?

I can't wait to tell Dolly. I hope she's having as lucky a day as me.

Chapter Five

Dolly

Lina Chen, 25, Glasgow

I'm not really sure how to narrow it down. Everyone has a good soul, underneath it all. It's hard to feel that through the wall. That's what matters more than anything, I think. That the person I fall in love with is good. Flexibility is a bonus. Oh, because I'm a Pilates teacher! Oh no, I'm mortified. My mam is going to watch this.

This might be an absolute fucking washout.

My fourth date of the day is with a sweet guy called Cobey who just really loves to surf. I'm not sure if he's so much looking for a wife as someone to help run his surf school at this point, but I admire the hustle. After all, I'm looking for a business arrangement of my own. Cobey is clearly far too nice to be that man for me.

'The thing is, there's nothing like being out there, on the waves. The peace of it, you know?' His disembodied voice matched with my delirium from many hours talking to straight men makes me feel like I'm either having a conversation with a god well into water sports, or I'm on a podcast.

'Yeah, I can imagine,' I say, emphasising my faux enthusiasm because I genuinely don't want to be impolite. I scribble down notes while I let him talk about his family history and why he set up the school, just to feel like I have something to do. It is a little worrying how well my cousin Jas's advice of 'let the men talk' has gone down with all my dates.

'We'll have to get you out there, once we're out of the warehouse!' he eventually says, with so much eagerness that I agree to it. He seems sound, just not what I need. Maybe when we can socialise without the pretence that I'm interested in him romantically, I can enjoy him more.

I've not surfed before, but I do have the kind of core strength and stability that I know helps. Regularly lifting Mum has given me way more muscle strength than people expect when they see me, because I'm fat, basically. People think fat people are all lazy food guzzlers with no discipline yadda yadda; all the stereotypes the world tells them we are.

I love food *and* I could probably out-bench-press half the men in this warehouse.

When I started working from home I missed the hustle and bustle of running round a kitchen, so I turned that energy towards becoming the strongest I could be. It's fallen off a bit, for multiple reasons, but the muscle memory is there.

Those perceptions and stereotypes are on my mind while I'm here, as you might expect. Like how they picture me, even though I'm not actually here to romance any of them. It's insidious really, diet culture and fatphobia and how easy it is to internalise all that. You can't always put it down, even when you logically reject it. It probably doesn't help I'm deeply aware of how straight-sized, slightly chubby women are treated on reality television, never mind fat women. I think I might be the first actually fat woman on *Wedded Bliss*. I think the show was a little worried about casting a fat woman – they made me talk it through with their team psychologists beforehand, but I suspect that was optics, feigned due diligence. After all, the psych teams are so often the ones who orchestrate storylines and breakdowns. Whatever I said must have been enough of the right thing, at least.

And even with all that anticipation, I wasn't expecting my first date to ask me if I liked to be up on someone's shoulders at festivals — a not at all subtle attempt to work out my body type.

Nice try, fucko!

I make a note in my diary to warn the others off Daniel the fatphobic tit. I hope no one gives him a second date, but then, you never know what other people think is a normal attitude to your partner's body. I'm incensed on behalf of all women who might come across him. I hope he gets a bad edit.

Marriage is supposed to be 'in sickness and in health' and I can categorically guess he's not interested in the first half. I've heard enough stories about men leaving their wives when they get sick.

Patriarchy's standards for women's bodies gross me out. Dates get to see each other on date three, and I wonder if this season will suffer the same issue as the regular American ones — the men don't come back for date four if they don't think you're absolutely perfect.

So, date one was a total mess.

My second date was equally nightmarish and kept going on and on about what an alpha he is. A real man's man who wants a little woman to be at home. I've been online long enough to get adverts for 'how to be an alpha' courses that show you how to be a True Man™ and I have been tempted to take one for a laugh. The most alpha person being a tall hot lesbian sounds like the start of a good anecdote. Anyway, I put this guy, Jackson, on my shit list with Daniel. With luck, he'll walk out of here alone, right into the nearest well.

Prospective fiancé number three, Ethan, was resolutely fine but kept asking me if I was interested in CrossFit, which, no, respectfully I'd rather die. I'm not convinced that he isn't just here on a recruitment drive.

I've never been gladder to be a lesbian.

We broke for lunch after date three, and I really wanted to ask Carys how she was getting on, but I got dragged into a conversation with the Hannahs about their dates, and felt it was important I paid attention in case any of them had a glimmer of interest in either of the dirtbag two (unfortunately yes). I barely had time to inhale the boxed salads production brought for us.

I guess this is my life now.

'So, when you look through to the future, like, how do you see your family?' Cobey asks me.

'I see marriage obviously, and children,' I say honestly.

Despite my cynicism, I've always assumed I'd get married. Just to another woman. We had to fight for that right, and I want it for myself.

And I like the idea of having a two-parent household, at minimum. I love my mum, but it's only us, and we're both falling apart. There's no one else to take up the slack.

Obviously, Mum is in that setup too, but I'm not comfortable talking about her with just anyone. Plus, I'm pretty certain my uterus would be classified as a hostile environment, which is another block.

'What about you?' I ask, trying to forget my real life for a moment.

'Oh yah, I love kids. Working with kids is so nice, but I want to have kids at home too.' I love the way he says this like kids are the same as takeaway versus frozen pizza. 'I'm not bothered about whether that's my own kids or step-kids or me and my partner adopt. I'm chill.'

The second part catches me off guard, because so many men on these shows seem to get obsessed with their genetic legacy, or whatever mad term they've come up with for it now.

'That's lovely, Cobey.' I make a new page for Nice Men and

put Cobey at the top of it. Congratulations, Cobey, you are officially the only man I'd vaguely consider marriage material. 'And if this all ends up with us married to different people, I'll be sure to bring my children to your surf school.'

I don't think I'm letting him down, because we both know the vibe isn't quite there. Still, it's nice to hear him enthusiastically reply, 'You better!'

We've still got time to kill, so Cobey tells me a bit more about his family – who sound like a horde of beautiful sun-kissed blondes who love the tradition of a Sunday dinner after a long morning on the beach running with their many, many dogs. He'll be a nice husband for someone here, I'm sure of it.

I reckon Carys would like him. They have a similar sweetness, and I think she needs an enthusiastic Labrador man to meet her where she's at. Maybe then she'll loosen up a little.

This morning, she was so tense. I thought she was going to cry when that glass of juice launched itself. I get being nervous, but it's more than that. When I can get her to relax, to talk to me, she's a different person.

I hope her dates are going better than mine. It would be nice for her to find a good man to fall in love with, even if I'd be a few percentages gutted about it. At least this protectiveness is a safer feeling than attraction. Unfortunately, I'm also still into her, but that'll go with time. I'll get over it.

The end-of-date jingle plays, and we say our fond farewells. I walk out into the door-lined corridor, a little thankful to leave the room. We've shuffled around every date, and I'm not sure if that means the men get to stay in the same room, or if the show is keeping us all moving so no one gets too comfortable. It's the only time we get a bathroom break but the mini-fridges get restocked, so it's not all bad.

Time for date five. I'm moved along by a woman who

introduced herself as Ewa ('like Ever'), passing Niamh and a Hannah or two.

Whit ends up two doors down from me and mimes a rather graphic finger in mouth vomiting motion. I guess her last date went badly.

I've got used to waiting for the light, as though we're walking into a radio studio that's recording. At least it's not as anxiety inducing as waiting for our names to be called at the doctors; I've spent way too much time waiting in reception rooms for one lifetime.

The light flicks on above my door just as I see Carys totter into the corridor on the heels she cannot seem to walk in. She sends me a frantic wave, almost knocking herself over with the motion of it. I try not to notice the pretty pink flustered blush on her cheeks. God. I can't believe I am into such a total dork. I give her a salute as I step back into my heterosexual present and future, leaving the real me in the corridor.

Maybe Mum was right about all this being a fool's errand. But I still have one more date today, and five tomorrow. There's still all to play for. I'm not ready to give up on our future just yet.

I plonk myself down on the velvet couch – this one Mrs Hinch grey. There's a dull ache in my lower back, the one that's pretty much always there by the end of the day, and I wish I could grab some painkillers but they're in my room. I can feel the end-of-day puffiness that comes with doing a little too much when you have this annoyingly weird disease.

Fuck it, I can knuckle through one more date, and then I'll lie down.

I'm pretty sure I've worked out where most of the cameras are now. In here, they're hidden by dried flowers. Another room used funky ceramic statues, and one an abundance of feather boas. I'm not quite sure who was in control of the small-scale decorations, but they've had a whale of a time.

I hear a noise that sounds like I'm no longer alone. Part of me wonders if the men are even on the other side of the mirror. Their voices could be piped in from anywhere in the warehouse. We only have to be in adjoining rooms for the face reveals, after all. How much of this is an illusion, even more so than I know it to be?

There's no time for wondering about how the sausage gets made.

I call out a cut-glass hello.

'Hey,' replies one of the deepest voices I've ever heard in my life. 'Nice to meet you. I'm Warren.'

'Hi, Warren, I'm Dolly. Nice to . . . hear you?'

Warren's laugh is belly deep, and I can imagine his body shaking along with each beat of it. The rumble of his voice reminds me of car tyres over gravel.

'Are you having a nice day so far?' I ask.

'Yeah . . . Yeah, it's been an interesting one. I'm still getting my head around it all, to be honest.'

'Me too. I keep trying not to look at myself in the mirror.'

He laughs. Good, finding me funny is key to staying off the bad list. 'Same. The first date I was like, man, I should have had a last-minute trim. I'm looking messy.'

'Right? I keep trying to touch up my lipstick. This can't be particularly exciting television.'

'I dunno, it's comedy value, isn't it? Think of the clips on *Gogglebox*. They probably got someone checking if they had food in their teeth.'

'Oh God, now I'm worried that was me,' I say, pleased with the back and forth we've got going. 'What do you do for work, Warren?'

'Dolly, I'm a professional basketball player.'

My ears prick up. Proper athletes (not your regular lower league football player on *Love Island*) tend to come on reality dating shows like *The Bachelor* for career reasons: fills time between seasons, helps them and the sport find new fans, and usually the management scores decent pay for the appearance too.

Not that I know enough about basketball to know for sure what camp he's in.

'Oh yeah? Who do you play for?'

'I'm between contracts at the moment, which is why I'm here. But I played college basketball in the States and then I've played for some teams in Europe.'

'So, is it basketball off-season right now? I don't follow the game myself so I'm not familiar with the calendar.' I know this should make me seem interested, because another of Jas's recommendations was to pretend you don't know things so the men can explain them to you.

'No,' he says, and I notice the caution in his voice. 'I got injured last year, just before the new season when I was trying out for new teams.'

'Oh man, that sucks.'

'It really sucked,' he says, and then laughs again. 'I do not recommend breaking your leg as an adult.'

'I'm sure kids would argue it also sucks for them.' It pleases me that he finds this funny too. Okay, Warren, let's keep cooking.

'Yeah, but when you're a kid, you've got someone at home all the time to look after you.'

'And you didn't have anyone to look after you?'

He sucks his teeth. 'I did, but it didn't work out, unfortunately.'

'Or fortunately for me?'

He replies with a deep, slow chuckle. 'Okay, girl. Anyway,

I should be back to full strength later this year, so I'm hoping to get back to it.'

I want to make it clear what I'm here for. How do I word this carefully, in a way that won't get cut out, or won't be used to edit me into looking like an absolute bitch? The edit is the only thing I can't totally control, so all I can do is aim for Strong Female Character, a woman who knows what she wants and is confident to ask for it, and hope that storyline is more compelling than Harridan.

'Warren, can I ask something? I just want to understand what you're looking for in a partner. As you have quite an intense career with a lot of travel, I imagine you're looking for someone who has their own things going on too?'

'Yeah,' he says, and I can almost hear him nodding. 'The personal support matters to me, as I've said, but I'd like to have a girlfriend, or wife I suppose, who has her own career and aims too.'

'That's *very* good to hear.'

'Oh yeah?' There's a smile in his words. 'Tell me about it.'

This is it. If we end up together, this section will definitely be aired, so I have to get the wording right. Warren is the first man I feel I have any compatibility on paper with, and while there might be some other men tomorrow, I'm not holding out hope. I need to play my hand.

I take a deep breath. 'Well, I am a chef by training, but at the moment I primarily make lifestyle and recipe content for socials. I want to grow my audience and find on-camera work. I want a partner who is going to support that, and if they wanted to be part of it, that would be lovely but there's no pressure.'

He's quiet for a moment and I feel my heart racing in my chest. 'I think we're on the same page, Dolly.'

We dive quickly into the stuff that I know will never be

aired but which I consider extremely necessary: the political stuff. Even in a fake relationship, this matters. I wouldn't befriend or remain friends with anyone who believed in things that I fundamentally disagree with, so the same standards apply to a fake fiancé. Yes, we both agree abortion is medical care. He's supportive of LGBTQ+ rights – obviously that's a same-same from me, the World's Best Ally to the gays and *definitely* not a card-carrying member. He was raised Christian but doesn't really follow it, though his church was quite progressive. I'm a Christmas carol ceremony level of religious, aka I like the aesthetics more than the content.

While we're not really supposed to talk about physical appearances, Warren and I do veer that way – he asks me if I've dated people of colour (yes) and I ask him his views on societal fatphobia because if this fake marriage is going to work he will absolutely get trolled online for marrying a fat woman.

Our conversation barrels along as we size each other up. I had started to lose hope that I'd find a pragmatic man, and yet here he is.

I swear I hear a couple of doors in the corridor close, which means they've given us more time. Another good sign that production think our chemistry is good television.

'Can I ask what motivates you, Dolly?' Warren asks, and I smile as he says my name, like it's the sweetest thing in the world. 'Like, you're so ambitious, both of us are. But I want to know what drives you. Where does that ambition come from?'

Of course he wants to know if I'm just a gold-digger, or a gold-digger with a heart. I had really planned for my backstory to be a second date conversation, when I could be sure I could trust my prospective fiancé.

'You can take your time,' he says, and that makes me want to trust him.

I tell him about my mum, and our unconventional family

life. How I've been looking after her since I was a teenager, and how that changes your ambitions, drives and desires. I give him the Spark Notes version to get us started.

He is quiet as I speak but I feel his attention, the reverence to my truth.

I take a deep breath before the next bit, the politics we hadn't got to yet. Bringing up benefits is always a risk because even people who consider themselves left wing can be very into bootstraps and self-reliance. 'And the support we get from the state . . .'

'Is *never* anywhere near enough,' he finishes with such utter disdain that I know he's familiar with the panic that comes every time the government decides to reform the welfare system.

'My Auntie Carol helps out a lot but she's getting on herself,' I say to camera with a cheeky wink. Soz, Auntie C.

There's a long sigh from Warren, and for just a second I worry that I've misread his frustration. 'The thing is, the way it's all set up, is that they make it impossible for one person to support someone else alone. And carer's allowance is a joke.'

Relief rushes through me. 'God, isn't it? What other job would you get less than a hundred quid for thirty-five hours' work? The public would revolt.'

'I've long considered revolting,' he says with a sad laugh. 'The councillors in my ends are pretty good with helping us find any bits of cash or support we didn't know existed, but it's mad that we have to rely on so many people to keep going.'

'Can I ask,' I begin gently, 'who you're talking about? And to be clear, if it's yourself, that's not a deal breaker to me at all.'

'I like hearing that from you, but it's not me. My little brother is disabled, quite complex stuff, and needs a lot of equipment around the house, and a powerchair to get out and about.'

I can just imagine the bills for servicing that every year, the new batteries, the spare parts, never mind the electricity to charge it. Most people assume that all that is covered by the council or the NHS, because it *should* be. I managed to buy Mum a comfortable manual chair to take her out in occasionally, and people were horrified by how much it cost to get a decent one that wouldn't make her arse go numb in five minutes.

We're still a few brand deals off a powered one, but I'll get it for her. By hell or high water.

'If I can work hard, I can make sure Connor never wants for anything. Then we can stop waiting for someone else to say yes, alright, he does need this or that, after three feet of paperwork. The game has meant I'm away from him a lot, but the money I've sent home has helped refit the house so it is accessible for him. It's a decision I'd make every time, even though I miss him and my parents when I'm playing.'

'You get it,' I say quietly.

If I was the type of woman who could fall in love with a man, I think this would be the moment. But I've found a kindred spirit, an ally, hopefully a friend.

'Warren?'

'Yeah, Dolly?'

'I hope this isn't indelicate to say, after everything we've just talked about, but I really like you. And I think we're on the same page. I think you might be the man I've been looking for.'

'I feel that way too, Dolly. See you again?'

The sound rings out that says our date is over, and for the first time I really don't want to leave this room, even though my back aches, and my pelvis is twinging and tender. I do really want to keep talking to him.

'It's a date,' I say with a big smile.

Even though this isn't a romantic connection, I feel a flutter of something rush through me. I think it's a kind of love, the sensation of how powerfully each of us feels about our people back home. The understanding of how much we love our family. We can share that, we can build a strong relationship on those foundations.

There's a few seconds before the microphones cut out.

'I can't wait to hear you again,' he says.

We both laugh and it feels good. 'Warren, I think you and I are going to be the couple to beat.'

'Is it?' he says with a deep laugh. 'You know what, Dolly, I think you're right.'

Chapter Six

Dolly

Warren Baddoo, 27, London

Family is what drives me. And that can be family in a family-unit kind of sense, or friend-family, or community. A community is just a bigger kind of family. Like, when I look out for my neighbours, that's family too. Life's too short to not open your heart to other people. Yeah, I guess the team is a family too — were you trying to get me to say that? Haha, you're sneaky. Hang on, let me try it again so you can edit it in. [Clears throat] You know, a basketball team is kind of like a family too. How was that?

The walk back to the women's quarters smarts. There's no time for me to hobble, so I brisk-walk even though it feels like the lower parts of my belly are burning up.

I'm the only one in the corridor so my suspicions that they kept me and Warren talking seem to be right.

The fatigue hits me like a train. I feel drunk on it; no need for all the alcohol they have on offer.

It feels like past midnight. I knew it would be long hours, but not having a clock to check is very strange. No wonder that guy from *Love Island* used the sun loungers as a quasi-sundial. Too bad there's no sunlight in here, or I could fashion something with all the bronze cups.

Still, despite the lateness, pretty much all the women are in the living room. They cheer as I walk in, which is a nice boost. There's quite a lot of booze littered around, in stark contrast to last night. I guess now we're making decisions and claiming men, they want everyone a little looser. They must have restocked the place while we were on our dates, because the stuff is everywhere. If it's not a fridge bursting with fizz and pink wine, it's a shelf groaning with spirits.

Bridget must have had a good last date, because she's dancing around filling glasses, with a more intense spring in her step than usual. Good for her. Someone has to find actual love on this show. Hopefully it's not some of the walking red flags I met this morning.

'Come join us, babe,' Bridget calls, waggling the bottle like a maraca so bubbles escape out the top.

It's tempting, but what I really need is some meds, and a lie down. Ewa, the production assistant from earlier, comes to collect my mic pack. I hope she gets to clock off at some point soon too.

'I'm going to do my ablutions, darlings,' I say with a real *Ab Fab* accent, and they are all just sufficiently drunk to find that hilarious enough to let me leave without protest.

I walk to the bedroom as quickly as possible, desperate to get out of the skirt that is pressing down on my inflamed tummy, and lie down.

When I open the door, I almost crash into Carys coming out of our ensuite, with a sheet mask on her face.

'A ghost!' I cry in surprise. I'm a little drunk on exhaustion, so I follow it up with a spooky *ooo* noise.

She laughs and swipes at me with her hand, her fingertips just about grazing my arm. Despite a day of emotional intimacy, the only people I've touched all day are Ewa, the original mic guy whose name I didn't catch, and Carys.

'I think I'd be a rubbish ghost.' The section of mask over her nose flaps about as she speaks.

'You could be a friendly ghost. Like Caspar?'

'Would I get to be friends with Christina Ricci?'

I bite back my thought that I'd like to be much *more* than friends with Christina Ricci. 'Could be. Are you all done in there?'

Carys practically leaps out of the way. 'Oh, of course! Go ahead!'

Even with a paper sheet on her face layered with snail mucus or whatever they put in them, Carys is too cute, wearing a button-up pyjama shirt with matching shorts in pink plaid, with a tiny cactus embroidered over the chest pocket. Because *of course* she is. 'I like your jarms,' I say, to explain away the possible staring I've just done.

Mine are just some basics from Marks and Sparks which are probably a little too unsexy for the show, but I've got sexier ones stashed for when they'll be filming me and my fake husband later. For now, it's all cotton, baby.

I grab them and nip into the bathroom for a quick shower.

I knew I wasn't bleeding yet, but I'm still reassured to see bloodless pants. I was worried the stress of the last twenty-four hours could bring it on. That's the thing with endometriosis – it doesn't give a single flying fuck, which frankly, you'd expect for a disease that grows random bits of flesh all over the insides of your body for no discernible reason.

The shower helps the ache in my back. I'll say this for them, the production team invested in a good hot water supply with better pressure than at home. I let the room steam up a little as though expelling the show through my pores.

When I step out, I assess the damage in the mirror. My belly is swollen. We're not quite at six months pregnant levels of pre-period today, but it's tender to the touch, and I wince pulling the waistband of my pyjamas over it. And while I don't have cramps, there's some niggling twinges that threaten to kick off. I neck back some painkillers and, just in case, an anti-spasmodic – thank you to the doctor who told me medicine to stop your guts cramping up stops endometriosis shenanigans in its tracks too. Fingers crossed my body will behave, at least until I'm out of the pressure cooker of the warehouse.

Even though I'd rather climb right into bed half damp, I take my time to do my full skincare routine to make up for the fact I'm going to be in full beat for weeks on end because of the cameras.

With one imminent disaster sorted, it's time to return to the bedroom I'm sharing with an unfortunately adorable redhead in novelty pyjamas who I'm trying to stop being attracted to.

At least she seems happier this evening.

When I walk back in, there's an interloper in our room. 'And who is this?'

Carys startles, moving herself in front of the creature on her pillow.

'I'm not judging. They're cute,' I insist.

'He's called David,' she says coyly, and a pretty blush rises on her cheeks. She rests a hand on David's furry brown head.

Some people are funny about soft toys; I'm not. And I probably would have brought my stuffed panda with me if I wasn't half-convinced she was a biohazard given I haven't washed her in . . . some time.

'Hello, David.' I mime reaching for his paw and shaking it, without touching him due to the aforementioned understanding of soft toy potential biohazard state.

Carys laughs and it's almost musical, high and glittery. I could drink it.

She covers her mouth with her hand. 'Hello, Dolly,' she

says in an old man voice that I think is supposed to be David Attenborough.

'He's *so* polite.'

'He's very smart,' she says, returning to her actual voice. She leans towards me, conspiratorially shielding her mouth from him. 'But does sometimes smell a bit fishy.'

I hesitate. 'Does he really?'

She shakes her head. 'Oh no, sorry. I just mean, you know, he's a capybara. They're aquatic.'

'Ohhh. Are they? Sorry, I mean *of course*,' I say and laugh. 'Well, David, as long as you keep your paws clean, I'm sure we'll have no trouble at all.'

Carys smiles at me so wide that her eyes crinkle. God, she really is so pretty. That disconnect from Carys this morning feels even wider. I feel like I've met three versions of her – the Carys managing an emergency, the one shaking over juice, and this one, relaxed and smiling and pretending to be a capybara.

'How did your day go?' she asks.

'Not bad,' I say, wondering how honest to be with her. 'I think my last date was a solid contender.'

'Oh yeah?' She cocks her head like a puppy.

'Yeah ... Warren? Have you met him yet?'

Carys checks her notebook and then shakes her head. 'Sorry, I'm so bad with names. No, not yet! What did you like about him?'

My brain runs quickly through the list of things I can't say. 'He's very kind. I think we come from a similar background too. I don't know, I don't want to get too excited just yet, but he was my best option by far today.'

'That shared background is important, I think. To some extent, not always, but like, having someone who *knows* you, who gets where you came from. That's huge.' Her eyes take on a soft, dreamy look.

I hate to say it, but I feel a sag of disappointment in my chest. 'So, who is he then?'

She laughs and that pretty pink blush warms her face again. 'Is it that obvious?'

'Very.'

It's for the best that I nip this crush in the bud, even if it's a sharp reminder that I seem to be the only queer in the warehouse.

'Patrick. He's a vet. He's . . . he's really nice.' She tells me about their date, about how he likes someone called Colonel Brandon, which makes me worry she's secretly well into the military, but she insists is a Jane Austen thing. They both like animals so that's fair enough really; I bet he knew what a capybara was.

'Good. I look forward to meeting him tomorrow.' For a second, she looks very panicked. 'So I can suss him out for you!'

Instantly, Carys relaxes. 'S-sorry,' she stammers.

I wave it off. 'Honestly, no stress. It's weird that we're dating everyone. I'll give him a proper grilling. Make sure he's good enough for you.'

That also gets a blush. Maybe because she's thinking about Patrick in damp Regency clothing or whatever straight women enjoy. 'Thank you. I . . . I haven't had the best luck with dating recently.'

I look theatrically around us. 'Whomst among us in this warehouse has?'

She giggles and it is annoying that I still get a kick out of making her laugh.

'What's your dating life been like?' she asks. 'If you want to talk about it. Don't worry if you don't!'

I shrug. 'I've not dated much in the last few years, but I've had a few relationships that lasted a while. Nothing ever really stuck.'

This is true, or at least, partly. Pip, Ayesha and Josie all stuck around for about a year. Either they called it off or I did. The usual break-up reasons in your mid-twenties – someone moves away, someone wants to get married sooner, you have an irreconcilable difference over what constitutes fidelity. They were heartbreaks, at one time, but now they're a soft-focus memory, an old picture tucked between pages. Then there were the more casual affairs, one-night stands or several-night stands. Sometimes several nights spaced out over the course of many years. In a small city like Liverpool, you end up picking up with the same girls over and over. Even the one dyke bar in Manchester yielded some repeat hits.

But with balancing work, looking after Mum and my uterus throwing increasingly uglier tantrums, sex hasn't exactly been on my mind. And who needs romance when you've got lesbians on TikTok who rescue cats for a living and who are conveniently across an ocean so you can't dream too deeply about them? A parasocial crush you keep to yourself is underrated.

Okay, I heard it. I need a life.

I turn the attention back on Carys. 'No luck for you either?'

'No, not really.' She gathers David into her lap. 'Just a high school boyfriend that lasted too long, and not much luck getting a third date since. Do you have any advice?'

'About what?'

'About ... picking the right one, I guess?'

'If I had any insight into that, I'm not sure I'd be on *Wedded Bliss*,' I deflect, because really I'm not sure I know much about love first hand. I've been agony aunt to various group chats over the years, but if you stop replying, people stop adding you, make a new chat, move on. It feels like I'm out of the game on friendship as much as romance.

'True. You'd be blissfully wedded,' Carys quips. Her hands

knead at David in a way that, were he a real live animal, I'd be concerned for his health.

'What's worrying you? Pat the Vet seems like he's a sound lad.'

It takes her a minute to speak. 'Just thinking about the person fitting into your life, which feels like a bizarre thing to consider for a first date, but I love my job on the city farm. How many other city farms are there in the country? What if the person I like doesn't live in London? Patrick is in Yorkshire, I think.'

I might be rusty, but I'm not entirely convinced this is actually what she is thinking about. 'I mean, you could go work on a *country* farm.'

'They just call those farms,' she says a little sarcastically, and then claps her hand over her mouth. 'Sorry, that was rude.'

I burst out laughing. 'No, please! I enjoyed that. A little glimpse of bitchy Carys.'

She groans. 'My evil side. You can't really be rude on the farm, so I have to lock her away in the attic of my mind.'

'Careful, Jane Eyre. She might burn the house down.'

'It was Rochester who locked her away,' Carys corrects me with the teacherly manner of a librarian who can't resist a fact-check.

I shrug. 'I've never been particularly interested in the men in those stories.'

Not that I've had much time for reading either, but *Jane Eyre* was my GCSE English set text and burned into my mind. She should have just gone upstairs, freed Bertha, and they could have run off together. That would have been a way better book. 'So you're worrying about how he will fit into your life?'

'Or me into his. I don't know. I think I'm too deep in my head.' She looks up at me. 'You said Warren was the only good one today. What was so bad about the others?'

'Well, for a start, Warren didn't ask leading questions about my weight.'

'No!'

'Yes.'

'Is that why some guy asked me how many times a day I went to the gym? I just thought he'd got a good deal.' She shivers with disgust and flips open her notebook to a page that has *DANIEL* written on it, with a gigantic X underneath.

'Ha, snap.' I show her my own expletive-filled summary.

'Imagine not respecting the sanctity of the experiment,' she sighs, lying back on her bed covers.

I mirror her, wishing I had something to hold. 'That's one way to put it. I don't know, the other four weren't all bad. Just not someone I'd take home to my mum.'

She rolls onto her side to face me, David squashed against her cheek. 'Tell me about her.'

I instinctively glance up at the corner of the room, even though I know there's no cameras filming us in here (in theory). I wonder how long it'll take me to lose that particular habit, or the sense I'm being watched at all times – the price I'm paying for possible stability.

Still, I want to trust her, and even though I have the mild horn for her now, Carys could be a good friend. I like the little weirdo.

Just to be safe, I flick off the overhead light, swapping it for the lamp on the bedside table. It feels safer somehow to be low-lit.

'So, yeah,' I begin slowly. 'It's just been me and her for pretty much my whole life. She was a nurse for a long time, so she's very good at medical advice – which the whole bloody cul-de-sac knows.'

Carys giggles, and I wonder, sourly, if she's thinking

about that in her future life with Patrick, the whole neighbourhood bringing their mangy cats or depressed goldfish to their door.

This is enough to make me wuss out from telling her the whole truth about my mum. 'What about your family?'

'Oh well, my mum and dad have been together since they were teenagers.'

'Wow, congrats to them.'

'Yeah. It's impressive.'

'But, I imagine, a lot of pressure on you to find your person,' I half ask, half suggest, putting several pieces together at once. 'Do you have siblings?'

'Two. They're not married but they've had more success in dating than me.'

'How's that?'

'Well, they've had recent relationships that last months.'

'Maybe you're just better at weeding out the wasters than they are.'

She makes a little noise that I take to be somewhere between a yes and a no. I'm not sure I really want to get back onto Patrick and how nice that's going to be when my hormones are acting up – aka the time I'm most likely to burst into tears – so I change tactics completely. 'How did you get into being a farmer then?'

'I'm more of an educator.'

'You're not educating the cows, surely? Wow, this farm is incredible.'

She stifles her snort-laugh on the back of David's head. 'No, silly. I teach the kids, show them what cows look like. You know one of the kids thought a cow would look snake-shaped? I was worried he was going to have a conniption when I showed him the real thing.'

'Generation alpha are not okay,' I sigh.

'Oh, they'll be alright. Eventually. I'm sure we were bizarre as children too.'

'That's true. I wanted to be a mortician.'

Carys sits up suddenly. 'Sorry, what?' She sounds less horrified and more excited than most people are when I drop this neat bit of lore.

'My mum watched a lot of *Six Feet Under*.'

'And that show somehow made you want to be a mortician?'

I shrug. 'It sounded cool. Like, you're helping people in a very tough time, and creating a ceremony that the person would have wanted. I guess it's technical and arty, in the same way food is,' I explain. 'Wait, that doesn't sound very good, does it?'

'As long as you're not eating people,' she says with a fake shiver. 'No one needs prion disease.'

'I feel like that might be horrors territory, so please do not explain what that means.'

She giggles in a way that suggests it might be, very much, the horrors. 'I understand what you mean, though. It's about nourishing, caring, providing a service that makes people happy, right?'

The feeling of being seen is a warm light in my heart. 'Yes. That's most of it. And I really miss that part. I trained in a really busy kitchen. When I transitioned to creating recipes and food content for social media, which was much more convenient, I missed the immediate feedback of *seeing* someone enjoy my food. The comments are nice, though people are always doing mad substitutions. Plus the chefs were as likely to say 'good job' as throw a spatula at the wall, so I can't be too rose-tinted glasses about it.'

'I'd love for you to cook for me,' she says, not really knowing how much that means to me.

God, this crush is getting out of control.

'Come on then, what did you want to be then? A vet?' I kick myself for saying this.

'No, everyone always thinks that. I wanted to be something way more specific.'

'Go on, I love specific.'

'Okay, well,' she begins, and I see her fingers pitter-patter across David's fur like she's playing the piano, making music of her story. 'Watching nature documentaries was really my thing when I was small.' She pauses for a second. 'I didn't have the best time in school, but I found a lot of comfort in them. I'd watch all kinds, though I always went back to David Attenborough. I'm monogamous, I guess.'

I laugh. 'Maybe you should be marrying him?'

'Oh no,' she says, suddenly serious. 'I could never live up to his wife Jane, though I think he'd be a very kind husband, which is all I want. Anyway! One day when I was off school, I saw a documentary about how roads cut across natural migration pathways for animals, which is a huge problem. It's the same problem for badgers in the UK as it is for orangutans on palm oil plantations. It made me so sad for them, but hopeful that we could fix things, now that we understand what we did wrong. There's always possibility for change, to make things right.'

I don't think I've ever met someone like her before. When she looks at me, it's like looking at stardust personified, because she glows with passion. Imagine being a person who could make her glow as much as talking about animals does.

'So that's what I wanted to do,' she says, dragging me back to the moment. 'I wanted to be the person who made the crossings for hedgehogs.'

'Hedgehogs?' I laugh a little and I see the stardust falter. 'No, I don't think it's silly. I'm just surprised you chose hedgehogs when you just mentioned orangutans.'

It takes her a moment to believe me, I think. 'I'm really more of a hedgehog kind of girl,' she says eventually.

'Sorry, I didn't mean to laugh.'

'It's okay. I laughed about you wanting to be a mortician.'

I'm relieved she's not upset, but I can still see a kind of closing up inside. Carys looks at me now, and her body seems held purposefully, like a ballet dancer. 'I can't imagine you on TikTok. Not because you're not beautiful and funny, but I don't have an account so to me it's just the animal videos I see getting reposted to Instagram.'

'Yeah, I'm not really filming animals over there.'

'But it's not just recipes? You said lifestyle content too. What is that?'

I wonder how to explain this if all she sees are videos of foxes and raccoons being friends. 'Do you ever see –' I take a breath, raise my voice into the influencer tone, and say, '– *come with me for a day in the life*?'

She bursts into giggles. 'Yes, I know them. That's vlogging, right?'

'That name signals to the youths that we are ancient crones, but yes, I do a variation on those. So instead of just sharing a recipe I might be like *what I eat in a day as a girlie who doesn't restrict*, or *what I eat to power my workout*, which always confuses people when they see a fat girl.'

She thinks for a moment, tapping her fingers against her chin. 'I guess mine would be like *come with me for a day in the life of mucking out the pigs*.'

'Probably *A Day in the Life on a City Farm*, unless you wanted to do some kind of aspirational montage of faeces. You've only a few seconds to hook people in, so you essentially are laying out the thesis statement of what's to come so people stay watching.'

'That's very smart. You can help me make some when we're

out of here then. Maybe it would be good to show people what I do for a living? Talk about food chains and green spaces and stuff.'

'You care a lot about it, don't you?'

'Yeah, I do.' She sighs happily, almost the same tone as when she talks about Patrick. 'I know it sounds counterintuitive but a lot of it is about the people. Bringing children to see farm animals and touch them and learn about them for the first time. It's kind of magic to see their eyes light up.'

'And you love animals,' I say, thinking about her and Patrick probably bonding over their favourite sheep breed or something like that.

I admittedly was not expecting her to launch into her favourite sheep breed, something called a Castlemilk Moorit. One of them unexpectedly had twins. 'Lonnie decided that two were way more than she had bargained for.'

'Fair enough, really.'

'My sisters are twins so I can see it, but her plan was to starve one of them.'

'Oh. Less fair.'

'Nature can be brutal,' she says, very matter of fact in the way only animal people can be. 'So I took him home and bottle-fed him.'

'In your house?'

'Yeah, my housemates thought it was cute for a bit but he kept nibbling their stuff. I'd take Smudge to work every day and he'd follow me round everywhere.'

'That sounds so cute. Is he still like that?'

'Mostly but he quite likes being a sheep.'

'You must miss him.'

'Yeah, but I don't have to pick up poo off my bedsheets anymore.'

Carys sighs deeply, rubs at her eyes with a knuckle like she's trying to bore something out.

'Are you alright?' I ask.

'Yeah, I'm fine. I'm just tired now.' She brushes me off in a way that feels very practised too.

'You know, you can talk to me about anything you want,' I say slowly, and I notice her gaze, though aimed at the floor, intensify slightly, as she's taking in what I say. 'It'll stay between us. What's said in the bedroom stays in the bedroom.'

Carys bursts into laughter.

'Yeah, I heard it,' I say, laughing along with her. 'Perhaps not my best choice of words.'

She turns over, lying on her back with David up on the pillow next to her head, and lowers a silky eye mask over her eyes. I almost don't hear her whisper, 'Thank you, Dolly,' before she falls into soft rhythmic snores.

Her ability to fall asleep in about twenty seconds should be studied. I, however, am destined to be wide awake for a while longer.

My hand feels itchy without my phone. Healthy, I know. Phone might equal job, but phone also equals Mum. Talking about her here feels like a summoning of worries. I know Auntie Carol and Jas are with her, but looking after her has been my job for years. I wish I could call her, even if she's still angry with me, because then I'd know she's alright, if a bit pissed off.

I wonder what she'll think when she sees me on TV. I'm pretty sure the first dates episode will air in a couple of days – I asked Louise about the airing schedule and she was purposefully vague about it. They don't have a strict every night schedule like *Love Island*, or dump it all in several goes like *Love Is Blind*, so it's hard to tell when the real world will creep in.

But it will. It's inevitable.

I wonder what people will have to say about Warren and me. Will I find a better match tomorrow? Somehow, I doubt it.

When do I bring up with him that I'm a lesbian in it for the money?

I'm pretty sure Warren is my best bet. Now all I've got to do is convince the world that I'm in love with him.

And stop thinking about Carys and the delightful little noises she makes in her sleep.

Chapter Seven

Carys

Patrick Stringer, 31, Harrogate

I've had some lovely dates the last two days, yes. I do have a top three, yes. Sorry, it's really hard to answer a question without sounding like I'm answering a question. I'm a vet! All I do is answer questions. What was the last question? Who am I most excited to see again? Sorry, yes, I know I'm not supposed to repeat the questions either. The answer is Carys, she ... Wow, she was really wonderful. It's strange. I only heard her voice but ... Yes, Carys. I'd like to see Carys again.

Do we need to take that from the top?

I'm so relieved when my tenth date, and second full day on camera, is finished that I almost keel over right there. Cobey is nice, but I took in barely anything because halfway through us talking about his surfing school, the room started to spin.

The light is off, and I know that if I don't take a minute to breathe, I'll throw up all over the date room.

The exhaustion of masking from talking to people and being so very conscious about every little movement I make is so heavy that I feel drunk.

The room is soft focus, and I'm not entirely sure if that's the ambient lighting or my nervous system crumbling.

I breathe slowly, as the quiet seeps into my bones. There's not been a second of silence all day until now; five dates with five men over God knows how many hours. And over lunch, Bridget really wanted to discuss her current ranking, which is absolutely fine, but I had to grind my teeth to stop the floating feeling that comes with my brain processing too slowly.

I knew this was going to be tough for me, but I didn't think I'd be so close to a shutdown on day fucking two.

I try to store up the quiet. The fizzing in my body starts to let out, like when you very slowly open a bottle of Coke.

I know there's the expectation that we'll talk about our dates in the living room. I want to be a part of that, but I also could do with a monk-like existence of no speaking or talking for a few hours first.

There's a knock, and for a moment I think it's on the mirror partition, but then I hear Reb's voice behind me. 'Carys, babe, you alright?' Her head appears around the door.

'Yes, sorry,' I say, forcing another smile onto my face. My cheeks hurt with all the smiling I've been doing today. 'I just needed a moment to gather myself.'

The rest of Reb slides into the room, and I try to feel the jolt of despair at losing my silence. 'Me too,' she whispers, and then slips her phone out of her back pocket. 'I'll tell them we're having a heart to heart, so we can have five mins' silence.' She slides down the door to the floor, shuts her eyes, and signs a lazy thumbs up in my general direction. Poor Reb, has she had a break?

I vaguely remember that all chats with our chaperones would be off camera, so I chance that we're truly alone.

I drop the still-plastered smile, kick off my uncomfortable but pretty shoes, flop back onto the couch, and zone out. I've never been more thankful to share a space with someone when

I'm so overstimulated that I'm angry at inanimate objects. Was this couch always so pointy?

The buzzing in my body turns to a background hum by the time Reb's phone vibrates, and I pick up my fuzzy notebook and discarded heels, walking barefoot down the corridor with Reb.

'Pretty sure bare feet in here violates some kind of health and safety,' Reb says, in between yawns she stifles with her phone screen. 'Can we pretend I didn't see it?'

I nod. 'Pretending mode, activated.'

The irony isn't lost on me.

'You and the girls have dinner and drinks coming any moment, so we'll be filming in the hope you'll talk about your dates.'

I suppress a groan. 'I was hoping you were going to take my mic pack.'

'Look, between us, the sooner you say your piece, the sooner you can go to bed,' she says in a lowered voice. 'They just need the shot.'

'Okay,' I say, steeling myself. 'I do need to eat anyway.'

'Precisely. Right, got to dash.' Reb squeezes my shoulder, then disappears down the corridor of doors to backstage.

As I slowly walk back to the dormitory, I can't help but think about the network of glass and wires and cameras that must be in the walls around me. It's all very *Truman Show*, or probably five different episodes of *Black Mirror*.

It's a very peculiar thing to know, for certain, that you are being observed. Not that that's particularly different from how I feel just existing as an autistic person; it feels like someone's always waiting to catch you out.

Is this how the farm animals feel when we have school visits? God, I hope not. I don't really have time to spiral about the emotional wellbeing of the animals in my care right now.

When I walk in, my eyes find Dolly immediately, in the middle of the group of women. She's radiant as ever, curled into the corner of the couch with her arm slung over the back. She and Whit whisper together.

As the door closes, all eyes turn to me. Her smile is the one I return.

She drags over a footstool and pats it. Dolly wants me to sit with her? Oh, it's so nice to have a friend. I'm pretty sure we're friends.

I take the seat, and Bridget plonks a bronze cup of mysterious fizzing alcohol in front of me with a 'hiya, butt'.

Priya seems to be leading the main conversation. 'So if we all had ten dates, that means we've all dated all the same men, correct?'

Everyone nods, some less enthusiastically than others.

'So are we going to talk about who our top threes are?' Niamh asks, sounding casual, but her eyes flash like she's ready for a fight to break out.

'No way,' says Whit, crossing her arms at the wrists in an X. 'That's a recipe for disaster.'

'Or good television,' murmurs Dolly, which earns an eye roll from Whit.

Dolly's glance meets mine, and we giggle.

Her eyes drop to my lap. 'Darling, unless you are trying to start a WikiFeet, I would put your shoes on while they're filming.'

That's when I realise the heels are still clutched in one hand, the notebook in the other. I have no idea what WikiFeet is, but it doesn't sound good, so I stuff my hot feet into my nasty little shoes and grit my teeth.

Dolly pats my knee, her touch soft and warm, and I feel slightly less irate about my shoes.

'Look, guys, maybe we should be compassionate about this,'

says Lina, once again the voice of reason in our group. 'All of us will have connections with more than one man, and there will be overlap, so I think it would be really mindful if we didn't have this kind of conversation right now.'

'Bores. You're all bores,' grumbles Niamh. 'In that case, did anyone else get the guy who was obsessed with teeth?'

Priya rolls her eyes. 'We talked to everyone, Niamh. That's what we just established.'

'Right, and did he talk to you about teeth?'

'Sorry, did you say teeth?' asks Dolly.

Whit leans forward excitedly. 'Oh yeah, he wouldn't shut up about his—'

'TURKEY TEETH,' chorus the Hannahs with Whit, though they have more enthusiasm and volume than I'd expect for the topic of teeth.

I resist covering my ears with my hands and instead plunge my nails into my palms to quieten the fizzing.

Dolly flips through her notebook. 'I can't believe I missed out on hearing some genuine banality. Who was that?'

'Billy,' sighs Hannah C. with a swoon.

'Sorry,' I begin, my voice louder than I expected. 'What are turkey teeth? I work on a farm and—'

'No, not from a turkey. From *Turkey*,' insists Hannah C.

Hannah S. looks over to me. 'I thought he meant the bird too.'

'Well, turkeys just swallow their food whole, along with rocks, which help grind the food up in their stomach,' I say, and realise with horror I've gone into fact-dumping mode. 'Haha, or something like that!'

It's too late. Everyone is confused.

Except Whit. 'That's incredible. You know, I haven't taken stones out of anyone's stomach yet. There was a big one in someone's—'

'I *really* do not think we need to know the end of that sentence!' cries Priya.

'Booooo,' calls Niamh, who I realise now is actually quite merry.

'Thing is,' continues Hannah S., 'they never come with heads at Christmas, so how would you know?'

'Could we move on from turkeys and whatever horrors Whit was about to unleash on us?' Lina asks.

Priya sighs. 'Well, Billy never mentioned teeth to me, so perhaps I have that to look forward to.'

'It's a bizarre thing to be obsessed with. He even asked what my favourite floss brand was,' Hannah S. says.

'Maybe he's an orthodontist?' offers Lina, who seems to have reluctantly accepted we are not moving on from teeth.

Bridget shakes her head. 'No, that's Whit.'

'I'm training to be an orthopaedic surgeon,' Whit sighs. 'Bones, not teeth.'

'Aren't teeth bones?' Hannah S whispers, and Lina shakes her head. 'That's not right, is it.'

'No, that's Malachi,' says Bridget, who spots it when Whit bursts into a huge smile. 'Oh hiii, we've got lovestruck here.'

Whit dips her head to hide her smile. 'It was just a good first date.'

'I thought he was nice too,' says Priya, sipping her drink, and I feel weirdly annoyed that she's ignoring our agreement not to talk about the good dates. 'And Patrick.'

My stomach drops. Priya is a knockout. If the walls come down on date three and there's a choice between Priya, a legitimate grown-up with thick flowing hair, or me ... I'm not sure anyone would think twice.

There's a hand on my wrist, and I glance up to meet Dolly's eyes. Her gaze is electric, intense. I find eye contact uncomfortable at the best of times but, somehow, I feel safe looking at her. I give her a small smile, answering the question I think she is asking me, and she pats my wrist as she sits back.

'Patrick's a bit too nice for me but wouldn't it be lush being a doctor's wifey?' giggles Bridget. She looks over at me. '*You'd* suit, I think, Carys.'

It feels a bit pointed, but I'm still glad for it.

'Technically he's a vet,' I say.

Bridget waves it off. 'That's just details, babe.'

Whit laughs. 'You might find you care more about the details when you need a surgeon.'

'You say that but you human doctors only need to know people. Vets need to know all about the insides of cows and guinea pigs and chickens.' Bridget places her hands on her hips. 'Really I think people surgeons could work harder.'

I'm not quite sure why I'm now picturing animals performing surgery, but I think it's the tension making my head spin.

'I agree. He's a good 'un,' whispers Dolly, and this gives me a different kind of spinny feeling. I guess I'm just glad she sees what I do.

'And Warren is lovely too,' I whisper back.

'Much nicer than the alpha male creep I dated yesterday,' she mutters under her breath.

I know who she means. He was my ninth date today, and immediately gave me odd vibes. I feel awful saying that, because I'm sure I don't make the best first impression, but he kept talking about traditional gender roles. I was so tired by that point that I just let him talk on and on, and he barely noticed I hadn't said anything.

Maybe that's the point. Maybe that's what he wants.

Luckily, the others seem not to have heard our back and forth, because Bridget is needling Lina about her dates.

'I have no idea who I like or don't like, if I'm honest with you. I think I need to give them a few more dates.' Lina throws her hands up in the air, slopping a little of her drink. 'It's just so hard! And weird!'

'That *is* the show, Lina,' says Bridget rather sharply.

This seems to land badly for Niamh. 'Come on now, being here is different. It's intense. That's what Lina means, yeah?'

'I just don't have a sense of their heart,' Lina says. 'It's not like you can see an aura through a screen.'

There's an awkward quiet that I feel the urge to fill with enthusiastic support.

'That's very true. Hopefully, spending more time with them will help us all.' It makes Lina smile, at least.

'God, don't you think it would just be easier to date a girl?' groans Hannah C., flopping back on the couch.

That doesn't seem right. Why would it be *easier* just because we're the same gender? I think of Miri and Sara in the street on the way here. That didn't seem *easy*. I can't work out how to say this out loud without citing them as an example, but I can't do that without giving away that Dolly and I met already, which is a strict no-no.

Dolly, however, snorts so loudly that she startles half the group.

'What's so funny?' Hannah C. has what Ang would describe as a *stink face*.

'It's the line my lesbian friends hear all the time from straight girls,' Dolly says casually, but I can feel the warning underneath it. Protective. Maybe she's like that with all her friends. 'People are people, no gender is easier than another.'

I wonder ... I wonder if having lesbian friends and being part of the LGBTQ+ culture means Dolly has, I don't know, kissed a girl, like the Katy Perry song. I don't know why I'm thinking of that.

'Hannah C., that's kind of homophobic,' Bridget says in a serious tone. Beside her, the other two Hannahs nod.

'Well, I'm sorry,' Hannah C. says, sounding not remotely sorry. 'I just thought it would be nice.'

Hannah S. starts talking about her experience as a wrestler and everyone mistaking her for being into women because of her job, and I wish I could listen but I'm having a small crisis because oh God, am *I* being homophobic by assuming that Dolly might be into women just because of who her friends are?

Crap, am I just thinking about this because we're sharing a room? Is this the school changing room all over again, where anyone caught looking at each other too long was called 'a gay'? That happened to me a few times, and I don't think I was even looking, but so much of my own behaviour reported back is baffling to me, like another person did it.

It's just a thought. Thoughts are neutral, right? It's the act that's bad. God, I don't even know.

I have to close the door firmly on those thoughts to pay attention, while studiously not looking in Dolly's direction, which is quite hard because she's sitting next to me.

'Have you ever gone girl?' asks Bridget like it's something scandalous. Maybe it is when we're on a dating show about men. The way she said it makes me feel a bit strange either way, especially after she told Hannah C. off.

Hannah S. frowns. 'What, like the movie? What's that got to do with lesbians? I haven't faked my own death if that's what you mean?'

'Urgh, spoilers!' groans Whit. 'I never get time to watch films.'

Priya taps her fingernails against the bronze cup. 'It was a book first.'

'Or *read*. Though maybe I should put audiobooks on when I'm cutting. Might be better for me than listening to Taylor Swift all day long.' She spots me perking up. 'Bit weird to say, but there's nothing like slicing someone open to "Look What You Made Me Do".'

'You scare me,' Dolly says with a smile.

'You know,' Lina begins slowly, 'I'm not sure I've ever really thought about the gender of the person I'm dating. Like, yes, I know I like men, but I don't think that means I'd ever rule out women? Like Dolly says, people are people, and I think it's perhaps not such a big deal for me.'

The sound of the room blurs, like I'm suddenly underwater.

Is that ... possible?

How can it not be a big deal for her?

And I thought people *know* when they're kids, isn't that the whole 'born this way' line? Maybe this is just another social rule I've misunderstood; it wouldn't be the first. Or maybe I'm just naive.

The conversation moves on before I can ask Lina what she really means, because everyone is suddenly arguing about CrossFit, because it seems one of the men is an instructor. What is CrossFit? I keep picturing angry strong man cartoons working out together.

They must have started arguing about something because the volume of the room shoots up, and now I really do have to cover my ears. I don't even know what started it but suddenly Lina stands up on the couch and claps her hands once. 'That's enough.' Everyone falls silent. She's a Pilates instructor, I think, so I guess she's used to wrangling rooms of stressed-out, hangry women. 'Arguing brings bad energy, and fighting over men is not very feminist.'

'Now's not the time for cat fights, ladies,' calls Lucas Nguyen's familiar voice. I'm not sure calling it *cat fights* is very feminist either, but there we go.

Somehow, he's in our dormitory, the cameras trailing him. It's funny seeing a popstar, or ex-popstar I guess, wandering around.

I school my face as Lucas struts over, carrying a shiny red box. 'It's time for you to request your second dates. You can select as many men for second dates as you like, but the date will only happen if the match is mutual.' He spins to the camera that has followed him in and gives it a winning smile. 'We're all about consent here on *Wedded Bliss*.'

He turns back to us to continue his speech. 'If both of you request a date, then you'll continue your stay in the warehouse and have a second date, still unseen. But if you get no mutual matches, you'll be sent home.'

There's a collective gulp as this sinks in. I didn't realise we could be sent home so quickly. This is all moving so fast.

'Let's get voting, ladies!' Lucas calls.

I'm surprised to see Reb still working, but she rushes over with a stack of paper and pencils, handing a set out to each of us. It's all so retro; a bit like voting in a UK election – put your X in the box next to your candidate's name.

It's weird to know that, right now, Patrick is looking at his own version of the list. Will he pick me too? I hope so. I mark an X next to him.

I'm not sure if it's eyes on your own page, like with voting, but I can't help notice Dolly checking off a few men. She catches me looking.

'Nosy,' she teases, but I'm confused.

'I thought you'd just pick Warren,' I whisper.

She shrugs. 'Still keeping my options open.'

They say if you go looking, you'll find something, though I know that's more about men's phones than the voting paper of your roommate on a reality television show. But still, my stomach squirms when I see the X on her paper next to Patrick. What is she doing? I thought she wanted to size him up for me, but did she actually mean for *her*?

I feel hot all over and I'm not sure why, because if she

likes Patrick, then *fine*, she should be with him, but she liked Warren, didn't she? That's what she said. I would step aside if there was something between them. Is this jealousy?

God, I hate neurotypicals sometimes. They never say what they mean!

I put an X next to Warren. And then a few more men, because it's not about her, actually. I should just be sensible, and give a few of these men more of my time, because Lina's right – it's hard to know them in just an hour. I barely heard anything Cobey said, so I should give him some more time at least.

I fold up my slip, and as I reach to put it in Lucas's box, my hand collides with Dolly's, attempting the same thing. I swear I get a little electric shock, but she doesn't seem to notice.

My roommate. My first friend here. The woman I watched stride into traffic. I don't want to feel strange, complicated things about her. I don't want us to feel like we're competing for the same man. I don't want to be angry with her. I just wish I understood her a bit better.

She gives me a big warm smile that I struggle to return.

'Gosh, I'm tired,' I say, rubbing my forehead with the back of my hand. I hope the movement covers any springing tears.

'Me too,' she whispers back. She's acting like nothing is wrong so maybe nothing *is* wrong. But why does it feel ... bad? Some flavour of bad I can't parse.

'Okay, ladies, I'll be back in the morning to hand out the good, and possibly some bad, news,' Lucas says.

I've officially had enough of the day.

As I excuse myself to bed, I hope that across the warehouse, Patrick is thinking of me too.

Script/Vox Pop Hannahs

[The Hannahs sit on a couch together.]

HANNAH C.   It's so frustrating that people keep mixing us up.

HANNAH P.   And not just the other women! The men keep mixing us up. But we don't even sound the same. Hannah C. is from Jersey!

HANNAH S.   I don't know why the women can't tell us apart when we all look so different. Yes, we are all blonde, but we're not even the same type of blonde. I'm dirty blonde, Hannah C. is honey blonde, and Hannah P. is butter blonde.

HANNAH P.   Exactlyyyyy.

[They all nod in sync.]

HANNAH C.   It should be easy to remember. I'm the engineer.

HANNAH P.   I'm the surveyor.

HANNAH S.   And I'm the professional wrestler.

ALL TOGETHER   We're unique!

Chapter Eight

Dolly

Jackson Smith, 25, Leeds

I just think a man should be a man in the relationship. I believe in gender roles – I think it's good for a couple to divide up the house. My role is to support my future wife in the home, her role is to support me as the breadwinner. It's a relationship style that's worked for a reason. I'm a traditional kind of man. I want to be the alpha, haha.

If the atmosphere last night was weird, then breakfast is much worse.

We're all waiting to find out who got mutual matches, and will be off on dates. It's even getting to me a little, and I end up rooting through the fridge for ingredients to make something with. I've got too much nervous energy for cereal.

I end up with a fairly large spinach frittata made in not really the right pan, so it sticks, with a kicker avocado salsa on the side. It's a recipe I've shared online before, a comforting reminder of who I am and what I'm here for.

There's enough for everyone, and I get a buzz when Whit, Lina and Carys come over with empty plates, ready to try it. There's a few of those perfect, eyes-closed bliss moments as they eat.

Carys was asleep when I got in last night, and I can tell

something is up as she's polite, but distant. Probably for the best given I'm trying to neutralise this crush.

Neither of the Nguyens return with the big red box.

Instead, some fresher-faced production assistants hand out pink envelopes to each of us in the living room, in front of everyone as the cameras pile around. This is new, I've not seen them do it on camera before. Maybe they're hoping for cat fights.

The room hushes as everyone waits for someone to go first, so I rip open mine. It's not quite a dance card, but inside I find a schedule of dates for the next two days. Warren is tomorrow, thank God, and today I have dates with Patrick and inexplicably . . . Malachi? The nice Scouse guy Whit said she really likes, but crucially also a man whose name I *definitely* did not request. Not just because Whit is cuckoo over him, but because he is looking for love. Hopefully he'll find that with Whit.

So why do I have a date with him? I'm not naive enough to imagine the showrunners won't influence decisions along the way, but manufacturing date choices seems . . . strange. Are they trying to create tension between Whit and me?

I wonder who else has scored a second date with someone they didn't pick.

I glance round at the others and everyone seems vaguely pleased, or they're hiding it well. None of the women are going home yet – pretty expected, as usually the first to go are the worst offenders on the men's side. Preferably the man who asked us all how heavy we were.

I head back to the kitchen to clean up, like a good cook. When I'm done, Whit and most of the other women have left, presumably to get ready for their dates.

The only person left standing is Carys, a bright smile on her face. I guess she got her second date with Patrick too. It might not have been my smartest moment to request a second date with him, but Carys is my roommate, and I want to look out for her.

That's what I'm telling myself anyway. Platonic mode.

Her little outburst on the first night about not knowing how to pick a partner made me worried that he was perhaps not as boringly normal as he'd appeared in our first date, where I'd written him off as another nice man looking for a wife.

But knowing that she really likes him has, I don't know, kicked up my protective side. I want to interrogate him for her. I don't want her to get her heart broken.

And if my crush is going to get squashed, realising the man I am up against in my own mind is good for her will help with that.

'All good?' I call across the empty room.

'Yes. We've got a second date this afternoon. Patrick and I,' Carys says, a little breathless. 'And you? With Warren, I mean?'

Okay, so I guess from her sharp tone that she clocked me picking Patrick and is slightly pissed off about it. 'I get to see Warren tomorrow. I'm really looking forward to it.'

I want to tell her that I'm not interested in Patrick, like I need to do with Whit, but she says a little loudly, 'Well, I'm going for a shower now, bye!' and scuttles away.

So much for that.

My dates aren't until after lunch, which I take to be a few hours from now, so I decide to go for a run in the gym: an activity that is mindless enough to take my brain out of my body.

About twenty minutes into my jog to the boppier tracks of *The Rise and Fall of a Midwest Princess*, Whit hops onto the treadmill next to me in the outfit she put on for her date, tailored high-waisted trousers and a pretty embroidered silk shirt. To my surprise and confusion, she kicks off her heels and starts running.

I slip out my slightly sweaty ear buds. 'Good date?' I ask, as she turns up the speed to levels I've never imagined running at.

She growls in response, then seems to realise she's not actually used words. 'It was a fucking shitshow,' she bites out.

I hit pause on my treadmill so that I can concentrate better and eliminate the risk of falling off mid-sentence. 'What happened?'

Whit keeps her eyes straight ahead as she quietly says, 'They sent me on a date with *that arsehole*.'

'You'll need to narrow that down for me,' I say lightly.

'Jackson.'

I recoil. 'The one obsessed with being an alpha male?'

'That's the one.'

'Why?' I say, meaning really why on earth would you pick him.

'Fucked if I know. I didn't ask for a second date for obvious reasons! The man has something wrong with him.'

I don't disagree with that. Clearly, it's not just my matches the show has fiddled with.

'Did he say something to you?'

Whit slams the emergency stop with her fist, and slowly comes to a halt. 'Nothing that was exactly *about* me but ... he just reminds me of my really controlling ex from when I was a student.'

'Oh Whit. I'm sorry.'

She shivers. 'He gives me the same feeling. Like all my skin has turned to goosebumps, and not in a good way. It's bad enough when there's a partition in the way; I do not want to be in the same room as that man.'

'Do you need a hug?' I ask, and she steps over to my treadmill so I can wrap her up. She's almost as tall as me, but tucks her head under my chin and bursts into tears. I let her cry it out, and when a couple of the Hannahs try to come into the room, I signal them to get lost for a few minutes. Whit deserves her privacy right now. The tension leaves her body in a big rush as the tears dry up.

'You're safe,' I tell her. 'I've got you. You're safe.'

We stay that way until she stops shaking. She steps out of my hug, wiping the tears from under her eyes, and suddenly freezes. 'Shit, have I ballsed up my makeup?'

'I think a refresh might make you feel better.' I take my pinkie finger and delicately dab away a few globs of melted eye liner that have peppered her cheeks like ashfall.

'Did that fix it?'

I press my lips together. 'Not really, no.'

She looks up at the ceiling and groans loudly. 'Bloody cameras. I hate thinking about makeup at the best of times. I never wear it to work so I don't have to worry about it going wonky.'

'I imagine there's a lot more at stake what with the sliced-open person in front of you. Do you want some help?'

She goes to hug me again but springs back. 'Sorry, I've got sweat dripping off me. I should fix that first.'

'It's probably some of mine, honestly.'

'That's friendship.'

I follow Whit to her room and wait while she showers. She's in and out quickly, covering her hair so it doesn't get wet. Once she's dressed, she sits down on the bed and I take off the remains of her old makeup for her with cotton pads. It reminds me of teenage sleepovers. There's nothing quite like the wealth of touch between teenage besties, but this feels close.

Eventually Whit takes over because I only just about know how to do my own makeup well enough, but I play assistant by handing her products as she requests them, like I'm assisting her in surgery.

The shaking seems to have stopped by the time she attempts mascara. 'Do you think they gave the men some kind of priority? Like, they said it had to be mutual, but do you think that's actually true? Like on *Married at First Sight* when only one person wants to go home, and they have to stay another week.'

Relieved to be out of range of the cameras, I lower my voice and say, 'The production team will be manipulating us for the best television. We have to remember that.'

It strikes me then that I don't actually know any of the job titles of the production team that rush around us, only their names. For all I know, Louise isn't an assistant or a runner; she could be orchestrating the whole story. Sure, it could be unethical, but this is reality television. When has that stopped them before?

'Whit, they've sent me on a date with Malachi and I didn't pick him, and I doubt he picked me either.'

'A much better forced choice,' she concedes.

'Yeah, but that's probably because they're trying to stir up some kind of drama between us.'

Whit gives me a look of horror. 'Those twats.'

'Twats, definitely. But I'm glad you like him.'

'He makes me feel like I've got love shooting out my arse,' she says dreamily.

'That sounds painful.'

'It's lovely, I promise,' she says with a laugh. 'I guess this messing round with our dates is the whole 'and whatever the production team deem necessary' part of the contract we signed.'

'You shouldn't have to see Jackson again,' I say decisively. 'What's your handler's name?'

'Hellie.'

'We should go talk to her to make sure you're not sent on any more dates with him, and be clear that this is about your safety. They have to be careful with mental health and contestant care, so they'll take you seriously.'

I hope, at least.

It's not like reality television has a particularly stellar record with contestant care, be it on or off camera, or after the shows.

They seemed quite thorough when we signed up as we had psychological evaluations, medicals, hell even STI tests, but then, they still made someone like Jackson part of the main cast, a man with clearly unhinged views, and gave him to Whit, a woman with a history of abuse. Unfortunately, a pattern I've seen before on dating shows.

When Whit's face is restored to its former television-approved glory, she pulls me into a squeeze. 'Thank you. Love you.'

'Love you too.' It comes easily, and I know it's true. You can't be stuck in a niche situation with a handful of people without forming sudden intense attachments, but I can see us being friends long term. Provided she doesn't mind all the things I lied about for the show.

I walk back into the living room, which is mostly empty bar a Hannah and Bridget doing nails – I need to ask them for some pointers later.

I stride straight to the door leading to backstage, rap my knuckles on it and ask for Louise.

'Darling!' she cries with excitement. 'Had a good workout?'

I had completely forgotten I'm in my *actually at the gym* outfit aka some ratty old leggings and an old band t shirt that's shrunk in the wash a few too many times, rather than the hot red outfit I wore the first night. If I'd been thinking right, I'd never have walked into a cameras-on area wearing this. This is the kind of outfit and body combo that gets posted in the *Daily Mail* with my head cut off to shame people for not going on weight loss drugs yet.

'Yes, thanks,' I say, forcing my thoughts past how see-through the arse on these leggings probably is. 'I just wanted to check something about my schedule for the next two days?'

'Yes, you've got dates with Patrick, Warren and Malachi.'

She says this without a moment's hesitation, not even a glance down to her phone. I know it's her job to know where I am at all times, but this seems . . . off.

'The thing is, I didn't pick Malachi?' I tilt my head to the side like Carys does, hoping that it looks curious and naive, not aggressive. 'I mean, it's lovely to get more time to hang out with him, but I didn't pick him.'

'Oh, the show reserves the right to try you on subsequent dates with contestants if we felt that a match was under-explored,' Louise says flatly. 'It's a good thing, darling. And we find that it reduces the possibility of regret once we get to the honeymoon stage.'

Now *that* I know is horseshit. Regret means drama. The group honeymoon in one big house is the first time all the engaged couples get to see each other in real life, meaning sometimes they realise that the person they wrote off earlier in the process is their type on paper, so to speak.

What are they up to?

There's two ways to play this: suspicion or flattery, and I choose the latter.

'Of course, thank you, Louise. That's really thoughtful. Malachi is really nice,' I say, putting on my sunniest voice.

I remain convinced that good edits are a result of good relationships with the production team, and I'm not about to risk getting some kind of bitch edit, even if I can see the love triangle they're trying to plant up. Nice try, guys. You've got a lesbian in the mix here.

She takes my hand and pats it condescendingly. 'You just have to trust the process.'

I'm struck with the sudden urge to bite her. 'Of course. I'm just so excited to be here!'

'Call me if you need me!' She bounces away back down the corridor, leaving me standing at the open door.

~

'Hello?'

'Hi, Patrick?' I call into the nothing.

'Is that Dolly? Wow, hi, Dolly!'

Bless him, he is nothing but enthusiastic. I can see why Carys likes him.

'It is. How are you today, Patrick?'

'I'm so good. What a delight to see you today!'

The tone of his voice tells me two things – that he's perfected the art of appearing personable at all times and that he absolutely did not check me off on his second date preferences sheet. Love triangle number two, perhaps? I wonder what they're doing to the other contestants.

'It's always nice to be called a delight.'

I decide not to hint to him that I know he didn't pick me; that sort of thing could be reused badly by cameras, so instead I just lean into a nice chat.

The sexual chemistry between us could be described as 'dead in the water', so we talk about the people we're actually interested in.

'Warren is the best, genuinely,' Patrick says after mentioning that they are roommates. 'And he speaks very highly of you.'

'As does my own roommate,' I say. 'Of you, I mean.'

I imagine him smiling to himself on the other side of the glass.

We talk about family for a little while. I wonder if he and Carys will get married, and fill the world with adorable, very enthusiastic children.

I need to check his closet for skeletons but our chat is all superficial, and I'm conscious of how much longer this date is going to last if production also realise it's dry as a dead well.

And so, I ask, 'Tell me, do your dates usually ask you to treat their pets?'

'They really do. I had one girl bring her cat to the date. It had a big abscess on its head, and she was expecting me to resolve that in the middle of Pizza Express.'

I bork. 'NO!'

'Yes! And the worst part is I did help the cat out – I drove us to the practice I was working at the time, on my day off. And then, she told me we were more cut out for the doctor–patient relationship than a romantic one.'

'The neck of her!'

'Veterinary care is expensive,' he sighs. 'But still. It was rather inappropriate.'

'I can't believe she subjected the dough balls to that.'

'Yes, I couldn't quite look at the garlic butter dip the same after draining that abscess,' he deadpans, and I die laughing.

Once I've composed myself, I return to my mission. This is what friends do, after all. I'll do the same to Malachi later for Whit, obviously. These two interactions are identical and definitely do not carry the weight of any jealousy, nope nope nope.

'So, it's a big jump coming on here to get married, isn't it? Have you been in a serious relationship before this?'

'Is this an interview?' He laughs nervously.

'I'll tell you if you pass,' I joke.

'I've been in one serious relationship, yes. We were together eight years, and broke up about six months ago.'

Wowee. 'What was her name?'

'Peony.' He says the word quietly, reverently. I can hear the love in the letters. I don't think this is just nostalgia or respect; this is being still hung up on your ex, I'm certain of it.

Poor Carys. Does she know?

'Do you mind me asking what happened?' I say, aware this will absolutely make it to television as his backstory.

'We, err. Well. I moved to Harrogate to set up practice, and she was in Newcastle doing her PhD. We'd been long distance before that too, and we were getting to the point where we could move in together ... I just didn't want to pressure her when she was busy with her work.'

'So you ended it?'

'No, I just said it probably wasn't a good time for us to live together. And she ended it.'

Oh, this absolute dummy. I would eat my hat (if I had one) if Peony didn't actually want to move in with him. The last thing a girl wants is being told what a man thinks she might want. I bet she feels like he took away her agency. Mistake dating career-minded women 101 right there, Pat.

I manage to steer the conversation back to my (fake) dating history – several boyfriends in the past, no one caught my eye for years, need a man who is career focused yada yada yada. Pip, Ayesha and Josie become Paul, Andy and Josh.

But all the time, I can't help wonder if Carys knows about the Peony situation. And if she doesn't, should I tell her?

When our date ends cordially, I find Carys in the corner of the empty living room reading a book. The tip of her nose keeps bouncing up and down as her nostrils flare in and out. Her eyes shine with excitement. I guess it's a good book. In another life, I see her in a patch of sunlight, curled up on Mum's couch with a cup of tea, the pair of them swapping reads.

She notices me, and her smile is hot like the sun. 'Dolly!' She snaps closed the book, and pats the seat beside her, like she's been waiting for me the whole time.

I'm relieved that she seems to have returned to her old self after her shortness last night. Perhaps that was like the first night where she just powered down from being too tired?

'Good book?'

'Better company.' I try to ignore the flip in my stomach.

That's when I know I can't do it. I cannot be certain that telling her about Patrick's hang ups isn't more about me than her. Nothing is ever going to happen, and I need to let it die. I need to friendzone her.

Patrick is a good man. He'll tell her.

'Who were you out seeing this morning?'

'Cobey,' she says, without the dreaminess Patrick is afforded.

'The surfer dude?'

'Yes, he's very nice, I think. We get on well.'

'Yeah, I liked him too. We agreed to buy each other a friends-drink when this is all over. Are you going to ask for a third date?'

She wriggles in her seat. 'Not sure. Maybe? I kind of panicked last night and put an X by too many names because I felt ... I suppose bad missing people off who had been nice to me?'

'I think the key question is do you want to marry him?'

She taps her fingers on the hard cover of her book. 'I'm still working on that.'

'That's fair,' I sigh. 'I suppose the other way to think about it is do you want to *stop* seeing them, and if not, then you keep going and try not to worry about the wedding part.'

She's quiet for a second. 'You just went on your date with Patrick?'

I'm relieved she's brought it up. I twist in my seat to face her. 'Hey, I just want you to know, I'm not interested in Patrick. I just wanted to get to know him, that's all.'

'Really? You don't have to pretend if you *do* like him.'

'No, he's very nice, but –' I try not to say *clearly hung up on someone else* '– nothing more than a friend for me. I was just checking out my friend's possible future husband and making sure he's good enough for her.'

I feel a smidge of guilt when a beaming smile breaks across her face. 'You're the sweetest.'

'I just wanted to be explicit, so you didn't get the wrong idea.'

There's nothing I can do about how this storyline will be edited eventually, but I've said my truth and Carys knows it, and that will have to be good enough.

When she shakes her head, her pinned-up curls start to come loose, bouncing around her cherubic face. 'Never. You've a good heart. And, umm,' her tone changes suddenly, 'I have to admit I went on a second date with Warren this morning.'

'Right,' I say as neutrally as possible. 'How was that?'

'He's a nice man but the same for me as you. I mean, with Patrick.' She groans. 'I'm getting my words mixed up. I mean we're just friends.'

'Thanks for telling me,' I say. 'Maybe we can go on double dates when we're married and out of here?'

'I'd like that.'

Carys is suddenly called away by her handler, Reb, a woman I've never seen below a nine out of ten on the stress scale.

That went better than I thought it would, at least. And now that I've got Carys out of my head, maybe I can focus on what my marriage to Warren will bring. Stability, I hope. The marriages aren't legal (though they were on that failed Australian series of the show) but if we felt it would protect our families more, perhaps we could.

A few years of fake marriage so that we can absolutely rinse everything we can possibly get out of our flash in the pan fame, use that to establish our own careers, pool our resources to be most effective, and then, finally, we'll have a mutual amicable divorce. Or, well, fake divorce. Real breakup. Or a fake breakup? God, even I'm getting tangled in it.

I think that's a good basis for a partnership, going old school, marriage as a business arrangement. It's a tried and tested method that's worked for centuries. I wonder if it's still technically a lavender marriage if he's straight?

Once tomorrow is over, hopefully I can just date Warren. I am clearly not going to find a better match than him. But I can't help but worry that *he* might.

I will absolutely have to tell him, at some point, that I'm one hundred per cent only interested in the girls. I'm not a *she plays footballs on Saturdays* bisexual, or even someone who could be tempted to fall in love with a man, even as nice as one as he seems to be. I'm not so conceited to think that he might fall for me, but I'm just realistic about how jeopardy, stress and close proximity can change things for two people even only mildly attracted to each other. I hope if he goes along with this, he's not breaking his own heart.

That's one of the many things Mum objected to, the idea that I might break hearts just to secure a future.

I think I'll know for sure when we see each other on our third date. He'll be able to see it in me. After all, it's not like we can outright say *hey, let's pretend to be together to beat all these saps and win the money for the people we love* out loud, not least because this show drops couples they don't believe in.

I just have to hope I'm right, that we have an understanding, and that things are smooth sailing.

Chapter Nine

Carys

Malachi Campbell, 29, Liverpool

I'm Malachi, I'm twenty-nine and I'm from Liverpool, born and bred. That phrase always makes me laugh — I used to think it meant like baked, like a loaf of bread ... Oh no, I can't bake. But I'd learn if Whit asked me to. [laughs] I know, I'm so down bad it's pathetic. I don't even care what she looks like, her energy is just ... Oh yeah, but you know surgeons are all jocks, so she'll probably have me doing parkruns and eating my macros. I don't mind. I'd do anything for her.

I managed to stay annoyed at Dolly for about half a day, right up until she walked over as un-glam as possible in her exercise clothes. It was like I saw a bit of the real Dolly, the home Dolly when she's not filming.

I have to believe her when she said she was looking out for me. I heard she went to talk to production about Whit's horrible dates, after all. Maybe she's just a very involved friend. I'm unused to that.

I'm always reading things wrong. I can add it to a list as long as the Trans–Siberian Railway.

I think, if I'm honest, I'm a bit intimidated by her. When she's around, I just want to listen to her. Even impress her.

It's lunchtime, on my second day of too many second dates

due to my over-X-ing – a totally new form of self-sabotage, I think.

I'm starting to feel really burned out again and kind of demoralised. I came here precisely to give up on men who I didn't have any connection with, and yet, by choice (or, if I'm honest with myself, like twelve per cent spite, at least), I ended up spending hours with the very same men I left the apps to avoid. Am I just doomed to repeat the same cycle, even here? I love routines, but this seems a bit on the nose.

Maybe I should have kept my eyes on my own page and just picked Patrick like I wanted to originally.

Lina finds me curled up in the corner of the living room. 'You're going to crease your dress,' she says, untucking the length of it around my legs. My bare skin misses the gentle touch of the fabric, goosepimpling under the air conditioning, but she is right, and then I'd have to iron the dress, which I truly do not have any energy for. 'And probably over-stretch your hip flexors if you stay like that.'

'Sorry,' I say, not quite sure why I'm apologising when she's not my Pilates teacher. I wriggle out of my compressed depressed pretzel into a slightly more socially acceptable way of sitting. 'Thank you.'

She gives me a warm smile. 'We've got to look after each other.'

'How have your dates been today?' My voice is croaky from overuse.

'It's been interesting,' she says, very diplomatically. 'But I think I've narrowed it down to three men.' She hesitates. 'I'm not sure if you are comfortable with talking names?'

'No, it's alright,' I say, unsure how I'm feeling in truth. I'll know in a couple of days' time when it's finally been processed. 'Tell me.'

'I think I'm going to ask to take Billy, Cobey and Zack for

the dates where we see each other.' I get the sense she's looking at me for reactions to the names, but I'm so tired all I can do is keep my enthusiastic smile static.

'Oh, Cobey is so nice.' I am pretty sure Billy is the man who talked about teeth, and Zack seems to have slipped my mind entirely. 'Can you surf? I feel like a life with Cobey involves a lot of surfing.'

'No, but Pilates means I have a good core. I think I could manage it,' she says, entirely seriously. I cannot imagine being so certain about your own capacity.

I tell her in turn about Patrick. 'He's really the only man I'm interested in pursuing, I think.'

'Yes, you have similar energies,' she says sagely. 'That's important. Relating to each other not only emotionally, but cosmically.'

Even though I'm not quite sure what she means by cosmically, my mind slips to her proclamation the other day that the gender of her partner is not that important. For some reason, it's been playing in my head, over and over, ever since. That happens sometimes with phrases. My brain sets up its own little radio station that only plays that song.

But then, when I do think about it, my skin feels tight, or like it's about to vibrate off my bones.

I think one of the hardest parts of being autistic is that my processing is off by a few days, and while my nervous system might be able to react and say *oh this is Good or Bad*, I won't really know what that *means* for a whole other day.

And this feeling doesn't feel Bad or Good, so I'm just stuck with it. I know that, really, I just need to ask her about it.

'Lina,' I begin, trying to gain control over the wobble in my voice. My palms feel sweaty. 'What ... I mean ...'

She takes my hands in hers, which doesn't entirely help because I'm just worried about sweating all over her. 'Talk to me,' she says, lowering her lovely lilting voice.

It's Lina, I tell myself. She's nice and calm and thoughtful. If I'm going to ask anyone, maybe she's the right person.

'The other day when we were talking about ... who we date. You said—' I have to stop to clear my throat, and I'm so nervous that I forget to restart my sentence.

The gap widens too long, and I'm so grateful when Lina fills it. 'Oh, about not really caring about their gender?' Her dark eyes are curious. 'Is that what you were thinking about?'

'Yes,' I say slowly.

'What do you want to know?'

I'm not sure Lina realises how enormous this question, among a sea of enormous questions, is. 'How did you know?'

'How did I know what?' She's being patient with me, I can tell. That calming teacherly nature that I think is just Lina through and through.

'That it's not important to you?' My throat feels tight, like I've just swallowed a load of chips when I'm dehydrated. 'I thought ... Isn't it, isn't that important for a lot of people?'

'Oh,' she says, and I'm relieved that nothing seems to have changed in her manner. 'Well, ever since I was a little girl, when I dreamed of my future of getting married, I was never particularly fixated on it being a man. It just didn't occur to me to think much about that.'

She doesn't seem upset that I've asked, but I suddenly feel hot all over. 'You didn't think about it?'

'It's hard to explain really,' she says, leaning back on the seat. 'I think when I talk to some people they have a very fixed view on their physical type, like who they are attracted to. But I've never had a type. I don't quite see that as important to me. It doesn't mean it's not important if it's important to you. Like, let's be clear, it doesn't make me more evolved.' She says this part with a smile. 'But for me to be attracted to someone, I don't think it's that important.'

'Have you ... dated women then?' Why does that feel wrong to say? I know we're on camera, but gay people exist. I'm an ally, for God's sake. I need to get a grip.

'Someone I dated as a teenager came out as trans when she was older, and looking back, I think we both kind of understood that relationship to be queer,' she says with complete calm. 'And my last regular dating situation was with a non-binary person.'

'But you came on here?' I say, trying not to sound totally confused. 'A show specifically about marrying a man.'

'Oh yeah, but that's because of the Yes,' she says, as though this is a totally normal thing to say.

But then, given how this conversation is going, who am I to say what is normal or not?

'The ... Yes?'

'I was doing this thing all last year, saying *yes* to whatever came across in unexpected ways. My friend Geena did a reading for me, and there were lots of the expected cards – Hanged Man, Four of Cups, you know – the cards were telling me that something new was coming and I should grab it.'

'So you applied because of tarot cards?'

'One of the producers slid into my DMs on my work account and invited me to have an interview. I think I skipped a few steps because of it. They said they wanted a good mix.' She shrugs. 'I suspect that means diversity of their contestants and they didn't have anyone else Chinese yet. Or a tarot reader. Anyway, when that happened, I was right in my Yes period, so I went for it.'

That sounds so much more magical than my reality. I applied to *Wedded Bliss* at two in the morning after my third wedding in a row in *one* summer. All my uni girls are married now. We'd been flatmates and therefore friends, and, well, I'd never needed to look beyond them. Harriet and I both did

Biology, Nettie and Yolly both did languages, and we spent every other waking moment together. A perfect quad. And, over time, that quad inevitably became a ... octagon? Mike and I were still together from high school, Harriet met Rob in Freshers' Week, Peter worked at the publishing house Nettie did her first internship at, and Yolly and Benjamin work at the same primary school together. When Mike and I broke up, our group became a ... septangle? I have no idea about shapes. The three of them were all so coupled up, and fate never intervened for me in the same way. Which is why, after watching Harriet get married at a perfectly dilapidated barn with cottagecore chic, I lay alone in my hotel double bed, filling out an application form. I'd love to be able to blame alcohol, but I had been so worried about making sure the whole wedding went without a hitch, that I didn't drink a drop.

I think I'd have preferred it if this romantic magical story had felt more like my choice, and less like desperation.

'And yes, it might mean now I end up with a husband,' Lina continues. 'But who knows what life will bring. Not every relationship is forever, and that's fine with me.'

I manage to laugh, despite the squirming of my insides. 'I don't think we're supposed to imply marriage isn't forever on here.'

Lina smiles. 'Maybe not, but I'm not being cynical. Just realistic. People come into our lives for all sorts of reasons, some of them make a home in it with you. That's the beauty of life, sharing it with someone.'

'Yes, that's true,' I say, assuming it must be.

I try to stop fiddling with my dress, but that turns into pressing my nails into my skin instead. My body feels alive with confusion.

It's a very weird feeling, the sudden understanding of how other people are just out there living their lives without analysing every moment.

Most people don't understand what masking is, and when they do they presume it's literal – a mask you wear. And it kind of is, in a way.

What they often don't understand, in my experience, is that mask has been built from countless hours of research. Not just trial and error and making notes then adjusting, but literal research: pouring through magazines, books, television shows, interviews. Seeing how people talk about themselves or understand the world. I can't tell you how many memoirs I've read. I've been learning, gleaning, assessing what information I should take with me and incorporate into the palatable version of Carys I present to the world, whether it be a turn of phrase to add to my small talk script, or a way of sitting that seems elegant.

The worst part is that you worry talking to people who don't get it might think it's manipulation, or that it *is* manipulation, so you don't talk about it. But you don't know how else to be, either.

No one gave me the handbook on how to be a person. All I have is the one I cobbled together myself.

And Lina has shone a very bright light on a set of rules and expectations I thought were canon to all people. Born this way, straight or gay, you know from birth or you don't, and it's all serious.

I miss what she says at first because I'm so deep in this thought spiral, but I catch it when she repeats, 'Is there a reason you asked me?'

In truth, I don't know. And I don't know why she's asking me. But then, why was I so curious?

'No!' I say, far too loudly. 'No, it's not that. I just … I'm trying to learn more about LGBTQ+ people! I guess this was one of those "born this way" kind of moments for you that people always talk about?'

'Maybe for me, but that's not true of everyone. Not everyone is certain of their own attraction to each gender from birth, same as not everyone is certain of their gender.'

'They're not?' I whisper.

'Well, no. That's how Sasha came out later.'

I shake my head. 'Not gender, I was thinking of attraction. Sexuality.'

'Oh no, not everyone knows,' she says, so relaxed that she starts doing stretches. I feel so stiff that I should probably have a go too but I can't move because a bombshell is being dropped on me extremely slowly. 'You have to consider compulsory heterosexuality.'

'What's that?'

Lina gestures around us. 'The idea that heterosexuality is the only option, or the best option, or the right option. Depends what you've grown up under. It makes realising you have attraction for women *as a woman* much harder because you've just been told your whole life that men are the only option. Unless you've fancied girls and known what it was or had an incredibly close childhood friendship with another girl and understood what *that* meant, it's hard for women to identify that as attraction, not admiration.'

'How would you even tell the attraction from a friendship?' I manage to gasp out.

'With a woman?' She asks this with a bit of surprise. 'All the same crush feelings, probably with a side of guilt for worrying I was objectifying her or assuming she was into me.' Lina laughs, and it's not unkind, but it's spinning me out.

I want to be sick and I don't know why. Sweat pools in every crevice and I feel my face flushing hot. 'Okay, thank you, Lina!' I say, getting to my feet.

'Are you alright?'

'Yes, I just . . . need the toilet!'

Not totally wrong. I crash into our ensuite, thankful that Dolly is out on a date right now and doesn't have to hear me throw up. Autism, for me, means that instead of identifying the feeling, my body just evacuates itself. I think I'm like a sea cucumber, ejecting my innards at any sign of danger.

I can't help it, but I'm replaying memories of high school. Year eight, that sudden friendship with Marina that felt intense and special and like nothing else I'd ever felt before. We would tell each other everything, share a bed, walk around holding hands. Just like all the other girls.

Except ... it wasn't. *I* wasn't like all the other girls, I knew that.

It probably didn't help when someone asked if we were dating, and Marina scrunched up her perfect little ski slope nose and proclaimed loudly that she was 'not a fucking lesbo'.

But, to me, it always felt different from any of the other friendships I'd had, and perhaps that's why, when Marina decided that she didn't want to be friends with someone quite so intense, it hurt so much.

Mike quickly came along and filled the hole in my heart, mostly.

For so long I'd chalked up that disaster to *just* autism, tragic as that sounds, but now I'm wondering if perhaps it was more all along.

After whatever that was burned up in flames, I told myself I'd never let myself get confused about a girl again. I liked boys, that was evident. I'd just got confused, overenthusiastic perhaps. Maybe watched too much *Orange Is the New Black*.

What if I was wrong? What if I've spent my life trying not to admit to myself something I've suspected for so long? I think hearing someone say it so casually, like it's not the end of the world, is just so terrifying. Because all this time I've thought it was the worst thing, a terrible mistake I had to hide, else people might not like me the same, and yet Lina just said it out loud with ease.

The rules I've been living by might not exist and that is petrifying.

Have I been locking myself away for no reason?

And is this the reason I can't stop wanting to talk to Dolly? Why I want to impress her, or make her laugh? Why I can't stop thinking about the moment the Goddess stepped out into traffic . . .

When you mask this hard, you get used to telling yourself sweet little lies. No, it's not that bad. You will get over it. It doesn't hurt. Stop overreacting. It all adds up to a habit of lying to yourself, and just because I'm aware I'm doing it, doesn't mean I can necessarily stop. Sometimes it means I can't quite follow my own train of thought.

Is the reason I've been thinking that Dolly would be perfect for me if she wasn't a woman because I like her? Her caring, kind nature. Her wit. I feel like we connect in so many areas, which makes us a great friendship, even if she is neurotypical.

Fuck.

So I've been objectifying her in my own head, and sharing a room with her . . . I bet she's felt uncomfortable this whole time. But she's friends with lesbians. She must be used to that? God, I'm making excuses.

But then, sometimes I catch her looking at me, like she's reading something on my skin. Could that—

'Carys?' Reb calls through the door. 'Are you alright? Lina came to get me.'

Bless sweet Lina.

'Um, no,' I call back. 'I've been sick a few times.'

That's a bit of a lie. It was just once, and entirely bright yellow stomach lining because I've not eaten anything for hours (likely part of the problem).

'Okay, honey, do you want me to call a doctor?'

I'm not sure any GP can help me with this particular existential crisis.

'No, I just think I need to sleep it off.'

I close the lid and flush the toilet, and manage to open the door without getting up.

'Oh, you do look bad,' Reb says, which is not actually comforting.

'Can I get out of filming this evening?' I croak, admittedly hamming it up a little.

I can't help but notice Reb's nervous look, the way she glances down at her phone for confirmation. 'Erm. I can ask.'

'I think we should send her to bed,' calls Dolly's disembodied voice, and urgh, she's the last and somehow the only person I want to see me right now. 'She might be contagious, and you don't want your entire cast of women going down with the shits and voms. Let the girl go to bed, and the rest of us can make sure we're filling any gaps on content today.'

She's been looking after me so well this whole time, but I don't want her to see me covered in vomit. Not right now. I bum-shuffle backwards so that I'm more hidden behind the door, pretending to fiddle with the toilet paper while Reb taps away at her phone.

'Okay,' Reb says wearily. 'You're cleared for tonight. Dolly, are you fine to still share the room if she's sick?'

'It's not a problem at all. Then someone's keeping an eye on her too.' The last thing I want to think about, when I have my head in the toilet, is the possibility of Dolly watching me.

'Do you need a hand getting into bed?' Reb asks, and I get the sense she might collapse if she tries.

'No, I'm just going to stay down here a little longer until it's definitely stopped.'

Reb passes me a bottle of water. I take it and sip slowly, the cold liquid a balm to my hot insides.

'Okay, we'll leave you be. Everyone out,' Reb calls, as she pulls the door behind her.

It's only when I lean my head down on the toilet seat, pressing the cold bottle to my wrists, that I hear Dolly call through the door. 'I really hope you feel more yourself later.'

If only she understood the irony of what she'd just said.

Chapter Ten

Dolly

Zack Allen, 31, Kent

You want me to explain what a nice guy is? Isn't it obvious? I'm nice. I'm respectful. Perhaps I don't look like some of the other guys in here – Warren's a basketball player for God's sake. Unfortunately, that's often what women really want, and that's really why I came here. I wanted someone to fall in love with me, for me. To see how good I am, without all the other distractions of looks and that. What's that? Oh yeah, well, my type is usually petite and brunette.

I'm glad I didn't have to go hard on Reb, who looks to be stuck together with masking tape at this point, because really, it's not on, making contestants work when they're vomiting. If someone is going to reinforce the protections for contestants' health, it should be our handlers. Apparently, it's just me.

Hopefully production won't hate me.

My evening date with Warren is a silent disco, which is really just me dancing in a room with headphones while trying to hear his disembodied voice through the speakers. Honestly, kind of a nightmare, but we have fun anyway. Turns out, my partner in crime is a total goof. I can't wait to see the footage of him attempting the worm, which ended with a loud crash as he backwards wormed into the side table his sushi was on. He took it well, laughing it all off, which is a good sign. Being in the public eye is going to be hard enough without having a sense of humour.

I try to slip back into mine and Carys's bedroom as quietly as possible, but I find her awake and reading with the bedside table lamp on. She looks peaky, with big dark lines under her eyes like Mum gets when she's done too much.

'Hey,' I say quietly. 'Did you get any sleep?'

Her eyes dart up to me over the top of her book. 'No,' she croaks. 'But I'm feeling better for the rest.'

'Good, good. Don't let me bother you now.' I take my pyjamas and go to the bathroom for my wind down in the hot shower. I try not to stay in there too long, just in case Carys needs to call someone on the porcelain phone again.

I wish I could say that there's nothing like seeing your crush post-vom to dispel the feelings. I feel the urge to fuss over her, but I remind myself I don't know her that well, and she hasn't asked for it. Just because I'm a carer for Mum and used to doing everything for her doesn't mean I can just slide into that role for Carys. That feels like overstepping a boundary I've laid down for myself too, if I'm honest.

When I go back into the bedroom, the light is off and Carys is breathing softly, so I slip into my bed ready for my scheduled twenty minutes of wishing I could use my phone.

Her calm doesn't last very long, and soon she's tossing and turning. 'Dolly?' Carys's voice sounds in the dark.

'Yeah, Carys?'

'Oh God, sorry. I'm disturbing you, aren't I?' she splutters, and I'm suddenly confused as to why she even spoke my name. There's a rustle that must be her blankets being thrown back. 'I'll go lie on the couch instead. Sorry!'

She starts to get up, and I'm so confused about what's

going on, that I say quickly, 'I was already awake. It's fine. Are you okay?'

Carys stills, possibly lying back down. There's a long beat that makes me worry she's about to say no. 'Just worried about tomorrow.'

'About seeing him in person?'

'Yeah.'

'What's worrying you?' I regret giving in to my own curiosity when I add, 'Worried you won't fancy him?'

I can hear the blankets rustle again as she fidgets. 'No, it's more like ...' She sighs deeply. 'I ... I'm not sure I want to talk about it. But my mind is whirring. I can't shut it off even though I don't want to talk about it.'

'We can talk about something else if it would help distract you?' I offer.

Another long beat of silence, followed by a low whisper. 'Can I ask you something?'

'Of course.'

'I know we said we wouldn't, but I want to ask you about ... the day we met.'

Well. That wasn't what I was expecting.

Even though the room is pitch black, I instinctively glance round for cameras. I've not found any in here, and trust me, I've looked hard. There still could be microphones. Just because I've not seen them use security footage from the contestants' bedrooms in the US series, doesn't mean the UK series won't.

'I ... I'm not sure that's a good idea,' I say firmly. 'Not when you're feeling so ill,' I add, just in case we are being watched.

I half want to climb onto her bed so we can talk, but that's the kind of thing an incognito lesbian on a dating show absolutely should not do if she wants to *remain* incognito.

'Well,' she begins, 'I was just wondering what your experience is with conflict, between two parties such as those that you were novel to.'

It's so formal, like she's on a legal drama, that I have to stifle a laugh.

It's true I didn't know them, but I swear I have seen Sara somewhere before. There must be some kind of old saying about the queer community being all your exes and their exes because sometimes it really does feel that way. A geography-less village within a country.

'Well, it's quite easy to resolve conflict when both parties are clear about what ... said conflict is,' I say, trying to adopt her strange legal tone. 'I recall an instance of conflict between two people in particular that was resolved.'

God, I'm not smart enough to fake legal jargon. I'm not even positive what I've said makes any fucking sense.

'Are you familiar with parties such as theirs?' I can feel Carys's eyes on me through the darkness.

'You're losing me,' I lie.

'You know.'

'I'm not sure I do.'

She's suddenly hovering over my bed.

'Jesus Christ!' I gasp. 'Did you have to sneak up on me?'

'It's dark! The sneaking is inherent!'

I push myself up because lying below her when all I can see are her bright wild eyes is making me feel all kinds of strange. 'What do you mean?'

'*Women* like that.' Her words are barely audible but still manage to hit me in the throat. Why is she asking about this now?

'You can say *lesbian*, Carys,' I whisper back.

'I didn't want to presume their sexualities,' she hisses.

I resist rolling my eyes because sometimes straight people

can be a little too sensitive around queerness and our language, even if it's a good thing when they correct other hets. Either that or they've watched too much *Drag Race* and end up appropriating slang from Black ballroom culture that they've never heard of.

'Fair,' I say gently. 'But yes, I know women like that.'

'Oh.'

It's been a long time since high school where I wasn't so much out there as never mentioning it, but this small *oh* sends a shiver down my spine in a familiar, terrifying way.

Fuck, have I just let it all slip? Has she worked me out? Is she going to call me out for being here and queer (not in the general way, in the heterosexual reality dating show way).

'Is there something you want to ask me, Carys?' I say it in our normal volume, hoping that it comes across as unafraid.

The question weighs heavy in the air, and her perfume scents on my tongue. I've trusted her this long, but I've been burned before by straight people's good intentions.

She shuffles away, back into her bed. 'No, I just wondered if the parties have resolved their conflict.'

Okay, so we're back to this. 'Hopefully,' I say, my stomach still squirming.

It's so quiet that I almost don't catch her say, 'I think they really loved each other.'

'And their cat.'

'Leonard.'

'You remembered the cat's name?'

'I never forget an animal's name. I'm not so good at people.'

Given she just appeared at my side like a ghost, I can't really argue. 'I think you're doing okay.' It accidentally sounds a bit like a question.

I hear a snort that at first I think is laughter, but there's a bitterness, I'm sure of it. 'If only. People are hard. I barely understand myself as it is.'

'You worry about that a lot, don't you?' I feel like I can be more candid in the dark, especially now we've stopped talking like drunk Shondaland lawyers.

'About misunderstanding people? Yes. Misreading the room. Saying too much.'

'Well, if I ever do something you don't understand, you can just ask me. I'd rather we talk about it than you worry, because chances are there's nothing. If I was pissed off at you, you'd know.'

We both laugh at that, but she still sounds so hollow. What is going on with her? I don't think this is just some kind of bug, unless it's one that's taking over her brain too.

'Thanks, Dolly, I'm going to sleep now.'

She falls asleep quickly, her breaths deepening, and I try not to think about the way her cinnamon hair must be splayed across the pillow.

It's quite depressing that even when I think she might possibly be gayvestigating me, I still can't stop thinking about her.

~

Overnight, we'd voted for our third dates – the first time we get to *see* our matches in person, even if across a partition – and I'm so fucking relieved to get a mutual match from Warren. To my frustration, production seem intent on throwing Patrick and Malachi together with me, so they appear on my date card too.

The full cast of women are still here, though I get the impression a few men have been dropped for definite as there's no mention of Daniel or the second-day guy so painfully unmemorable I forgot his name.

Everyone is nervously preening. It's not so much love at first sight, but confirmation of possible love at first sight. For all the other girls, today matters a hell of a lot. Generally it seems to be the women who can look past not being that attracted to the men at first – but the dudes? That's another story.

Once again, I am extremely grateful that I'm not here for actual romance, because I know exactly the kind of reactions mid-size girls in shows like this get when they are revealed to their men – always dudes who say they have no type and then proclaim it is 'petite'.

I have to trust that Warren is not going to do that to me, given our tentative, unspoken potential arrangement that I hope he's considering too.

If I'm honest, I'm kind of surprised the show let me on because usually they keep clear of fat people, particularly fat women, for this exact reason. Perhaps this should have been a sign to me that contestant care is not their top priority, as much as they proclaimed it might be.

Just then, Louise bustles over to me. 'Is Carys still unwell?'

'I thought she should probably sleep as long as she needs to,' I say, trying to sound polite and not narked.

'Right, but we *do* have a show to film,' she says in that specific-to-sickness-condescending tone that I've heard far too many times in my life. 'Was she poorly overnight? If not, then really she should be up and ready to film. This is a team effort, after all.'

I choose not to respond to this blatant fishing with the information she's after. 'I'm a deep sleeper,' I say sweetly. 'Let me take her envelope through to her with a cup of tea and see how she's doing.'

The millisecond of a look Louise gives me could curdle milk, but she wipes it away in a flash. Scary, really. Reminds me of Carys in ways I can't put my finger on. 'Fine, that seems like the best course of action. But give me a call when you know how she's doing. Dates start in an hour.'

I want to note how pointless it is for her to give me a deadline, what with the lack of clocks in here, but I shouldn't start a fight, even if I really want to.

Once she's gone, Lina sidles up to me. 'Is Carys *actually* alright?'

'I think so. I will go wake her up in a second,' I say, walking to the kitchen to make Carys that cup of tea I promised Louise I was going to make.

To my surprise, Lina follows me. Not that we've not got along, but we've not really had much to say to each other. Slightly on purpose on my part if I'm honest. That comment about being chill about gender made me want to keep my distance only because the last thing I need is another queer woman clocking what I am.

Last night's questions from Carys were bad enough.

'I think I should tell you something,' Lina begins, her glossy black hair falling over her shoulder like a curtain of rain.

'Go on,' I say. She doesn't speak until I start running the tap to fill the kettle.

Lina covers her mouth with her fingers and her words come out low and fast, just audible to me over the sound of the water. 'Carys was asking me about being attracted to women, all prompted by me talking about gender. I think she's feeling unsettled, but I'm not sure why. I'm telling you because I think you care about her as much as I do, but don't repeat this.'

The lid of the kettle closes with a loud clack in the new silence between us. 'Right,' I say, trying to get this settled in my head. Before I can ask anything else, Lina announces she has a date to get ready for and leaves me in the kitchen holding a very full kettle.

What the hell was that? Was Lina really telling me what was going on so I can look after Carys, or was this a warning? Was Carys needling Lina because she suspects me? And if so, has Lina worked me out too? I hadn't anticipated another queer woman in here (whether that's a label she'd even use for herself, I will have to find out another time) and perhaps that was naive of me. I can't be the only one in here keeping secrets.

I try to suppress the shake in my hands as I set the kettle to boil, teabag in cup, a teaspoon of sugar that drops golden crystals all over the counter.

I'm safe. I'm fine.

I don't have time to worry about this because I've finally got my face-to-face date with Warren. I need to focus on Warren. What's Carys going to do without internet anyway? It's not like she has any evidence that I might be a lesbian. The production team would probably think she's on one.

Probably.

But I should make sure I keep them sweet today, just in case.

Script: See and Touch Dates

[Karina stands in an empty date room, when the mirror slowly lowers.]

KARINA   Over the next few days, our couples will come face to face. But will they like what they see?

[Karina turns to look through the gap left in the wall, finding Lucas on the other side. She looks to a camera shooting over his shoulder.]

KARINA   I know I do.

[Karina winks into the camera. Lucas spins round to face the same camera.]

LUCAS   But there's always a catch. On the first date, there is strictly no touching. We want our couples to get to know their partner through the other senses – sight, smell and ... err ... speech. I'm not sure that's a sense.

KARINA   But then tomorrow when the barriers come down, they will be able to touch. But, once they've seen each other, will any of them come back for more?

LUCAS   I hope so! Or this will be a very short show.

[Karina lightly smacks him on the arm while laughing.]

KARINA   Now let's check in with our couples to see who is on the path to *Wedded Bliss*.

Chapter Eleven

Carys

Cobey Worthing, 28, Newquay

I guess I'm looking for a woman to ride the waves of life with me. Not literally, like it would be super cool if they could surf but the raw power of the sea isn't for everyone. That's why I think Lina and I are a good match – she's so chill, and I'm so chill, and together we're just ... chill. I hope she likes me. Do you know if she likes me?

I think there might be something seriously wrong with me. It's reveal day, the day I finally see Patrick's face, and yet I can't stop turning last night's conversation with Dolly over and over in my mind.

'*I know women like that.*'

That's what she said, wasn't it? But does that mean what I think it means?

And why do I care? I mean ... I'm pretty sure I know why I care. I think. Maybe.

Dolly is already gone when I wake up, which either means she's up abnormally early or I've slept in. From the murmur of noise outside the door, I think it might be the latter.

Sleep didn't refresh me at all. It's not like I had a meltdown. It wasn't *really* a meltdown, though therapists of the past might disagree with that. Not that I've listened to them much at all, which is probably at least part of the reason why my nervous system feels mysteriously aflame most of the time.

They couldn't understand my inability to name a feeling as I experience it. Most of the time it's three days later that I finally work out what the Good or Bad feeling actually meant. They call it alexithymia, which is a fancy name for 'I have no idea how I feel about anything right now'.

But I don't really have days. I need to work out what I'm doing with myself asap.

Someone knocks, and I sit up very straight, pulling the covers practically up to my chin. 'Hello?' I squeak.

I cannot tell you how simultaneously relieved and alarmed I feel upon seeing Dolly carrying a mug. 'Thought I'd bring you a cuppa for strength. I put about twelve sugars in.' She sets it down on the bedside table next to me.

Dolly wears a white shirt dress, belted at the waist and unbuttoned to show the dip in her throat. The colour reminds me of white calcite crystals, shining in the light. The dress is paired with gold hoop earrings and softened with a pinkish-nude lipstick that matches her heels. She looks incredible. Grown up. Marriage material.

Not the sort of thing I could wear and carry a mug of tea without disaster striking.

I don't know how I didn't notice what I'm now unable to ignore.

I whisper what's supposed to be a thank you but the frog in my throat sends it garbled. I'm not even sure which language I used.

She raises her arched eyebrows. 'I'll take that to be a thanks.'

I want her to sit down and stay with me, but she stands, probably to stop her dress wrinkling. Like she's ready to walk out any moment.

God, I feel so needy.

Dolly continues to be immune to my inner turmoil. 'Look,

production were hassling me about how sick you are. I'm not digging, but what do you want me to tell them for you? If you don't want to go out, I'll get Reb to fight that battle for you.'

There's a hot hollowness in my chest that I can't name, but I think that it's more than just being overwhelmingly thankful. I realise what Dolly has proposed is what my sisters meant about reasonable adjustments – more time, more rest, they'd suggested, like it was something I could just ask of a show filmed on crunch time.

Dolly might not know I'm autistic, but she's still trying to advocate for me.

Would she understand if I told her? So few people know. Again, not because I'm ashamed but there's only so many times you can hear *oh we're all on the spectrum* or *you don't look autistic* without wanting to melt down right there and then to prove a point.

But I feel like I could trust Dolly with it, somehow. Maybe that's just wishful thinking? Or, most likely, the assortment of feelings I'm having about her.

She doesn't rush me, but she waits. Most people try to fill my thinking gaps with more words, which just slows down the conveyer belt of thoughts even more. Every bit of sensory information has to get processed in order or the conveyer belt grinds to a halt or explodes, so sometimes it takes me a minute to process.

It's hard to think when I can smell the heady, glorious musk of her perfume. I tend to wear anything that smells like sherbet or Parma violets, but on her, the deep ouds and leather notes seem almost delicate.

God, I need to get a hold of myself. I came here for a reason, and that reason is on the other side of the warehouse waiting to meet me.

'Um.' I test out my voice, and it seems to have returned to normal. 'I'll be out in a moment. I think I needed the sleep.'

'You must have. I was clattering about this morning and you didn't stir even a bit.'

Her eyes don't quite fall on me, which, while typical for me, is unusual for her. Am I making her feel uncomfortable? Perhaps she can sense the weird attachment feelings coming from me? Or maybe my questions last night made her feel strange.

'Are you feeling nervous about today?' I ask instead.

To my surprise, Dolly barks a laugh. 'Yes. No. Probably. I'm dressed in bridal colours for some reason.'

'It's a lot, isn't it.'

'All a bit *Blind Date*.'

'I don't know what that is,' I say, a little embarrassed.

'Surprise, surprise? Our Graham?' she says in an extremely good Scouse accent. 'Cilla Black? Liverpudlian icon, red hair, nasty little Tory?'

'Not ringing a bell, sorry.'

Dolly waves a perfectly manicured hand, the tips of her nails rounded and dipped in soft pink. 'It's an old dating show from like the nineties or something. The contestant would pick between three people, the walls come down, and ta-daaa, yer man is there. Or woman.'

I resist the gulp in my throat.

'Anyway, it reminds me of this whole situation.'

Her accent is back to plummy, and I wonder once again why a girl from Liverpool, who can do such a perfect Scouse accent, sounds like she does. Maybe I'm projecting by thinking it's a kind of mask. Maybe she got a scholarship to a fancy school, or maybe her mum sounds like that too.

I wish that people came with Wikipedia summaries you could look up, and then ask them questions about. It would make getting to know people much easier. I just want to know everything about her.

Is it odd that I haven't thought that about Lina or Bridget, though?

'I was thinking more *Love Is Blind*,' I say quietly.

'I'm not sure we're allowed to say that name in these hallowed halls,' Dolly says with a smile. 'Need anything else?'

'No. And thank you for all this,' I say, and I push the blankets back to communicate that I'm getting up, and give her an out to leave. I've taken up more of her time than I should have this morning, after all.

When she does go, I feel hollow again. Maybe I'm just destined to feel scooped out, whether she's around or not. Lonely.

Perhaps one day I'll narrow down what the variations of that feeling actually mean.

I've had my reveal day outfit picked out since before I got here: a cream silk pussy-bow shirt under a forest green wool dress with a wide circle skirt, with sensible brown round-toed shoes. It's the sort of outfit that I hope says I'm a smart woman with my life together.

It's vintage librarian chic. Librarians always seem so grown up. They're pinnacles of information, bastions against the disinformation cycles, people who know how to abide by systems and rules. That's who I'm trying to be.

I wonder what he thinks I dress like, given he knows I work on a farm teaching children and adults. Probably bright dungarees, patterns, big wellies; not inaccurate.

But I can look like a nice man's wife too.

Now I just have to feel the part.

I walk out into chaos. Hannah C. is crying, comforted by Priya, while Hannah P. and Niamh look on slightly confused.

Hannah S. and Whit arm-wrestle over the kitchen island, and I feel warm as I watch the muscles in their arms flex.

Lina is doing a headstand against the wall, though actually, now I look at her, she seems quite serene. I didn't know you could be serene in a headstand, given I've never been serene upright.

I don't see Dolly.

'Oh fucken hell, babe.' I jump because Bridget has snuck up on me, waving a pencil in my face. 'Do you have a sharpener?'

'A what?'

'For my lip liner. It's blunt as a welly.'

'Oh no, I don't, sorry. Shall I see if one of the others—'

She doesn't wait for me to finish the sentence, flips to face the nearest wall mirror and rubs the dull pencil against the edges of her lips. Her pretty little face tenses up in a wince.

'Bridget, don't!' I try to grab it from her hand, but she dodges. 'You're going to get a splinter!'

'It's fine!' she bleats, tears in the corner of her eyes. 'If I don't think about it, it's only a bit unbearable!'

The colour does darken, but I can't tell if that's the product or a bruise.

'There.' She sounds pleased, and to be fair, her lips do look good. 'Gotta be fit for the first time I see my mans.'

I feel guilty for not making time for her in the last few days. After all, Bridget decided we'd be friends from the off, my fellow Welshie, and I've barely spoken to her while I've been having my internal crisis.

I knew Bridget was seeing a few different guys, but being awol means that I am out of step with her. 'Who are you seeing today?'

She counts off on her fingers. 'Billy and Zack today. Jackson and Ethan tomorrow.'

'Wow. That's going to be so nice.'

Bridget rolls her eyes. 'I'm not so sure. What if they're all mingers? What if they think *I'm* a minger?'

'No one could think that,' I insist.

'They might. I'm already sweating, babes.' She fans her armpit with the dull lip pencil.

I take it from her and hand her my notebook.

'Cheers,' she says, resuming fanning herself. 'I just know they're all seeing other women too, and I want to look the hottest. Even if I don't want to date all of them after this, I want them to want me most still, you know?'

I'm partway through untangling why she might care about men she doesn't like wanting her, when she bursts into laughter.

'I'm joking, babes. Your face was a picture. But look, I do look fit, though, don't I?'

'Y-yes,' I say, feeling an old familiar discomfort at telling another woman she looks beautiful. It feels odd in my mouth, like if I loosened control on the words they might fly out and I'd say something too effusive. 'You are going to knock them out.'

I'm not quite convinced that's the right way to say that, but she seems pleased.

'Good.' She steps back and admires her tattooing work. 'Sparks are going to fly, at least on one side.'

'Sparks?'

'Yeah, babe. Like, that magnetic, lightning feeling you get when you look at someone and think *oh they're a bit of me*. These men are all nice and I fancy them, but I'm here for a spark.' She cups her mouth with her hands and shouts up at the ceiling, 'Strike me down with love, baby!'

Sparks. I've not felt sparks since Mikey, right at the beginning. I think.

'What about you? Excited to see Patrick?' she asks. I guess Bridget has been keeping up with me better than I have her.

'Yeah,' I say, unconvincingly. Until now, I'd not considered that Patrick might be seeing more than one woman today.

The front door to the dorms slams as Dolly walks back in, with some of the production team in tow. They call us over to get mic'd up, while Dolly goes to stand with Whit, her back slightly to me so I can see the black wire of her mic snaking around her neck.

If she's just seeing Warren today and things don't work out, does that mean tonight might be the last time we are together? If we both get dumped, we will both have to leave the warehouse.

My stomach hurts at the thought.

Because she's a good friend. Because she lives far away and it'll be hard to stay in contact. Because because because definitely not because I might—

'Carys?' I'm summoned from my thoughts as we are corralled to our doors, ready for our dates.

The wire snaking down my back makes me shiver. I do not look at Dolly.

Light on, cameras in the walls roll. Action.

When I walk in, the mirror barrier is still there. This feels like it could be a date just like any from the last few days – me and a plush couch, staring at my reflection, and trying not to panic.

Except I know that that divider is going to fall any moment.

I sit down neatly. If the barrier is going to suddenly crash down, I want him to see me looking my best. My most controlled.

'Morning!' Patrick calls cheerily, his voice coming through the speakers as usual.

'Hi! Hi, it's me, Carys.'

'I know, Carys.' I swear I can hear the smile as he says my name. 'I'd recognise your voice anywhere. How are you doing today?'

'I'm nervous,' I admit, and then immediately regret it. 'Not about seeing you. More about—'

'Revealing ourselves, right?'

'Yes.' I'm thankful that he gets it. 'I hope you like me.'

'I adore you, Carys.' My heart flutters in my chest. He

adores me? Patrick *adores* me? I'm not sure a man has told me they adore me before.

'Carys and Patrick?' A voice sounds from the speaker, though I can't be sure who it is. 'The barrier is going to come down in a moment, so could you both please stand? We need to remind you that this date is strictly no touching.'

'Oh gosh, here we go then,' Patrick says. The same Patrick I'm about to be able to see.

I stand up slowly, trying to keep my quivering heart and soul inside my body. 'What if we close our eyes,' I rush out, 'and then when the barrier is fully down, we open our eyes at the same time?'

'Okay, I've closed my eyes.'

I close mine. 'Promise?'

'Promise. I'd make it a pinkie promise but this is a No Touching Zone.'

I giggle. 'Hands where I can see them, Stringer.'

There's a rumbling as the barrier comes down.

My fingers yearn to flick to shake out the nerves and redirect all that energy out through my extremities.

But I am being filmed, and Patrick is about to see me for the first time. I don't want his first impression of me to be frantic, even if that's how I feel inside. Even if that's how I feel a lot of the time.

I clutch my hands together in front of me, the way I've been practising since I was small. It looks delicate. It looks quiet.

It feels like an age passes before the noise stops.

'Are you ready?' Patrick asks, and I jump slightly because this is the first time I've heard his voice in front of me, instead of through the speakers.

He really is right in front of me. Suddenly, he feels so much more real to me. I can hear the rustle of his clothes as he moves, the sound of him breathing. I think I can even smell his perfume, the washing powder he uses, his shampoo – all creating a warm, surprisingly floral smell. Clean, fresh, lovely.

Patrick is *here*.

I just have to open my eyes.

'Yes,' I say, throwing a huge smile onto my face. 'On three? Three.'

'Two.'

'One.'

There he is.

The first thing I notice are his eyes. A deep soft brown, with the start of crow's feet pinching at the corners as he smiles. Those crinkles mean he's a man who smiles a lot. That matches up with the Patrick in my head.

His smile is open mouthed, handsome but sweet too. His fluffy brown hair is short and pushed back, and he's taller than me, which is no surprise because I've always been knee-high to a gnat. He looks exactly like who you'd want looking after your sick pets.

Patrick is a beautiful man.

My God.

I laugh. I don't mean to, but it comes out in a rush, and I clap my hands over my lips to stifle it.

But then he does the same. And we're giggling together, watching each other through this tiny partition, suddenly very real.

'Hi, Carys.'

He watches me as I watch him. I wonder if this is how fish in an aquarium feel.

I manage to stammer out, 'Hi.'

'This is really weird, isn't it?' He laughs awkwardly, and I join in, enjoying the blended sound of our laughter. He laughs from deep in his chest, down in the diaphragm, a laugh from his soul. 'I can't believe it. You're right *there*,' he gasps.

'You've been right there all along,' I echo.

I could fall in love with him. I know it. I can feel flutters in my stomach, in my chest, like butterfly kisses.

And yet there's a voice in my head that whispers should I be feeling more, doing more, saying more?

The butterflies aren't sparks, after all. Sparks mean electricity, passion, wanting. Should I be trying to tear down this barrier to get to him, or is that unrealistic? What are the other women doing? If I knew what everyone else was doing, maybe I'd know how I'm supposed to act here. Am I doing attraction wrong?

I'm not sure, but I'm enjoying the stillness of watching each other.

And then I remember that we are being filmed. I school my face into a huge smile, just in case I wasn't smiling enough while I was looking at him. God, I hope I was smiling? Resting bitch face was a term coined for autistic women when they've just got a neutral face. But the last thing I want is a ton of people watching my expressions, posting online about how cold I'm being with him.

I spring to life, clapping my hands together. I laugh with the kind of childlike glee I know people think is cute, but of which I feel so little right now. 'Welcome to my tiny room,' I say, gesturing around at my half of our joined space.

He does the same, and we giggle.

God, he's a nice man. And I'm glad to see him. I am. I *am*.

Our conversation speeds by in a blur of excitement, picking up from where we left off. He tells me about his family because I asked, and I try to listen, but the whole time a few questions ping around my head.

Shouldn't I be thinking about kissing him?
Am I doing this right?
Do I look excited enough?

I wish I was the sort of person who could be present in a

life-changing moment without worrying if I'm experiencing it correctly.

I know I like him. That's not in doubt.

I wish I wasn't so worked up, so unsettled. I adjust how I stand but that doesn't seem to fix how I'm feeling either, and I laugh at what seems like the right time in the middle of his story about being trapped on a farm by an errant border collie who kept herding him into a corner – but did I? Did I miss the moment?

I'm missing *this* whole moment by living so inside my own head.

I know that my sisters Ang and Del would tell me to go easy on myself, but they don't have to live in a brain like mine. They don't have to monitor themselves.

It's just weird that there's one person I haven't felt like this around, or at least, not to this extent. When we talk in our bedroom, I wear the mask lighter. The script quietens enough for me to hear her.

Is that why Dolly appears in my mind, even when I'm looking right at the man I'm dating? Or why what I feel when I'm around her feels closer to how I feel about Patrick than any of the other women?

I'm not sure I can ignore all the mounting evidence, and the things I've hidden for so long. Or the suspicion that I'm not so much barking up the wrong tree as ignoring half of the forest.

But just because I might like Dolly, that doesn't mean I can't also like Patrick, right? I am sure I like him. I am.

Does Dolly like me?

It's a question I've tried really hard not to look at, to push away into the corner of my mind, because she's my *roommate*.

But then, sometimes, I think she looks at me in the way I want her to look at me. That deep, soft look you give someone when you feel more for them than just *I don't mind sharing space with you*. Is it wrong to hope that she does? Maybe it's just like what Bridget said this morning, about how she likes the idea of being wanted. Being wanted does sound nice.

But it feels like more than that, this hoping.

God, it's bad enough that I think about her that way, but to assume she could like me back just seems ... I don't know. As if I'm imagining she's some kind of predator? No, actually, it's not that bad but ... oh, it's all so tangled up and I just wish I could *know* if I was imagining all this or lying to myself.

Because it feels like lying but I can't tell in what direction. Am I lying to her in the friendly way I act? Am I lying to myself about the ways I feel about her or Patrick?

Masking feels so much like lying sometimes; maybe I'm just manipulating everyone around me all the time into thinking I'm a nice person they might want to fall in love with.

Is this what Lina was talking about? Compulsory heterosexuality?

'Would you like that, Carys?' Patrick says, jolting me out of myself.

Fuck, I really did not hear him this time. 'Sorry,' I say breathlessly. 'I um ... got distracted by your eyes.'

Not entirely a lie. Eye contact is extremely distracting.

He blushes at the compliment. 'I asked if you'd like to have another date with me?'

'Oh!' I cry. 'Yes! Obviously!'

It's only when I leave that I realise what I've committed to: a date where we could touch.

Am I ready for that? I could tell him I like to go slow, that I need time, but what if he reads that as lack of interest, or that I'm weird? If I want to be with Patrick, I have to give it my all. Give *him* my all (or as much as is permitted on a streaming television show).

I just wish I could stop thinking about Dolly, down the hallway, looking at Warren, wishing she was looking at me.

Chapter Twelve

Dolly

Look, if I wasn't a lesbian, I would be all over Warren. He is objectively, incredibly handsome. His skin is deep, dark brown, and I've never seen a man so assuredly rock a goatee. And his muscles are, as one might expect, rather massive. I'll admit I wasn't expecting a basketball player to be so stylish. He's dressed beautifully in a rust orange suit, with a grey turtleneck underneath.

I *almost* feel guilty that this hunk of a basketball player is wasted on the secret lesbian. Except that he's here for the same reason as me. Romantic love isn't important. We're here for a different kind of love, familial love.

I imagine some people closed their eyes when the barrier fell, but I kept mine wide open, as though I wanted to catch every second of him.

When the barrier is finally down, Warren tilts his chin up to me, and just says, 'There's my girl.'

I can imagine the internet losing their mind over that. Props to him, the man knows how to lead a scene. I wonder if he's done any acting before. He must be, at the very least, media trained if his management company sent him on here.

We show off our outfits to each other in a string of whoops and claps, none of which feels fake at all.

It's a nice thing to actually like your future fake husband.

After I got mic'd up this morning, I had to wait in the living room because he obviously had a morning date. So I made notes of things to ask him, and when I got bored of doing that, I started coming up with recipes for our wedding day. Presumptuous maybe, but hell, shy bairns get nowt.

We must have been in here a while, as production bring us food. They asked for an order, and I picked a poke bowl, a mess-free option as long as I am careful. The thing about being fat in public is that if you are perceived to be a slob, people judge you way harsher than if you were thin.

Still, that neurosis aside, we sit eating together like we're at the end of a really big table rather than a strangely divided figure-eight room.

Our chat is lovely, really. We talk about expression, romance, displays of affection and our love languages. All things that I maintain are as important for friendships as for romantic relationships. Given we're doing both at once, it seems even more important that we manage to discuss it, even in a coded way.

I must admit I feel relief when he says he's a man who thinks there's a time and place for public displays of affection. Me too, my guy.

Posh Louise pops in to give us a stack of cards with questions to ask each other, which we have a good laugh with. Warren gets a little silly about it – he loves to say *negative* in this robot voice that makes me cackle every time. About halfway through, I hear some of the doors outside close, followed by footsteps in the corridor – another sign that they're prolonging our dates. Personally, I think we make good television, even if it is a tad premature to think the showrunners plan to follow our storyline.

We end up designing our dream dinner party for so long – we both love barbecue as high cuisine, with elegant flavouring, great tableware and good guests. I can just see the weeks of content we could get out of the recipes for that, the brand deals we could work towards. He casually drops his near-million followers to me, a number I know will have soared once this show starts airing. Before the show, mine was more like 300k, with good engagement. I wonder what it is now.

By the time I get back into the dormitory, I get the feeling that it might be evening. Time moves strangely here, and I suspect that they might even be waking us up and starting filming at different times to stop us from getting too comfortable. It's a little unsettling, especially because I'm so used to living on a routine of checking my timers to see how long it's been since Mum had whatever dose of which medicine.

The traditional slightly hesitant cheer goes up when I walk through the door, and when I do the traditional happy jiggle, it reaches a crescendo. I wonder if anyone's cheer got dramatically cut short today. I do hope no one had a bad date, even if they were Warren's morning date.

We all know that tomorrow several of those mutual matches are going to be, let's just say, less mutual. There seems to be something about the heterosexual male experience that means they can barely look past someone who isn't delivered to them exactly as they ordered (read: blonde and petite).

I'm hit with relief that I didn't get that vibe from Warren. No hesitation, no comment while I ate, no asking about going to the gym. None of the usual humanoid red flags I've seen waving in front of chubby-to-fat female contestants on other reality shows.

The atmosphere in the room feels mixed. Everyone is broken up into small groups, and I can see Hannah C. delicately tapping her fingertips under her eyes while Bridget looks on with the kind of forced *I'm here helping* look that I've seen on other 'girls' girl' contestants. I know Carys likes her, but she gives off something . . . well, *off* to me.

I suspect that Hannah P. might have been one of Warren's dates that he broke off yesterday, because she gives me the stink eye from across the room. Noted, girlie. I'll keep my respectful distance.

I also suspect, from Priya's watchful eye, that she might have been Warren's morning date. It's a match that I can understand: she's smart, has her life together, seems keen to provide, and even if she's a bit over-serious to me, she probably would balance Warren. Sorry, Priya.

At the end of the date, I made my position clear. 'So, Warren. I really like you. I like what we have going, and I want to make it clear that I'm *only* seeing you in the experiment.'

'Wow,' he had gasped, hand on heart. 'Dolly, wow.'

'I'm not asking you to end any of your other connections, because I'm sure you have some and it's a lot to think through. But I wanted you to know that, if you want me, I'm right here.'

It was a good line, I think. He didn't say anything, but I'm hoping he'll end things with Priya. That'll be the final sign he's in. After all, we're not going to be fan favourites if either of us go catching feelings for someone else, so hopefully he sees that if he does like Priya. Love triangles always play trickily, and once you're engaged, the audience explicitly frowns upon it. The fans of *Wedded Bliss* are here for a magical love story.

We're going to give that to them and reap the benefits in financial security. A fair trade.

I make my excuses to go freshen up, and head to our room.

Carys is already back, slumped on her bed. For once she seems unbothered that she's creasing the hell out of her outfit.

Her eyes are faded, distant. The colour, which was already pale, seems washed out.

'Carys? Are you alright?' I ask.

She doesn't respond in words, just a tiny shake of the head.

Her arms are wrapped around David the capybara so tight that the poor creature looks half-strangled.

I push the bedroom door shut behind me, making sure it doesn't slam. The last thing I need is to alert the others that something is up or one of the camera-hogs will be here comforting her provided it's on film.

I sit down on my bed and wait for her to elaborate.

'I'm having a bit of a day,' she says finally, her eyes fixed on the wall.

'Do you want to talk about it?'

She nods but I watch as she searches for the words. 'Dolly, do you ever wonder ...' Carys begins, but she trails off, her eyes focused somewhere else.

'Do I wonder what?'

'If ... if people are lying.'

I really do try to hold back the laugh, but it comes out as a little *ha*.

She barely responds. Only her eyes sliding over to me suggests she even heard me. I wonder if she's been drinking.

I clear my throat. 'I think that people lie about all kinds of things, all the time. That's the human condition. I don't think it's necessarily a bad thing, but I guess that depends on what they're lying about.'

She nods but says no more. What happened today? Did she have a bad date with Patrick? I feel like if they'd broken up, someone would have warned me. And I can't imagine him saying anything that bad to her. After all, he's just a mild-mannered Yorkshire man who likes mojitos and seems besotted with her, but then, I have seen some of the dogshit ways men speak to and about women on dating shows. I shouldn't be *that* surprised if he has.

Did she find out about his ex-girlfriend? The one with the flower name. Peony, that was it.

Or maybe one of the women gunning for Patrick said something to her?

'What about people lying about love?' she continues. 'Like, about the way it feels. How you are supposed to act.'

She turns her gigantic doe eyes up at me, and a pang shoots through my heart.

Fuck, she looks so sad. 'Should I get Reb?'

'No!' she blurts, which is more than enough answer for me. 'Will you ... will you stay with me?'

I ignore the swirling in my stomach. 'Did something happen with Patrick? Did he upset you?'

Carys's cinnamon curls bounce as she shakes her head. 'No. He was a total gentleman, as always.' There's not a hint of sarcasm, which is a relief. That's not really Carys's style.

'Okay, good. I'm glad he was nice to you,' I say, hoping to see a glimmer of a smile, but there's nothing. She's just curled up like a sad prawn.

'Can you elaborate on what you meant about lying about love?'

She stops and starts a few times, and I can see she's getting frustrated with herself from the clench of her fists.

I reach over the gap between us, and take her angry claw, expecting it to unclench in mine, but it stays clammed up. 'Take your time. There's no rush.'

I try to ignore the way the back of my neck prickles when she looks at me.

'The sparks,' she whispers.

Or at least, that's what I think she says. 'Sparks?' I echo.

'Yes. I hear all this talk about sparks, fireworks, about feeling something deep in your chest when you see them. And then also about *just knowing* when you've met the right person.'

'Well, yeah,' I scramble, trying to follow what she's saying. 'The fireworks? That's attraction, really. That's not always the same thing as love.'

She shakes her head, and the moment her eyes move off me, I realise how hot I felt under that gaze. 'I just wish it was clearer.'

'When you have them?'

She doesn't answer me.

'Is this something the other girls said?' I sigh. 'Look, between us, I think some of them are ... protesting a little too much, you know? Trying to convince themselves.' *Or the audience*, I add silently. 'Not everyone moves at the same pace, after all,' I insist.

'It's not just them,' she sobs quietly, and I realise that she's really crying. 'There's all these stories about sparks, the overwhelming feeling of it. I'm used to being overwhelmed by feelings but ...'

Ah. I see we're talking about something much bigger than just Patrick here, potentially.

I move to sit beside her, offering the packet of tissues I keep by my bed. She takes one with a wet smile, and dabs at her eyes.

We've not been this close when we talked before. I mean, we have, but we weren't sitting-on-the-same-bed close. It feels intimate. I can smell the sweet-sherbet perfume she douses all her clothes in.

Focus, Dolly. She's talking about fancying her future husband. Stop thinking about how she smells.

The crumpled tissue lands in her lap. I don't want the snot to ruin her pretty *Mad Men* dress, so I pick it up with my nails and replace it with David. I feel like he should be here for emotional support.

The weight of Carys's head on the top of his squishes his face down to look very strange, and I have to stifle a laugh. Carys peers down at her capybara. 'Oh sorry, David.' With a couple of quick squishes, his face is pretty much back to normal.

'But when you met Patrick today, you liked the look of him?' I ask, trying to get us back on track. 'And that guy you dated for ages.'

'Mike. His name was Mike.'

'Did you ever get the sparks with him?'

'I think I loved him, in some ways?'

Okay, that feels like a question dodged, or perhaps she's still answering questions I've already asked. God, I'm really out of my depth here.

'To be fair, you were a teenager. I don't think it's weird to not be deeply in love with him when chances are you were just the first two people who mutually fancied each other.' I'm of the age now where friends, or, well, mutuals I suppose now, are divorcing the men they married right out of secondary school.

'I don't remember sparks, though,' she says finally, as a fat teardrop lands on David's ear. 'Does that make me a shallow person? We had sex and I didn't . . . maybe I didn't . . . I mean I wanted to. I liked doing it. But does that make me shallow?'

I feel like there's like five layers to this conversation I'm missing and yet somehow we are talking about Carys's teenage sexual exploits. 'Speaking from experience, and not to slut shame myself,' I begin, and I get a little thrill when she laughs. 'But let me just say that love is not always an essential component for orgasms. For some people it is.'

I can't quite tell if that's what she's getting at, hinting at some kind of asexual or demisexual identity? I dangle the idea anyway, just in case. It would be a lot of pressure to be here if she was. 'Do you think perhaps you need that connection to feel attraction to someone?' I say carefully.

Really, I'm not sure if it's my place to float this aro/ace spectrum to her. But given the situation, examining how she feels about romance and sex might need to come sooner rather than later. I'd rather risk a little clumsiness than miss it, if it's the answer. I know straight women aren't often given the encouragement or space to think about what attraction *really* means for them.

After considering it for a while, she says, 'That's not really the issue, I don't think.'

'Then maybe you just weren't that into him or in romantic love with him, in the end,' I offer gently. 'Like I said, that's not uncommon.'

'That makes me sad, though. He deserved better than that.'

The size of her heart genuinely baffles me sometimes. 'How did it end?'

'He broke up with me when I was at uni so he could follow his dreams.'

'Which were?'

She sniffs loudly. 'Being in a One Direction tribute band.'

Dear God! I pretend to cough to cover my laugh, and reach for my huge bottle of water with my name on it to chug it down. I drank too much show wine on my date today to handle this delicately and I need to sober up stat.

Carys bursts loudly into wails, hopefully not because of me laughing. The racket such a small person can generate is kind of incredible.

'Well. That's ... unique. Have to admit I wasn't expecting that,' I say stiffly.

'He had a good voice,' she concedes, hiccupping slightly.

'Who did he play? Harry?'

'Niall.'

'Oh, so he was Irish?'

'Not even a bit.'

This is so absurd that we both burst into peals of laughter.

At least she's crying for a different reason now. She laughs so hard that she has to clutch my arm so she doesn't fall off the bed.

This is hysterical, or maybe literal hysteria setting in. Call the old timey psychologists! We've got a pair of wandering wombs.

When I can finally speak, I gasp, 'Not even like how Americans say they're Irish when they mean like five generations ago?'

'Nope. English all the way down.'

I'm at least a quarter Irish on Mum's side and Scousers are a different breed, so I feel confident when I say, 'That might have been one of the problems with him then.'

'One of *many*,' she giggles, and I feel relieved to see her smile again.

Mike's bizarre career choices aside, we still have spark-gate to address. Plus I really am too gay to know anything about One Direction beyond who was even in the band.

'So . . . Patrick?'

'It was fine, I think.'

Wow, endorsement of the century.

It appears she realises how flat that sounded, and continues, 'I mean, it was lovely to see him! I like him a lot! I'm just . . . I feel like there's so much going on in my head all the time, and right now, when there's so many other couples happening around me, it feels like I can't make all that noise quiet again.'

'Okay,' I say, mostly to signal I'm listening rather than I'm following. 'Like the sparks?'

'Yeah. I worry that perhaps I've been looking for sparks in the wrong places.'

What does Carys mean, looking in all the wrong places? I almost say, this is a heterosexual dating show – what righter place exists than this? But I manage to stop myself at the last second.

'Well, if this has come about because you've seen Patrick, did he and Mike look alike?'

'Not at all. Mike's really fair, Patrick's dark with chestnut hair. Different faces too. 'It's not that I don't like Patrick, though. I do. *I do.*'

Speaking of girls protesting too much ...

'Right. So he's not your type?' I'm struggling to find the thematic link between a vet and an off-brand Niall. I'm about to say this, hoping to get another laugh out of her, but then she looks at me.

Really looks at me. I feel like I'm the one in the spotlight.

Carys has the kind of big sad eyes you could fall into, and keep falling. She doesn't make eye contact much when we're alone, which I think is why, when she does, it's like looking at the sun.

I swear it's just the amount of time it's been since I last kissed someone that makes me glance at her lips.

'I—' she begins but stops suddenly.

'You can tell me.' I take one of her hands in mine in an act I tell myself is platonic.

This seems to surprise Carys. I'm about to withdraw my hand in case it's too much, but she squeezes back.

What the hell am I doing? Hurting my own feelings for definite.

But then her face has changed. Gone is the sadness.

Her pretty mouth falls open. Her cheeks are flushed from crying, but ... If this was anyone else, I would think she ...

No. That can't be it?

Heat prickles at my neck.

She's straight.

She's *straight*.

Isn't she?

'Dolly,' she whispers my name like a promise. 'They're both men. That's what they have in common. I think ... perhaps I've been lying to myself about who I am for so long that it's all coming out now.'

Oh fucking hell.

I *am* in trouble.

Sirens might be blaring in my ears saying *get away, get up and move, stop looking at the pretty redhead*, but I cannot move.

No wonder I can't stop looking at her. I never did fall for straight girls.

She drops my hand and while my skin yearns for her touch again, I'm relieved for the space. 'Sorry,' she says, jumping up. 'I don't know what I'm saying. I shouldn't assume. I just ... I wonder if I've been burying the real me so deep for so long that it's spilling out now. Erupting?'

'Like a volcano?' I say stupidly.

When she laughs, it's like a burst of fire in my chest. 'The metaphor is a bit tortured but it will do. I think it's not that I don't like men, because I think I do, but I'm starting to realise that I like women too.'

I am hit with a barrage of feelings.

Relief, that this whole time she wasn't asking about my connection to queer women because she was investigating me.

Terrified about what happens next.

Thrilled that she might, possibly, like me.

Shut up, brain! I'm still sitting on her bed, which feels dangerous, even if she's pacing back and forth.

God, how the fuck do I navigate this conversation without outing myself? 'That ... sounds difficult.'

'Sorry, I shouldn't— I didn't—' she splutters, whirling back and forth. 'Fuck, I've made you uncomfortable, haven't I? I'll ask for a room transfer.'

Before I can think it through, I grab her by the wrist. 'Carys, stop. It's fine. I don't feel uncomfortable.'

Not in the way she thinks, at least. I can't let her think that she's coming out to someone who's having a homophobic reaction about sharing a room with her; that would break her heart.

'And I'm not going to repeat what you've said outside these walls. That's your business, not theirs,' I add.

'Thank you.' She's so short that we're basically the same height when I'm sitting down. The knowledge makes my lower belly melt. 'When I was a teenager,' she continues, 'I thought I liked girls, but I hid it from everyone. I told myself I'd got it wrong. I don't think I was wrong.'

And when Carys turns her face to me again, all prettily pink-smudged with sadness, I see something else there. 'You've ... never felt that way about a girl before?' she says.

It's a whisper, barely there, but it hits me like a wall.

What am I supposed to do? Lie? Obviously, and yet.

I know that coming on *Wedded Bliss* meant locking away that part of me, but I can't quite bring myself to say the words.

If this were anywhere else, I'd be candid. I'd be honest. I'd tell her it's normal. I'd try to desperately ignore the soft falling-open of her mouth.

To say that here could be dangerous. Could jeopardise everything.

But then she's looking at me, with expectation and, I realise, hope.

Oh God, this isn't just about her fancying some kind of arbitrary woman, is it? Could this be about *me*?

I feel aflame just looking at her, and my brain unplugs itself. 'I— yes. Carys— I ...' I lick my lips, my mouth suddenly wet with the thought of kissing her.

She unpicks my hand from her wrist, and threads her fingers through it, so we face each other, palm to palm.

'That's why I asked, Dolly, about the girls on the road. I ... I wondered if the feeling I was missing might be right here. I wanted to know it wasn't just me.'

Her eyes dip down to my lips.

'We can't,' I gasp.

'But you want to?' The little squeak in her voice, the wish fulfilled, makes me want her even more.

When I look at her parted cherry-red lips, at her heavy-with-wanting eyes, all I can see is how lit up with desire she is.

Desire for *me*.

Our eyes lock together once again, and I'm spellbound.

'Are you sure you're not just confusing friendship?' I babble, knowing that I have very rarely looked at someone I considered only a friend like that. Nor have I held hands, sat this close, thinking about kissing my friends I didn't also want to sleep with. 'I know it's really intense in here. And we've grown close,' I protest further.

'I think we both know that's not it.'

My heart thuds in my chest as she takes my other hand too, uncurling her fingers in my palm.

God, it's been so long since I've been touched that I shiver. I forgot how addictive the feeling was. This is like the fresh water I've been wandering the desert for.

This is the first time I've wanted something for myself in a long, long time.

'It can't all be just a story, can it?' she whispers, and I start to unravel. 'The sparks?'

'Carys,' I whisper, pleading but I'm not sure what for. To stop? To keep going? Maybe both, in separate universes, so I can taste her and this remain a fantasy at the same time.

'If you don't want this, I'll stop.' Her voice is low, breathy, and so close I can taste it.

I'm high on the girl with the cinnamon hair, and the sweet-shop scent of her.

'I don't want this to stop,' I croak. 'But I can't . . .'

One last ditch plea for sensibility, even sense has long fled this room.

It feels like an electric shock when she leans her forehead

against mine. She steps closer, standing between my thighs, and my body aches at the closeness of her.

'I won't move a muscle more,' she whispers. 'It's up to you, Dolly.'

God, it's too addictive to hear my name in her mouth. 'I think you are so much more than just an experiment.'

I know then that we've crossed a threshold. There is no turning back from this. Whatever Carys and I are, it's an inevitability.

From the moment I saw her in the road, this spark of fire rushing to help, I knew I liked her, wanted her, thought about her all the time. And it's only got worse the more I've got to know her.

'I want you. And ... I think you want me too.'

'Bold of you,' I manage to shudder out.

I bite my lower lip, letting it drag through my teeth, and think about what it would feel like doing that to her own pouty bottom lip.

We move in infinitesimal increments, like a gravitational force beyond both of us is drawing us together slowly.

Our hands unclasp, and she cautiously slides her hands up my arms, over my shoulders, only stopping when they reach my jaw.

'I thought you weren't moving,' I tease.

When I put my hands in the small of her back, she gasps, and I'm certain that I want to hear that sound over and over. If she wasn't standing right between my legs, I'd press my thighs together to feel the deliciousness.

I'm drunk on her.

When the soft tip of her nose brushes against mine, it's my turn to gasp.

'Please,' she begs. Her breath dances on my skin. 'Dolly. Please kiss me. Just once.'

All my weak protestations die at her words. I don't have it in me anymore. I don't want to hold back.

'Just once,' she pleads. 'I want to feel the fireworks.'

Just once?

If that's all we can have, I'll give that to her.

Just once.

'Kiss me then,' I say, drunk and cocky and desperate for this agony to end.

She moves so slowly that I might break in two, still clutching my face in her hands like she's about to devour me, or drink me. I'm about to beg her to do either of those.

And the relief of her lips finally on mine is a rising symphony.

I see stars when she nudges her lips open, and as I dip my tongue into our kiss, she makes this beautiful little sound.

Our mouths move easily in sync, like we've been kissing forever, or like our bodies recognise each other from a past life.

I'm hungry for her, and it's my turn to moan when she steps forward, pressing her body against me.

My God, I want her.

I dot tiny kisses on the curve of skin where cheek meets nose, and she melts against me, whining softly into my hair at the touch.

'Dolly,' she pleads, dropping her hands from my jaw to run them through my hair.

I trail kisses along her face, under the softness of her chin, and along her jaw.

Her skin tastes of the coconut moisturiser I try not to watch her slather on every day, and the rhubarb pie perfume she dabs at her delicate little wrists. There's an undercurrent of salt that I could lap forever. And a deeper flavour all her own that I could enjoy forever.

She tastes incredible, and I wonder what the rest of her tastes like; sweet and salt and heat. At just the thought of it, I come apart, a deep pulse between my legs rushing through me like a wave.

Our kiss deepens as she tugs at me, begging our bodies to get closer.

Carys steps back suddenly, tearing at the buttons on the front of my shirt dress. It opens, and she peels it back hurriedly, so it pools around my waist.

In return, I whip the dress off her, and the pussy-bow blouse melts off her pale shoulders. She stands in front of me in a matching lace set – of *course* she wears matching sets.

'If this is going too fast, we can—' I blurt out, but I'm interrupted by Carys unleashing a frustrated growl and climbing into my lap, straddling my hips.

She's right there, on top of my heat, and if she makes one goddamn move, I'm going to die right here.

Apparently, she's feeling the same kind of intensity, because she looks down at me finally and whispers, 'Oh my God.'

'Hi,' I whisper.

'Hi.' She kisses and slowly begins to grind against me.

I'm so overwhelmed I almost tip into orgasm right then. God, she could make me come apart in a second.

'Fucking *hell*,' I whisper, as I kiss along her bare shoulder and up her neck, nipping slightly at the soft juncture between the two.

All that separates us are the remains of my dress and her knickers, which if you know anything about women's clothing is basically nothing.

I bury my face in her chest as she moves again, suppressing a moan in my throat. Each grind shoots electricity through both of us, and I hear her breathing heavier, and heavier.

Fucking hell.

She tips my chin up to her, and she looks as drunk on this as I feel. 'I feel it.'

'The sparks?'

'Everything. Technicolour.' Her voice is high with relief.

There is nothing hotter in the world than knowing someone found their meaning on your lips and is now revelling in it. I'm giddy on her, on it, on *this*.

'Do you want—' I begin.

'Please.'

'— me to touch you.'

'I said please, didn't I?' she says with such a bratty edge to it that I almost flip her over right there.

I slide my right hand up the bare skin of her inner thigh, and she moans at the touch.

'Shh,' I whisper.

She looks down at me desperately as I grip her hip with my left hand to keep her still. 'I'm not sure I can be quiet.'

'If you want me to make you come, you'll have to be.'

She looks genuinely shocked when I say the word *come*. Perhaps she's not used to speaking plainly in the bedroom. 'I promise I'll try. For you, I'll try, Dolly,' she whimpers as I slide my thumb to the front of her underwear, the fabric already soaking wet. She's hot, and when I stroke her, her body roils with pleasure.

When she finally comes, the noise is a high little bleat, nestled into my hair.

'I can't breathe when you do that,' she gasps, her mouth falling open to reveal the pretty shell-pink of her mouth. She unclasps her bra, and her nipples are the same colour as the inside of her mouth. She's all peaches and cream and I want to lap her all up.

'Do you want me to stop?'

'I never want you to stop.'

'Good girl.' I bring her to orgasm with my hands again, drunk on how pliable she is under my touch.

She drunkenly kisses me, eyes heavy, and I have no idea if it's been minutes or hours since we first kissed. It feels unreal.

'My turn,' Carys demands. 'You might have to show me what to do.'

She steps back to pull off the rest of my clothing, only sidetracked by my, frankly incredible, breasts. Her eyes turn hungry, and soon she's flat against me, my nipple in her mouth.

'Fucking hell,' I gasp, as she grinds herself against my leg. 'Are you going to take those knickers off, or do you want me to do it for you?'

She locks eyes with me as she steps away and drags them down. First hers, then mine.

When we're completely naked, she pushes me back to lie on the bed and kneels between my thighs. Normally I want to sit up when being viewed from this angle, guaranteed that my head and neck become one, but under her intense gaze, I'm not afraid of how I look. I'm what she's been waiting for.

'You're the most beautiful person I've seen, Dolly.'

I can't get enough of her saying my name. I can't get enough of her.

I drag her up to lie down next to me, and she trails her fingers down over the soft roll of my belly. Her eyes flash as she slides her fingers between my folds.

'You're so wet,' she gasps.

What she lacks in finesse, she sure as hell makes up in enthusiasm and I'm so gone on her that I'm dying after only a few movements.

I reach over, waiting for her permission, and when she nods into my mouth, I slide my fingers inside her.

As we fuck, my mind can't help thinking of all the other things I want to or could do to her. How well she'd wear a strap. How I want to learn all the tiny spots of her body that spark under my touch.

I want to be fluent in Carys. In the ebbs and flows of her body. Every inch claimed under my ownership.

It's the most stupid want, because it can never happen. Not the way I'd dream if I weren't about to get engaged to another man. The last thing I'm going to do is make Carys a dirty secret on the side; she deserves so much more than that.

All I can do is give her the best orgasms of her life, and send her on her way, out into the world to kiss so many other girls. To find the fireworks everywhere.

It'll hurt to say goodbye. But for now at least, it's perfect.

She's everything I ever wanted.

Too bad I can't keep her.

Just for tonight, we'll see all the fireworks.

Chapter Thirteen

Carys

I can't believe I did that.

Any of it.

But my God, I felt the fireworks, all through my body.

Repeatedly.

I wake curled against Dolly in my single bed. I can't believe how lucky I am to be with her. To have kissed her.

To have her like me back.

So much has changed in the last few days that my head is spinning even though I'm still.

I hadn't expected us to have sex – I hadn't expected anything at all.

I wanted to kiss her once she told me that she felt something too.

Everything else took me by surprise, in the best way. A lot of that was me letting go of worrying about what I could or should be doing, and just enjoying the moment with her. With *Dolly*.

I didn't know sex could feel so freeing. When I knelt between her legs, I was praying at an altar.

Just the memory of last night is enough to make heat pool between my thighs, and I press them together happily.

There's only been a few times I've gone all the way on a first date, and that was back at the beginning of my dating journey when I hoped it would make men like me. Needless to say, it didn't seem to change things for them.

But last night, despite the speed of it all, everything just felt right. I wanted her, and she wanted me right back. It was complicated and yet, that part, that wanting, was totally uncomplicated.

I'm not sure I've ever been wanted like that.

And I've obviously never been with a woman that way before, and it was just ... incredible. I've enjoyed sex with men, but with Dolly, I experienced something so astronomically different from before.

Even though no one is listening in, I'm finding it hard even to bring the thoughts forward, like I'm still wrapped up in how I'm *supposed* to speak about being attracted to her, never mind think about her. Compulsory heterosexuality apparently has a lot to answer for.

It's still such a tangle.

I think she's worth untangling that for.

I wriggle round in her arms, ever so slowly, so that I can look at her. Luckily, she doesn't stir, so I can look all I want. Not in a creepy way – I'm not a teen vampire in the corner of her bedroom, I'm fairly sure this is allowed.

I decide to practise that untangling, so that when she does wake, I can tell her exactly what it all means to me. What she means.

Even deep asleep, Dolly takes my breath away. She is the most beautiful woman I've ever seen. I thought that the day I saw her step out into traffic, but it's different now. I've seen her beauty in ways I couldn't imagine appreciating before – how she looks naked, how she looks when she orgasms, and the way her eyes soften when she tells me I'm beautiful.

Tangled up in the sheets, she's a model in a Renaissance painting. All curves and dips and softness. She's so deliciously soft. The dimples on her arms. The flowing wave of her thighs – the same ones that gripped around my hips and waist last night as she cried out in pleasure.

It's all of her. The long dark eyelashes flutter in her sleep. Dolly's plump lips still bear the ghostly stain of her red lipstick; how many more kisses will it withstand? Her hair is all mussed, and fuzzed with old hair product. I must admit, I feel a little proud that that's partly my doing.

I have to resist the temptation to stroke back her hair or kiss her, because I don't want this quiet moment to end. Plus, it's more nerve-wracking staring at someone when they're wide awake. I'm not done drinking her in.

Still, I'm giddy on it all. Not just last night, but my feelings for her. The certainty of working out what was going on, the relief, the joy of it all.

I don't know what this means in terms of a wider identity for me. I know some people like labels, but am I allowed to take my time? I'll have to ask her that when she wakes up. There must be rules about it. I just don't want to take up any space that isn't mine.

At least, maybe I don't need to carry the shame around it all any longer. That will take some time too.

I guess I can leave heterosexuality behind.

'You're watching me.' Her voice is low and croaky, and it takes everything in me not to kiss her straight away.

I feel heat rush to my cheeks. 'Only a little.'

She opens one eye. 'Morning?'

'It might be. I woke up a little while ago, and I can't hear anyone else up yet. Did you sleep okay?'

'Evidently.' She turns her head and squints, not fully committing to the movement yet. 'I think my bare ass might be hanging out the bed.'

We wriggle closer together, and I pull the blankets around us, distributing them more equally.

'How are you feeling?' I venture, a little nervously.

'Sleepy.' Dolly is not a morning person, even after sex it turns out.

'Come on, give me a proper answer,' I whisper, trying not to feel bruised by her diminished enthusiasm.

She looks at me under heavy lids. 'Sore.'

For another monosyllabic answer, it really jolts my nervous system awake. I did that. Me.

'Sorry,' I say, not sorry at all.

'Don't be. It was incredibly fun and absolutely worth it.'

Fun. Well, yes, it was fun, but it was more than that for me. It's not a bad word by any stretch of the imagination, so why does my heart ache a little?

Wasn't it more than fun for her?

Perhaps I'm expecting too much. After all, there were a lot of firsts. I don't want to assume but I guess the only first part of it for her was on the set of a television show.

My heart suddenly staccatos in my chest and I try to push out any thought of the situation we're in. I don't want the real world to rush in. The only thing that exists right now is Dolly and me in this too-small twin bed.

'Though,' Dolly continues, stretching out her legs. I can't help but feel a flutter in my chest as I wait for her to say something profound about us. Instead, what she says is, 'I'm not sure Rihanna's entire makeup empire could hide the bags under my eyes.'

Oh. Well, never mind. I'm getting too caught up in the narrative in my head as usual, and I need to just experience the moment as it happens.

'You look beautiful,' I insist, kissing her on the tip of her nose.

She smiles, wrinkling the tip from side to side like a cartoon rabbit. 'In the lowlight, sure,' she agrees with a wicked smile that I want to kiss off her face. But she stretches again, distance growing between the two of us. 'In high definition? Perhaps not.'

'I don't want to think about the show,' I say a little sharply. 'Let's just enjoy this.'

She yawns, and I shiver with delight as her fingers find my thigh, stepping up to my hips. Every touch is a joyful pinprick.

But the bubble has been broken. I can't stop thinking about what's outside the door. How we're going to navigate today. What we're going to tell production. What I'm going to tell ...

No, shut up brain.

'What?' Dolly says. My eyes, which were probably off-focus looking at the wall while I drifted inside my own stream of thoughts, snap back to her concerned face.

'Sorry. Nothing.'

'Tell me.'

'I just ...' I begin, unsure where to start with all the things we are going to have to talk about. 'I think I just want to talk about last night.'

'Okay.' She rubs the sleep out of her eyes. 'What do you want to talk about?'

This question feels too open and is the kind that makes my brain itch. It's still all too big – the fact we kissed, fucked, fell asleep naked, told each other we liked each other (not in that order) and now, as a result of that, probably need to talk about the ramifications. Plus the whole I need your advice as a ... Hell, I don't even know how she identifies. That seems rude, given the circumstances.

My train of thought grinds to a halt under the weight of all the things we need to talk about.

The gap of silence must have been too long, because suddenly Dolly is out of my arms and sitting up against the headboard, the covers pooling in her lap. All I can feel is cold air where she once was, like my body is highlighting all the places she once touched me in neon. It's jarring.

'Sorry,' I whisper, frustrated that I can't get the words out or in the right order, especially now she's moved.

I'm still trying to find the words when I hear a door across the hallway open and close. That means someone else is awake, probably another of the early rising team like Whit or Lina.

I can't help but notice the way Dolly nervously looks at the door.

'Come on, we should probably start getting up.'

This might be the first time she's ever stopped waiting for me to speak and that *hurts*. I'm so used to other people doing it to me, but Dolly? She's always let me take my time.

'I think—' I begin before I'm ready, but I want to stop her from getting up and out of this bed. In the gap, I notice her glancing at the door again.

'Tell me?' I can tell she's trying to sound patient but failing.

Fuck. I'm fucking this up.

'I just wanted to know if I should start packing now?' I blurt. It's not really what I wanted to say at all; the logistics of moving on through this experiment were literally at the bottom of the list.

Dolly's eyes soften and she takes my hand in both of hers, cradling it like a bird that's flown into a window. 'Do you want to? I mean, if you think that's the right decision then obviously I support you. You need to know that production might kick up a fuss about breach of contract, even at this stage. It's probably not as bad as if you're engaged but . . .'

This is not quite the answer I was expecting, but then talking with neurotypical people always feels like it takes a few goes for us both to translate each other. 'I . . . I don't know? I'm just trying to wrap my head around what we should do.'

I can't help but notice the way Dolly's eyebrows rise slowly. 'We?'

'Yeah?' I say, unsure if this is quite right either. I wish conversations didn't feel so slippy to me.

Her brows slowly furrow into not quite a frown, but a question, I can tell that much. 'What do you mean? You want me to come talk to production with you?'

I blink. This feels off course too. Because, yes, I think we should talk to production, but wouldn't it make sense to bring this whole situation to them together? Perhaps we speak to Louise and Reb at the same time?

I realise belatedly, that I've been blabbering my thoughts out loud.

'Carys,' she says slowly, and a nervous ache grows in the middle of my torso. 'What do you think is going to happen today?'

'We don't have to,' I say, waving my hands. It all comes out in a nervous rush. 'I don't want to pressure you, or anything, and I know you probably want time to break things off with Warren first. But maybe we can talk about the easiest way to tell production so that we can leave without ruffling too many feathers. Or, you know, whenever we decide to go? I don't want to rush you.'

That ache turns into a pit when Dolly shuffles off the bed stiffly, roughly throwing last night's dress back on. She doesn't look at me the whole time.

Still turned away from me, she takes one long deep breath in, like she's preparing to monologue. 'Carys, what are you talking about?' she asks, her voice steady and flat.

'Us?' It's supposed to be declarative, insistent, but it comes out as a question. I can't get a handle on any of the words or how they sound because my heart is beating so loudly in my ears that I can barely hear myself.

Dolly looks up at the ceiling, and I understand this

behaviour. It's not the same as my lack of eye contact, which happens because it's easier for me to concentrate if I don't have to think about reacting or emoting or reading the other person properly. The kind of not looking Dolly is doing is about not wanting to look at me. And that is terrifying.

'Carys,' she says slowly.

Why won't she look at me?

'Carys, last night you said it would be *just once*.'

The whiplash of this conversation is unending, and I scramble through the script of last night to try and remember what she's talking about. 'I said I wanted to feel the fireworks.'

'Just *once*,' Dolly insists.

'I don't think I said that. I meant . . . like . . . *for* once.'

'Carys, you said *just once*. I remember it. I wouldn't— I went along with you because I thought we understood each other.'

That can't be right? Wasn't it obvious that I meant much more than a one-night stand? Because after we kissed everything changed?

Didn't it?

Panic floods through me because she's misunderstood or maybe I've confused things by not being clear.

Dolly shakes her head and backs away from me slightly like I'm a wild animal. I feel like one, caged and ready to snap.

'Fuck,' Dolly whispers, wiping her hand down her face.

'You're coming with me,' I say, cursing myself that I forgot the pesky question mark again.

'What?'

'I'm leaving.'

'Yes.' She nods once as though this was the obvious part.

'And you're coming with me?' I ask properly this time.

But there's a familiar look in her eyes, that look of pity and regret, the look I've seen too many times.

'Aren't you?' My voice falters.

Dolly closes her eyes for just a second, and I watch in slow motion as she kneels on the floor next to the bed to take my hand.

I wish I had put my clothes on too. With my free hand, I clutch the sheets up against me, as though they might protect me from the emotional barrage that is coming for me.

'Carys,' she says, very slowly like she's talking to a frightened animal. 'I really enjoyed what we had together last night, and I'm really glad that you seem to have got some clarity on some things. I am so happy we had that moment last night, and I'm sorry if there's been some confusion about the boundaries going forward.'

It feels stupid to hope that she's going to say she wants to be with me.

And yet I do.

Right up until she says, 'But Carys, I'm not leaving the experiment. I'm staying, and I'm going to marry Warren.'

I didn't realise you could feel your heart break in two.

'Why?' The words are barely more than a whisper.

'My reasons haven't changed.'

'And they are?'

I feel the frustration radiating off her. 'I have responsibilities, Carys.'

Responsibilities? What is she even talking about? She's never mentioned having responsibilities. Does this just mean she doesn't want me?

I can't do this naked, so I pull on my pyjamas as she stands up and moves away from me. The distance feels like a wound.

'So you're going to marry a man you don't love,' I say, and I hate that I can hear the desperation in my voice.

'Yes.' She says it so flatly, like this is a totally normal thing to say. Wait? She doesn't love him?

'A man you *can't* love,' I murmur as I realise what's going on.

Now she looks pissed off. 'That's right. I'm a lesbian.' She slow claps. 'You worked it out.'

'And last night didn't change *anything*?' I'm hot and angry and I know I should be pleading or supplicant, but I am just so fucking furious. 'You're a *lesbian*, Dolly.'

'Keep your voice down,' she growls, her eyes dancing to the door. 'A little note from me to you: I'm almost certain that we've both had plenty of people throwing that word at us pejoratively, but I've reclaimed it for myself and I'd rather you didn't weaponise it either.'

I feel scolded.

'Fine.' That stings and I feel dizzy, because she is right. But that doesn't override the shaking, horrible bad feeling coursing through my body.

I swing back to desperation as the spinning, spirally feeling of rejection claws at me. There must be some way we can salvage this.

'What if we recouple? Together?' I suggest hurriedly. 'That way you don't have to leave the show, if that's important to you? Would we be their first same-gender couple? That must be a big deal.'

The look she gives me now is harder to read, sadder. 'You know that's not what this show is, Carys.'

I don't really, because I barely watched it beforehand, which continues to be one of my most pointlessly self-sabotaging decisions. Apparently it was a lucky guess that there's not been an LGBTQ+ couple yet.

'Do you know how little airtime queerness gets on reality TV?' Dolly continues. 'That's why we're always relegated to our own spinoffs – *The Queer Ultimatum* not *The Ultimatum*. That one season of *Are You the One?* where everyone was bi-sexual for a gimmick. The *I Kissed A* franchise that has only queer people dating the same gender. Perhaps, if we're lucky, one couple a season on *Married at First Sight*.'

Obviously I have no idea what any of these shows are, which means I can't argue back. I can feel the tears welling up because everything she's saying is so fucking sensible and all I want is to hear her tell me that she wants to be with me. Is that stupid? I feel stupid.

She looks quite sad when she says, '*Wedded Bliss* is not ready for lesbians. Nor are, in my opinion, half the brands out there waiting to work with a nice heterosexual couple from the show. The exact brands I'm banking on giving Warren and me some financial stability.'

This makes me angrier, this time on Warren's behalf. 'So you're just going to lie to him?'

Dolly's hand goes to her forehead like I'm giving her a headache. 'He and I have an understanding.'

'What does that mean?' I cross my arms, deeply aware that I sound like a toddler asking *why* over and over. 'Explain it to me.'

'Fucking hell, Carys,' she hisses, fully exasperated with me now. 'It's not about feelings for us and that's fine. That is the relationship we are building, that works for us. Centuries of marriages were built on business arrangements.'

'But you're faking being in love with him,' I point out.

'Well, yeah,' she says, like I'm stupid. 'We've got to sell it, haven't we? This is a *television show* after all. Most of us are not actually here to find someone to fall in love with.'

This stings. Not just because that's exactly why I'm here, but it's just another reminder that I'm operating on another planet from most people. '*I* am,' I say quietly.

'And look how well that's going,' Dolly whispers, not unkindly.

My last remaining hopes crumble into dust. She doesn't want me. She doesn't want me, not enough to give up on this business arrangement for the chance at something real with me.

What's so wrong with me?

I drop back down onto the bed, the room still spinning.

'I can give you some names of people to look up on the outside,' Dolly continues. 'They'll be discreet but can talk through all this early coming out stuff, if that's what you want. Guide you towards some help, some community. There's plenty of that in London at least. It's a lot to process your own sexuality, especially when you realise at an inopportune time.'

I feel like I might be sick.

'Carys?' Dolly reaches out for my hand but I cannot cope with processing her touch right now, or all the different meanings of it, so I slap her hand away.

She looks surprised and hurt.

Fuck.

Shame hits, and I want the floor to swallow me.

This wasn't how it was supposed to go.

Clearly, this is enough to run Dolly's well of sympathy dry. 'Carys, I have responsibilities. I have made commitments. I can't leave the experiment just because you're having a late-in-life-lesbian crisis.'

'I'm *twenty-seven*,' I hiss, as though that's the most egregious part of this conversation.

I can't believe it. She's breaking up with me. After last night, she's breaking this off.

'We're not together, Carys,' she says, and I realise I said some version of this out loud. 'There's nothing to break up.'

Nothing?

Is that what she thinks of me?

Nothing?

I need to get out of here. I need some air.

Dolly stands between me and the door, her face buried in her hands. 'God, I *knew* I shouldn't have slept with you. Of course this would be a mistake.'

Heat races through my veins. I can't tell if I'm going to cry or scream. 'I'm not a mistake. I'm not *nothing*.'

'I'm sorry. That was too harsh. I'm just panicking.' For the first time since I've known her, she actually looks rattled. Perhaps I look more unhinged than I realise. 'I didn't mean you are a mistake. But us, *this*, right now was a mistake.'

'Only because you're saying it is,' I say, stumbling over the words. 'Only because you're doing this instead of choosing me.'

She groans in frustration. 'What did you think was going to happen, Carys? That we were going to skip off into the horizon in some Sapphic bliss?'

I thought that maybe I was it for you. Like you might be it for me. I can't get the words out.

Even though I don't speak, she can clearly tell what I'm thinking and feeling. I never was very good at hiding either from my face, and Dolly seems to have got quite good at reading me in the short time we've known each other. 'I'm sorry if that's what you were hoping for, Carys, but that's just not possible. I can't give you that.'

'So this was just casual for you?' I whisper.

The worst part is that she hesitates. I think, for a second, that she's going to tell me that no, this wasn't casual, that this meant something to her, as much as it did to me. That when we kissed, the fireworks meant something to her too.

But instead, she says in a firm voice, 'Give yourself the space to process all this. It must be really hard what you're going through, but Carys, you can't imprint on me because I'm the first girl you kissed.'

That's cruel. I didn't expect her to be so cruel. Maybe that was my first mistake.

I feel my broken heart shatter. I can't believe I trusted her with my body and my heart and *me*, only for her to stamp on everything with one of her perfect high heels.

'I'm not some *duckling*,' I sob.

I can't look at her any longer so I flee into the bathroom, locking the door behind me, and I walk straight into the shower cubicle, pyjamas still on. I sit down on the floor, because my legs are far too jelly to stand up any longer. My body shakes from all the feelings threatening to explode out of me and I know that if I don't do something drastic, I'm going to have a meltdown.

The last thing I want is for Dolly to see me even more broken apart than I already am. I don't want to give her the satisfaction.

I spin the temperature all the way into the blue and turn the shower on full blast. The shocking cold water runs into my mouth, down my throat, slicing through my hair to my scalp. It's a delicious relief to start with.

Eventually I start to shiver.

And, when I finally feel human again in all the worst ways, that's when I finally really cry. The tears wash away down the plug, like they were never there.

I spin the temperature up and, seeing as I'm already here, wash away the remains of last night, of Dolly, just like she wants.

Clean at last, I step out into a towel. I hope it's not obvious I've been crying, so I wipe the steam away from the mirror to check. It mists up again quickly, blurring my reflection, but I'm not sure I recognise the person I catch a glimpse of.

What the hell am I doing?

This, all of this, is just so unlike me. Maybe ... maybe my sisters were right to be worried about me coming into this experiment. Perhaps they correctly predicted that being slowly driven mad by masking twenty-four-seven and overstimulation from the god-awful lighting and all the constant socialising I'm having to do all while knowing I'm being filmed, watched and dissected by the public would eat away at me. They didn't tell me that, but they asked me, over and over, if I was sure about going on this show.

It's not like I'm not used to experiencing, and expecting, scrutiny from those around me. Ever since I was little, I've been so hyper-aware of how I'm being perceived. All that has been kicked up to eleven since I've been here. There's no downtime, except when I sleep, and I'm pretty certain I'm not getting enough of that.

There's a saying about how pressure turns coal into diamonds, like it might make the best of people if you just try to get through. I'm not so sure about that. There's no sparkliness about me right now. Just sharp edges and confusion.

I really wish I could call my sisters. They'd give me a good talking to, help me work out what I should do next. When I was little, I really struggled with thinking things through before I acted. Mum used to call it *getting Carys'd away*.

I know that if Ang and Del were here, they'd make me talk through things in order, to untangle the knotty tangle of panic in my chest. A rat king of anxiety.

Let's look at the facts, in order: I'm sleep deprived and overstimulated and out-peopled. This is probably the most difficult thing I've ever done in my life, and you can't make good choices when your brain is throwing itself against a wall.

Sleeping with Dolly is a perfect example of that.

So, okay, I like women. I think, after last night, that's pretty undeniable, and I've spent a lifetime denying myself truths for reasons I don't fully understand. To fit in, to camouflage? Because I was too scared of being too many deviations from normal? All of the above, maybe.

And with all that understanding and unmasking, of a kind, of course I might get . . . over-excited.

Maybe Dolly was right, just a little, about the 'imprinting' thing. Did I just latch onto the first person who showed me true kindness who was also within touching distance, and just misconstrue attraction for love? Sexual chemistry for romance? I'm not sure; it definitely felt like a crush.

It was a crush. And crushes can be got over, even if they sting.

Ang would tell me to give myself grace. *Who hasn't had an inappropriate crush in a trying time?* she'd say.

Dolly's pretty much the only person I've even remotely dropped my mask in front of in here, which is a pretty big deal to me. No wonder I would feel close to her, carried away with the fantasy of it all. Given this whole experiment is about romantic fantasies and longing and promises ... maybe it's understandable that I got confused about what I really want.

Because what I want is Patrick.

Oh no, Patrick.

A pit opens in my stomach as I realise I've basically cheated on him. I mean, we're not official yet, but I'm pretty sure the social contract of dating multiple people in *Wedded Bliss* doesn't extend to sleeping with your roommate.

I feel so embarrassed; I've never cheated on anyone before and, if I'm honest, I'd held that as a badge of honour. Proof that I was potentially a good partner for someone, despite everything else.

Not that I've told Patrick that I'm autistic yet. No wonder I glommed onto Dolly for getting it without being told what *it* was. I haven't given Patrick that same chance yet, to be kind and understanding. To listen to me, and to not be afraid if I'm a little strange.

If I do, will I fall even deeper for him? I feel like yes, I could. I will.

I will definitely tell him I'm autistic before we're married. Probably.

Should I tell him about last night? I'm not sure I can. I don't want to start off a relationship on a lie, but maybe this is one of those occasions where it's okay to omit the truth to save everyone's feelings. If I tell Patrick, he'll be upset and confused. And today is supposed to be our date where we get to touch, even kiss, if we want to. I want us to focus on building the foundation to our marriage, not destroy it.

No, I can't tell him. If I can chalk this up to some kind of madness, maybe it's okay not to tell him.

I'm not sure how long I've been in here but it hurts that Dolly doesn't knock or try to speak to me. I know she's still in the bedroom, so I'm going to have to face her.

So, what am I going to do?

I replay our conversation over and over, and I keep snagging on something. The mysterious responsibilities she's never mentioned. I mean, no, I didn't tell her I was autistic but that's my business.

I mean, she's an influencer. Isn't that a job with money? Brand deals, isn't that something? Surely more money than my hand-to-mouth salary combined with living in London in a house with three to four other strangers. I'm pretty sure she still lives at home too, so that's rent free. Meanwhile, I regularly see the bottom of my overdraft. But I've seen some of the labels in her clothes. I know they're expensive. And that accent – I don't think she could be *that* desperate for money.

If she's a lesbian and came on the show to find a husband, there can't be pure reasons for that. Does 'responsibilities' just mean she's after money? For what? She must already have money.

I don't think anyone owes anyone else the inner workings of their sexuality, but also, this is a heterosexual dating show. Not only is Dolly denying someone their fair chance at finding love, but she's lying to herself and the world too.

What if Warren could have found someone to fall in love with, but instead he's with Dolly? There's no way he knows for sure. That's not the sort of arrangement you can agree on camera, surely? The show is about love! She can't be sure of his feelings.

I don't understand it. I don't understand *her*.

If she came on this show for money and fame or whatever but has been telling me and all the others she's here for love, then she's been lying the whole time.

No wonder I would foolishly leap to the idea of us leaving together or recoupling if I thought she was here for honest reasons. Would I have even kissed her if I'd known?

In fact, has she said anything truthful this whole time?

It's pretty rich for her to get angry with me this morning when I was just upset and confused, especially if all that is because she's been talking a big game about her priorities and Warren and love. She didn't have to be so fucking *mean* to me.

That's when I realise: it's all her fault.

Yes. That's it. It's Dolly's fault I'm in this mess, crying in the bathroom, feeling guilty about cheating on Patrick.

Sure, I can take responsibility for getting confused and carried away, but I was working off faulty evidence, wasn't I?

None of this would have happened, none of it, if Dolly had been honest with me.

And now, what? She wants to win the show. I guess that stability she is after is taking home the nest egg grand prize money.

There are real couples in here, falling in love and wanting to start a life together. Bridget and Whit and Lina are all here for love; don't they deserve a true shot at happiness and the money too?

I'm sure they deserve the hundred thousand pounds more than Dolly and Warren do. Patrick and I certainly do.

Does she even believe in love?

She's making a mockery of it all. Of all of us.

The sanctity of this experiment matters to me. I came here to find love, and I think I'm going to find it with Patrick.

God forbid I let two people who are *faking* love win. That would ruin everything.

And then, an idea forms. No. Is that too much? I swear I heard one of the Hannahs mention people get kicked off dating shows if production don't think they're genuine.

If I reported her to them, they could send her home.

But ratting them out is risky. If the others found out it was me, would they think I'm a bad person? Everyone else seems to like her, probably more than they like me. I'm sure Warren is popular on the boys' side too.

Plus, if she went home, I wouldn't have the satisfaction of seeing her lose to me.

Because I think I can beat her.

I can do more, I can push more. After all, I am very familiar with making myself approachable, friendly, trustworthy to strangers. I know how to be the adorkable, cute character that people expect and find they like. I'm good at corralling an audience at the farm. I've spent my life training myself to be just enough and not too much.

She might be a faker and a liar, but I'm a high-masking autistic woman; we're similar but I'm a different breed.

I'm the most formidable opponent Dolly Doherty could ever come up against.

That prize money is mine. Mine and Patrick's.

Or at the very least, I'll do everything in my power to make sure it's not hers. I just have to be a little bit better than her at everything. I *know* I can do that.

This decision feels dangerous, but it feels right. Excitement threads through my body in little thrills.

I'm not going anywhere. I'm staying, and I'm going to make it her problem.

~

When I leave the bathroom, Dolly is nervously pacing around between our beds, dressed in fresh clothes, but halts when she sees me. She watches me like I'm an animal in a trap. 'Are you okay?'

I ignore her question. 'You're right. This was a mistake,' I say, my words clipped and short.

'Carys, please. I didn't mean it in a bad way. It just happens sometimes. People get—'

I cut her off with a wave of my hand. 'We can be adults about this.'

I can tell she doesn't quite believe me. The panic on her face is delicious.

Good. Squirm, bitch!

I busy myself getting dressed while she waits silently, unsure how to progress this conversation. Welcome to my life.

I'm surprised she doesn't just leave.

'Do you want me to help you pack?' she asks eventually.

'No thank you,' I say, concentrating on the zip that runs up my side. I dry my hair quickly and shove it up into a bun.

If I get ahead of this, I can control the narrative – the thing that'll piss her off the most.

'I'll put in a request for a room transfer,' I say, choosing not to say *so I don't have to look at you again* because I'm being an adult right now.

'What do you mean?' I can hear the panic in her voice.

I go to the door, pull it open just a crack and turn back to her. 'I'm staying. I'm going to marry Patrick. May the best woman win.'

Chapter Fourteen

Dolly

Lina Chen, 25, Glasgow

[Lina shuffles a stack of tarot cards] *Come on, we'll just do a one-card pull for you. Perhaps to see what your next few months are going to look like?* [A hand appears to take a card from a flared pile. Lina turns it over and nods her head slowly] *Now, don't be scared, but you did pull Death.*

Oh *fuck*.

I'm not sure this could have gone worse if I tried to fuck it up more. And I completely fucked up that chat by getting frustrated and mean, but fuck.

Everything was going perfectly to plan until last night, and now I have a freshly hatched baby-gay about to detonate all over everything I've worked for.

This is my future. My mum's future.

What does 'may the best woman win' mean? Is she going to out me? Is she going to tell them that Warren and I are fake?

Fuck, I knew I shouldn't have told her anything. I should have just told her I was more into Warren. There were so many more sensible things I could have done than reveal my grand plans like a shite villain in a movie.

There's still time to stop her, so I grab Carys by the wrist before she can close the door. 'Carys, please. Don't be an idiot about this.'

Carys spins, snarling. It turns her pretty face ugly. She yanks her hand out of my grip, and I feel my nails accidentally dig into her skin as she moves. She yelps and holds her wrist to her chest.

'Fuck, sorry.' I want to check her skin over, but she won't give up her hand.

'Oh, let me get this straight,' she says with zero irony. 'When I make a plan, I'm somehow an idiot. You're just smarter than the rest of us, is that it?'

'I shouldn't have called you an idiot,' I admit. 'But you can't just stay here to spite me.'

She laughs. 'Don't underestimate me.'

'I'm *not*. I'm worried about you!'

I am. *And* I'm worried about her messing this up for me. But she's not going to listen to me if I keep being a cunt to her.

'You can't worry about someone you don't give a shit about,' she snaps.

'I *do* give a shit, Carys. That's why I'm trying to talk you out of making a bad decision.'

'You're just scared I'm going to beat you. You're scared that Patrick and I make a better couple than you and Warren do.'

I hate that my traitorous body finds it hot when she is literally threatening me.

And while I never had notions of winning this thing, she doesn't need to know any more details.

'What about Patrick? You were oh so concerned about whether I'm lying to Warren, and yet you're going to lie to Patrick? The guy is *in love* with you.'

That is somewhat of an exaggeration and I should feel bad about it, but I don't.

'And who is to say I don't like him back?'

'*You* did!' I feel like I'm going insane. 'That's what all last night was about!'

'I didn't say that at all. I was just confused, clearly.'

Maybe she didn't say that. Did I imagine it? All I can remember are the horny sirens blaring in my ears that I should have listened to, then I wouldn't be in this total shitfit of a situation.

She straightens the collar of the latest in a parade of identical twee tea dresses. 'I know I'll feel it when I kiss him.'

'And what if you don't?' God, shut up, Dolly. Why are you even asking this?

'I will. He matters more to me than anything in the world.' She looks me up and down like I'm muck. 'I said this was a mistake. I was just confused. Let's forget it happened.'

'So you're shoving yourself back in the closet?'

'Dolly, it doesn't *matter* if I like women when I could love Patrick. I'm not like you.'

I don't stop her as she walks out the door, leaving it flung open.

Well. That's fucking that, isn't it.

How the hell did I fuck this up so badly that she went from *kiss me and show me I'm queer* to *run away with me* to *I'm going to ruin your life* in less than twelve hours. Not that I know what time it is because there's no fucking clocks here!

Jesus, this must be a lesbian drama world record.

Whit appears in the doorway. 'What's with the gob?'

'Did you hear any of that?' I ask nervously.

'Not the content, just the tone.'

Hopefully no one else heard anything. I want to explain everything to Whit, but I spot the mic immediately. Anything I say, production would hear. God forbid someone heard us arguing and sent her to get the details.

We're out of sight of the cameras, though.

I shake my head, as I slowly say, 'A stupid argument about Patrick.'

I have to hope that her surgeon training means she's used to improvising with communication.

She watches me for a moment like I've grown a second head, but then nods. I hope that means she understands I'll explain it to her another time. 'Ah, I'm sorry. Let's get some breakfast in you. Don't want you hangry.'

Whit takes my arm and leads me to the kitchen. Carys is nowhere to be seen, and we're apparently the only women dressed and ready.

She said she was going to ask for a room swap, didn't she? I just have to trust that she's not telling them anything else.

Would she do that? The Carys I thought I knew wouldn't.

Whit lets go of me to pour us both cups of coffee from the dispenser, and I scramble for a reason for our argument. Do I go scorched earth like she has, or take the higher ground? The public love the former, but you can easily be spun as a villain. Grown-ups tend to do better long term.

'Basically, I'm worried Patrick isn't that into her,' I say finally.

Whit looks over her shoulder and gives me a searching look. 'Because . . . he's into *you*?'

'No, no,' I insist. 'Did he ever mention his ex to you? They were together for years and only just broke up before he came on here.'

'What?! No, he never mentioned her but we only had one date.'

Whit hands me a steaming cup. It's not good coffee, but it's drinkable. I live for the day I can brew my own again, rather than this burned filter stuff.

'Well, he told me a lot. Things with his ex-girlfriend seem kind of messy, recent and serious, which is not good for Carys.

I was trying to warn her about it, but I think she thought I was making a play for him.'

'To be fair, weren't you dating him up until yesterday?'

'Yeah, but I was trying to suss him out. We've got no more dates. Urgh, she's a sweet kid. I don't want her to get her heart broken.' I do realise the irony of this statement. 'I think he does like her, but if he's hung up on someone else, what if he regrets the process? I wonder if I should speak to her again, but I don't want to upset her.'

I worry I'm hamming this up so much I'm going to smell like bacon.

'At least he's no Jackson,' Whit scoffs.

'Which is that one?' I say, trying not to look at the door that leads out to backstage.

'The alpha male. The one Bridget is gone on.'

I can't help but pull a face. 'Well, don't look at me; I already fucked up my first attempt at talking someone round from a red flag. I'm not volunteering.'

Whit pats my hand. 'You're such a good friend.'

'Wow, thanks,' I laugh nervously.

'I meant that as a compliment. Sometimes I just sound sarcastic,' Whit insists. 'It'll be alright. She'll come around and realise you were just trying to help.'

I worry at my lip, still tender from where Carys playfully bit it last night.

Will she tell them about me and Warren? It's not like she can prove anything, and if she wants to beat us, she needs me to stay in the experiment.

But then if she did tell production I was a girl-kisser, that would unleash too many questions that might taint her own image.

God, I wish I knew what the fuck was going on.

'Hey, tell me what's going on with you?' I ask Whit, eager

for distraction from my potential impending outing. 'You get to see Malachi last night?'

Her face lights up. 'Oh did I!'

'Okay, hello! Tell me more.'

Her shoulders soften as though she's just stepped into a warm bath. 'He's so beautiful, Dolly. And he is such a kind soul that I really did not care what he looked like because I was already gone. But it doesn't hurt that he looks like a bit of me, you know what I'm saying.'

I pull her into a hug, more for me than her. 'I'm really glad for you.'

'Thanks, beauts.'

As we break apart, I notice the ache in my arms from less wholesome activities last night. Perhaps I should be doing more weights. Maybe these gym girls I'm surrounded by are onto something, not that I suspect any of them are doing *exactly* what I did last night.

Not that I plan on having sex again any time soon, especially not with Carys fucking Cadwallader.

'Who are you thinking about?' Whit's eyes sparkle with mischief, and I'm just about to splutter an excuse when she asks, 'Was *Warren* all you ever hoped for?'

How to answer that? Yes, he's the perfect fake-husband-to-be (provided he proposes). He's objectively handsome. Do I feel anything remotely sexual towards him? No. Looking at him is like looking at a really good statue in the Walker.

'Babe, he's a basketball player,' I say, hoping this will carry me far enough. I think back to the many photos of the WNBA players I've seen over the years for what attracted me most. 'Those *arms*.'

She sucks her teeth. 'I knew it. I *knew* that voice was the voice of a hot man.'

'I can confirm.'

'Do you know if he saw anyone else?'

I hesitate because I'm not supposed to know that he's also seeing Priya and Niamh, but I wheedled that out of him. And as good as it might be for the show to stir up some jealousy and drama, the last thing I need is any more of that.

And as if on cue, in walks Carys with Reb in tow. For some reason, Bridget is also with them, her head high like she's a teacher about to bust me for bunking off for a fag behind the sports centre. Carys's head is low, her face smudged in pink and red like she's been crying. She and Bridget hang back, while Reb walks over to me with a harried look. 'Hey, Dolly, can you come with me for a second? Louise wants to talk to you.'

I follow Reb through to backstage. I just about manage not to look at Carys until we are level, and she flashes the quickest sharp smile at me from behind her mouth.

What the hell am I walking into?

Reb leads me out to the small kitchen area to wait for Louise, and as I take a seat, I can't help but notice one of the doors a little away from me open and close. Through the gap, I see a flash of screens, at least one for every single date cubicle, plus several angles in our living quarters.

'Hey, babe,' says Posh Louise, sliding into a seat next to me. In her hand is a gigantic insulated cup with the *Wedded Bliss* logo on the front.

'Hiya. No day off today?'

'What's one of those?' she says with a sigh. 'We're all stationed down the road so if anyone has a crisis we can come get you.'

'Am I having a crisis?'

'You tell me.' She takes a long sip from her jug.

'Hey, can I get one of those?' I ask idly.

'No,' she says briskly.

'On *Love Island* they'd give us one,' I tease.

Posh Louise raps her knuckles on the table, clearly not

having any of my nonsense today. 'I've just spoken to Reb about your little incident with Carys.'

'I wouldn't call it an incident so much as a spat,' I say, keeping my voice easy breezy.

'As far as I'm concerned, as long as you haven't punched the girl, all is fine. The only thing is that Carys has put in a room transfer because of your argument over Patrick.'

Interesting that Carys picked the same argument cover as me. I mean, it makes the most sense – what else are two heterosexual women most likely to fight about on a high-intensity show that ends with weddings?

It's weird that we're somehow on the same page even when we're fighting, or whatever this is.

'Bridget's roommate Lina is going to swap with Carys, so you'll room with her. That alright? While she packs, you can stay out here and do some interviews for us.'

I try to school my face so that the surprise I feel doesn't leak out. 'Interviews?'

'Babe,' she says, fixing her eyes at me over the rim of her glasses. 'Arguments over men is what the show lives for. Work with me here. You've already made paperwork for me and I *haaate* paperwork.'

Provided I stick to the same script as what I told Whit, this should play alright. Yes, there'll be differences between Carys's and my versions of the story, but as they say there's always three sides to any story – hers, mine and the truth.

'Of course.'

Louise beams at me. 'Good! I knew you wouldn't let me down.'

While Carys had occupied the bathroom, I'd got dressed into my loungewear set but I'm still wearing last night's makeup, plus some of Carys's. 'Louise, can you get me some of my makeup before you stick me in front of the big lights?'

'Oh, but it's so much more authentic if you look like you've just been pulled out the fight.'

She gets up then frowns. I try not to be offended as she leans across the table to get a better look at me. Even more so when she turns on her phone torch. I can only imagine just how many chin hairs she's lighting up. 'Actually, on second thoughts, I'll get someone to go get your makeup for you.'

'Thanks,' I say flatly.

When I get back to the dorms, a few of the girls are sitting in the living room, but the atmosphere is off. I guess everyone knows about our fight now.

Lovely Lina gets up to greet me. You can always trust a Scot to be sound, so I know we'll be alright in this weird shift around.

'You doing okay?' she asks, her voice lower than usual, which is impressive given how soft-spoken she is.

I answer honestly. 'Not really.'

'Are you a hugger?'

'I'll take one if you're offering.'

I wish I could turn off the part of my brain that thinks about what this will look like on TV, but given Lina is much shorter than me, and has to discreetly turn her face to the side so she's not directly motorboating me, I can't escape into the hug completely.

Posh Louise strides in purposefully followed by one of the other handlers, a man who looks like he could blow away in a strong breeze, who Lina tells me is called Liam. They gather the remaining women into the living room.

I take a seat on the couch next to Lina, who insists on holding my hand as though I'm going through some personal bereavement rather than having my roommate choose to leave our shared space. Perhaps she can sense the gay drama.

Whit perches next to me on the armrest. 'You good?'

'I will be.' I try to look like the *girl who is going to be okay* meme that Jas sends me whenever I've had a vaguely trying day.

I try not to notice Carys and Bridget hanging back, choosing to stand behind another couch instead of sitting, for maximum distance.

In walks Karina Nguyen, looking even more modellish than usual. Her long hair is curled in loose waves, as though it's just something she did the other day, all casual like. She's poured into a figure-hugging gold dress that's utterly incongruent with the assortment of pyjamas and loungewear the rest of us are wearing, but that's the show, I guess.

This time she's followed by her husband, Lucas, dressed in a slim, tailored, brown suit that beautifully complements his dark brown skin tone. He's incredibly handsome, and I notice several of the girls go gooey as he approaches. I wonder how Karina feels about seeing that: proud or jealous?

Together they look fresh from the red carpet.

'Hello, ladies,' calls Karina in a sing-song voice.

'Hello, Karina,' we chorus back, with a few people awkwardly adding 'and Lucas' at the end.

'It's so nice to see you all again,' he says. 'I've been spending time with the men you've been dating and I can see just how lucky some of them are.' It appears that Lucas is the kind of man who can gently call a whole room of women absolutely smoking, in front of his wife, without coming across as a total lech.

'As you're aware, the show airs a few days behind what's going on in here, and so last night the first episode aired,' Karina explains.

This sends a shiver down my spine. I didn't realise they'd tell us this – the last thing we need is to think about the public reactions. God, I hope my mum hasn't been screaming obscenities at my behaviour at the telly. She hasn't even seen the worst of it yet. I hope no one will.

Lucas smiles as Karina looks to him to continue, and I wonder how much they rehearse these bits in private. 'As part of that, we decided this year to involve the public a bit more in the decision-making process.'

My stomach drops. This is new. What do they mean they've involved the public?

Clearly, the other girls are as horrified about this as I am because you could slice the tension with a knife and serve it up on a pretty plate. But none of us say a word, because you're not supposed to. Not when the hosts are talking. All we can do is non-verbally react, and boy, are they getting their meme's-worth from some of our faces captured by roving cameras.

'What that means,' Karina continues, her voice steady and calming, 'is that we'll be polling the audience on who they think are the most compatible couples, and in turn that'll be an opportunity for you guys to win dates, or extra things for your wedding package.'

Okay, that's not *so* bad. I can work with that.

'And if we end up with a lot of engaged couples, it *might* just help us decide which storylines to follow to the honeymoon stage.'

I relaxed too soon.

Normally, every couple you see on the US series goes on honeymoon, bar perhaps one or two who break up immediately. I know from the post-show podcasts that if a couple is dropped for mysterious reasons (let's be real, often the contestants of colour), it might be because production don't like a couple's storyline.

I felt confident playing the game when I just had production to tangle with, because I did the research. I studied hard, I read every single testimony from contestants, all the behind-the-scenes interviews, every leak on Reddit, for fuck's sake.

And now, to find out that it might be just down to the public is ... Well. It's a variable I hadn't considered.

Lucas takes a thick piece of card out of his inside jacket pocket. 'In fact, we've got some preliminary comments you might be interested in.'

Everyone gasps, and not just because we're trying to make good television. Whit's fingernails bite into my shoulder.

'We asked the public which couples they thought were the most genuine out of all the current pairings active in the first episode they've seen, which includes the early days of the experiment,' Karina explains.

'As you might remember, *Wedded Bliss*'s core themes are Communication, Cooperation and Compatibility, so we wanted the viewers to consider all aspects of that,' Lucas adds.

Yeah, fucking right. This is a popularity contest. Public votes always are. And the white couples tend to be the ones who come out on top.

Karina gives us all a beauty queen smile. 'We thought you'd like to know the top four pairs, as voted by the viewers.'

'In ascending order.' Lucas clears his throat dramatically, before shooting a smile right at what I assume is the camera production told him to just look down. 'At number four, we have Lina and Zack.'

There's a smattering of applause and Lina blushes bright red. All nice to be chosen, but *Zack*? I didn't even know she was dating him, let alone why the public like him. I'm pretty sure the only thing I wrote down in my notebook was how many times he brought up being a nice guy and how nice guys are often misunderstood. Boke central. Now we're roommates I probably have a moral duty to talk to her about that. As long as I don't kiss her too.

'Our third most compatible pairing is ...' teases Karina, 'Dolly and Warren.'

Now this is a surprise. I let the relief and excitement I genuinely feel flood my face. Hopefully this means we've got a good edit. I wonder if that means the general public have seen Warren and me talk about our family yet. The world isn't kind to disabled people, but the people who look after them? Oh yeah, we get all the cookies and everyone thinks we're saints. It frustrates the hell out of me usually, but here the cookies mean something. Saintliness could turn into cold hard cash.

I wonder how my mum feels about that. Probably as bad as she felt when I told her I was coming here.

I wonder who has beaten us through. I hate myself for looking, but I glance over at Carys who is standing too-still, almost robotic. She does that sometimes, when she's around everyone at once. Clams up tight like she's hiding herself away.

I'd feel sad about it if she wasn't planning to fuck me over.

'The public think our second most compatible couple are Patrick and Carys!' announces Lucas.

She looks so genuinely happy that I almost wonder if I completely imagined last night. Or this morning. I don't think she's a faker on my level, so maybe she really does like him.

Everyone applauds and I try to forget how the blush she wears matches the one she wore in bed after I made her come.

Jesus, how down bad am I that even when I'm pissed off at her I'm still thinking about it.

I think, deep inside, I don't want to believe us having sex was just some experiment. One last-slash-first experience with a woman before she gets engaged to a man.

Why does that sting?

If she wants to commit herself to heterosexuality to get back at me, well, good luck, babe!

I'm so busy in my own thoughts that I miss the beginning

of Karina announcing the winners, but I hear Whit's name so clearly that I'm one of the first people on my feet hugging her. She looks so overwhelmed but so happy, jumping up and down in mine and Lina's arms.

Lucas waits patiently for us all to stop screaming. 'As winners of the compatibility vote, Whit and Malachi win an extra date this evening. Dinner for two outside the warehouse!'

God, they get to leave? This place is so all-consuming that I forgot I wasn't born and raised here.

Whit punches the air. 'Hell yes!' I guess she's not beating the *all surgeons are jocks* allegations.

'That seems to have gone down well,' laughs Karina. 'Now, ladies, I hope you're all ready for your big dates today. As I'm sure you'll all remember, today is your first Touch Date.'

How could I forget? Yesterday I got to see Warren, today I get to, well, touch him, as much as is consensually on the cards.

The air is thick with excitement, and just a touch of horniness.

'And possibly your last as you'll be encouraged to narrow your matches down to just one this evening, and hopefully it'll be mutual,' adds Lucas, which is a major downer.

Even Karina rolls her eyes at him, before snapping back to her calm TV presenter energy.

'Engagement is on the horizon,' she continues, and it just kind of hits me that the date we get engaged on will be our *fifth* date. Mad that some people think they can fall in love in that little time.

'Compatibility comes in many forms,' Karina continues. 'Can you trust in the connection you've built with your partner so far that you'll find more of that together?'

I feel like eyes are on me, and I catch Carys watching me. Our eyes meet, and I feel a spark of that tension from last night. Before she reached up and clutched my face in hers. Before she kissed me. Before before before.

Her face morphs into a scoff, and she looks away. I wonder if she was remembering the same thing. I hate how much thinking that hurts, even if it was my choice to cut things off, if you could really call it a choice.

Bridget must see this because she gives me the stink eye too.

If Carys wants to paint me as some kind of villain, fine. And if she wants a fight, then let's fucking go.

Unfortunately for her, I know both her and Patrick's weaknesses.

She picked the wrong bitch to cross.

Chapter Fifteen

Carys

@mellytonin: has anyone made a fancam of Patrick yet?

@pinkee341: @mellytonin here you go babe [attached file, Pat4eva.mov]

@pisswizard: omfg Carys and Patrick are endgame <3 I can't wait to see them together

---

Second most compatible couple. Well, well, well. That's something, isn't it?

Suck it, Dolly.

I want to rub it in her face. Your fake relationship only came *third*. Not as convincing as you guys think you are, clearly.

It feels so good to be right. I knew I could be better than her, and the public just proved it. Patrick and I are the real deal, and the *Wedded Bliss* audience can see that too.

I wonder what people like about us. We're quite silly, a little giggly. Maybe that's it? Our chemistry. And I know now that we look good together too.

It's perhaps a little vain to say, but the validation that the public think we're a good couple makes me even more excited to see him today.

Sure, it's not quite the same as winning, but at least a couple who are in love are in first place. It would have been nice to win a date out of the warehouse, but I've already got a grand prize waiting for me today – Patrick.

Today, I get to kiss him. If he wants that, of course. I hope he wants to kiss me one day.

Karina and Lucas are whisked away quickly along with the camera team, and only Reb hangs back. 'You good?' she asks me.

I nod. 'Great. Thank you so much for your help this morning.'

Bridget slings an arm around my neck. 'Don't worry, babes. I'll look after her.'

Reb gives me a tight smile. 'Make sure to have some breakfast. You've got less than an hour to get ready, or thereabouts.' And with that, she excuses herself.

It's so funny that they speak in time we have no way to read. Maybe neurotypical people can naturally sense it better than I can.

I'm already dressed and have absolutely no stomach for eating so I'm relieved when Bridget whisks me into our new shared room for help doing her hair.

'I want to curl it for the special occasion,' she giggles excitedly. 'But I'm awful at doing the back. Will you give me a hand?'

Before I can agree, she sits down at her makeup table with her back to me, and hands me her styler. She has one of those fancy Airwrap things that always terrify me a little because I always think about your hair getting sucked inside it and having to chop it off at the roots. But Bridget's a hairdresser, so she knows better than I do.

Luckily, I've had a lifetime of doing my sisters' hair.

I start sectioning off her long caramel locks. In the mirror, I catch Bridget looking on approvingly, which gives me a little thrill that I'm doing it right.

'You're a star, babe. I can never get my arms akimbo enough to do that bit so it's always flat as a pancake from behind, and if they're filming from that angle when we kiss it'll look dreadful.'

'Oh . . . yeah,' I agree, having not thought about that at all. My hair is still pulled up into a severe bun.

Reading my mind, Bridget says, 'Babe. Are you going to keep your hair like that today?'

I glance in the mirror and the bun is so tight that it's given me a startled look from the unnatural tilt of my eyebrows. 'I shouldn't.'

'I'll do you after, don't worry.' Bridget squeals and I almost drop the expensive hair whooshing contraption. 'Oh God. I hope he's a good kisser. He is *lush*.'

I realise I'm not sure who she means. I know she's been dating a few men — Jackson, Zack, Billy too, I think — but I have no idea who she's seeing now. She kept her cards close to her chest about who she liked most, and I've been too self-involved to pay attention.

That's another thing I've not liked about the last few days. With all this Dolly mess, I haven't been a good friend. I want these friendships to last, and while Dolly's turned out not to be the person I thought she was, I think Bridget and Lina could be long term if I put the effort in.

'Zack?' I guess.

'Well, yes, but I was thinking of Jackson. I'm seeing both of them today.'

'And Zack's not lush?'

'He *is*.'

'But not totally your type on paper.'

'Exactly, babes.'

I drop a fresh warm curl, letting it bounce in my hand. 'What do you like about Jackson?'

'He's just very smart, you know. And look, I said I'd never date another rugby boy, but he's ex-rugby, so all the bod and none of the lifestyle.'

'Have you dated a lot of rugby players?'

In the mirror she catches my eye. 'Babes, I'm a little slice and I live in South Wales. What do you think?'

We both laugh, and I love the throaty sound of her big laughs. 'I'll have to take your word for it. I feel like I've been out of Wales for so long. Things have changed and keep changing. I mean, two actors bought the local football club and now where I'd mooch round town as a teenager is all over Disney+. It's so weird.'

'Surely no weirder than filming a dating show for another international streaming service.' She gives me a wink.

'True. I think that part hasn't hit me yet.'

'Oh, it's hit me like a fucking truck. Hence dragging you in here to be my lady's maid.' She blows air out her cheeks in one big whoosh. 'I think this is looking good.'

'I think we're done,' I say, pleased with my curling work. They're not perfect, but they match the pattern Bridget had put into the rest of her hair without creating too much of a seam at the back.

Bridget cranes around, trying to spy the back of her head in the mirror. I look around for a second mirror to hold up behind her, but all I have is one of the tiny circle ones for plucking your eyebrows. I make do, and hold it up for her. 'I knew I should have snuck in one of my big mirrors from work.' She grunts frustratedly. 'Oh well, I can't see. I'll have to trust you. Luckily, I do!'

She hops up, and doesn't quite place a kiss on my cheek

as much as kiss the air next to me, so as not to disturb our makeup.

'Your turn.'

Bridget is so gentle at undoing my hair and brushing through it that I almost fall asleep. 'I'm going to put some heat and product into it, give you some body,' she says confidently, and I let her do whatever she wants to.

Bridget is beautiful, but I feel no fluttery feelings from her stroking my head. I'm not getting confused by our friendship or our closeness. I can think she's stunning and like her a lot, without mistaking it for more.

And I thought all that about Dolly, in the beginning, before I got all tangled up in my confusion and her lies.

I just have to remind myself that this is what a normal adult female friendship is. You can be close without it being romantic.

I don't really have any close men friends other than a few of the guys at work, and I would never be so touchy-touchy with them. So all the physical intimacy I've had with men has been with men I'm dating.

Maybe that's why I got so confused with Dolly. I couldn't separate out the crush. And given I find so much social stuff confusing, it's no real wonder I got that all mixed up in my head.

I feel calm under her touch. You're supposed to feel comfortable in a friendship, not nervous, and Dolly made me so nervous sometimes. Was that a red flag I missed?

Luckily, I can't see any here. Bridget and I are close in age, but most people would think I'm younger from the way we dress. She's in a white tailored two-piece – a crop top paired with long flowing trousers belted with a gold buckle. Before I got here, I thought that my mustard jumper with short sleeves tucked into a goldenrod plaid circle skirt looked quite smart, but now I'm worried it makes me look like I teach arts and crafts to forest creatures.

'Should I ditch the tights?' I murmur, as I look at my reflection.

Bridget scrunches up her lips as she gives me the once over. 'No. You look like *you*.'

I get up and grab a very important accessory from my wardrobe. 'Will you still say that after you help me pin this beret in place?'

She laughs and takes the matching hat from my hands. 'Of course. He's going to love you. I bet he already does.'

I watch as Bridget presses a few hairpins between her lips, and gently sets my beret over my hair, tilted a little way back so it doesn't close up my face.

Even now, I'm looking at her lips and I feel nothing, even though Bridget is an objectively beautiful girl.

And sure, there's men whose lips I could probably look at too and not feel anything, but that's different. Being attracted to men never came with a side serving of dread that I was doing something wrong.

I guess that's a change. The last few years, I'd have been too rattled by terror to even do that for long, too worried that I was going to get found out. Now, I feel ... nothing.

That's one thing I owe Dolly for – she's shown me the boundaries of my own attraction to women. What I'm supposed to do with that knowledge, I don't really know. It's not like it's relevant to me, especially if I want to marry Patrick, is it?

'Why are you staring at my lips, babe?' says Bridget.

I immediately worry that I've made her uncomfortable. I guess old neural pathways take longer to die. 'I was wondering if you found a sharpener for your lip liner in the end.'

'Oh! Yeah, my handler Ewa brought me one because they

were worried about the health and safety implications of me getting infected from it. Fair enough.' She laughs throatily again. 'Are you excited to kiss Patrick?'

'Yes,' I say quickly. 'I am.'

'Well, you're cute as a button. He's going to love it.' She shapes my beret one last time. 'All done. Shall we mynd?'

Back in the living room, I manage to nibble down some toast and butter without getting it all over myself, and before I know it I'm back on my too-warm velvet couch, looking at the mirror barrier between mine and Patrick's rooms.

'Hello?' I call, hoping to hear Patrick's voice.

When he replies, it's like a melody. A very Yorkshire one, but it's music to me. 'Morning, Carys. How are you?'

'Good,' I say, and I can hear the nerves in my voice. I'm going to kiss this man today. The last kisses I had were disastrous, let's put it that way. This will be like the ultimate redo.

Yesterday, I was so nervous about seeing him, and his reaction to me, that I couldn't enjoy it.

But now that I'm faced with the prospect of touching him, kissing him, holding him, I feel excited. *Finally.*

Plus, this will be closer to a normal date than just staring at each other like animals in a zoo.

The mirrored barrier slowly falls, but this time I watch.

There he is.

When I look at his deep brown eyes, the way his stubble glazes his jawline, I feel something. I really do. Happiness, I think. Pride that he chose me back. The kind of warmth in my torso that feels *safe*.

'Hi,' my potential future husband says.

'Hi,' I say back. 'You know, I'm not sure I'll ever get used to hearing your voice come out of your mouth instead of from around us.'

Thankfully, he laughs at my awkwardness. 'I know the

feeling. And look, we don't need to rush this. We can take our time, if you'd like? It won't change how I feel about you. I can wait for you.'

That's when I know for sure that I was right about everything. Despite all the confusion, he really is my lighthouse in this storm of an experiment. I know without any doubts that Patrick is the thoughtful, kind, beautiful man I want to spend the rest of my life with.

If it was proposal day, I'd get down on one knee right now.

'I don't want to wait,' I say, a huge smile bursting across my face.

Patrick wears a smile that must mirror my own. 'Then, let's not.'

I race across the tiny room, pushing myself through the divider hole into his side, and I throw myself into his open arms. He tilts his head down, and I reach up on my tiptoes, and we kiss.

Our first kiss is a collision of lips and tongues and a little bit of teeth, and we laugh giddily through it. It's a silly kiss, but it's *us*. He tastes of sweetness and spice, like a sweet cup of flavourful tea, poured straight from the pot. I know I could kiss him over and over, forever.

I fit against him like we were made for each other.

Everything is so different now I can be close to him and even touch him. Patrick is no longer a voice through a speaker or a face across the room; he's a living, breathing person. And one who wants to kiss me!

All the feelings I had for him locked in my heart explode, becoming manifest.

I'm so dizzy on him that I force myself to take a step back, so I can look at him up close.

'Hi again,' I say.

'That was one hell of a greeting.'

'The first of many, I hope?'

'I hope so too.'

I take his face in my hands, and his eyes soften. 'I can't believe it's you.'

'I feel like I've been waiting for you forever.'

I bring him down to my lips and kiss him deeply.

When we break apart, we press our foreheads together like we are in prayer. A communion of us.

'Wow,' he says, lightness dancing in his voice.

We break into giggles again, and I bury my face in his chest. He smells like fresh books and nights in front of the fireplace. This is the smell of home, I think. My home. Our future.

I feel so lucky that our magical first kiss is recorded, so in the future I can watch it whenever I like. I wonder if it looks as wonderful as it feels, like a storybook romance come true.

Patrick breaks our kiss to look at me, tilting my chin up with his hand. His touch is so gentle, and I can't help but think about him caring for sick or old animals, healing them with his hands.

'Carys, you know you're the only woman I'm seeing, don't you?'

I didn't actually know this for sure but hearing it out loud fills my heart with hot air.

'You're my only date too,' I whisper, because he needs to know he's the only reason I'm here.

'That's wonderful to hear,' he says.

We kiss again and I wonder how many kisses you can fit into a happy lifetime.

'I want you to know that ...' He clears his throat. 'I have something important I'd like to ask you tomorrow.'

Oh my God. He's really going to propose to me? Patrick really wants me? Out of every woman he could have, he wants me!

'I know it's unconventional to tell someone in advance, but

I know you don't love surprises, and I want you to have the time to think it through, like I have had.'

He's so kind.

'You know me so well,' I swoon.

'It feels like I do. I hope that I do. I want to spend every day learning as much about you as possible.' His thumb strokes gently across my bottom lip.

My body is alive with wriggling feelings that I can't pin down. Excitement yes, nerves, anticipation that I know I have to wait until tomorrow for it to happen, relief that he told me it's coming.

I'm worried he thinks I'm not excited about it, so I push forward the biggest smile I can. 'I promise I'll think about it, though I really don't need to. I know my answer.'

He smiles so wide that his eyes crinkle just a little in the corners.

And now I understand. All the difficulty, all this strife with trying to cope with being on the show while hiding my autism and getting all confused, this is what it was for. I might have gone through something difficult and upsetting, but I am leaving with a beautiful husband.

And yes, I'm not quite ready to drop the mask with Patrick yet, but when we're alone at the apartments, I'll be able to show him a bit more of me.

Their kisses are different, I think idly. Dolly's were hungrier, like we were trying to devour each other.

I cringe at the thought. Get out of my head.

I kiss him again, not to prove anything to myself, but as a reminder that this is real. He is real. We are real.

'This is so nice,' I say purposefully as I nuzzle my face into his neck. His scent fills my senses, driving away any last thought of Dolly from my traitorous brain.

He presses a kiss down on the top of my head and it makes me want to cry in a good way. Relief, I think.

Lord, I'm going to be a mess tomorrow. I'll need to borrow some waterproof mascara.

Obviously I'll be saying yes. I don't think I need to worry about making good decisions any more, at least not while I'm in the arms of the man I could fall in love with.

My future is right here, with Patrick.

Chapter Sixteen

Dolly

@bigbaby: omfg warren is so fit i might die pls resus me so i can die again thx

@RealiteeTea: I keep seeing people say Patrick and Carys are endgame and hello??? Have you seen Warren and Dolly? [fire emojis]

@havenmaven: I just realised Dolly is Dolly Doherty! I've been making her sweet potato curry pie every month – it's foolproof. tiktok.com/DollyPie

@thehafofit: I swearrrrrr I met Dolly on a night out years ago ...

Game face on, Dolores.

That's what Mum would say to me.

Well, she would if she remotely approved of me being on here. When she meets Warren, when he tells her why he's here too, she'll understand.

She's always been a practical woman. Just like me.

The divider comes down again slowly in what I assume is

designed to prolong the anticipation of seeing someone you want to bang.

Warren and I go straight for a hug, arms clasped tightly round each other.

We only have maybe a minute and one chance to get this right.

I know for a fact that *Wedded Bliss* never makes their contestants reenact anything because it always plays strained and fake. Other shows have made that mistake before, with two different kisses edited together, and immediately spotted by the audiences.

My hands work quickly, as I pretend that I'm just overwhelmed touching him for the first time. Over and over, I whisper sweet nothings, I laugh, I make enough verbal noise to hopefully cover what I'm really doing. My hand slides up his back which, wow, he *is* absolutely jacked, until I find what I'm looking for.

As the wire unclips from his mic pack, Warren clocks on to my plan.

His admittedly huge hands are already at my waist, and stroke over my own pack, tucked into the back of my high-waisted trousers – thank God I thought to wear separates today.

I'm a big tall girl, so it's not normally an easy feat to lift me off the floor, but Warren sweeps me up into his arms and swings us around in a circle, just as his fingers flick the wire out.

I can't help but admire his finesse.

We did it. We're off mic, and for the first time, production can't hear us. As long as we're quiet and make as much additional noise as we can, any hidden mics shouldn't be able to pick us up.

'One year minimum,' I whisper hurriedly right into his ear.

He kisses my cheeks. 'Prenup if we have to legal it.'

'Obviously,' I laugh loudly, as though he's just whispered something sexy to me. Just in case I'm wrong about this, then they have something to play. And if they have had to turn the sound up high to hear us, I'll have blown out their speakers. Sorry, audio team, but needs must.

I say more sweet nothings against him, the usual stuff about how good he smells, how tall he is, wow look at your muscles, while he whispers some more conditions. 'A fake I love you moment today. I'll propose tomorrow.'

'PDA okay, lie about the sex, we can discuss later,' I whisper back.

'And honesty with our family.'

We finally stop spinning and I feel so dizzy that we have a genuine funny moment of him plonking me down, before we collapse onto the couch. I'm not even sure whose room we're in now.

Outside, I can hear the hurried footfall and anxious shouts of the production team scurrying towards us to fix the sound problems.

I lean back to look at him, and we seal the deal with a smile.

'Third place?' He grins like he's very proud of himself.

'I think we can do better. Let's make it first, shall we?'

Louise bursts into the room. 'Sorry to interrupt. Something's gone wrong with the sound and I just need to check the mic packs.'

'Oh shit, sorry.' I spring up and lift my shirt up enough so she can see it. The loose wire falls out, hitting the carpet behind me. 'Do you want us to do it again?'

She grits her teeth and I hope that she's not actually in for a bollocking for our behaviour. 'No, no. It's okay,' she says, as she picks up the end of the wire. 'Ignore me, just focus on each other.'

We lock eyes, smiling as Louise whizzes round us, checking and rechecking our mic packs are working.

The minute she's gone, I say, 'Are you going to kiss me then?'

Warren smiles cockily, and I *know* the girlies are going to be yelling all over socials about this moment. He slides one hand up the back of my head, fingers threaded through my short hair, and before I know what he's doing, he dips me low.

'Wow,' I whisper, as he holds me in his big strong basketballing arms.

I wait for him to move first, and he kisses me tenderly, slowly. This is a man who is familiar with lip balm, I can tell, because his lips are so plump and soft. He tastes like honey.

I don't *feel* anything for him romantically or sexually, as expected.

But a nice kiss is still a nice kiss.

It's not my first time kissing a boy. I may have come out the womb pretty certain I liked women, but even I kissed a few boys during spin the bottle at parties – a small price to pay to kiss the girls I *actually* liked with plausible deniability. Those were much less enjoyable, a few bitten lips, a few washing machines, but worth it because I got to snog Mikaella Matthews for the first time.

My stupid horny brain flicks back to last night's hungry kisses with Carys.

I concentrate on Warren, on pretending, on selling our romance to the audience who might vote to send us on fun dates, and to the brands waiting to have us represent their eco-friendly washing liquids or matching organic cotton sweatsuits or green juice powders or whatever.

The one thing I know for certain is that that was a kiss for television. He's Prince Charming, and I'm swept up in him. It's a kiss that is going to be talked about for *months*. Perhaps there'll be gifs, fan edits, dissections of our (excellent if I do say) technique.

I'm sure that'll do him well in the future too. Once we're broken up and he can date again, the girlies will be clamouring for him.

I'm positive Jas will be giving me top marks for my convincing performance of heterosexuality.

When he finally rights me, I can't help but laugh. 'God, sorry. I'm lightheaded.'

'Was that not from my kiss, though?' He raises just one eyebrow, his lips falling open ever so slightly, and I am *positive* there'll be gifs of that inevitable close up.

I place my hands on his chest to stabilise me. 'You leave me breathless.'

'Lucky me,' he whispers, drawing a finger down my jaw, and tilting my chin up just enough so we kiss again, 'that I get to kiss a woman like you.'

'I can't wait to be with you properly,' I say with just enough suggestion that the audience will know it's going to be hot when we're engaged.

'Baby,' he says so smoothly that I almost forget this is fake, 'you're even more beautiful in real life, and I fell in love with your soul through that barrier this week.'

'Love?' I whisper, eyes wide.

'Yes. I love you.'

I gasp. 'Warren, I love you too.'

I'm almost tempted to somehow engineer us back into a dipped kiss, but instead, I just go for another sweet one.

'I can't believe I found you,' I say.

He smiles down at me. 'We're going to be unstoppable, Dolly.'

Script: Episode Five, Proposals

Scene: Proposals episode intro
Location: Men's dormitory

[Medium shot of Karina and Lucas standing together.]

KARINA Welcome to a very special episode of *Wedded Bliss*. The Proposals episode!

LUCAS I'm so excited to see which of our guys decided to propose, and which couples are going to leave today engaged.

KARINA Me too. Isn't it so thrilling?

LUCAS I think some of them are just excited to get out of the warehouse!

KARINA Yes, but that's a surprise! The men have chosen places all around the city to pop the big question.

LUCAS That's right, I hear we're headed to a city farm, the top of the Dome, a boat on the Thames, the London Eye and Parliament Hill today. We've got a whirlwind filming schedule! But who will say yes?

[Close up on Karina.]

KARINA Yesterday, our remaining pairings were able to touch for the first time. And today, they are putting their relationships on the line. How many couples will be on their way to saying 'I do'?

[Close up on Lucas.]

LUCAS   Which of our couples are on track for
             wedded bliss, and who is headed right to
             breakup central?

[Karina winces.]

KARINA   I hope everyone finds a love as special
             as ours!

~

Scene: Proposal
Couple: Carys and Patrick
Location: Tower Hamlets City Farm

[Introductory shots of the city farm, interspersed with footage of the couple with overhead drone footage of the farm and its boundaries against the city. Shots of Carys introducing Patrick to various animals. Carys and Patrick sit at a picnic table in the middle of a green area.]

CARYS   I can't believe they let us come here. I missed
             all my friends. I really thought Buttercup
             would put up more of a fuss about me being
             gone so long.

[Cut to a shot of Buttercup the goat looking nonplussed in the background.]

PATRICK   Well, I wanted to bring you somewhere special,
             and I know this place means a lot to you.
CARYS   It does. I can't wait to show you round
             properly. You still haven't met Gerri the
             parrot who hates everyone but me.

[Close up of Patrick laughing.]

PATRICK I know we've talked a bit about what our
life will look like together. But I wanted to
reassure you that I'm not going to take you
from here. I can see how happy it makes you.

CARYS But won't that mean we have to do long
distance? If your job is in Yorkshire
still and—

[Close up as Patrick reaches over to grab her hands.]

PATRICK Shh, don't worry. We can manage this. And
I can work all over the country, so we can
take our time and look for the right job
for me.

CARYS And it's not that far on the train! I love
taking the train!

[Close up on Patrick as he reaches into his pocket, and takes out the ring box.]

PATRICK *[whispering]* I hope you won't think ill of
me for not getting down on one knee, but I
will fall right over if I try and get out of this
picnic table.

CARYS *[giggling]* I won't. I mean, I will! For the
other bit. It feels wrong to say 'I won't'
right now.

[Close up on Patrick opening the ring box.]

PATRICK Carys Cadwallader, getting to know you has
felt like finding another half of me. I think
you're one of the kindest people I've ever met,

	which makes sense because you've dedicated your life to working with animals and teaching children. I love that about you. That goodness makes me want to be more like you, and to learn from you. I can't imagine my life without you. Will you marry me?
CARYS	I will!

[Medium shot as the pair laugh and Patrick places the ring on Carys's finger.]

~

Scene: Pre-proposal interview with Lina
Couple: Lina and Zack/Cobey
Location: Thames riverside

[Close up on Lina as she looks out over the river.]

PRODUCER	*[voiceover]* So, can you tell us about what's happening today?
LINA	I am pretty sure I'm getting proposed to twice. You'd think that would be a good thing but ... I have to break one person's heart.

[Cut to shot of Zack and Lina sitting in the centre of an old cinema, with theatre-style velvet seats. On screen are images from Zack and Lina's dates.]

LINA	*[voiceover]* I really love his energy. He's just so sweet and thoughtful.

[Cut to aerial shot of Lina and Cobey on a tugboat sailing down the Thames.]

COBEY	I wish I could have got you a fancier boat.
LINA	It's a very nice boat, Cobey.
COBEY	But I wanted to bring you to the water. It's a metaphor thing, isn't it.

[The boat lists suddenly and Lina retches over the side. Cobey leaps to her side.]

LINA	*[voiceover]* Haha, yes, he's very attentive. I'm just worried it'd be such a big life change for me.

[Cut back to the cinema where, on screen, Zack kneels down and holds out a ring. Still seated, Zack presents the ring to Lina.]

[Cut back to Lina looking over the river.]

LINA	It feels very head and heart at war. I don't know. What do you think?

~

Scene: Proposal
Couple: Dolly and Warren
Location: Primrose Hill, sunset

[Opening shot on slow zoom of Dolly and Warren standing at the top of the hill, the sky pinkish orange behind them as the sun sets.]

DOLLY	It's so beautiful up here. I've never seen London look like this.

[Warren slowly gets down on one knee, and holds up a ring box to Dolly.]

WARREN	Dolly Doherty, Queen of my heart. I want to walk through this life at your side. Will you do me the honour of marrying me?
DOLLY	*[breathlessly]* Warren, I couldn't dream of anything more wonderful.

[Warren slides the ring onto Dolly's finger, stands up slowly, and they kiss. This time, she dips him.]

~

Scene: Close out Proposals episode
Location: Men's dormitory

[Cut back to Karina and Lucas in the studio.]

KARINA	Wow! What an incredible set of proposals. That leaves us with five engaged couples, our Blissfuls: Dolly and Warren, Carys and Patrick, Bridget and Jackson, Whit and Malachi, and Lina and Zack.
LUCAS	An incredible season so far, I think. Unfortunately, we'll be saying goodbye to the rest of our contestants – for now!
KARINA	Our five couples will now head to beautiful Corfu, on a honeymoon like no other.
LUCAS	That's for sure – because they'll all be sharing one villa! This is the chance for our couples to spend time together in person with the support of the friendships they built in the warehouse.
KARINA	And allows them to see how their partner shows up for their friends, in social situations, and in shared living. Are they a giver?
LUCAS	Haha, I hope so!

Chapter Seventeen

Carys

Whit Vempati, 29, Manchester, and Malachi Campbell, 29, Liverpool

[Malachi and Whit sit on a sun lounger together.]

WHIT	Hello, fiancé.
MALACHI	Hello, fiancée.
WHIT	You know, every time I see that written down, I think the word is finance. And I keep half-calling you 'my finance'.
MALACHI	*[laughs]* You can call me your finance if you'd like.
WHIT	Financier. What's one of those? That sounds even posher.
MALACHI	Isn't that a little biscuit thing? Didn't they make them on *Bake Off*?

[They look to camera.]

PRODUCER	Erm, yeah, it's a French almond cake.
WHIT AND MALACHI	*[together in bad French accents]* We're financiers!

'God, you'd think they'd at least spring for a hotel room for us to get changed in,' Bridget moans. 'What's the budget for this show, three quid?'

It's pretty impressive that with only the poor lighting of this restaurant's bathroom, Bridget manages to expertly apply false eyelashes. She doesn't even break her flow of chat. If I try to talk while doing anything around my eyes, I will absolutely poke one of them out.

As if on cue, I dink myself in the eye with my eye liner from just *thinking* about talking. 'Shit,' I moan, dabbing at the black ink leaking off the front of my eyeball. I look a little possessed. I groan and cap my cursed pen in frustration. 'You'd think having to do my eyes every day for the last week I'd have got better at it.'

Bridget looms next to me, her eyes wide and owlish. If she was an owl wearing just one false eyelash, that is. 'Those cat eyes are going to have to be sisters, not twins, babe.'

My senses flood with the smell of her perfume, makeup, clothes, hair, everything all at once. I love Bridget but she's a very scenty person.

I can feel the hot licking edges of my brain starting to shut down after the last few days.

Yesterday and the day before were the proposals, taking place all around London. None of us girls knew about the excursion part or where we were going so I was on edge all day. Production took us out in our couples for a few hours at a time, along with our chaperones and some cameras, before returning us to our dorms.

Which means that the rest of the time we were just hanging out, waiting. Less than ideal for me because that sort of quiet structureless time means I find something to be anxious about, even if it's just the concept of waiting for something else to happen. The only distraction from that was getting annoyed that I couldn't escape from Dolly, who just seems to be *everywhere* all the time.

Luckily, Hannah S. ended up trying to teach us some wrestling moves, and we started on a human pyramid until production told us to knock it off for health and safety reasons.

Then it was just back to waiting. Waiting for my life to begin.

Obviously, my proposal from Patrick was lovely, but wow, it was intense going back to the city farm after feeling like I've been in the warehouse for ages. I didn't even get a chance to speak to any of my colleagues but it's probably for the best when I was so hyped up.

The ring is a new bit of sensory information I'm having to process all the time. I keep thinking something has landed on me, and I'm realising how often I accidentally bash my hand into things because I hear it go *dink* every time, and then I panic I've broken it somehow.

I didn't get the best sleep last night because Bridget was telling me excitedly about her engagement to Jackson, and she was so happy that I didn't want to cut her off. I'm positive I'll like him better in person. I don't remember much about our date – everyone keeps referring to him as the alpha when Bridget isn't around, and it just makes me think about that discredited wolf study where they threw a load of wolves who didn't know each other into the same place to see what happened. A bit like *Wedded Bliss*, really. Plus, it's not as if I haven't made terrible first impressions before, and people have been kind to me. I'll extend that grace to him too. For Bridget too.

I glance over at Bridget, now just finishing up her second eyelash. 'These are sisters too,' she laughs, moving on to her lips. While I'm relieved that she seems to be sharpening her lip liner, she has fashioned a scarily pointy end that she stabs onto her lips with vigour.

'I'm not sure it's always supposed to hurt,' I murmur.

She winces. 'Beauty is pain!'

'Everything is pain,' groans Lina, who is plucking her eyebrows.

I can't disagree with that. Today has been a challenge. The last thing I want to do is have a public, televised autistic meltdown, but I can feel my hard limits getting closer and closer.

I don't want Patrick to see me like that, just yet. I want time to explain all that ... eventually. I just hope I can hold it off.

We had all thought that today would be a day off after we've been on camera for the best part of a week, but when the five of us girls woke up, the other girls – the Hannahs, Niamh and Priya – were already gone, like they'd vanished overnight. No one will tell us if any of them got engaged, or what's happened to them. It's like they never existed. We didn't get to say goodbye.

We remaining girls were shuttled off to the airport, along with our handlers, in a big taxi. I knew that we would be flying somewhere, but having a flight sprung at me on a tired morning was not ideal.

Typically, Dolly was sitting next to me in the car, and I tried not to look at her at all. Her long legs kept knocking against mine, and it's quite fascinating how only a few days ago that would have sent my heart into a tizzy, and yet today it's just annoying. I made sure to look out the window the whole way.

Then there was the airport. Normally, when I go through security, I wear a sunflower lanyard so that people know I'm autistic and might need extra time or clearer explanations. Obviously I didn't pack one with me, and even though I know I could get one from the accessibility desk, Reb was stuck to my side like glue. If I picked one up, they'd know I hadn't been forthcoming about being autistic. I didn't want to fuck things up.

So I knuckled through, without headphones or sunglasses or any help. I could just imagine my sisters screaming at me about this in future, but I didn't really have a choice except to slide the mask back on.

What made things worse is when I got to the x-ray bit, I kept being rushed and then I dropped everything, and the only person who came over to help was Dolly so we had this awkward moment kneeling on the floor, surrounded by all my things, trying not to look at each other. I mumbled a thank you, because I'm not rude, but I couldn't trust myself to speak any louder without my brain popping.

Once we'd got through, I told Reb I had a killer migraine (not a total lie), and donned headphones, sunglasses and some emergency extremely minty chewing gum to focus on. I wish I hadn't packed David in my checked luggage.

I didn't see Patrick until we were at the gate, where he was sitting with all the other men. Forcing through overstimulation to greet four men I've half spoken to through speakers wasn't ideal, but once I managed to whisper out that I had a migraine, everyone got me to sit down and left me alone for the best part. That's the lonely price of it; sometimes you only get to watch while everyone finds this part easy.

On the flight, they sat us in our couples, rather than with our handlers. It was lovely, but still kind of strange, as quietly sitting next to Patrick on the plane was the first time we've been together without also being on camera. Around us, I could hear the other couples chattering away and taking selfies. Patrick put his arm round me so we could curl up and fall asleep. The rhythm of his breathing was like a lullaby. Even though we've only touched a few times, I can't get over how natural that intimacy felt.

It's not lost on me that after filming, we'll be sharing a bed. It's a step up. I'm going to have to wear my sleeping headphones to adjust to the noise, but I'm a little glad that we won't yet be alone. We can work up to it.

So now we're in a Greek restaurant bathroom. It's frustrating that they didn't take us straight to the big house we're going to be living in for the next couple of days, especially after an early morning and a flight. We arrived to cameras, lights, production staff we'd never met before, all waiting to start filming us couples having our first evening meal date together.

'I can only assume this scheduling was done by a man,' groans Dolly's voice from one of the stalls. 'A woman would never expect us to get ready in a toilet.'

She's not wrong. The five of us only just about fit, and also it has all the delightful and intense scents and flavours of a bathroom. On top of that, the ruffles on my peachy pink dress are starchy and keep tickling my neck and arms. I could balance it out by dulling my other senses, but I don't think I'll get away with sunglasses as it's too late in the afternoon – I'll look too obviously autistic or, worse, like a diva.

Whit walks out of one of the stalls dressed in a cream waistcoat paired with matching trousers. 'This was the worst colour I could wear. Please tell me I don't have anything gross on me?' She spins around, and I double-check her for unmentionable substances.

'You're good. And you look lovely.' I try not to look at her bare and very toned arms for too long, because I'm admiring *not* ogling. Important distinction.

'Thanks,' she sighs. 'It's so much effort. I'm not used to thinking about what nice outfit to wear every day. I'm a surgeon; give me back my scrubs.'

'I'm starting to miss my farm fleeces,' I agree. 'Here, take this sink. I can squeeze in here.' I pick up my makeup pouch and move one sink along next to Bridget, who is also nearly done.

'Thanks,' Whit sighs, peering closely at her skin in the mirror. Her makeup bag is organised so that every product or tool has its own little slot, and she opens it out flat to take out one thing at a time. I wonder if she's always been this way, or if it's the side effect of the operating theatre. She groans as she dabs foundation on with a beauty blender. 'Not gonna lie, but the daily full face is testing me.'

'I keep breaking out,' Lina says in sympathy. It looks like she's painting little stars on her cheeks. I guess it goes with her flowy skirt and crocheted crop top. The kind of clothes I'd find from searching 'hippy aesthetic' on Pinterest. 'Well, look. This is novel at least.'

'What is?' I ask.

'I'm not sure I've got dressed for dinner with four other women in a restaurant bathroom before,' she continues. I like the way Lina always tries to find the silver lining in every cloud, even a toilet.

'Yeah because it should not be novel, right?' Bridget's accent goes full throated with irritation. 'It should be fucking *pre*-novel! Anti-novel!'

'I'm not sure that . . .' Lina clearly decides better than to try and argue grammar with a furious Welsh girl. 'It *would* be nice to be in a dressing room.'

'Any room that smells less like piss,' Bridget adds as she contours her nose with highlighter.

It's Whit's turn to groan. 'I did ask if it was alright to go *before* I wazzed.'

'I'm not gonna deny you your human right to wazz, Whit,' Bridget says seriously. 'My complaint lies with production, and their decision to place us in this wazzy room.'

'Could everyone stop saying wazz?' I sigh, picking through the lipsticks in my makeup bag.

'Hush, Whit and I are busy unionising,' Bridget says.

'Okay, I think this is as good as it gets,' Whit announces, throwing her beauty blender back into the makeup bag.

'Whit, babe, you could literally go out there in a pair of ASDA bags, and Malachi plus the whole world would be too entranced by your beauty to notice,' Bridget says, and Whit bobs coyly.

'Fuck my life. Help! Someone is going to have to get me out of here,' cries Dolly from the stalls. 'These loos were not made for my ass. I think I'm stuck.'

I probably shouldn't help her. But she did help me at security. Maybe we can be civil in public.

'In the loo?' gasps Lina, rushing to the toilet door in a cloud of glitter. 'You fell in?'

'No, I'm—' The door half opens and closes, something rattling ominously. 'I'm caught on something.'

Bridget throws her hands up in the air. 'This bloody wazz room!'

'I'm coming in,' Whit says.

'Coming *in*?' Dolly cries. 'Where? There's no room in here!'

Whit wedges herself into the door Dolly is currently trapped behind. 'Here, stop waggling your arms around and let me assess the situation with my highly trained surgeon eyes.'

'I want you to free me, not slice me open!' Dolly protests.

'Stop moving or you'll rip it.'

Whit and Lina seem to have a handle on it, so I go back to finishing my makeup. When I do, I see Whit in the mirror, bending down to free Dolly's dress that seems to be caught, her beautifully curved legs bare where the dress has pulled away.

I focus on keeping my eyes on my lips as I slick on my lipstick.

'Oi, Gog,' Bridget says, catching my attention. She lowers her voice to a whisper so I have to lean in close. 'You spoken to her since you moved out?'

I shake my head. 'Not really. It's fine. I'll just keep my distance.'

'That's going to be harder here. They'll be getting us all to hang out together more.'

I grit my teeth, unsure if this shade of pink is clashing with the peachy dress.

'Just remember, you got the man in the end,' Bridget continues. 'Hopefully Patrick will be smart enough to keep away from her too.'

It didn't take much for everyone to accept that we'd irrevocably fallen out over Patrick. No one even really tried to reunite us, which is a relief but also would be a bit sad if it was anyone else.

With a cry of success, Whit wrangles the door open slowly to reveal Dolly in a black and silver patterned silk dress with a huge slit going all the way up one thigh. It's not so much an outfit for a beach holiday as a fancy dinner, but it works. The woman really can dress.

Too bad she is, personality and priorities wise, dreadful.

Whit does a quick check over her outfit. 'I'm not sure anyone has ever stepped out of a toilet looking so beautiful.'

Dolly blows her a kiss, and I feel a sour twist in my stomach.

When everyone is ready, we leave en masse, abandoning our things in the bathroom. The men are already seated at individual café-style tables covered with a white cloth, decorated with flowers and lit candles.

Patrick stands as I approach, and pulls out the seat for me to sit down. Before I do, I kiss him on the cheek, and I feel his mouth curl up into a smile. His cheeks are blushed as he sits back down. I think he's shyer than I expected.

I'm discovering new things about him all the time, even though I know him already. There's so much more *new* to discover.

Maybe I got a little used to having him behind a barrier. Now he's just . . . here. All the time. I can't quite believe it.

'You look beautiful,' he says, just as a waiter appears to take my drinks order, so I hope it won't look too weird on camera when I order a water, a Diet Coke, and a glass of white wine with ice cubes in it. Patrick's half-finished beer sweats in the evening heat.

'You too,' I say, hoping it's not too weird to continue the conversation after that gap. 'Look beautiful, I mean.'

I want to make sure he feels as loved as possible, but I can feel the mask working overtime, the grinding of each gear and muscle.

What I really need is to lie down alone, in the dark, with my headphones, David and no one else. That would reset me.

But then, Patrick looks so handsome in his all-white linens, the shirt unbuttoned just enough so I can see the top of his chest. I want to be the kind of woman he deserves. That means I need to be switched on.

Is it really even masking when it's your partner?

The waiter returns with drinks in show regulation bronze cups. Unfortunately, with my trio of drinks, it does look like I'm about to play one of those hide-the-ball tricks that swindle tourists. Even more so when they hand us *another* pair of goblets so we can toast.

'We look like we're hosting a medieval ball,' I laugh awkwardly.

Patrick raises his eyebrows and shakes his head as he surveys the table. 'If so, we're hogging all the mead.'

I glance over at the other tables where everyone has a much more normal number of cups.

'Perhaps we're the King and Queen,' I suggest.

'Oh dear, I'm not sure I'm ready to suddenly rule a country as well as a ball,' Patrick says, tugging at the collar of his shirt. 'This scenario is rapidly getting out of hand!'

I giggle and take a sip of ice cold water, the sharpness of it a delicious knife through my foggy brain. I'm so glad he likes to be silly with me.

If he's willing to go along with pretending to be royalty

with me, maybe unmasking will be okay. He'll come into my world, and understand how I see it.

Gasps and cheers erupt behind me, and I crane round to see the Nguyens arriving, in matching and surprisingly chic Hawaiian print outfits.

'Good evening, couples!' calls Karina. 'Let's toast. Congratulations on your engagements!'

We all raise our glasses of fizzy stuff, clinking echoing around us.

'Babe, you're supposed to look me in the eyes,' groans Zack behind me.

'Am I?' Lina asks.

'Yes. Or it's really bad luck. Let's do it again.'

My neck starts to ache but I watch as they re-cheers. I can only see the back of her head, but I can see Zack's expression turning from annoyed to pleased. My stomach squirms a little, though I'm not sure why.

Meanwhile, Lucas laughs and claps his big hands together once. 'Let's not start this off with bad luck! It's always good to be cautious.' I wonder if he always sounds like this, or is this his television presenter voice?

'We're here tonight to explain to you all how the next section of the show is going to work. As engaged couples, you each have a starting wedding budget of twenty thousand pounds!' cries Karina excitedly.

There's a chorus of *oohs*, and I join in even though I have no idea if this is a good amount of money for a wedding or not. It just seems like a huge sum to me.

'Throughout your time in the villa, and beyond, you'll have the chance to win extra money for your budget,' Lucas continues.

'But,' Karina's voice turns cold and serious, 'put a few steps wrong, and you might get hit with a *penalty* too.'

God, I wish I'd watched this show before I came on it because I have no idea what's going on. Patrick mugs pantomime shock, and the others perform similar overegged reactions. I can't read the truth in it.

I risk a glance in Dolly's direction, and I can see she's not happy about something.

'As you know, you'll be sharing not just the honeymoon villa, but the *bedroom* with your fellow couples.'

What? All ten of us in one room?

'We see it as an opportunity for PG-rated group bonding,' Lucas continues with a laugh. 'And in the daytime, you'll be competing against the other couples to win prizes for your wedding. We'll be testing your compatibility, your ability to work together, *and* how much you guys are into each other.'

I feel a bit strange when Lucas waggles his eyebrows.

'And if you and your fiancé don't keep within PG boundaries in the villa,' continues Karina with a warning tone. Dolly sits up a little straighter. 'Then *all* of you will suffer a penalty to your wedding budgets.'

Oh.

Gasps and complaints sound all around us.

'Oh my God,' whispers Bridget. Her fiancé Jackson looks like someone just died.

Even Warren makes a convincing complaint noise.

'That's right, folks, it isn't time to explore each other's bodies,' says Lucas smugly. 'Just yet. It's still all to come.'

'Haha, cum,' laughs Zack, and I feel like I want to strangle him.

God, can these people not hang on a few more days? It's not that big a deal, right? I look at Patrick and I'm obviously attracted to him, but I'm not ready to sleep with him. Especially not in a bedroom with eight other people in it.

I know, hypocrite, but still.

I was mentally preparing for the new sensations of sharing a bedroom with Patrick. Sharing a room between ten of us—

Patrick touches my wrist, sending a jolt of electricity running through me. It's not a romantic firework; it feels like a taser. I startle, flicking both my arms akimbo, which manage to knock over two of the four glasses directly in front of me, Diet Coke spilling all over the white tablecloth, and all over Patrick.

I want to cry. I jump up, trying to clear up the mess. But there's nothing to mop it with, so I'm just moving glasses away from the liquid splashing everywhere. 'Oh God, I'm so sorry.'

Patrick is somehow next to me. 'It's okay, Carys.' His voice is so soothing it makes me want to cry more.

I stand numbly, unable to move, and he wraps his arms around me, squeezing tightly. The pressure quietens the frenetic buzzing in my brain, just enough that I can breathe. It's not quite a meltdown, or a panic attack, but I feel sick and tired and on the edge of one or the other.

'It's alright,' Patrick repeats, stroking my back like he might comfort a scared animal. Perhaps that's what he likes in me: I'm just as feral as some of his patients.

It was just a startle, I tell myself. It wasn't *him*. I was just too het up to process a sudden touch.

When I turn back, a waitress has cleaned up and production have managed to reset our table with a new tablecloth and drinks. Patrick once again holds a chair out for me. It's like nothing ever happened, except for his damp shirt.

'Let's reset and get Patrick a new shirt?' a voice calls.

'I'll be back in a moment,' Patrick tells me, as he leaves.

I dig my fingernails into the creases on the inside of my fingers, where the skin is thin. It hurts but helps, like the cold water in the shower that morning. Pain is clarity. If I can focus on that feeling, it dulls all the rest – the hurry and panic. I close my eyes and succumb to it.

Time warps and slows, but I hear heels clop over the pathway towards me. When I open my eyes slowly, I see Karina crouched down by the table next to me. 'Hey,' she whispers. 'You doing alright?'

I swallow, because no, but I'm not ready to say *Karina Nguyen, I think I'm on the edge of having some kind of menty b.*

'Don't worry about it. It's just a couple of drinks. You should see how many things I've broken on sets over the years. This is my second pair of heels today.' She makes a big oopsie face and I can't help but giggle.

She has something hidden under her shirt, and when she pulls it out, I see David. Karina squeezes him onto my lap, under the table, and covers him with a napkin. 'There, now the cameras won't see him either.'

'How—' I begin, my words slack with confusion. My heart fills because, wow, Patrick must have got him for me. He's so kind, so thoughtful.

Lovely Karina gives me the sweetest smile. 'I hope you don't mind but when Dolly told me how helpful he is to you, I sent her to get him out of your case.'

Oh.

When I look up, I see Dolly watching me from across the restaurant garden.

I deflate. I'm sour. I'm *angry*. I'm ... grateful, even if I don't want to admit it. I hate how Dolly can pull so many feelings out of me at once.

Was she just doing this to show she's better than me? Or to get a rise out of me? This is a perfect way to get herself in good standing with Karina too. God, she's *such* a pretender.

I bet Dolly Doherty has never cared about anyone in her life.

But then, is that true? She is always there when chaos tries to swallow me. And she talked about her responsibilities, whatever the hell those are.

Dolly gives me a small smile and turns away, and I suddenly feel cold.

She didn't have to go in my suitcase without asking, even if it was for a good reason. I mean, I would have been fine without David. Probably.

I'm glad he's here – rubbing his ears always makes me feel so much calmer. But now I've got a giant capybara toy hidden in my lap, and I hope to God that the producers don't notice and film him. The general public aren't kind about adults carrying soft toys.

I feel the mask clamp down over my face as I smile demurely, straighten my posture, and forget the fact I was almost about to scream-cry in the middle of this restaurant.

It's under control. I'm in control.

'Thank you, Karina,' I croak out.

She blows me a kiss and totters away on her gigantic heels.

Patrick returns, freshly dressed in another white linen shirt – perhaps he has a cartoon character-style wardrobe built of the same few pieces in multiple colours.

'I hope I didn't ruin your shirt,' I say.

'Don't worry, pet,' he says, his eyes crinkling as he smiles. 'It'll all come out in the wash, won't it?'

Well. No, not necessarily. If that cola stain settles in, it'll be a pig to get out. Some things have a habit of getting their claws into you.

I know what he means, though. Even if his phrasing was a little off, I hope that Patrick's easy-going nature will rub off on me. He was so calm even though I fucked up.

'Are we ready to go?' calls Lucas across the garden.

They count down for the cameras to come back on.

'So, you were telling us we can't sleep together?' Bridget gasps. 'What about kissing? You've got to let us kiss.'

'Like I said, keep it PG. Kissing is fine, but any and all sexual acts will be considered fineable,' Lucas explains.

'Oh my God,' says Dolly, her eyes wide, and I know she's faking it because she's not going to sleep with Warren. That must be in their little fake dating agreement rules. 'Why are you guys planning on shagging when we're all in one room?'

It's a fair question.

'There's probably other rooms,' says Jackson as though this is obvious.

I concentrate on taking a sip of my drink, and suddenly the conversation has moved on and the Nguyens have left, and now a waiter is handing me a menu that I have to try to read. I say, 'Two of those,' to whatever Patrick ordered and hope it's something I'll like.

The cameras are still on us when the food arrives. Luckily, Patrick had ordered souvlaki with some dips and veggies and chips, things I already like and can probably force myself to eat. My hands are shaking so much I worry I'm going to fling it everywhere, so I concentrate incredibly hard on eating 'right', which means I'm too quiet.

Patrick notices. 'Are you okay?'

I put down my cutlery and give him a mega-watt smile. 'Yes,' I say too emphatically.

His smile falters a little, like he doesn't quite believe me.

Maybe I don't need to lie so hard? After all, he was so understanding when I knocked the drinks everywhere. 'I'm just *so* tired,' I add as a qualifier. Neurotypical people find *I'm tired* easier to understand than *the audio landscape of scraping cutlery against plates and mouths chewing around me makes me want to die*. It's the kind of white lie that conveys how I feel ... ish, in a way they can understand.

It seems to work. His shoulders soften, and so do his eyes. 'Me too. That nap on the plane was a good start.'

'It was. But I could do with like twelve more hours.'

He reaches forward but doesn't take my hand, just rests his palm up, waiting for me to take it. I do, because I don't want him to feel rejected, and because choosing to do it gives my brain time to process the movement. It's nice. His hands are warm and a little scratchy.

'We'll have a good sleep tonight,' he promises.

I want to laugh, but that would be strange and a tad cruel when Patrick doesn't understand my brain in full yet. I don't want him to misconstrue it as me pressuring him into sex, or rejecting him. I just smile and nod.

I know I won't sleep tonight. When I was a teenager, school used to take us to this lakeside camp where everything smelled mouldy-wet, and we built the same failing canoe out of big plastic tubs every year. We stayed in big dormitory rooms of, at minimum, eight of us, and I never slept.

It wasn't just the lack of sleep, though. I'm not great in group activity situations. At the same camp, I'd regularly get in trouble for wandering off when I was supposed to be doing something, and I also got used to accusations of not being a team player. No one knew I was autistic then either, so they just thought I was rude and mean and uncooperative.

That's what I've spent years filing away. Now I know what's wrong with me, I can hide it. Make myself palatable. Likeable.

Unfortunately, I worry that Patrick is about to meet that version of me.

'Yeah,' I say, with a smile. 'I hope so.'

I pick up the cup with the wine and take a long drink, as though it was water. As far as Patrick knows, it is. The ice cubes clink against the bottom of the cup as I drain it.

Alcohol dulls my senses. Being slightly drunk will make tonight easier.

Or at least, I can only hope.

Chapter Eighteen

Dolly

Cobey Worthing, 28, Newquay

Yeah, obviously I'm quite gutted. I really thought that we had something in the warehouse. I just ... I hope that Zack will grow to be the man Lina deserves. She must see something in him that we can't, which is somehow how it is! But ... I just hope he's good to her.

For a man as proportionally massive as Warren, he's quite a considerate bedmate. Gave me a chaste kiss goodnight, keeps to his side, showers before bed, doesn't snore – a dream man. I almost feel bad about hogging him.

Unfortunately, the rest of my roommates are less dreamy. All I can hear is snoring and ... well, less wholesome sounds. I must have fallen asleep for a bit, but I'm awoken by Bridget and Jackson giggling in the bed next to ours.

There's no ignoring that. And not just because of the threat of slashes to our wedding budget, because I'm positive they're literally fucking under there.

Instead of lying here listening to coitus in action, I get up to fetch a drink of water, grabbing my phone as I go.

I make sure to whack Bridget and Jacksons' entwined feet as I squeeze past them. 'Keep it PG, campers,' I hiss.

They ignore me. Obviously.

It's a fancy house. If we weren't stacked together like sardines, I'd probably enjoy it more.

The kitchen is decorated in stark white, and once I've gulped down some water, I'm wide awake.

While the others are racking up fines, I may as well do a little exploring and try to work out if there are any cameras in the building. I'm pretty sure it's just someone's house, not a specifically built set, so the likelihood of them being in the walls is low, but still. A secret lesbian on television can't be too careful.

It's like being on a film set, but in my pyjamas. And no one else is here.

Well, not *my* pyjamas. The show regulation sexy pyjamas. It's so ridiculous. I *brought* slinky, sexy pyjamas to wear but production insisted all the girls wear these matching sets with our names embroidered on the tit – as though I'm going to mix up my size 24 top with Bridget's size 6 one. Please. They're a rip-off of the *Love Island* merch and presumably are being sold on TikTok shops or Instagram affiliate links right now. The men have matching slinky boxer shorts that remind me of the Boots 3 for 2 Christmas present options for men.

I wasn't going to argue in case I got accused of not being a team player.

I wander into the living room, which might have the highest concentration of bean bag chairs outside of the nineties. I wish I could call Mum. She loves shit reality TV décor, always complaining about the neon light signs on *Love Island*, or the chairs without supportive backs. If I had my phone, I'd take pictures for her.

She'll have seen probably two episodes by now, I think, so will have seen me 'falling in love' with Warren. I wonder what she makes of that.

I swallow down the rise in my throat, and as I turn,

something catches my eye. Through the window, I see a lone figure standing by the pool.

Unfortunately, I would know that silhouette anywhere.

I could go back to bed, ignore whatever Carys-created drama is happening.

I could.

I hate how much I notice about her. At security when she needed help and wouldn't ask for it. At dinner too. The confused, icy look she gave me presumably when she realised I got David for her. I hate that these instincts just kick me into auto-drive when I really should be keeping clear.

I'm pretty sure Patrick was one of the actually just snoring contingent. I could make him deal with this.

Why *is* she standing out there in the middle of the night?

I wonder if she's finally realising that you can't re-cork champagne, or lesbianism. Well, you probably can preserve opened champagne with some kind of rich person device, but I'm a girl from Crosby who doesn't even buy the real stuff in the first place. Gay panic is my expertise, not champers.

Bringing Patrick in to assist in a queer crisis is not going to help. Hey, babes, I know you're reconsidering your whole relationship to attraction and desire, but here's the man you're supposed to marry in a few weeks!

Yeah, no.

The temperature must drop a lot overnight because even standing inside in my tiny show regulation pyjamas is making me wish I'd brought a proper fleecy dressing gown. She's outside in the cold.

Seeing Carys's bare feet is the last straw.

My carer instincts kick in, powering me forward before I can think twice.

'Carys?' I call her name softly as I approach.

I didn't mean to startle her, but I think she's on a hair

trigger. When she spins round and realises it's me, the look she gives me is a mixture of confusion, upset, maybe not anger but something.

'What do you want, Dolly?' she snaps. Her body a sharp line, all taut elbows and folded in on itself.

Well. Fuck me then!

I'm only human, so I can't help but be annoyed. 'I saw you were awake and standing out here at two in the morning,' I hiss, conscious of waking the others.

Carys blinks a few times. 'How do you know it's two?'

I point up at the sky. 'Well, that big fucking thing called a moon is kind of a giveaway, don't you think?'

She rolls her eyes. 'It comes out in the day too.'

I almost say, *so do people who aren't lying to themselves about being queer*, but I hold the barb in.

'I wasn't being *literal*,' I say instead.

She doesn't reply, but looks up at the sky. 'Usually, I have to set alarms to remember everything,' she says, kind of dreamily. 'The one thing about being here is that I've surrendered all life administration to the production team. It's nice not thinking about dinner.'

I'm not sure why we're having this conversation out in the cold. 'Can't relate,' I sigh, desperately missing my kitchen. 'Not cooking is so strange.'

'Does Warren cook?' she asks for some reason.

'A little.'

'Good, your relationship is so amicable,' she says, and I think she's aiming for sarcasm but doesn't quite land it.

'It is,' I say, calm as possible. 'We're honest with each other.'

'I doubt that,' she snaps, and it's annoying that she's right, because I still haven't told Warren that I bat for the other team exclusively.

'Okay, fine, there's a few details missing.'

'A few! Dolly, are you always this good at lying to yourself?' Her voice hitches. 'At lying to your fiancé?'

'It might be fake, but it's solid. Has Patrick talked to you about his ex yet? Peony is as big an omission as my lesbianism.'

I regret saying that immediately.

Carys's eyes flash wide and angry. 'Urgh, just ... *fuck off*, Dolly.'

She storms away a little and I let her go while I panic about saying my truth out loud. I look around where we are on the patio, not caring if I make it obvious that I'm actively looking for cameras because if they see this, they'll have heard what I just said.

After a few minutes, I come up empty. Either way, it's too late now. If production have cottoned on, I'll hear about it tomorrow. It's not like, if I even found them, I could rip the equipment out of the walls.

I need to be more careful about what I'm saying just to get back at her.

I'm about to leave, but she's standing by the edge of the pool in a way that worries me. No one should swim unaccompanied.

I might want to, but I can't leave her alone out here, even if we're just arguing and probably making it worse.

Come on, Dolly, be a grown-up. Be the bigger person here.

I give her a few moments to cool down, or to curse me under her breath, and slowly approach.

In the moonlight, I see the sheen of tears on her cheeks and neck. Her mouth is a flat line, all from a tense jaw. Like she's trying to engage every muscle in her body to hold herself up. There are no further words, no movement, nothing else from her. She has that trapped animal look again.

'What's wrong then?' I say a little too brusquely.

I've said the magic words, because the statue begins to crumble. Her body vibrates. I don't think it's a panic attack, but her eyes are wide and unfocused.

It's kind of like a look I've seen on my mum's face, when she's in a really bad state. She doesn't say anything, because I don't think she *can*.

'I'm going to get you a glass of water. Then I'll be right back.' I speak slowly, like I'm talking to a feral cat I need to convince to eat. Or to not bite me. Again. In a less fun context.

Her eyes flash to me, huge and pleading.

'Just me, I promise.'

On light feet, I tiptoe back to the kitchen. Now is not the time for wine goblets. She needs something with a handle. I take a mug and fill it.

When I get back, Carys hasn't moved.

'Come sit down. It'll be easier to drink this.' I don't touch her, but I point the way towards a bench seat on the far side of the pool.

No one should be able to hear us from here.

Once sat, Carys takes the mug of water in both hands when I offer it, and sips slowly. The wildness in her eyes dulls.

I don't know how long we stay there, totally silent, but it's long enough that I start to get really cold. I can't tell if she doesn't register how cold it is. It's like the icy air doesn't touch her.

'I should have brought some blankets from the living room. It's like a bean bag emporium in there,' I say, feeling the need to fill the silence.

'A soft furnishings only zone.' Her voice is croaky, slurry, almost like she's drunk.

We go back to silence, and I retrieve two lurid neon blankets, because it's clear she's not going back inside any time soon. I resist the temptation to wrap one around her. She takes it, gathering it in her lap, stroking the fleece like it's a real creature. Or David, who I'd be tempted to get if I wouldn't wake someone.

Carys sets the mug down on the bench next to her. 'Thank you for the water.'

'That's okay. It looked like you needed some help.'

'You didn't have to do that,' she says, which is true. 'I've not exactly been the nicest to you in the last ... however long it's been.'

'Days. A few days.'

'It feels like weeks in here. And we've only been here for a few hours.'

'It's confusing,' I agree. 'Err, sorry it means you didn't get space from me for very long.'

'Or anyone else,' she adds, shuddering as she glances at the house. When she looks back at me, she appears just about as thrilled. She bites down on her lower lip. 'We're still not friends.'

'Fine.' Seems a bit rich, but then she didn't ask me to come out here. I'm the sap of a knight who keeps willingly rushing to her aid.

I decide to give her a pass, temporarily, because of whatever the hell is going on with her right now. People say stupid things when they're hurt or sick. That's what Mum and I do when she's being a snappy little shit. Let it wash over me in the moment; we talk about it later. Who knows if it's the healthiest dynamic, but it means we don't leave anything festering and we talk it out when the pain has passed. I know that when my endometriosis is bad, I'm pretty inhuman. As if it's heard me thinking about it, just then my uterus gives a sharp twinge. Not now, dickhead. I'm busy.

'Call this a temporary truce then?' I offer. 'I'd feel awful if I let you freeze to death out here.'

'Why? That'd improve your odds.' The little curl of a smile is infuriating.

'I don't think I'd get a great edit out of it, do you?'

This seems acceptable to her. 'Fine. You can stay.'

'Look, do you want to talk about whatever is going on?'

My asking resurrects the upset. Her knees bounce under the blanket, and while her eyes aren't wild, they look scared. What the hell has happened?

'Did something happen with Patrick, Carys? You can tell me.'

She stops and starts a few more times before seeming to deflate before my eyes. 'It's just *so* loud.'

Huh? 'Loud?' I repeat, just to be sure that's what she said.

'In the bedroom,' she sniffs, rubbing at her eyes.

'Patrick?'

'No, no,' she stutters. 'This has nothing to do with him. It's just the noise. It's constant.'

Okay, I'm not really following what she's saying, but then my mum gets ratty about noise and light when she's feeling really shit. I think of Bridget in the bed next to me snogging Jackson's head off.

'From my bed, I've got the joy of surround-sound make-out sessions,' I say, trying to lighten the tone. 'I swear I can *hear* us losing cash with every slurp.'

'It's not just that.' Her fists clench on the blanket, knuckles whitening. I can see her getting frustrated with herself as she fails to find the words.

'Tell me,' I urge.

She looks up at the sky, blinking tears. 'I've been overstimulated for days and I'm very close to—' She stops again, takes a breath. 'You can't repeat this,' she begs.

'I won't. You know I'm good at keeping secrets, after all.'

She laughs at that, a huffy sad kind of noise. 'Yeah. You are.' She takes a deep breath. 'I'm autistic and you caught me in a shutdown. Or maybe a meltdown, I can't tell yet. It's just bad.'

So many questions jump into my throat, but I swallow them down. This is not the time to make her explain. 'What would be helpful for me to do when you feel like this?'

'The water helped.' She heaves suddenly and I think she's about to vomit, but it passes without any expulsions. 'Sorry, my nervous system gets a bit confused during, or after or . . . I'm not sure it's technically done.'

She sips at the water again, a few round drops landing on the blanket as her hands and lips shake.

'When I'm overstimulated it's like . . . every sense is too much,' she whispers, her voice muffled and low like she's talking through cotton wool. 'Even talking hurts.'

I recognise the pain on her face. I know that look. The low ache in my belly is a sign that my own personal pain is right on track, but hopefully will do me the solid of skipping the honeymoon.

'Do you need quiet?' It's not really quiet out here in the true sense of the word, because there's cicadas and the lapping of the sea, but it's all the kind of sound you might put on to fall asleep. Certainly nicer than the sound of skin slapping together. 'No chatting?' I clarify.

She nods, and we sit in silence for a long, long time. It would almost be companionable if there wasn't everything going on between us, truce aside.

I hope, for Carys's sake, no one is filming right now, or that, if they are, the loud cicadas will cover our whispering. Does she realise that might have been on tape? They'll have a field day if they are filming – one secret lesbian and a secret autistic in one fell swoop.

Thing is, I strongly suspect that she's been hiding this from not just the cast, but production. Not to be big headed, but she told me pretty much everything including her inside leg seam, which I've also explored thoroughly, so I suspect that if Reb or someone on the team knew, Carys would have confided in me earlier.

Would they have let her on if they'd known? Is that why she's gone undercover? No reality television show is perfect on duty of care because half the drama comes from them ignoring those responsibilities, but UK shows have been pretty tight on mental health in the last few years at least. Neurodivergence isn't the same as mental health, but the extra duty of care involved means they probably view it the same.

I know there have been some testimonies from autistic reality show contestants who've talked about the specific struggles they've had with the structure, namely the purposeful lack of sleep or sensory downtime, the constant requirement to socialise, all the change.

I don't know enough about autism to say it definitely puts some of her behaviour in perspective, but if I was slowly being driven mad by being on a reality TV show, I might act a little unhinged too.

It's not like I don't care about her, because I do. I just also happen to think she's acted like a tit of late. But I don't want her to hurt. In fact, I want to wrap my arms around her, tell her it's okay, that she's safe.

How embarrassing that I still like her, even when she's a total bitch to me.

Over time, her posture relaxes. She goes from firm as a well-baked biscuit to something looser, not yet relaxed but close to it. Her breathing evens out too.

'Thanks,' she says eventually, signalling the end of our silent meditation. 'I feel like I can hear myself think again.'

'Sorry to ask another question, but what else do you need?'

'Sleep. But it's so much. It's so much in there,' she moans, and my heart breaks a little for her.

I think back to her sleep kit that was always on her pillow

in our shared bedroom. 'Do you have your ear plugs? Your sleep mask?'

She shakes her head. 'They're in my case somewhere but I couldn't see it and then I got stressed out and ... Well. Now we're here.'

'Okay, I can find some for you.'

'It's not just the sound,' she sighs.

God, I can imagine. Several of the men have particularly potent feet, and then there's all the perfume and hairspray. Plus, the unfamiliar beds and sharing suddenly with Patrick, a man she's functionally just met.

I'm so busy thinking about the hellscape of the bedroom that when she groans and flings the blanket off her suddenly, I startle. 'What's happening?'

'The tag,' she gasps.

'The tag?'

'In the back of the top. It's just ... so loud.' Carys points at the middle of her back with skewiff arms.

I peer round, careful not to touch her, and see a very square-looking tag sewn into the back that is sticking out at an odd angle. I reach around to the back of my own vest top. The tag is stiff and itchy and kind of gross to the touch now I'm prodding at it.

These fucking pyjamas.

'I'll get it out. Hang on.'

I risk going back into the bedroom, and find what I need immediately. I'm a meticulous packing cube user, so a fresh pair of ear plugs, my spare sleep mask and my manicure kit are all in the same handy bag.

Warren sleepily opens an eye as I take it from the bedside table. 'All okay?' he mumbles.

I nod. 'I'll tell you in the morning,' I whisper, and his eyes close again.

As I walk back to Carys's spot, I catch her humming on the breeze. It's a familiar song, I grew up watching all her films with Mum.

'Marilyn Monroe, huh?' I say as I sit down beside Carys.

'*Some Like It Hot* is my favourite film,' she says.

'I thought perhaps you just had a thing for blondes,' I say glibly.

It's probably not the time to make jokes about our prior entanglement when she's so overloaded. Me and my big gob are always stepping in it.

But to my relief, she snorts. 'Maybe.'

No more barbs, Dolly. This should be a banter-free zone, for many reasons. Namely because you love banter.

'Okay, I have all the supplies. Are you ready for me to cut this tag out?'

'Should I take my top off?'

Before I can shut my stupid mouth I say, 'I won't stop you.'

'That's how we got into this mess in the first place,' she replies with a sigh. 'Are you going to cut this thing off me or just wave those nail clippers at me?'

'Turn round, will you?' I wedge myself at an angle behind her so I can see her back better. 'I can do it without you getting naked. You're an engaged woman now, after all. You've got to be demure and mindful and chaste.'

'These pyjamas aside.'

I laugh and I can't help it, because I'd forgotten how funny she can be when she's not giving me daggers.

I try not to pay attention to the long lines of her neck, the sprinkle of freckles across her bare shoulders. When she moves her cinnamon hair out of the way, there's the ghost of a mark, just now visible. A reminder of my last visit to this particular position.

God, is this what the next few years of my life are going

to be like while I'm in heterosexual mode? So desperate for anything that I'm turned on by the sight of a woman's bare shoulders?

I gently fold out the seam at the back of the top, the material catching just under her shoulder blades.

This close, I can smell the sugar of her perfume. I've missed it.

Luckily, the label isn't sewn in particularly well – probably part of the problem to be honest. I could cut the thing off, but then it'd likely leave an even sharper edge. The skin where it must have been touching is angry and red and raised into little hives. I make a note to find some insect bite cream as that might soothe it for her, though I definitely should not offer to put that on for her. That's Patrick's job now.

Working with the nail scissors is painfully slow, one stitch at a time. I wedge my phone in my top, the torchlight guiding my snips. It takes a little physical contorting, but I manage, very slowly.

God, imagine if they're filming this debacle.

I notice goosebumps begin to gather along her bare upper arms, as Carys's calmer nervous system finally registers the cold.

'Sorry, I'll try to be quicker,' I say, as she shivers.

'It's just a bit of cold,' she says tightly. 'I'll be fine.'

'You've been out here a while. I don't want you to catch a chill.' It's easier to be honest when she's facing away from me.

'You should.'

'What?'

'You should want me to get sick.'

'Why would I want that, Carys?'

'I said I wanted to beat you, didn't I?' She chuckles, but all the fire has gone out of it. 'Getting sick would get me out of the way. That would be smart gameplay.'

'Yeah, but then you'd get sympathy votes from the public for being all adorably snotty, wouldn't you?' I tease.

She laughs. 'So you think I'd be adorable?'

'To thousands of people who don't know you, sure.'

'Touché.'

This is getting alarmingly close to banter.

The last thread snips easily, and the tag comes away in my hand.

'All done,' I say. 'Better?'

She pulls her top back up, and her eyes close like she's slipping into a warm bath. 'Thank you. I can't tell you how horrible that felt.'

'You're welcome.'

Carys looks at me then and it feels like time slows down, just for a moment. I think she's about to say something, perhaps acknowledge the almost friendly atmosphere between us. I wonder whether this truce can last.

Instead, she holds out her hand.

Into her open palm, I drop the packet of ear plugs, and the sleep mask, which she slides onto her forehead like a bizarre Alice band that rucks up all her hair.

'Do you think you'll manage back in there? We could set you up a sun lounger out here as a bed, like the dedicated boys do in *Casa Amor*.'

She looks nervously back towards the house. 'I'll *try* inside. It might be okay now I'm ... you know. Calmer.'

I nod. 'Do you want to—'

'No.' Her cheeks flush. 'You were going to ask if I wanted to talk about it, right?'

'Yes.'

She bites the side of her bottom lip. 'You keep this secret, I'll keep yours.'

I resist the urge to point out that I'm now keeping two for

her, but I can only imagine what kind of speech she's given herself about how straight she is now. 'A trade and a truce. Careful, Carys, someone might suggest we're friends.'

She drops her eyes to the floor. 'I don't think anyone will think that.'

That hurt. I guess whatever connection we had is over. In every form.

'Whatever you want, Carys.' I pull the blanket round me and stand up, ready to go back to the bedroom.

And yet I still wait for her, because I'm a sucker for punishment.

'Sorry. I just . . .' Her big sad eyes look up at me and I feel a twinge in my chest. I'd do anything to make her not look so sad. 'I just think it's for the best. So neither of us gets confused or hurt.'

Oh. A dagger to the heart might be less painful.

Maybe she's right. We should just keep away from each other. After all, I think she's repressed and forcing herself to marry Patrick to prove something to herself, and she probably thinks I'm some conniving hag out to steal all the pure-hearted couples' money.

She hovers at the precipice of the house. It must be really hard to subject yourself willingly to something that could cause yourself pain.

'I'm too wide awake, so I'm just going to enjoy the fresh air for a bit longer,' I lie.

I walk into the living room area and pick up some of the throws and cushions. The implicit *I'll be here if you need me* hangs between us. I'm not sure I have the will to say it, or if she is prepared to hear it, but it's there between us, its meaning shining like a neon sign.

I couldn't stop putting someone else's needs before my own if I tried.

With her eyes on me, I feel exposed, like she's seeing the raw me, the fundamentals. Like I've seen her tonight.

There are things I want to say but I swallow it down as she silently watches me for much longer than a casual glance. There's meaning, if she'd only say it. If I'd only ask.

But neither of us move. She nods, and I hear a ghost of a *nos da* as she leaves.

I pick two lounge chairs close together, and on each set out the throws and cushions. Too bad I don't have anything to do other than look up at the night sky. But maybe that's a good thing? Perhaps I've spent so long looking after Mum every day or creating content or replying to comments from bed that I've not had downtime like this.

A digital detox, isn't that what rich people are always going on about? This is probably a good thing.

I breathe out the tension and take in the fresh Greek air.

I'll only stay up a little while, just in case.

Just in case she wants to escape and come back outside.

Just in case she needs me.

Chapter Nineteen

Dolly

@weddedblessed: Question! Are they filmed like all the time in the villa? Hidden cameras etc. Anyone know?

@loml: I don't think so @weddedblessed, are you thinking of Big Brother?

@laughingwithsalads: I think you are both thinking of Love Island @weddedblessed @loml Do you really think there are hidden cameras in the walls?

When I next open my eyes, Warren is standing over me.

'Hello.' His amused smile tells me that I've been out here all night.

'Hey,' I croak, my throat dehydrated and claggy all at once. I rub the gunk out of the corner of my eyes. 'I'd ask you what time it is but ...'

'I haven't learned to read the sun yet. I heard looking directly at it was like really bad for you?'

'No, really?'

'Mad, right.'

The blanket I'd slept under is kind of damp with

condensation and the sun is low in the sky so it can't be too late in the morning.

I feel lowkey horrendous. I can't believe I fell asleep out here.

When I sit up, the blanket falls away to reveal a huge bite on my thigh from some horrible insect.

'Oh, that looks nasty,' Warren sympathises.

I poke it and it *really* stings. 'I'm going to hunt down the little fucker and murder it. No one steals my blood without my permission.'

'I worry that you've thought about that this much.'

'What? The permission to steal my blood?'

He raises his eyebrows as if to say *yes, you fucking weirdo*. Poor man for being stuck with me. 'Why were you out here? Was I hogging the bed?'

'Not at all. You were a delight.' A hesitation. It's not really my story to tell, after all. 'I couldn't sleep, so I came out to look at the stars.'

'That's pretty cute.' He perches on the sun lounger, which rocks dramatically, and we have to hurriedly adjust our weight distribution so it doesn't tip over. 'Oops. I don't think these were built for two.'

'It can't contain this much bodaciousness.'

He shakes his head. 'Dolly, who has said bodacious since the nineties?'

'Is it not vintage? Maybe I'm bringing it back.'

'No. How is my future wife so uncool?'

'Soz. Have you been up long?'

'Nah, I came to find you after they turned the lights on. Big switch. Blam!' He flicks out his hands like an explosion.

'Oh, that sounds miserable.' My stomach swoops, hoping Carys's sleep mask was firmly affixed. 'Is everyone up?'

He shakes his head. 'Bridget and Jackson are still in bed. Suspect they're both naked under there.'

'So much for our wedding budgets,' I murmur.

'We could be alright if the rule is no oral, no sex.'

I try to resist the urge to point out that, for a lot of us, those are one and the same. 'You mean no penis in vagina.'

'Bit clinical, but yeah.'

'There must be hands rules.'

He laughs deeply. 'Thinking about getting or giving?' He holds his up like he's under arrest. 'These hands are innocent.'

I laugh. He's such a goof. 'Thinking about not being fined thousands of pounds if someone touches a penis.'

'Do you think they include wanking?' He looks genuinely worried.

'I wouldn't put it past them to outlaw masturbation,' I sigh. 'They want us as insane as possible, remember?'

'How would they know? If there are cameras in the bathrooms, they're going to have so much footage of us taking shits.'

I burst out laughing. 'They'd deserve it.'

He does raise a point. How are they going to know who has been doing what unless there's cameras in the bedroom? I doubt they're relying on us snitching because no one ... well, most people wouldn't be stupid enough.

I'm not sure I'd put it past Zack to complain or Jackson to brag openly.

'In a bit I'm going to make some breakfast with Patrick and Malachi. You want some food? I was thinking crêpes as they're easy.'

'God, yes. That's nice of you.' I'm quietly relieved to hear I've snagged a fake husband who thinks making crêpes is easy and doesn't expect me to always cook.

'Patrick suggested it. Carys seems poorly, so she's sleeping in. But we've all got to eat.'

Good, I think. And apparently say.

'Good?' he asks, tilting his head like a puppy.

'Someone needs to get a good sleep in here. I can't wait to sleep in our own private room. Right now, we've got the worst of both worlds – a shared dorm and surround-sound frotting.'

He laughs, and I join in.

'Anyway, speaking of our probably rapidly dwindling wedding fund, they left us big folders to look through before filming later,' Warren adds.

I blink in the bright light. 'Sorry, you need to define "big folders" a bit more for me. I'm pre-caffeine and slept on a plank of MDF.'

He smooths back my hair from my forehead. I can feel it sticky and brittle in the morning heat from last night's texturising spray. 'Go get dressed, I'll get the folder. Meet back here in fifteen?'

'Call it thirty. This –' I gesture to my aching body '– is going to need some serious intervention.'

There are two shared bathrooms with weirdly less privacy than we had in the warehouse as my modesty is only preserved behind a misty glass shower door, as people wander in and out. Is Warren right? Is this a no-cameras space?

It's complicated with *Wedded Bliss* – the American series generally only shows footage from camera setups rather than fixed cameras built into the set like on similar shows. But this is a new series, a new production team, and I can't trust that we're not being constantly observed.

No one is mic'd up yet, but could they still be recording what we say?

With my logical reality TV expert brain on, I do feel like if they had listened in last night, Carys and I would have been called in for a chat already. I hate the anxiety of not knowing if I've been caught out.

Maybe this is how Carys feels all the time with neurotypical people scrutinising her. I wonder how the hell she's coped this long.

I spend ages looking and once again find nothing concrete. Maybe the bathroom *is* off limits.

I find Warren and Malachi in the kitchen where they have taken over a counter with huge jugs of batter, lemons, sugar and syrups. It's not the messiest kitchen I've seen, but I have to resist the urge to clean up after them.

Whit sits on a barstool at the counter, her hair piled up messily and secured with a clip. 'Morning, beaut,' she says when I saunter over. She kisses me on the cheek. 'Warren, have you seen your girl?'

Warren's spatula clatters to the counter and he whistles. 'Heyyy.'

I resist the urge to do a twirl, but I know I look good. The brief wasn't strictly swimwear, but I wear a bronze two-piece. The plunging bra has a purely decorative, faux-functional bow tied under my boobs, paired with high-waisted pants edged with frills. I was briefly worried the bottoms would read *child's swimming nappy* on camera but as soon as I put them on and they hugged to my curves and belly, I knew they were smoke-show material.

There'll be comments online about how fat girls can't wear bikinis, but if I listened to what fatphobic knobheads said I'd never get anything done. Instead, I just hope that some girl with a body like mine sees me on camera and thinks, fuck it, I'm going to look that hot too. The importance of hot-and-fat-girl representation can't be underestimated. I know it for a fact – unfollowing all the accounts when I was a teenager and following a load of beautiful fat fashion babes radically altered my view of my own body, and gave me a lot of decent tips on where to get good plus-size clothing, instead of endless recipes for smoothies.

'Thanks, I try,' I say, flicking the sharp edge of my hair.

'Okay, I'm really gonna do it,' Malachi says. With so much concentration that his tongue peeks out the corner of his mouth, he flips a crêpe. We all hold our breath as it flies through the air and somehow lands in the pan perfectly rotated.

We all react like our team just scored the championship goal.

'Good morning,' says Louise, manifesting like a very posh spirit summoned by cheers. 'Just a reminder that we'll be filming a challenge in about an hour, so we will need to come mic you all up.'

Okay, so they need mics on us for that – is that confirmation that the only footage they're going to use is anything they come in to film? Louise starts to leave and I wonder if I'm in the clear.

'What are we doing today?' I ask, wondering if I can wheedle stuff out of her.

'Just a fun little couples challenge,' she says, with a sniff. 'Your pancake is burning.'

'It's a crêpe,' Malachi insists.

'Well, it's on fire,' she says as she leaves.

That's an exaggeration. It's not on fire, but the edges are catching.

I lean over to grab Warren's abandoned spatula, free up the catching edges of the crêpe and tip it out onto a plate. 'Turn the heat down a little,' I say. 'More fat, less heat for the next ones.'

Malachi gives me a thankful nod, and pours fresh batter into the pan. He's a good lad for a boy from Bootle. My true accent keeps sliding out when we speak, like something about the word *crêpe* is a Scouse activation code.

'I always forget you're a trained chef,' Whit says.

'Hang on, then why are we cooking?' Malachi says teasingly. 'Wasn't it Patrick's idea? He's not even here.'

'He conned us,' gasps Warren. 'Here, I made you an iced coffee.'

True husband material. When he passes over the lidded plastic cup, I make sure the looks are long, just in case. It's good practice, either way.

'Did you look through your binder yet?' Whit asks, pointing to one on the counter.

It reminds me of an all-inclusive cocktail menu at a fancy hotel. *Reminds me* is probably the wrong phrase; perhaps, what I imagine they might be like. We don't exactly have fancy resort holiday money yet – I really hope we get a brand deal that means I can take Mum for some sun on her bones one day.

'What's in here exactly?' I ask, even though I know the answer.

'It's the catalogue that has all the options for your wedding, like the rings and stuff,' explains Whit.

'And we can just look through them?' I ask.

Warren shakes his head. 'Nope. Louise asked us to wait until we're mic'd up. But someone peeked already.'

Whit covers her face. 'It was looking at me!'

'Is that before or after the challenge?' I murmur, thinking aloud.

Before, they get lovey-dovey footage. But if a couple fucks up the challenge, they might have two royally pissed-off people trying to fight their corner over wedding linens. Smart producing.

'I hope it's an active one,' Whit says, stretching her legs. 'Like, a race or something.'

'As long as we're not rating the attractiveness of the other gender.' I raise my voice for this part. 'Sorry to say, men always get it wrong by not putting their fiancée first.'

'Noted!' laughs Warren.

'I would *never*,' says Malachi, who looks genuinely

flabbergasted at the idea of rating his model-looks doctor fiancée less than number one.

The boys serve up crêpes for us, leaving some in the oven for Patrick and Carys. I want to ask where they are, but I need some Carys-free time this morning, especially after the strange intimacy of last night.

The sweet, tart crêpes wake me up, somewhat making up for my poor sleeping spot choice.

'Do you think we'll win money in the challenge?' Whit asks.

'Enough to counter the fines Bridget and Jackson are racking?' I scoff.

'Bridget and Jackson's what now?' Bridget says, striding into the kitchen in the world's smallest high-waisted bikini. Not to be indelicate, but I'm not sure how she's keeping her insides *inside* that thing.

'Fine hatting,' Malachi fills in, which is both ridiculous and seems to work, given Bridget wears a trucker cap, her ponytail sticking out the back.

'Yeah, I'm regretting not bringing a big hat,' Whit explains. 'Look, Lina's got a big hat too.'

Across the pool, Lina is completely shaded by her massive hat that has *Out of Office* embroidered on the underside. An interesting choice, because I'm pretty sure Lina has never worked in an office. She's too much of a free spirit for fluorescent strip lighting.

I wonder why she and Zack are over in the corner. Do they not want to come hang out and make crêpes? My resounding impression of this Zack dude is that he's not outright evil like Jackson might be, but he seems kinda yuck. Maybe I have overly high standards for men.

'Maybe they'll let us out so we can go get you a big hat? I'll buy you the big hat of your dreams,' Malachi croons, and Whit goes to him for a kiss. Gosh, they're sweet like sugared crêpes.

I'm not sure Bridget bought what we were saying, but she makes up a green juice from powder that smells like the gunk you get on the Mersey sometimes.

Malachi and Whit move off eventually, too loved up to pay much attention to the rest of us.

There's still no sign of Patrick and Carys, even when we've washed up our plates and pans.

'Ready for a beautiful day in paradise?' Warren says in that slow, deep voice. A flash of a smile.

We walk over to a big squishy seat in the sun that reminds me of soft play centres. It's warm under the sunshine already.

Last night is playing on my mind. I've not cheated on him, because we're not really together, but we talked on the way here about being exclusive, just to be safe. And that means I probably need to be honest with him, as much as I can, about who I am.

I wander round to grab some suncream from a table nearby, scoping the area for cameras. We're still un-mic'd but I can't relax about it yet.

'Can I ask you something?' I ask as we settle down. I flip open the lid of the suncream and pour a splodge into my palm.

'Shoot.' Warren settles his bucket hat over his eyes, like makeshift sunglasses.

'Did you think you'd fall in love here, like at all?'

He flips up the brim of his hat to peer up at me with one eye. 'Why do you ask?'

'Just curious.'

Warren sits up, removing the bucket hat from over his eyes. 'I was open to it,' he says, as he picks up the suncream and starts slathering it onto his long, muscular arms. 'To falling in love.'

My throat feels dry. Maybe Carys is right – am I denying Warren a chance at falling in love with someone for real?

'But none of the women sparked anything in me, until you,' he says, and I catch his meaning. 'What we have ... it's the best situation I could possibly imagine. And I think that, in time, love is going to come.'

I lick my lips and taste suncream, all synthetic coconut. 'I think so too.'

Love, not romantic love. Partnership. Friendship. Family. Those are the kinds of loves that we are working towards.

'We align on so much,' he continues. 'I think we make a good team.'

I want to be honest with him about the fact that I'm gay as the yellow brick road, but now isn't the time. When we're alone in our new apartments, provided they aren't bugged either, then I'll tell him. It makes sense to hold off a little longer.

'Me too.' He's missed a few streaks of suncream on his back, so I stand up and rub it in down the centre of his spine.

'See, you've got my back.'

I groan. 'That was offensively bad.'

He presses his hand over his chest. 'There's nothing wrong with being corny.'

'This is going to be a test of my sanity.'

'What about you? Did you think you would?' He swats me with his hand and I boop a blob of suncream onto the tip of his nose, which he rubs in aggressively.

I'm thankful for the distraction. 'Why do men always do skincare like that?'

'Like what?'

I mime the same action, rending my skin around like I'm getting an aggressive facial massage.

'Alright, alright, point made. You can teach me to be more delicate,' he says, laughing all the while. The change is so sudden that I almost jump when he reaches over for my hand.

'To be serious again for a second, Dolly, I don't have any regrets, if that's what you're asking me. Do you?'

I look at my future fake husband. Yes, he's lowkey famous in his career, far more than I am I guess. Niche famous. And he's also good. Kind. Funny. Caring. Someone I see myself reflected in. A man I can trust.

'None,' I say wholeheartedly.

'Then we're good. Don't sweat. You're too beautiful, and so is the weather, for either of us to be getting stressed.' He lies back, hat over his eyes again.

'You're a smooth talker, Warren.'

'Maybe, maybe.'

When this is all over, I really must find a nice girl to set him up with. He might just be a perfect man.

Production call us over for mic'ing up, but it all goes so fast and no one is willing to entertain my curious questions about what we're up to, so soon Warren and I are back on our big squishy seat with the enormous plastic binder. The lighting is good here, and I catch a roving cameraman come in, so I wave him over.

'We were going to go through our wedding binder if that's alright?' I say, my voice a little higher than usual. I don't know this team, they seem to be local, but he gives us the thumbs up to get going.

We smile and kiss and flick through the pages. It's all the vendors the show is using, and I recognise quite a few brands as being UK based.

The first few pages, which he skips past, are the ring options which he explains they already flicked through.

'Lucky I love my engagement ring,' I beam, flexing my hand in front of me. He did well; a tasteful diamond with small pearls around it, quite vintage, a little camp.

I flick through to the venue options. Some are in London,

which makes sense for production ease given we'll all be living there in apartments as of next week, and a few dotted around the country – I suspect some of them might be geographically close to our various homes as I spy one in Liverpool.

It would be easier for Mum. Though saying that, I haven't really thought about the logistics of getting her there. It's not that I don't want her there, I do. But a potentially whole-day wedding could be a month of spoons for her. And that feels like too big an ask when this isn't real. I need to talk to her about it, off camera.

God, I hope she's okay.

I push down the worries that threaten to spill up, and flick back through the pages. They've thought of everything: caterers, musicians, florists, entertainment, celebrants of various stripes and religions. Everything we might need for our televised nuptials.

The cameraman wanders off after a while, presumably because there's only so much of two people flicking through pages that a person can watch.

I know that we won't necessarily get our first choice of any of these venues, so I need to work out a kind of hierarchy.

The dream one, though, the one that makes my heart flutter, is the huge space in the Barbican glasshouse. The high ceilings, the light, the beautiful plants filling the space. If I was getting *real* married, that's where I'd want it to be.

I kept hold of my warehouse notebook, so we draw up tables for ranking options. Warren wants Nigerian food served by people who know how to cook it, so I defer to him as we build an ideal menu together. Our venue needs to be wheelchair accessible, which knocks out a good four or five, leaving us with the beautiful tropical glasshouse in London, a big country house, and a kind of plain registry office set inside a nice building near Liverpool.

It almost feels real. Except it's not real at all.

The sun is high above us, and I'm about to go inside to cool down in the air con, when a voice comes over the speakers announcing that group filming will commence shortly.

'Challenge time,' I murmur.

'Well then, wifey,' Warren says, standing up and holding out his hand to help me up too. 'Let's go win our dream wedding.'

Script: Challenges intro

[Karina and Lucas stand together in the villa's back garden.]

KARINA   Our first challenge is the River of Life, where couples will answer trivia about their partners and their relationship.

LUCAS   Get two matching answers? You both move forward together. Any disagreements mean you're stuck right where you are.

KARINA   And the first couple to meet in the middle have a chance of winning something incredible for their weddings. But that'll go to the couple who know each other best.

LUCAS   We're fair here. Second place gets second pick, and so on down the list. So it's all to play for! How do you think we'd do?

KARINA   *[laughs]* Darling, after twenty years, I'd hope we'd win.

Chapter Twenty

Carys

Transcript of a video from Reality TV content creator @missgoss

Okay, so I looked up the sales records of that house that they're all staying at which you can see in the image behind my head, and you won't believe who owns it. Zoom in on that name. Know who that is? Only the showrunner: Richard Lee Aldridge! This is just his house! Feels like the UK season of Wedded Bliss *cost about twenty quid. What do we think about that, Blissfuls?*

I walk through the villa, and she's there at every turn. In the pool. In the kitchen. Waiting for me on the sun loungers, where I left her last night. Doesn't she understand that I need to keep clear of her?

She starts to disappear down the garden, running through the lush green foliage, and I run forward, chasing her.

'Carys?'

'Dolly?' I shout. 'Dolly! Wait for me.'

Why won't she just stay here? Why won't she talk to me? It would be easier if she spoke to me.

She turns back to me and I swear she's wearing fewer clothes than she was a moment ago.

'Dolly?' I call.

She finally stops running. Her lips fall open, and I'm really going to kiss her again and—

In a shock of white light, reality pours in. And there is Patrick.

'Shit!' I shout, leaping back and whacking my head on the headboard. At the same time, he jumps back so I narrowly avoid headbutting him in the nose. 'Shit shit shit! Sorry!' I cry.

Patrick looks at me like I'm a horse about to buck.

'Sorry, I didn't mean to scare you,' he says, and I realise he must have flipped up my sleep mask. 'Is your head okay?'

'Yeah,' I grumble, thankful that my sleep mask is as thick as a blackout curtain and managed to cushion my bump a little.

He dares to come closer now I've stopped flailing round like an insane thing. 'You were shouting. I was worried you were having a nightmare.'

My cheeks burn with embarrassment. Oh God. Oh God oh God oh God.

'What . . . what was I saying?' I ask.

'You kept saying *slow down*, *wait for me*, stuff like that,' he says, now perched fully on the edge of the bed. 'Are you feeling alright? You look a little flushed.'

He puts the cool back of his hand against my raging hot shame skin.

'I think,' I croak. 'Migraine. I got up in the middle of the night and was feeling kind of funny.'

'I thought something was up. I couldn't wake you earlier so I just left you to sleep in longer.'

I sit upright, and the movement makes me swoon.

'You're probably still postdromal. Take it slow,' Patrick asks, keeping his voice sweet and low.

I wince as I nod, for full effect.

I don't have a migraine. I have post-meltdown brain ache and a heap of embarrassment that I was having a sexy dream in our not-quite-marital bed about the woman I kind of cheated on him with.

'I'm going to go get you some crêpes. Do you think you could eat?'

'Yeah,' I say, though I don't really know if I could stomach them.

I find an ear plug tangled in my hair; the other has vanished into the ether.

Patrick leaves, but doesn't close the door behind him.

'Hey, lovely,' Reb calls from the doorway. 'Can I come in?'

'Hi, Reb,' I say, waving half-heartedly.

God, it really is bright in here. I don't have to try hard to pretend I have a migraine because I can barely see.

'Do you have time for a temperature check?' Reb asks, and when I don't immediately answer she adds, 'You know, just to check you're doing alright?'

Oh God. I told Dolly I was autistic last night, didn't I? Has she told someone? We had a truce, didn't we?

Or did production somehow hear what I said? Fuck, I didn't consider that there might be cameras outside.

I try not to react, but honestly my un-masked facial expressions are pretty flat so she probably thinks I haven't moved a muscle anyway. 'What's this about, Reb?'

Reb looks at me like I might be a bit stupid. 'Babe, you can only seem to open one eye at a time.'

She's not wrong. I swap which eye is open, and in doing so open both, just to see if I can, but two is far too much. 'Oh . . . yeah.'

'This is your second migraine this week, and I know this environment can be quite stress—'

'No, no,' I say, waving my hands. 'Honestly, I think it was the wine last night. White wine sometimes hits me the wrong way.'

'Okay, I'll make a note so no one serves you any. Save your poor nice head. Do you think you can manage filming today?'

'Mmhmm. What are we doing?'

'I'm not really supposed to say,' she says with a sigh. 'But it's a challenge. Competitive. Whole lot of you.'

'Is it physical?'

'You have to stand up.'

'I think I can handle that.'

'Good. Good. Okay, I'll get you some painkillers, yeah? I'll send them back with Patrick. Oh. Sorry, can I?' Reb reaches forward and, with a bit of fiddling, plucks something out of my fringe. Upon seeing what it is, she practically throws it into my lap. 'Oh, err, it's an ear plug. Right.'

Poor girl looks ready to vomit. 'Okay, I'll leave you in Patrick's capable care, but do shout if you need more meds later, okay?'

I give her a thumbs up she doesn't even see, because she sprints out the door.

What a mess. I pick out the crusty bits from my eyes.

I think I can safely assume I wasn't overheard admitting I'm autistic. She didn't even mention mental wellbeing, so I guess the migraine excuse works.

But that dream. Dolly shows me one bit of kindness and I start picturing her in her underwear. God, what's *wrong* with me? I mean, arguably a lot of things but specifically in this instance, what is going on? I'm supposed to hate her. Am I just some perve who gets horny for kindness?

Patrick returns with a plate of crêpes before I can spiral too much, plus a glass of water and some paracetamol all balanced on top of a big book thing. Even I know that paracetamol is not going to touch a true migraine, but it'll take the edge off my situation at least.

I neck the meds quickly, trying to ignore the chalky taste of the tablets.

'Thanks for this,' I say, eyeing up breakfast.

'Ah, thank Malachi and Warren. They kept them warm for us.'

He's already rolled them up for me, lemon and sugar, and I try to be nice and say thank you, even though I'd rather have done it myself as I bet the balance is off. Most people don't put the best part of a lemon in theirs.

'So, production were handing out catalogues of all the wedding venues and options for us to go through on camera. Do you think you'd be up for that before the challenge?'

That explains the binder resting by my feet. I'm not sure I've got the brain for wedding planning today, but I don't think I've got a choice either.

The first not-sour-enough crêpe is claggy, and I have to unstick it from the roof of my mouth before I can reply with an unconvincing *sure*.

But then he asks me a question that makes my brain go completely blank.

'When you were a little girl, what did you imagine your wedding would be like?' he asks sweetly, stroking the long bits of my slept-on hair. 'I want you to have your dream wedding.'

I shove another bit of crepe in my mouth to buy myself some time.

The simple truth is that I am not sure I ever dreamed of a wedding. I knew I wanted to be married and have a partner, but I've never been able to picture the event itself.

That seems like the socially unacceptable thing to say to the man you're about to marry. But I spent so much time as a child trying to make sure I was Doing Human Right at every step that I didn't have much space to dream ahead.

Even when I was with Mike, I was more focused on being a good girlfriend in the moment than imagining the next stages of our lives. I love planning, but there were just too many variables when it came to building a life towards a specific event with one person.

It is somewhat impossible to imagine a future where someone loves you unconditionally when you can barely stomach yourself.

When I was small, I was so angry that I kept getting things wrong, *being* wrong, and not knowing why I kept fucking things up. I wasn't an angel – I said some things to people that I realise in hindsight might have been true but not kind – but even when I was kind and lovely, it didn't always work. I had to adapt, fit myself into being the right person for every relationship.

Carys Cadwallader is a different person to everyone. My family and friends and colleagues will probably watch this show and all agree I'm acting differently, but the how and why and true version of me will vary for all of them. I think my sisters know the most truthful version of me. My parents know ... someone who could be small and quiet and passive.

It's not lost on me that the version that Dolly has met is closer to the real me than the person I am around Patrick. She's even seen the spikier, unpalatable versions I never let anyone see.

That's the thing about masking; it's survival by splintering. Instead of a whole personality, I have a handful of wood chips.

There's only so long I can get away with chewing this quickly disintegrating crêpe. What would he want to hear? Does Patrick want a wife who knows what to ask for, or demand, even? What's a middle ground between the truth and whatever that could be?

'I couldn't imagine the event without the person,' is what I manage to come up with. 'A wedding is about two people. So what I want is what *we* want.'

Patrick takes it in, nodding slowly, and I worry for a second that he's disappointed. Eventually he says, 'You thought all that as a little girl?' He laughs but not unkindly, and kisses me on the top of my head. 'My sensitive girl.'

Well. He's not wrong.

Conversational masking is back in full gear, and I turn the question back on him. 'What about you?'

Patrick blinks in a machine gun splutter, followed by an awkward cough. 'Well. I mean. Yeah, I thought I'd get married before,' he says in a strained voice.

Now I regret asking. Peony. That's who he means, doesn't he? I only know her name because Dolly threw it at me like a grenade last night. Patrick still hasn't really told me about her, though I haven't talked much about Mike either.

'To an ex-girlfriend?' I say, wishing we weren't having this conversation.

'Yes, but we were young and together a long time. We hadn't planned anything. Things change.'

It's very clear that he wants to drop this. I feel stupid and selfish for bringing up his pain because I wanted to get the heat off me. That's not the kind of wife I want to be.

'I think that makes it very special then,' I insist. 'We get to pick everything from scratch together with no prior expectations. Just what feels right for us.'

He smiles tightly, perhaps the bitterness of the memory still on his tongue.

I shouldn't be jealous of Peony. It's in the past, I'm sure, no matter what Dolly implies.

'What about a big country house? Jane Austen style? You can be Colonel Brandon, I'll be Marianne.'

I know I'm not supposed to yet, but I grab the binder and flick through to the venues.

'Carys—' Patrick begins, but I cut him off with an excited noise when the page falls open on a big white stately home.

It's beautiful. The rooms inside are decorated with intricate wallpaper woven with bits of gold leaf. At the back, sweeping steps we can pose on for our wedding photos lead down to large lawns with beautiful topiary. The perfect place for a garden reception. There's even a marble columny thing like the one Lizzie and Darcy argue in in the 2005 version, though hopefully it'll be without the downpour. There's even accommodation so all our family could stay there too. A destination, yes, but something that feels homely too.

Patrick's face lights up. 'It's perfect. I can just picture it.'

We kiss a gentle chaste kiss. A good-morning-my-spouse kind of kiss.

'Okay, no more looking.' I slam the book shut with a sharp clap.

The excitement of finding our possible venue spurs me on. Patrick helps me up, and then Bridget arrives, insisting on helping me dress. She makes me sit on the makeup table pouffe while she does my face, which is very kind but I am wearing more makeup than I might have ever worn in my life. The foundation is sticky and tight against my skin, and I have to work not to notice it.

Even though it usually makes my tiny head look like a pea, we shove my messy hair into a high pony topped with a baseball cap that Lina lends me. It says *Pathological People Pleaser* on the front, which feels a bit on the nose.

Hopefully I look cute and sporty, not desperately hungover from the meltdown.

The overstimulation is still there, but it's duller today – not because things are better, but because my wrecked brain has given up trying to process half of the stuff around me. I notice I'm missing more words than usual when Bridget chatters to me about what the challenge could be, unable to fill in the gaps when every third word is missing. It's a beautiful white noise of sound, which sounds rude to say, but I'm not sure she expects me to listen.

When I finally make it outside, most of the couples gather by the lawn. Lighting and cameras are being set up, and I suspect that Lucas and Karina are on their way by the slightly nervous atmosphere from the production team. That means challenge with a capital C.

A gaunt man who I think is called Liam is laying down thin bits of card in rows along the grass. They kind of look like stepping stones.

'What's this for?' I croak, when Reb hands me a shiny laminated board and a felt tip pen.

Rather than answer, Reb announces to the group, 'We'll explain the rules in just a few minutes.'

I flex the fingers of my right hand, and try to hold onto the pen properly, but it feels strange, disconnected. Sometimes, after a meltdown or shutdown, I really struggle to write. The communication bit of my brain is the first to go, so not being able to speak isn't a huge surprise. But the writing goes too, though given there's more typing than handwriting in my life, I forget this quirk. Hopefully I can manage it, though people are weirdly judgy about handwriting.

I studiously ignore Dolly's glances from across the lawn.

'How are you feeling?' asks a cheery voice, and I look up to see Malachi wearing an unbuttoned Hawaiian shirt, like he's about to hit the beach. He's very muscly – I think Whit said he's in the early stages of training to be a firefighter. You probably have to be very fit for that. You know, physically fit! Not just handsome.

My cheeks redden as I try to find a place to look at him that doesn't feel ogly.

'Medium,' is all I manage to say, which is not really the right answer, but he laughs as though I was purposeful.

'It's a real medium kind of morning,' he agrees.

'Thank you for the crêpes. They were just what I needed.'

'I learned to flip one! Second best day of my life.'

'What was the first?'

I follow his look across the lawn to Whit, perched on a bench with her long legs crossed at the knees, her head thrown back in laughter as Dolly animatedly tells her a story.

'When I met her,' Malachi says. 'The love of my life.'

He says it so sweetly that I want to burst into tears.

Whit and Dolly must sense us watching, because they both look over. Whit and Malachi silently coo at each other, all exaggerated words and heart-hands.

I don't think they notice the weighted look between Dolly and me. Her eyebrows rise in a silent question, and I give her a quick little nod.

I've never been great at reading or conveying non-verbal communication but I hope I've conveyed *thanks for last night but we're back to not being friends and also let's not talk about it with anyone thanks*.

Her eyes drop and she turns away to fuss over Whit. My body feels cold all over, like I've just been shoved out into the snow.

It weighs on me that I'm able to be so much more honest with her than anyone else, even though we're practically enemies. Maybe the distance makes it easier?

Or maybe it feels easier because she's the only one I've given the chance to see me.

Still, I feel angry and embarrassed that she saw me like that. And, if I'm honest, a little hurt that all she could bother doing was look at me. Not even going to ask me how I am?

Maybe that's stupid – we said it was only a temporary truce, I said we're not friends. And yet, I still feel . . . dropped? Rejected.

I think that's even more embarrassing than her seeing me at my most vulnerable.

Reb returns, freeing me from the prickling in my head that could be the meltdown hangover or Dolly-generated. 'Do you need anything? I hope you're feeling a bit better.'

'I still feel awful,' I say before I can really think it through.

'Oh. You can sit this one out if you want?' she suggests hesitantly. 'It would ... have to be both of you, though.'

That decides it. I don't want either of us missing out, especially if there are prizes up for grabs.

'No, I'll push through,' I say, trying to sound confident.

'Good,' she says, a little too relieved. 'Migraines are a total slag.'

I burst into giggles that hurt my head but do make me feel better. 'They are.'

'Okay, time to get ready. Look, your man is here.'

Patrick replaces Reb at my side, and I beam up at him. He really is lovely.

Whatever this challenge brings, I hope we rise to meet it together.

'Look at our wonderful betrothed couples!' cries Lucas with CBBC level enthusiasm as he and Karina arrive, all shiny and golden.

They walk round to one end of the rows of cardboard circles.

'Now, together you will face many challenges and travel the River of Life together, but we wanted to get a read on how well you've got to know each other so far,' says Karina, her eyes wide in wild excitement.

The cue cards in their hands reflect the bright sunlight, and I try not to wince as the light flickers in my eyes.

'And so we brought you to a literal river of life!' Lucas cries with even more excitement.

We all look down at where they are gesturing at the cardboard circles and lines on the lawn. It's ... well, I don't want to be rude, but a little less impressive than they are making it out to be. It's not really a river either. We're on grass.

I realise my internal pedantry means I've missed Karina's short explanation of the game, though it seems to be just write an answer and hope it matches Patrick's.

And then Karina adds, 'The first couple to meet in the middle get to secure their dream wedding venue.'

A commotion of gasps surrounds us. I wonder if the other couples picked their venues while I was sleeping. Bridget and Lina exchange nervous glances and it dawns on me that there might be a rule that none of us can have the same venue.

I need that country house.

'We've hand-selected the best venues in the country, but who will get first pick? Let's find out. Couples? Line up!'

Okay, okay. This is important. I pull out the last remnants of my energy, knowing I'll pay for this later.

I line up at the starting point, Patrick directly opposite me. There are ten stepping stones between us, with a blue line in the middle. That means five questions with matching answers to win. We can do that.

To my left, Dolly and Warren high-five. I hate how confident they are that they can beat *real* couples. They can't know each other that well; he doesn't even know she's gay.

They have nothing on Patrick and me. We've been learning about what matters about each other – how we feel, how we act, what's most important to us. I mean, yes, he doesn't know I'm autistic yet, but we understand each other.

Urgh, I regret pretending that I'm well enough. I'm groggy, like the edges of the world are still a bit muffled.

'You've all had a chance to think about your upcoming wedding,' Karina asks, confirming my suspicions. 'Whit and Malachi, what do you picture when you think of your wedding?'

I try to focus as they gush about this little church near Malachi's grandma's home in London. Luckily, it doesn't sound like what we want. I mean, I don't think we're having a church wedding.

The conversation moves on to Dolly and Warren and my thoughts grind to a halt when Warren says, 'We're weighing up some options, but one I really liked that I didn't expect to be my vibe was the beautiful old country house.'

You've got to be fucking kidding me. Of course they want the same place we do.

I must have made a face, because Lucas suddenly says, 'Uh oh, it looks like we might have some competition on our hands. Carys and Patrick, is that your dream venue too?'

I'm glad Patrick answers, because he's good natured and laughs the situation off. 'Yes, that's the kind of place we imagined getting married in. But what will be will be! We're just lucky to have each other.'

He gives me a happy wink, and I plaster on a smile. I need to remember who I'm trying to be here – the good girl, the dream wife, the homely one. That's who I am. And pouting like a little demon is just going to get people hating me. So, I do what I always do, and pick the cute option. 'I'd marry you anywhere,' I say dreamily, brushing back his floppy fringe.

'Oh, aren't they *so* cute,' sing-songs Karina, pressing the cards in her hand against her chest. 'And much nicer than me. I was insistent on a big venue.'

Lucas laughs, wrapping his arm around his wife's waist. 'Yes, you were. Do we think we'll get some Bridezillas in the mix here?'

I hate that term, but everyone laughs so I smile along with

them. I can totally sympathise with people who panic when their day isn't going to plan.

'May the best couple win,' Dolly says, practically confirming the truce is over. 'Which is us.'

Everyone else laughs at her joke even though I know it's not one; that's just what she thinks. I want to walk over and beat her about the head with my square of shiny plastic board.

Fine, Dolly. Let's go.

'Are we all ready?'

There's a thundering cry of *yes* which makes me dizzy.

This is fine. Everything is fine!

'First question,' begins Karina, and I feel my heart beating out of my chest in a way it hasn't since I sat Maths GCSE. 'Men, what's your favourite thing about your wife-to-be? Ladies, you write down what you think they like best.'

The squeak of marker pens on the boards gives me toothache.

What does Patrick like about me? I try to replay his proposal in my head. What did he say? The reason we were at the farm . . . kindness! I scribble it down on the board and realise everyone else is already done.

'And reveal your answers!'

Luckily, Patrick has written 'she's kind' so that's a match. A huge smile bursts across my face as we step forward. One down!

It's no surprise that Whit and Malachi have matching 'smart' and 'dead clever' answers. As the only other couple who have stepped forward, they are in line with us.

I try not to look too smug about it.

'Oh babe, you think I'm funny?' Bridget says. Her board has 'sexy' written on it. 'That's nice.'

Lina and Zack's mismatch is awkward. Her answer is 'interesting' whereas he has scribbled what looks like 'bum'.

I try not to crane my neck round, but Karina announces,

'It looks like Warren wrote "intelligent" and Dolly wrote "funny".'

'I do think you're bare funny, though,' he insists.

'Bit big headed that I put "funny" myself, though, isn't it?' she says with an awkward laugh.

One thing I've learned is that nice and kind aren't always the same thing. Kind is about doing things for others no matter how it benefits you. I can't help but wonder if, actually, Dolly deserves the 'kind'. She's not nice, but she is kind.

Lucas is well onto the next question. 'Ladies, what's your man's favourite breakfast?'

I have no idea about this, so I just scribble down 'croissant'. That's what people are always eating in London – there's a reason we have a Pret on every corner. The city runs on cheap espresso and stale pastries.

Only Dolly and Bridget get this one right, with a peanut butter and jam bagel and protein shakes for Warren and Jackson respectively.

Patrick's answer is Marmite toast.

'That's your *favourite*?' Malachi gasps. 'Of everything you could eat in the world for breakfast, you picked Marmite?'

'It's a good source of vitamin B!' Patrick protests.

'Oh, that's tragic,' says Whit. 'Live a little, man. You could be eating waffles!'

'With Marmite?' Bridget asks, her nose rucked up in disgust.

Whit shivers. 'I hope not.'

I wonder if Patrick knows what my favourite is. I probably would have put crêpes because of this morning, but ... is that true?

This round brings Dolly and Bridget in line with me.

Lina is still standing at the start.

'Come on, babe, you know I also love a green juice,' Zack groans. 'I made you one this morning!'

'In my defence,' she says, wiping clean her board, 'it was kind of gross.'

'That's very rude actually.' His lip curls into a pout.

I really am not sure I like him. I thought Jackson would be the one I'd be having to work hard to like, but at least he's pretty on the surface about being, well, *him*. There's something about Zack that gives me the weirds.

I really thought Lina was going to pick Cobey. She didn't want to talk about it in the warehouse, and we've not had time since because my brain's been leaking out my ears.

It's always strange when your friend brings home a boyfriend that you can't quite work out. Maybe she sees something in him that the rest of us can't yet.

'Men!' shouts Karina, commanding our attention. 'What did your fiancée want to be as a kid?'

I scribble down my answer, realising quickly that there's not actually a name for the person who builds safe crossings for hedgehogs so they don't get run over. When I talked to Dolly about it back in the warehouse, it took so much context to explain. I guess conservationist would be close, but I'm not sure we've even talked about it?

Needless to say, Patrick doesn't seem to know either, because he's written 'veterinarian'.

Dolly would have got it right.

'Close!' I say truthfully.

'Hang on, what does that say?' Patrick leans forward and squints rather than coming closer and leaving his designated position. 'Hedgehog road-crossing maker?'

'I don't think that's a job, honey,' says Malachi, who has correctly guessed that Whit was born to be a surgeon. 'But maybe it should be.'

'You could make it one,' insists Whit kindly.

'Surely I get half a point?' Zack says, pointing between his and Lina's boards because he wrote 'teacher' and she wrote 'Yoga teacher'.

'No half points in this challenge,' says Lucas.

'Ew, a mortician?' cries Bridget, and I know she is looking at Dolly's board – strange to know I'd also have got that right.

'I know, but it wasn't to be,' Dolly says dramatically.

'OMG why?'

'It's a bit of a dead-end career, isn't it?'

I can't help but snort-laugh at that. She *is* funny.

Warren knew about her morbid childhood ambitions, so they step forward, putting both Dolly and Whit ahead of me, with Bridget and I tying in second. Lina has not stepped forward at all.

I need to catch up or Dolly is going to take our venue from us.

'Ladies,' says Lucas in a way that makes me want to shiver. 'How many people has your man slept with?'

Oh. Shit. We haven't discussed that.

'Really? Breakfast and body counts?' Dolly calls with genuine annoyance, looking from the Nguyens to production. 'Is that what we're going for?'

'Shut up,' hisses Bridget. 'I know this one.'

It turns out she does not, unless Jackson has upped his number on purpose. When they reveal their boards, Bridget fixes him with a narrowed look. 'I guess I got it wrong,' she mutters.

I guessed one for Peony, and get it right. He's only been with one woman before me and he nearly married her? That's a strong bond.

It depresses me to see Lina and Zack have variations of *he lost count*. They finally get to step forward, but Lina looks like she wants the ground to swallow her.

'Oh, Zack, that's not right,' Dolly groans.

'That's kind of slut shaming, babes,' Bridget points out through gritted teeth. 'Even if it's gross for Zack to not remember the women he's slept with.'

'I wasn't keeping count,' he insists. 'Wouldn't it be creepier if I kept like a spreadsheet of them all?'

'Weirdly specific!' quips Dolly, which earns a scatter of *oohs* from Warren and Malachi. 'And we're not disgusted that you can't do maths – it hints at the way you might view women as disposable.'

I hate to agree with Dolly, but I do.

What *does* Lina see in Zack? I don't think they're faking their relationship. Does she think she can change him for the better? I know love means sometimes you don't notice the sheer number of red flags a person is furiously and often proudly waving in your face. I hope she doesn't think we're being mean.

Everyone got that right, so I'm still behind Dolly. Whit and Bridget too, but I doubt Bridget cares about getting married in England.

'Men, what are your fiancée's biggest turn-ons?' Karina says with a cheeky smile.

Would Patrick even know this? We've barely talked about physical intimacy.

The only person here I've slept with is Dolly. Would Warren know?

That night flashes through my mind. The wave of her body, how her mouth fell open after each kiss in a gasp, locking eyes with her as she made me orgasm.

I can't help it. My eyes slide over to her. It's a jolt through my body when I see she's looking right back at me.

'Hang on,' Zack shouts. 'The rule is we're not supposed to be sleeping together in the villa, so how would we know?'

'You could have still *talked* about it.' Bridget says this a little too quickly. We are all very aware they should know the answer to this.

But she's right. It's clear other couples have had a conversation about sex.

We could have talked about it. Shouldn't we have talked about it by now? I like kissing him, and I'm excited to explore more, but we've never been a sexual couple from the off. It's cute, comfortable.

I look down at my board and write 'neck kiss' because that's probably right. I do like it, as long as no one breathes into my ear as that sensory nightmare makes me think of pigs rooting for truffles.

There are things I like that I'm not going to write down on my board. My co-workers and family don't need to know I like to watch. Neck kiss is more appropriate.

It's quite awkward when everyone flips over their boards.

Some of the men are a little too proud, but to my surprise Bridget and Jackson's answers don't match — she actually likes dirty talk, not eye contact.

No surprise, though, that Zack and Lina don't match, even if it seems intuitive that she'd like massage and touch.

Malachi coyly reveals that Whit loves him whispering in her ear, which makes me think too much about mouth sounds.

I knew Dolly would write 'compliments'. Her ego loves to be flattered, after all.

'And what did you write, Patrick?' Lucas asks, waggling his eyebrows. 'What is Carys's biggest turn-on?'

I see Dolly wear a small smug smile which is *so* obvious. I clench my teeth together, knowing my smile is turning grimacey.

I wish she would get out of my head, and also my life while she's at it.

My oblivious fiancé goes bright red. 'Aha, well … We

haven't explored that side of things yet, but I know she likes to have her hair stroked as she falls asleep, so I put that.'

'If it makes her fall asleep, maybe it's technically a turn-off,' jokes Dolly.

Everyone laughs and I feel under a spotlight. Why did she have to bring more attention to this? Why did she have to open her mouth?

'At least my thing is not about my *ego*,' I say, trying to keep my voice light and teasing, but I think everyone hears the bite in it.

God, I knew I wouldn't get the tone right. I try to be really careful about banter. There's been a few too many times when I was younger that I went too far, without realising.

Not that I care about Dolly's feelings, but I do care about how it comes across to the public. I feel like she's rubbing off on me . . . which is a horrible choice of words.

Still, there's a chorus of *ooos* from the other couples. Bridget flashes me an impressed smile.

'Guess Carys really wants to win that venue. Better catch up then, girlie,' Dolly jeers. 'Wait, do you need me to shout? You're so far behind me after all.'

God, she's right. One more correct answer, and she wins. I need to get two in a row *and* her to get them both wrong for me to beat her.

'Cat fight!' hollers Zack, which is met with dead silence.

I can't help the growl that escapes my lips. 'Be a good sport, Dolly. Lina's even further behind, so you're whacking her too.'

Dolly cackles. 'You're the one who is pointing it out, you weapon!'

Lina waves her board that has the word *massage* smeared all over it. 'Oh, please don't bring me into this,' she begs.

'But she's disrespecting you, babe,' says Zack.

'Stop joining in,' she hisses at him. I'm pretty sure I catch her add, 'You're embarrassing me.'

That's when I finally turn back to face Patrick, who looks at me like I'm a stranger. And that feels much worse than everything else so far.

'Well! What a spirited game,' says Karina, trying to get us all back on track.

Mean-spirited, more like.

'We have one last question for the ladies about their men,' Lucas says. 'Whit and Dolly, if either of you get this right, you and your partner win. If there's a tie, we'll go to a bonus round. The rest of you, this is your last chance to catch up, so ya'll better hope they don't know this one.'

Karina looks down at her cards and clears her throat. 'Okay, this might be a tricky one. Ladies, what does your man say is his biggest fear?'

God, I have no idea. Patrick is so steady that I can't imagine him saying anything. I pick mice and hope for the best.

Apparently it's heights.

'I'm a vet.' He seems upset I might accuse him of being scared of a patient, like it's a professional slight.

As awful as it is, I can only focus on the fact that I got it wrong and so haven't moved forward.

Somehow, Whit is the only person who correctly guesses that Malachi's greatest fear is 'falling down a well and no one hearing me and getting stuck there for so long I have to eat my toes' which is weirdly, verbatim, what he has written on his board.

Together, they step forward to the blue line, and seal their win with a kiss. I guess they really do know each other well, or have a psychic connection because that was highly specific.

'Congratulations, Whit and Malachi, our winners!' cries Karina excitedly.

Dolly and Warren take second place, Bridget and Jackson tie for third with Patrick and me.

Lina and Zack come in last place. 'Oh well,' Lina laughs

and drops her board to the floor. 'I've never really been one for winning.'

I can't help but notice the tension in Zack's body, the tightness of his mouth.

'Me either, babes,' sighs Bridget. 'Hopefully we still get to pick somewhere good.'

'Speaking of which,' Lucas says, 'Whit and Malachi, do you know which venue you'd like to secure?'

'Well, obviously we'd like to reserve the church, wouldn't we?' Whit smiles adoringly at Malachi.

Malachi drops his voice, and holds her so tenderly. 'Are you sure? I want it to be special for you.'

Whit kisses him on the tip of his nose. 'I love you for pausing to check that. But yes. Let's get married there!'

The Nguyens applaud as Whit and Malachi embrace, and I feel a hollow ache in my chest as I look at them, so deeply in love. They seem to take in every piece of each other. I'm not sure anyone else has built a relationship that even comes close to their intuitive bond.

When I look at Patrick, do the others see the same kind of love? Patrick looks at me like I'm sunshine, but not like I'm the world. I can shine on him, even blind him a little to what I am. But all I really want is for him to see everything of me, and still want to stay.

God, I'm so tired. I'm so tired that I want to go lie down and cry and not sit here listening to everyone who beat us talk about their wedding venue of choice.

I'm steeling myself for the punch when the Nguyens ask Dolly and Warren what their choice is.

To my surprise, and apparently Dolly's, Warren says, 'If it's alright, we'd like to check a couple of things before we decide? There was lots of good information about logistics, so we just want to check some things first.'

Are they allowed to do this? I can't tell if it would be worse to prolong this situation or just get it over with now.

Either way I feel like I'm going to pass out from standing up and trying for so long, and the fire in my brain runs straight to my mouth. 'So we have to sit in limbo while you make up your minds?' I say before I can hold back the words, and I *hate* the look that passes over Patrick's eyes. 'Sorry, I—' I stumble with hot shame flushing my face. God, why did I speak?

'We'll try and be quick about accommodating your wants while we check accessibility of the event space,' Dolly says, smiling a little too wide. 'I don't want to put you out.'

'That's not what I meant, and you know that, Dolly,' I insist, my voice turning whiny when I wanted it to be firm, confident, honest. I can't get control of myself. Work-Carys won't appear. Girlfriend-Carys is gone. I can't find the right mask to slip onto my face. I feel a frog lodge in my throat, and light whitens, like someone turned up the sun.

Dolly looks like she's about to say something else, when Warren calmly interrupts, 'I understand. We're cool. We will let you know as soon as we've made a decision.'

The Nguyens wrap up the challenge and make us give each other a half-hearted round of applause, but I am barely there. I don't process any of it. When they tell us the cameras are off, I sprint to the bathroom to vomit up all the feelings bursting through my skin.

Chapter Twenty-One

Dolly

> **@potatofiend:** sorry did Zack put his greatest fear as being cancelled! What skeletons are in his closet?
>
> **@5ft2bexact:** I know @potatofiend. Can you believe Jackson wasn't the one with the weirdest answer?
>
> **@regularsizedhorse:** To be fair to Warren big slugs are terrifying

Rather impressive they could get it all this quickly, but why couldn't we have had that upfront?

While the big country house having accommodation solved some problems and it's tempting to steal it from Carys, surprise, surprise, there's no lifts anywhere. Still, it's tempting to steal it from Carys just to fuck her over.

I really want us to get married in the Barbican Conservatory. I can't stop thinking of how warm and beautiful it will be under that sunlight, surrounded by plants. If I was getting married for real, this would be the place I'd pick.

But there's a few hitches: how do we get people there, where will everyone stay, how accessible can we make the rest of the wedding beyond the venue itself?

Warren pokes me in the gap between my eyebrows. 'Your brain is going to set on fire with all that thinking.'

'I just want to get it right,' I insist, peering at him over the top of my sunglasses. 'This is the first big decision, so it feels important.'

Warren nods slowly. 'Come on.' He stands up, taking my hand and the rest of me with him. 'We need to cool that brain off with a little dip, yeah?'

I immediately work out what he means. Getting in the pool is our opportunity to talk freely. Or free-ish. Every day, when we'd get mic'd up, the production assistants had stressed repeatedly that we could not get them wet without causing significant damage, and that we shouldn't spend too long in the pool either, presumably because we can only swim mic-less. I suspect they hope that most people don't want to ruin their hair and makeup so won't swim.

The camera crew have left us alone because, surprisingly, two people reading through email printouts is actually not that exciting, especially when Bridget, Jackson, Lina and Zack are playing with a hacky sack Lina brought with her (presumably from the early 2000s).

I still haven't worked out if there are hidden microphones or cameras. I just don't want to trust it. I got away with it last time but who is to say I will be as lucky again.

I instinctively press my hand over my pelvis. The dull ache of a flare is starting to set in, but I think I've got time before things get distinctly *Jaws*-level pool unfriendly.

We leave our mic packs on the sun loungers and, always a gentleman, Warren guides me down the pool steps into the warm water. I wrap my body around him like a koala on a tree. He's so tall and the pool is so shallow that he has to crouch so that our heads are at water level.

'Talk to me,' he whispers in my ear.

'I just worry that getting everyone there will be such a faff,' I say honestly. 'I don't particularly want to leave it to chance that they will understand the complexities of accessibility.'

Let's be real, given neither Carys or I disclosed our disabilities to them doesn't exactly fill me with hope that they will do a good job.

'Okay, so we'll handle it. We're a team, right?'

I lick my lips and consider it. 'We're a team. Can we pick the Conservatory then?'

He sighs happily. 'Good work on saying the thing you want.'

'I always say what I want, don't I?' I say, a little confused.

'Mmhmm.' His voice vibrates against my body and through the water around us. 'We will look fire in that natural light. Golden hour?'

'God, the photos would be perfect.'

'And, it has the bonus of not pissing off Little Miss Red. Unless you wanted that?'

I cackle. 'You noticed that?'

'*Everyone* noticed that. She's wound so tight. And why's she got beef with you exactly?'

I consider telling him the truth. After all, he knows everything else. But I'm too much of a coward to tell him the whole of it. 'Not sure. Unfortunately, I do enjoy winding her up. It'll make such good TV.'

'As long as people don't think you're deep in feelings with Patrick.' He leans back to look me in the face. 'Please, he's a nice boy but my ego couldn't take the rejection. The man spends his days with his arm inside a cow.'

'You know, people *love* a love triangle. Would you fight Patrick for me?' I bat my eyelashes at him.

'Absolutely not. I'm a lover not a fighter, baby. But I bet you'd love to have two people fight over you.'

'Honestly, I would. Is that bad? Am I very shallow?'

He bursts into laughter. 'Like this pool.'

It's my turn to cackle.

But when it cools, I realise that now is the time to tell him the truth about me, if not about Carys.

'But there is something I do want to tell you, while we're here.'

'Is it about you asking me if I thought I'd fall in love here, and how you dodged me asking it back?'

'You noticed that, huh.'

'I notice a lot. I don't want to make assumptions, but—' Here he begins splashing water with his hands, like he's tapping out a drum. I realise, with great love for this man, that he's being sure that no one will be able to pick up this audio, just in case. 'I didn't think you were interested in men full stop.'

'Well,' I say, feeling the shake in my hands as I clutch onto him like a life raft. 'Yeah. I'm gay.'

'That's cool with me, I promise.'

He stops splashing and instead walks us round the middle of the pool. 'Oh, my bestie is a Libra too,' he says lightly, like we've just been discussing astrological signs, instead of me coming out to my straight fake husband.

I glance over to the hacky sack and cameras, but no one notices us.

'Is she a basketball player too?' I murmur.

'You bet.'

'Perhaps you shouldn't invite her to the wedding, just to be safe. She'll be mobbed.'

'People love a Libra, huh.'

I snort-laugh.

I want to ask him about his own attraction, about whether he's strictly into girls or if he's ever dabbled. But that question is much more dangerous for him as I am pretty certain that being a professional sportsman is not the most queer-friendly career for men. I want to protect him.

I knew, in my heart, that this would be a safe conversation with Warren. It was never about him, but the geography, the surveillance, the safety. I'm so glad he understands.

I kiss him on the cheek. 'Thanks for being chill about it.'

'Listen to me when I say that there's nothing here to be unchill about. We're partners. I got you.' He squeezes me tightly, just to punctuate it. 'Even if our moon signs probably clash or something.'

God, this man. 'I adore you,' I tell him honestly.

His deep laugh rumbles through my heart. 'Don't go falling in love with me now,' he whispers.

'Darling, if I could love a man, you'd be it for me.' I peck him on the lips, and it feels real, in a way. We're not *in* love, but I do love him.

~

I was hoping that we'd get the afternoon off after a challenge, but they send us all out on individual dates. In reality TV land, a 'week' is often just a few days with lots of outfit changes. I suppose, with a tight budget, they want us in and out of this house as quickly as possible.

Inexplicably, they send Warren and me waterskiing and I have to submit to the fact that there will be footage of me with my arse waggling in the air circulating the internet in a few days' time. At least it's a good arse.

After we've humiliated ourselves, we give them good relationship content over champagne – conversations about our favourite things, the future, our wedding. Real couple stuff that gives Warren a chance to shine as a responsible husband and bastion of a thoughtful form of masculinity without the toxicity. I'm here for it, and I know his DMs will be flooded the moment we announce our notes app breakup.

We're dropped back home in the early evening, where

production serve us a buffet of grilled meats, pitas, dips and salad on the communal table – one of the few times we don't get filmed. I can't wait to get in a shower to get this salt off my skin, but I take advantage of being a fat girl eating off camera and shovel forkfuls of oily leaves into my face.

All the couples except for Carys and Patrick are here. I'm not sure what everyone else has been up to, but Malachi and Whit are splattered in dried paint, and Bridget and Jackson look a little too pink.

Unfortunately, I clock production preparing for more filming when they wheel by several clothing rails.

I jump up, and rush over to a very sweaty and tired-looking Reb who is pushing them in. 'Hey, babe. What's this?'

'Costumes,' she says flatly, before wincing. She turns to me, sleep-deprived and bruised dark eyes pleading. 'I didn't say that.'

I mime zipping my lips closed, and she gives me a look of relief.

Because we'd chosen the Conservatory, Bridget and Jackson got the okay to pick their venue, and so she tells us about how they've gone off-piste. 'I've had the Georgian drawing room at Cardiff Castle on reserve just in case,' Bridget explains. 'Good for us because it's *fit*, and good for them to get the free filming.'

'I'm impressed that you managed to get Sunset Motions to agree to that,' I say, knowing the venues often have agreed promotion deals.

She taps her nose. 'None of the venues were in Wales, were they. Told them they were being too Anglocentric and they shat their pants for not being woke enough.' She cackles gleefully. 'Win win!'

Well, fair enough. I can't act like I wouldn't also try to imply the show wasn't being inclusive enough to get my own way. Perhaps I've been underestimating Bridget. Not Jackson, he's very clearly who it says he is on the tin – a gender essentialist dickhead who thinks caregiving is an affront to his masculinity. I hope I'm wrong about him, for her sake, but I know I'm not.

Despite everything, I notice the moment that Carys wanders in, tucked under Patrick's arm, followed by a cameraman. They look . . . kind of uncomfortable.

They both sit down opposite Warren and me, with hellos from Patrick and nothing from Carys. Bridget asks them about their day, and Patrick explains they went to a sushi-making class.

I realise that they probably don't know that it's their turn to pick their venue.

'Hey,' I begin. 'Warren and I decided we're going with the Barbican.'

At this, the camera swings round, clearly filming us. Shit, I was enjoying wolfing down dinner, and I had to go and bring up something plot relevant. Everyone sits up a little straighter.

'That just felt right for us,' I continue carefully. 'And that means you guys get your dream venue too. A win all round.'

'Oh, Dolly, that's so kind of you,' Patrick beams.

I see Carys's eyes dart from me to the camera so quickly that I almost miss it. She's suspicious, but she knows it's time to put on a show.

'Thank you for always being so considerate,' she says, so sweetly that my teeth ache. 'Can I take the opportunity to apologise for my behaviour earlier?' Her eyes are wide with false sincerity.

I reach out and take her hand, ignoring the spark of heat that rushes through me. 'It's okay. Thank you for apologising. I get a little too competitive, so I'm sorry for my part too.'

She sinks a sharp nail into my palm and I try not to wince. 'No, really, it was *me* who was being out of line.'

Patrick looks very confused about what is going on, and Warren coughs to disguise his laugh.

'I know we're not here to make friends, and we don't have to be that,' I say, hammering home last night's point, because that's what she wants to hear, isn't it? 'But I really admire you for this apology. That's very vulnerable of you.'

Carys gently pats at our joined hands with her free one, and I feel her sharp fingernail hammering against my palm. I'm not quite sure if she's trying to turn me on, but there's something rife for psychosexual analysis happening to my body. It's frustrating to be so chemically attracted to someone who is in actuality a total mess.

'And I appreciate you for being so open to it. You're always so thoughtful,' she adds.

'Are you two quite done kissing and making up?' Bridget asks loudly.

I get a tiny thrill at the flush on Carys's cheeks. I hate to admit that fighting might be almost as fun as fucking her.

Finally Lina and Zack arrive, looking too oily like they've just stepped out of the massage parlour. 'Oh no,' she says, upon spotting yet more clothing trolleys being wheeled in. 'What are *those*?'

'Challenge time,' Bridget says, and I'm not sure if that's her own deduction or if she heard Reb and me whispering. 'I have my suspicions about which one.'

'Come on,' Whit sighs. 'Don't leave us hanging.'

Bridget smiles broadly. 'It's got to be the Pulse Race Challenge, babes. Sexy costumes and dancing. It's time to try to make everyone horny!'

I spy Carys's eyes flicking up to me and away, over and over. That, my friends, is gay panic in action.

This morning was bad enough. Basically any time one of the Nguyens' questions was about sex, she looked at me in the most *obvious* way.

Compulsory heterosexuality may be a deep closet to hide yourself in, but I wonder how obvious it is to everyone else that she keeps peeking her head out.

Fair play, it's not like the idea of all of us dancing around in tiny underwear masquerading as costumes isn't exciting to me. Carys must be losing her mind in among the mothballs.

I shouldn't enjoy this. I shouldn't. But, oh, this is going to be *good*.

Chapter Twenty-Two

Carys

@potatofiend: How do you look angry while getting massaged by your future wife? I swear there's something up with Zack!

@mellytonin: omg Patrick makes such good sushi I wish he'd make sushi for me

@missgoss: You could not pay me to go paintballing

It's quite possible that this is the longest day of my life. Why *why why* didn't I watch the show before I applied? Stupid me thought it was all cute dates and hopes and dreams, not trying to set everyone's heart racing through sexy dancing on national television.

When Reb came through and confirmed it was indeed the Pulse Race Challenge (as it's apparently dubbed) she gave me another of her *are you up to it?* looks. No, but what can I do? I'm going to crash out hard later, once I've given five men including my future husband a lap dance, apparently.

While I was still getting my head round it, we got sent up to our dressing rooms with the costume rails, along with an armband each, with a little pulse monitor hidden in it.

I didn't even get a chance to talk to Patrick about it. This will be the first time he's seen me in any kind of lingerie, and he's sharing the experience with four other men. Plus, he's definitely a little upset with me. While we were rolling sushi, he asked if I was feeling alright during the challenge. I know what that means. It's the sort of way my parents used to tell me I was acting out of order, enquiring whether I thought that behaviour was normal for me, with the implication that it's not acceptable.

I'm not sure I've ever felt quite so small. I cried and I told him Dolly got under my skin, and the tail end of that migraine meant I didn't use my best judgement.

He was kind, because of course he was, but I could still see that hesitation in his eyes. I can't lose him. That's why I have to show him that I care about him, and I'm going to do that by taking this challenge seriously. This way, he'll see I'm willing to do anything for us.

The first step is picking out a costume.

'I really don't think you're the hot little devil kind of girl,' Bridget says, contemplating the costumes in front of us. She wears angel wings, with a matching white lingerie bodice and thigh-high lace stockings. I cannot imagine wearing that at all, never mind on television. 'Though you definitely have a temper on you.'

'I don't,' I say sharply. 'I'm perfectly calm.'

She gives me a knowing look. 'Devil goes in the maybe pile.'

'How do you even do sexy? This might be the worst night of my life,' I moan.

Bridget cackles. 'Oh, no fear, babes. I'm pretty confident Jackson and I have this locked down.' She doesn't say it meanly, I don't think.

I can't imagine Jackson raising my pulse from sexy dancing. Anger maybe. Perhaps his tactic is just to stand there and say sexist things in my general direction. I'm trying, I am, but at dinner he kept talking about Traditional Family Values and I wanted to crawl under the table.

'We'd match. Angel and devil.'

She pats me on the shoulder. 'Sure, babes, but remember we *are* competing. We can matchy-costume another time.'

The devil costume goes back on the rack.

I wonder what Patrick has picked. Neither of us particularly exude sexiness, not like some of the others in here. We're cute-type.

I have no idea how exactly I'm supposed to get anyone's heart racing. The most beating mine does is from anxiety. Perhaps when it's my turn, I should ask everyone to think about their deepest existential fears. There's probably a rule against that.

Maybe Bridget's right. We won't win, but I can still give it my best. For him, for us.

But how to do that without grinding on the other men so enthusiastically that it makes him uncomfortable?

Clearly, Bridget has read my mind. 'Look, babe, one option you have is just to dance up on him and take the loss. Keep your pride?'

'What about the cowboy hat and the little shorts?' suggests Lina, who sits in a towel, redoing her makeup. 'You work on a farm after all? Kind of cutesy.'

'It's not about her story as much as what will get Patrick excited,' Bridget says, pushing the tiny shorts to the end of the rail. 'Unless. Does he have a thing for cowboys?'

'It's a maybe,' I say.

'A maybe on cowboys?'

'On the outfit,' I insist, unhooking the shorts and holding them against me. 'I'm not as confident as you, Bridge. I don't want everyone seeing my—' I gesture in the area around my crotch.

Bridget is perplexed. 'What? Your fanny?'

'Yes,' I hiss.

'Well, don't go bum-naked, and they won't,' she says flatly and clearly unimpressed that I can't manage to say *fanny* out loud.

'I don't think many of these leave much to the imagination, though,' I moan.

'That's the point!' She presses her palm against her forehead. 'You're hopeless, Carys.'

I discard another option that seems to be some kind of lingerie animal ear combo. 'What did you pick, Lina?'

'I've got an idea.' It's her turn to sigh. 'I'm not sure what Zack would like . . .'

'What do *you* feel sexy in, though?' calls Dolly. For a blissful few moments, I'd forgotten she was here. Well, not truly because she's so irritating that I always know when she's nearby. But she's been tucked in the corner doing her makeup, outfit chosen already. As she's the only one who wears plus-size, she had her own rack to choose from.

'Nothing,' says Lina a little too honestly. 'But I don't think that would be allowed.'

'We air after the watershed,' says Dolly. 'Go for the closest thing to that?'

Lina's face brightens, and she takes something from the rack that looks like a pair of tights and disappears.

I wonder what Dolly is going to wear. Has she gone for the 'little more than underwear' route? I flinch as I remember her on her back, and shove through the rack some more.

'Lads, I feel a bit creeped out,' groans Whit, still in a robe. 'Like, I know the rule is if we get everyone hot then Malachi and I win, but I feel kind of weird about that.'

'Same,' I sigh, discarding another *I'm a mouse, duh*-type outfit.

'It's just a bit of fun, babes.' Bridget slides the hangers along the rack in a sudden violent motion, revealing a very short, laced-up dress. 'That one.'

I don't have any time to say no. It's *so* not me. But it's better than the rest.

Costume secured, I take off the remains of today's melted makeup and work out what will go with this dress. A smoky eye, I think. I can probably do that.

The problem is the whole time Dolly won't shut up. I know she's just trying to give Whit a pep talk, but could she just be quieter about it?

I said I'd be good, for Patrick. I don't need to rise to her. Easier said than done when I'm filled with a hot, pricking irritation whenever she's around.

'Just keep your eyes on the prize,' Dolly tells Whit. 'Sorry to all you girls, but I think I've got the best teammate of the lot of you.'

This is when I lose it. *Dolly* doesn't even fancy her own fiancé, or any men! How would she even know what gets their pulses racing?

'That's a bit fucking rude, Dolly,' I snap.

Everyone goes silent for a long moment, broken only by Bridget going 'Oops' before giggling awkwardly.

'Carys, I obviously didn't mean it in a bad way.' I can tell she's trying to keep her voice steady to hide how much I've pissed her off. I wish I didn't like knowing that so much. 'I'm not calling your men uggos. I'm just trying to get everyone in the friendly competition mood, right?'

'Sorry, I just think it's a bit weird to imply we might all fancy your fiancé.'

'It's not that deep, Carys,' says Whit, patting me on the shoulder as she passes. 'Bridget basically just said the same thing.'

I feel the urge to defend Bridget but she just shrugs. 'Yeah, I did.'

'Dolly seems to think it's deep,' I insist. 'Doesn't that bother you guys?'

Whit says 'Nope' loudly but Bridget and Lina remain silent.

'See, they agree with me,' I say, overreaching, but I don't care. 'She's so blatantly here for the wrong reasons. We can all see it.'

'What even is the right reason?' Dolly murmurs, keeping her eyes off me.

'I just think we need to be careful of snakes in the grass,' I mutter.

I see her reflection change, ever so slightly, and her eyes dart to me.

Come on, Dolly, fight back. She can't always play the good guy, like earlier when she handed us the wedding venue like it was blessed bread, even though we'd spent the whole day worrying in case she took away my dream. Our dream. She can't just wipe away all that wasted energy with a gift.

I think for a moment that she's going to leave. Right up until her face turns into an exaggerated pout, like a sad cartoon duckling. 'Oh no. Is it easier to come at me when you're worried men don't want to fuck you?' she hisses.

'Dolly,' warns Whit. 'Just ignore her.'

'Sorry, Whit, but I'm a little tired of *insecure* people taking their own issues out on the rest of us.' Her eyes slide over to me, and her lip curls. 'It's embarrassing, really.'

'Fuck you,' I snap.

Lina gasps. 'Carys, that's not okay.'

She and Whit look at me like I'm unrecognizable. I went too far, didn't I?

The familiar pit opens beneath my feet and I'm about to fall ... right up until Dolly mouths, 'You already did.'

The girls could have seen that! My heart races as Dolly's eyebrows rise in a challenge.

'Alright, girls, save it for the lap dances or whatever,' Bridget says, dragging me away from staring angrily at Dolly. In the bathroom she shoves the dress into my hands. 'Don't blow your engine now. Just beat her.'

Script: The Pulse Race Challenge

[All the women sit in a row on a deep bench seat in dressing robes, while Karina and Lucas Nguyen, in matching gold lamé bikini and swim shorts respectively, watch over from the balcony upstairs.]

KARINA It's time for the Pulse Race Challenge! The spiciest *Wedded Bliss* challenge, where couples work together in a display of sexuality and confidence.

LUCAS Each contestant has chosen their own costumes and music in the hope that they will titillate their partner and the other contestants on the men's or women's side. Remember the winners will be the couple who collectively raise the pulses the most.

KARINA Okay, ladies, I'm already warmed up just standing here. *[She glances at Lucas and giggles.]* Now it's time for the men to get your hearts racing!

Music: 'Doctor (Work It Out)' – Pharrell feat. Miley Cyrus

[Patrick walks in wearing scrubs, pretending to check over the women by listening to their breathing and hearts with his stethoscope. Close up as he leans in to kiss Carys while the girls scream.]

LUCAS Now he looks like just what the doctor ordered.

KARINA Darling, I think he's a vet.

[Close up on Dolly laughing.]

Music: *Gladiators* theme tune

[Short excerpt of Zack dancing as a Roman gladiator grinding his crotch in the women's politely baffled faces.]

KARINA   I think that might be a thumbs down from the audience.

Music: 'Talk Dirty' – Jason Derulo feat. 2 Chainz

[Jackson walks in dressed as a devil carrying a pitchfork, and first grinds against it slowly. Long close ups on each woman as he dances. He places Bridget's heel on his chest, and licks all the way up her knee to the top of her thigh. Zoom in on Carys looking terrified.]

LUCAS   If evil looks like that, I'm not sure I want to be good!

Music: 'Hotel Room Service' – Pitbull

[Malachi wears black trousers, white shirt cuffs and a black bow tie. As the music begins, he rips off the trousers to reveal tiny sequinned black pants. Cut to the girls scream-laughing. Cut back to close up as Malachi picks up Whit, wrapping her legs around his waist, and carries her off.]

KARINA   Now that is service with a smile.

Music: 'Gasolina' – Daddy Yankee

[Warren runs in dribbling a basketball, oiled up so his muscles shine, and wearing only a pair of basketball shorts. He does some tricks to make the women laugh. Then, in a display of strength, he picks up

every woman in turn, raising them into the air and spinning them round. Finally, he takes Dolly into his arms, kissing her deeply, before throwing her over his shoulder in a fireman's lift.]

LUCAS   Well ... Wow. What do you even say to a man who can do that?

KARINA   *[looks to camera]* Pick me up next?

Chapter Twenty-Three

Carys

> **@mellytonin:** I love that Patrick didn't do the sexy dances. He's so loyal to Carys!!!
>
> **@regularsizedhorse:** Dear @WeddedBlissUK please find some men with rizz for s2
>
> **@wokemacarena:** I'm vomming at that leg lick

I thought after seeing the men go first, the waiting wouldn't be so bad. But after the screams of laughter and delight, I'm not sure I can make anyone feel that good.

Bless Patrick, he did a pretty good job and went the comedy route instead of trying to be sexy. Honestly I prefer that. I might have felt strange if I saw him lick another girl's ear, but Bridget seemed to enjoy watching Jackson do that.

It'll be less weird when he meets my family if they haven't seen him oiled up. Not that it's a bad thing, but I'd never hear the end of it.

Production pick the order we go in, I guess because they've cued up the songs.

It's Dolly's turn to go first, and I try to pay attention in a way that seems the appropriate amount. We haven't spoken since the dressing room – I think the girls were ready to put us in a timeout if we started up again.

She walks out in a navy silk robe and as the rumbling, fuzzy beat of 'Vigilante Shit' by Taylor Swift starts playing, she loosens it. The silk slides down her skin, and I hate the way my heart skips a beat as I follow the falling fabric tracing her thighs. Underneath she wears a completely see-through fishnet bodysuit under a black leather bodice.

The men gasp, she smiles, and my skin prickles.

One by one, she dances slowly on the men. It's all eye contact and slow movement, edging them closer and closer to begging.

I'm vaguely aware that the other girls are screaming next to me, and I know I should be doing the same. But I can't make a sound. My throat is caught.

It can't be that weird, can it? Maybe the other girls are getting turned on too. Voyeurism is sexy, and we're watching our men get turned on.

That's all it is.

That's *all* it is.

I can plead with myself but as she whispers something in Malachi's ear, I'm transported back to that night. The way she traced my skin, made me wait for her touch. I see it here now, in how she performs for these men.

When she gets to Patrick, she lowers herself onto one of his legs, and grinds her body along. I know she's doing that just to fuck with me, but all I feel is a deep pulsing heat between my legs.

Every gyration is a sense memory on my skin. I lick my lips, bite down on them to distract myself, but I'm flooded with the scent of her perfume, the ghost of her biting my bottom lip, and nipping down my neck.

Her final dance is for Warren, teasing, teasing. Never

touching. And when she finally does, with just a fingernail along his jaw, it's like I feel it on my skin.

I'm on fire. I'm wet. I feel like I want to die if she doesn't touch me.

It's only when Bridget nudges me and shouts, 'Doesn't she look fab?' that I wake up from the possession. I nod vigorously and laugh excitedly like the other girls, clapping along. I even throw out a *whoo*.

I try to get a hold of myself, I really do. I try to forget.

But when she turns around to face us as she lowers herself down onto Warren's lap, I can't stop looking at the crease between her breasts. I want to run my tongue down that line, all the way down.

Bridget nudges me again. 'You alright, babe?'

'Just nervous,' I bleat. 'And, you know, urgh *Dolly*.'

Bridget lingers a little too long on me. 'Yeah, babe.'

When the music cuts out, I'm pretty sure I can hear my own heart beating in my ears.

And when she stands up, Dolly looks right at me and smiles.

Fuck.

Chapter Twenty-Four

Dolly

@silksiobhan: Anyone notice Dolly kept looking back at the girls? Was she dead nervous or something?

@wishiwasachair: @silksiobhan I think Or Something...

@silksiobhan: Okay @wishiwasachair I'm glad it's not just me!!!!

I know Carys is watching, and wanting me.

When I open my legs, her mouth falls open. She remembers.

If she insists on lying to herself and being a total bitch to me in public, then I'm going to enjoy watching her squirm a little.

My curves look poured into the latex of this bodice and the men eat up every inch of me. So many men say they don't fancy fat girls, but I see their desire, naked and raw. I may not be used to seeing men writhing around underneath me, but I recognise the hunger on their faces.

Carys wears it too.

If I were less petty, I might want her to close her trap, remember to be angry at me instead of less obviously desperate to fuck me again lest someone notice. I *should* care that her naked desire might be seen, but I don't.

It's all for me, in spite of herself. And that is doubly delicious.

When the song ends, I turn away from the men, so they get a good view of my delicious rump, and slowly bend down to pick up my silk robe from the floor. I walk away with it slung over my shoulder, rolling my hips with every step. The men are still hollering, so hopefully I'm high up the rankings.

All I can see as I walk back is Carys, awkwardly clapping while trying to gather herself.

If the cameras do spot this, it'll be great fodder if they're still chasing the love triangle about Patrick, given I did just pretend to rub myself off on his leg.

I wonder what will crumble that relationship first: his love for another woman, or hers?

'Wow, dude, that was incredible!' squeals Whit.

'Oh my God, even I'm all hot and bothered after all that,' laughs Bridget, fanning herself with her hand. I see Carys shoot her a confused look.

'Hopefully the men are too,' I tease.

I should have known not to go there because misery guts immediately kicks off again. 'See? Just like I told you,' growls Carys.

To their credit, the other three look a bit fed up of her shit.

I display a frankly enormous amount of restraint in not immediately pushing her into the pool.

'It's a *game*, Carys,' I say, trying to bite back the snap I want it to come out as.

Lina takes Carys by the arm and turns her away from me. 'Is this kicking up some feelings of abandonment for you?'

'Or jealousy,' mutters Whit.

'I just—' she splutters. 'It's just—'

Obviously she can't say she thinks I'm a faker because I don't think they care. Or the truth, which is *this bitch broke my little gay heart* or *I am attracted to her and I hate it because it's a constant reminder that I'm lying to myself.*

'Come on, babe, don't be like this,' says Bridget, taking her other arm. 'I've got to go waggle my bits in front of Patrick next. You can't get bothered with me about it, so don't stress about her either.'

I slightly resent the use of *her* like I'm not there, but it feels like looking a gift horse in the mouth when Bridget's just trying to keep the peace.

With both Lina and Bridget on her arms, Carys looks like she's about to be escorted off the premises. 'Fine, sorry,' she says, not sorry at all. But she's embarrassed, and that's good enough for me. 'I'm just nervous and being a dickhead.'

She said it, not me.

Bridget dons some enormous, feathered angel wings that strap on over her shoulders, helped by Lina, who then agrees to go assist Whit into her costume.

That leaves just Carys and me to cheer Bridget on from the sidelines. We're alone, or alone as can be, and I know she's thinking about that too, from the furtive, angry little sideglances she keeps giving me. I don't put the robe back on, just to fuck with her.

The opening beats of 'Maneater' by Nelly Furtado play, and Bridget struts out, an angel in lingerie. There's not much left to the imagination, let's just say that. Bridget has the type of body that all the geezer boys on *Love Island* call a pocket rocket: toned, tanned and petite. The boys fall over themselves as she does moves that I didn't know existed.

'I thought we were okay,' I say, keeping my voice low, and speak without looking at her. 'After our talk the other night.'

'It was a temporary truce,' she says between gritted teeth.

'So that's it? I help you and you get to treat me like shit?'

'I'm not doing *anything*,' she says, but I can tell she doesn't believe it. 'You're the one who—' She abruptly ends that sentence.

While everyone is distracted by Bridget's aggressive humping, I lean over to Carys, who gasps when my mouth brushes her neck.

'Carys,' I whisper and she shivers in delight. Her body can't tell lies like her mouth can. 'Stop acting like a spoiled brat.'

I snap back to face the men, as though nothing has happened. Out of the corner of my eye, I see her reel at the sudden end to the moment.

I concentrate on cheering on Bridget as she sits on Jackson's face.

'Fucking hell,' laughs Whit as she and Lina return.

The music ends, and Bridget slides off Jackson to a round of applause from us all.

Lina performs to 'Toxic' by Britney Spears in a *Wedded Bliss* budget version of the iconic nude diamanté bodysuit, and mostly writhes around on the floor. Her final move is a handstand. Slowly, her feet fall to either side of Zack's shoulders so that her ass is in his face, and twerks mid-air. It's strangely captivating.

'I don't think I've ever seen anyone do that before,' whispers Bridget as though she hadn't just executed a gravity-defying performance of her own.

'I think I should start doing Pilates,' murmurs Whit.

'Oh well,' Lina laughs as the music ends and she runs right into Bridget's arms. 'I gave it a go!'

Suddenly autotuned *yeahs* sound all around us signalling that it's Whit's turn to dance, apparently to 'Pony' by Ginuwine.

We all go nuts as Whit walks out dressed in a firefighter's orange hat, low slung trousers hanging on by braces, and allover kind of sporty white underwear.

Look, for a straight woman, she has *incredible* lesbian energy. The gay corners of social media are never going to recover from this moment, not least because of the hose, which she wields between her legs like the world's largest strap.

'It's getting hot in here!' she yells, trying to hold the laugh out of her voice mostly unsuccessfully. The hose turns on, and Whit sprays a light mist all over the men, gyrating to the music the whole time.

It might be the best thing I've ever seen.

The men go feral. Warren laps the spray out of the air, Patrick whoops, Malachi looks like he's about to fuck Whit right then and there.

She is just *so good*, the perfect intersection of horny and silly and hot – like all good sex is.

After, Whit struts back to us with the biggest grin on her face as everyone screams and applauds. 'That was a bit good, wasn't it?'

I pull her into a hug. 'The absolute best!'

'I almost want to borrow this . . .' says Bridget, admiring her hose.

'You're up,' Whit says to Carys. 'Good luck.'

Carys runs her tongue over her cherry-red bottom lip. 'Yeah. Guess I am,' she says, flicking her long cinnamon hair over one shoulder.

She drops her robe at my feet. She is wearing the tiniest dress known to man with thigh-high patent leather boots.

Fuck me.

She struts out to the boys as the music begins. I don't immediately recognise the song, but the lines about having to taste her when you kiss someone else ring in my heart like an alarm.

The men are stunned that cute Carys can look like this, all wide-eyed, mouths hanging open. Patrick looks like all his birthday wishes came true.

The skirt of her little Oktoberfest-type dress poofs out so we can all see the bright white knickers she wears underneath. The back is laced up in a bodice, and I can't help but think about loosening those ties, slipping my hand up that tiny skirt. Insisting she keep the boots on.

When she steps one foot up on the back of the bench next to Patrick and leans forward to kiss him, I almost die.

I worry I look too clearly into this, but luckily, the other women can't look away either as Carys circles her bum in Patrick's crotch. He's the only one she touches.

I feel winded when the song ends and she walks over to us dusting her hands. Jesus, I can't believe that all it took was a dirty little dress to undo me.

'She was pretty good, wasn't she?' Bridget's eyes bore into me.

'Yeah. She was,' I say, and I can't help but notice the linger in her look. I worry that she has noticed the weird energy between us has a distinctly sexual tone. 'I'm going to talk to her. Try and smooth this fight out.'

Bridget pats me on the shoulder, and her wings flutter with the movement. 'I think that's a good idea, babes.'

Production rush in to remove our heart monitor bands, and inform us that we'll find out who won in the morning – probably an attempt to get us drunk, cocky and fighting over who was best for the drama.

The Nguyens announce we're having a party to celebrate our love or whatever. This will be the perfect opportunity for Carys and me to slip away to talk.

I bide my time as drinks are wheeled out, and someone sets up a kind of DJ booth. No one changes out of their outfits, so we look like we're having a themed sexy party.

Zack appears with a tray filled to the edges with shot glasses. 'Let's get this party started!'

It's quickly loud and raucous, and after everyone has accepted one round of shots, the cameras focus on individual couples dancing together.

I find Carys with Patrick, still blushing so furiously that I'm worried about his health.

I take her by the elbow gently. 'Can you help me in the bathroom with something?' That's the only place I can be certain we've got total privacy.

For a moment I think she's going to reject me. 'Fine,' she says wearily.

We unclip the wires from our mic packs and turn them off for good measure, leaving them in the bedroom. Production might not notice we've gone offline if we're quick.

I shut the door behind us, as Carys sits down on the closed toilet lid causing the layers of her skirt to puff up like a ballerina. I stay standing, which makes me feel even taller than usual, but I want to have the door at my back. My exit if things go wrong.

'We need to make that truce permanent,' I say. There's no point beating around the bush. It's not like we have the best communication when we're actively fighting, after all.

'We're fine.'

'We are not fine and the others are starting to notice.'

'Really?' Her eyes dash to the door. 'Do you think—?'

'Not if we put all this to bed now.' I regret my choice of words. 'I'm just not sure this is worth our energy. Can we not just be distantly polite for the rest of this process?'

'No.' It's a sharp little bite of a word.

I groan. 'Why? You don't even know *why* you're angry with me.'

'Yes, I do.' She seems as puffed up as her skirt. 'You're a liar.'

'Right, and what about exactly?'

'Marrying Warren.'

'Well, you're marrying Patrick when you're not even into him.'

She looks up at me with a curled red sneer. 'I'm not lying to him. I *am* into him.'

'I'm sure. And I bet he still hasn't talked to you about his ex-girlfriend?'

'He has,' she says with limited conviction.

'Well, there we go. We're all a bag of liars. You're no better than me or Warren or your future husband.'

Her nose wrinkles up in disgust. 'God, Dolly. It's not all about you. I can like him too.'

'So you *do* like me.' I'm so smug.

It's her turn to growl. 'Urgh, can you just fuck *off*!'

Her words echo off the tiles, and both of us spin our heads to the door. No one appears. The music outside must have covered her yelling.

'I don't want to talk about this,' she groans.

'That's what I'm suggesting,' I insist, though it rings a bit hollow when I've been digging at her. 'People are noticing that we're pissing each other off all the time, on purpose, and will put two and two together. If you care about your marriage to Patrick then you surely don't want that.'

Her eyes drop to her skirt. 'I just don't like what you're doing.'

'Fine. You don't have to. You can just fume quietly about how much you hate me, while we stay civil in public. If we both want to keep playing the Little Miss Perfect Heterosexual card, you need to agree to this. If we keep this up, everyone will notice the way we look at each other.'

She rolls her eyes. 'And how *exactly* do I look at you?'

'Like you want to kiss me, Carys.'

It hangs in the air, awkward but true.

'I don't,' she whispers.

'Do you really believe that? You've just turned all that off for yourself, have you?'

'Some of us can . . .' She begins haughtily, but she trails off as quickly as she's started. 'It doesn't matter.'

'We just can't get away with eye fucking each other across the sexy dance-offs either.'

'I don't imagine there'll be any more of those.'

I snort. 'I wouldn't put anything past this show. Just, can we leave it?'

'Only if you can stop implying that I'm a lesbian.'

'Actually, all I've said is that you obviously like women and are hiding that from yourself for some reason.'

She stands up suddenly, an angry little noise shrieking out of her. 'Urgh, this is what I mean, Dolly. You don't know me as well as you think you do but you always have an answer for why I'm wrong and you're right. I'm just stupid little Carys who has got everything wrong as usual.'

I look up at the ceiling, trying not to roll my eyes. 'I didn't say that, and if there weren't two marriages on the line, I wouldn't give a fuck how you act.'

Carys storms towards me. I think for a second that she's about to push past me out of the bathroom, but she stops right in front of me. God, she's beautiful even when she's furious with me, all that pretty pink an angry flushed colour. Raspberry red, perhaps.

I want to kiss the colour off her, even now.

'I thought you were good at hiding how you felt?' she says.

'I don't think either of us is good at that,' I whisper.

She sneers up at me. 'You think I still want you?'

'Yes. Carys, why do you think you get so angry when you look at me? When you see me kissing Warren?' Something like realisation flashes across her eyes. 'You don't hate me, Carys. You're jealous. You want me. That's been the problem all along. You never stopped wanting me.'

I don't even know how we started kissing, but we are. It's

hungry, angry. The tips of her fingers dig into the softness of my upper arms like I'm the last life raft, but also like she's trying to drown me. Pleasure and pain mingle together, and my head swims.

She can't get close enough, so I hoist her up by the soft meat of her hips. She wraps her legs around my waist, her arms around my neck, and she bites my bottom lip hard. I am so, so thankful I'm strong as she writhes around, trying to ride me. The heels of her thigh-high boots dig into the soft curves of my hips and I imagine her standing on me in them.

We were drunk on each other last time, but this is a different intoxication. It's all fury as she slides her fingers down between us, trying to pleasure both of us at once. I really regret wearing a gigantic fishnet bodysuit and a bodice. I couldn't have picked an outfit harder to get into.

When she hits the right place, I almost drop her from the rush of it.

'You were right. Happy?' Her pleading noises as she grinds are a melody, and they make me want to squeeze my thighs together from the delicious ache.

I set her down facing the mirror, me right behind her. Our height difference means we can see each other clearly in the reflection. I push her forward slowly, so her hands land either side of the sink. She's bent over, underneath me, and I can see she loves it.

'Say it,' I tell her.

She locks eyes with me, panting hard. 'Come on. Fuck me.'

Chapter Twenty-Five

Carys

> **@sourguts:** ngl is anyone not buying this love triangle?
>
> **@selfishbaby:** Omg rite @sourguts! Whyyy would Dolly want Patrick when she has Warren?
>
> **@pisswizard:** there's some bare Patrick slander in the comments today

I don't know what's taken over me, but I can't stop.

I don't want to stop.

The fireworks, or whatever the fuck Dolly does to me, are addictive.

And the worst part is, she's right. I *am* jealous. I've been so jealous of everything she's doing with Warren, so angry that she chose that lie over me, so desperate to kiss her again. Lying to yourself is a hard habit to break.

And now I'm in a bathroom begging Dolly to fuck me while everyone else parties downstairs. The sweet sticky alcohol that Zack handed out warms my veins, and numbs my thoughts.

All I can see is her. And me. In the mirror together and desperate for each other.

'As you asked so nicely,' Dolly says finally.

She gathers the fabric of this tiny dress in one hand, and kicks open my legs.

'This ridiculous skirt,' she growls, as she runs her fingers along the edges of my lace underwear. 'Did you choose the outfit you knew would drive me the most wild?'

I want her to rip my knickers off. I want her to make me come like she's taking revenge.

She slides her hand under the fabric and onto my clit so fast that I let out a cry of pleasure. My body ripples under her touch. The last time we slept together was a gentle discovery of each other's body. This is *fucking*.

I keep my eyes locked on hers while Dolly fucks me, and pushes her fingers inside me. I'm not usually an eye contact person because it is so intense for me, like being stripped naked. But now, it's a heavenly intoxication. I feel aflame.

'Come for me, Cherry,' she whispers.

That pushes me right to the edge of the cliff. My knuckles go white as I grip hold of the sink for dear life and watch this incredible Goddess of Wrath make me come.

I don't try to smother my moans, so she covers my mouth with her free hand. I lick the sweet salty taste of us, of me, off them.

I've never done anything like this before.

I feel *possessed*.

She spins me round, and we're kissing again. A hungry devouring where I can barely taste where I end and she begins. It makes me want to eat her right now, but before I can even attempt to undo that ridiculous outfit she's wearing, she hops me up on the sink.

Between my legs, she presses her body against mine, and I groan into her cleavage.

'Do you like the taste of yourself?' she says in between

kisses. 'What am I saying, clearly you do, you little egomaniac.'

Before I can say anything else, those panties are fully torn free and she buries herself between my legs. She licks, nips, hums into me, sucks at my clit. I have to steel myself against the worktop as I come, my hair tipping into the sink as I throw my head back.

She laughs and the sound vibrates through me, setting off another wave of body shakes.

Fuck fireworks, this is an earthquake.

I want to slide my hands inside her, touch the soft velvet of her folds and make her come half as much as she's made me. I want to prove to her how much she wants me. How stupid she was for rejecting me. For throwing away the opportunity to be with me.

'Can't you see, Dolly?' I gasp. 'You're addicted to me.'

I drag her up to kiss me. If I was with a man, I'd be embarrassed by how much I enjoy the taste of myself on his lips. But Dolly is just as degenerate as me.

She pushes one of my legs between hers, and grinds her pussy against my thigh. Seeing her use my body like that might be the hottest thing ever.

Dolly pauses her grinding to tear apart the fishnets, and with some undoing of her bodysuit, there's enough space to slide my fingers into her. She's so wet, it's unreal. All that for me?

On some level, maybe every level, I want her.

Maybe Dolly was right when she said we had to keep away from each other, but the sensible parts of our brains switched off long ago, sometime between kissing and now.

And if this burns everything out of us so we can have a truce then good.

When she comes, moaning into my hair, it's transcendent. There's a rattle at the door and we spring apart, our eyes wide with terror. Her pupils, dilated drug-wide only a second ago, change in an instant, the fury washed away.

'Who is it?' Dolly calls, as I scramble to pick up the remnants of the knickers from the floor.

Fuck, fuck, fuck, there's no way to repair these.

'It's just me, babes,' calls Bridget from the other side. 'I just wanted to make sure you hadn't murdered each other.'

'No, we're fine,' I say, opening the door but keeping my lower half tucked away out of sight because she will absolutely be able to see everything. 'Dolly couldn't get out of her bodysuit and we ended up ripping it. I'm just trying to help her fix it.'

Bridget's eyes dash between us, and God, is it obvious that we've been fucking? My hair is a mess, the ends damp, and Dolly's is all rucked up in strange shapes. Our cheeks are flushed, and lips bitten.

'It's been a bit of a struggle,' I laugh.

'Are you sure? Did you two manage to talk about everything?' I notice the soft slur of alcohol on her words and I hope to God that means that she won't be thinking too deeply about the scene she's stumbled into.

'We hashed it out,' I insist. 'It's fine, we're fine.'

'Okay!' Bridget smiles sunnily and I feel guilty for lying to her like this. 'You two can ... finish up your discussion.'

When she leaves, I expect Dolly to say something to me about what just happened. Anything.

But she just steps out the bathroom, spins round and says, 'Thanks for the chat. I think we needed that.'

'Right,' I say flatly, picking up my ruined knickers from the floor. I can get them on and it will cover my modesty until I can get a new pair from the bedroom. I'm not sure how Dolly is going to explain the massive tear in her fishnets right around her crotch.

'Truce,' she says.

'We can keep clear of each other,' I agree. 'This is for the best. For Patrick.'

'And Warren.' Dolly leaves without another word.

I look in the mirror, the same mirror I'd just been using for less savoury reasons, and fix my hair.

My hands shake as I'm hit with the realisation of what I've done. I've cheated on Patrick. We're engaged, and I just fucked Dolly in the bathroom. I *asked her* to fuck me. I chose to do this, knowing it might hurt him.

I want to cry or throw up but my body still hums with all the heady endorphins of sex. Sad and elated. Terrified and relieved.

A second time is so much worse. I don't want to be this kind of person for Patrick. I can't tell him, I can't, and that makes me even more awful. But I have to protect his feelings and myself, and I don't want to lose him.

I scrub at my hands and face, and I close all that feeling for Dolly away.

After a second time I'm not sure I can go on denying that I like women. As long as I focus on Patrick, it's not that important. I don't have to talk about it, to anyone ever.

It's just so easy, once you're used to pretending, to lock stuff away. Especially yourself. I've spent my life chaining parts of myself up.

First it was things I liked that everyone thought were corny, or I should have grown out of, like animation or Taylor Swift or animals. I locked all that away and learned better things to like, everything that they told me was good.

Then it was the way I looked at girls. How everyone was confused when I hadn't had a crush on a boy yet, so I just picked the one the majority of my primary school friends liked. When I eventually did like one, sometime before Mike, it felt like I'd fixed myself. But then I liked Marina too. And I knew that wasn't acceptable, so I locked that away. After all, if I still liked boys, why did it really matter?

And my whole life I've been tamping down my physicality. I want to bounce and shout and move when I'm happy. The same when I'm sad, I suppose. There's so much energy that courses through me that is apparently wrong.

I've spent so long being told that how I am, who I am, is wrong. Eventually you start internalising that. This is just another familiar part of that.

I turn the key and fix a smile on my face. I know the steps; I've been dancing it my whole life.

There's a knock at the door again, and Bridget is back. 'Babes, you good?'

I open the door and step out, mask fully affixed. 'Yeah. I will be. Sorry, my head is kicking off again after that shot. I might get changed into something else.'

I walk over to my bed and sit down, hoping that she can't see my falling apart knickers. From my bedside drawer, I take some paracetamol and neck it with some old water from last night, wincing at the dusty flavour of it. 'That'll sort me.'

Bridget seems unconvinced, and silently hands me my mic pack.

'Oh thanks. I took that off because I was worried I was going to be sick.' I know this doesn't make sense. The timing is off. But I've said it now, so I'm going to have to live with the lie.

'Is there anything you want to talk about?' Bridget asks warily.

'No, honestly I'm fine. Dolly and I had a talk.'

'Good. I told her to. Are you going to be friends now?'

'No, I think it's best we keep clear of each other. Treat each other like a family member we don't like but can't escape from, you know?'

To my relief, Bridget laughs throatily. 'God, do I? If I look at my Auntie Sally I get pissed off. Come on, you're missing the party.'

'I'll be down in a minute.'

When she's gone, I put on some new knickers and change into a party dress. I give the girl in the mirror one last glance, and try not to notice the cracks.

Chapter Twenty-Six

Carys

@silksiobhan: I wish Whit was gay and marrying me thank you

@wishiwasachair: Couldn't tell if Lina was trying to be the snake or Britney lol

@pisswizard: you're thinking of Slave4U not Toxic @wishiwasachair but yeah it was kinda serpentine writhing tbf

Despite the fact we've somehow only been here a little over twenty-four hours, we have to pack to leave as we're already done here. I'm not complaining. I'm glad to go, especially after last night.

And now, we sit outside post-breakfast waiting for the Nguyens to come for one final chat, and to announce the winners of the Pulse Race Challenge.

Patrick is so hungover he can barely sit up. Hopefully it means he doesn't notice I'm drowning in guilt. I go into caretaker mode, forcing him to drink sips of water, stroking his forehead, going through the motions of being a good partner.

Everyone looks worse for wear, so I guess Zack's shots game took multiple prisoners.

I don't look at Dolly.

The Nguyens arrive in matching white linens, like they're heading off on their own holiday. They do a bit of spiel to the camera, mostly talking about what a great 'week' we've had in Greece. I'd never thought about how reality TV shows manipulate time before, but it's so blatant.

'And now, time to announce the winners of the Pulse Race Challenge, who together raised the pulses of everyone the most,' explains Karina for the audience at home.

'The winners are . . .' Lucas pauses for effect. 'Malachi and Whit!'

Wow, their second win in a row. To be fair, I think all of us knew that Whit beat the rest of us girls hands down. I'm not sure I can look at firefighters the same way again.

But still, that's two wins, and two first choices in a row.

'Malachi and Whit win a . . .' Lucas does a little drum roll on his legs. 'Matching set of Mr and Mrs dressing gowns.' He turns to camera. 'Just like the ones you can buy on the *Wedded Bliss* shop, for wedded bliss in your own home.'

Oh. Well. That's pretty nice but seems like a major letdown compared to winning something for the wedding. While Malachi and Whit seem quietly pleased, everyone else seems a bit nonplussed.

'There'll be more opportunities for our couples to win things for their wedding throughout the coming weeks, all the way up to their wedding day,' Lucas adds when he sees the sea of deflated faces.

'We're so glad you've had a wonderful time here,' says Karina, smiling. 'But remember, only a few days ago we warned you that getting physical would yield fines to the groups' wedding funds.'

'And we can confirm that there were several breaches of this rule,' Lucas says seriously.

My heart thunders in my chest. Please, dear God, please say no one saw us. Or heard.

Patrick is pale, but I think that's still just the hangover. He whispers, 'Wow, okay,' and laughs, looking at the others with his mouth hanging open with overblown shock. It almost feels worse that he has no clue that he might be about to find out I cheated on him in front of all our friends. And the Nguyens!

Lucas clears his throat. 'Let's get to it, shall we?'

'Our cameras caught at least one act of masturbation from . . .' Karina pauses for effect while we reel at the news that someone was jacking off in here.

'Zack,' says Lucas.

'I knew he was a wanker,' murmurs Bridget next to me, and I have to bite down on my lip so I don't laugh.

'Sorry, dudes, I'm not about to let my nuts go blue for a few quid!' Zack laughs.

Whit screws up her face in, not quite disgust, but some kind of pity. Poor Lina looks as if she'd quite like to disappear.

'And in total, the fine is three thousand pounds,' Karina adds.

Lina makes an inhuman noise you could roughly categorise as a frustrated groan by way of death rattle. '*Zack*,' she hisses. 'For a wank!?'

I never thought I'd hear Lina Chen say *wank*.

'It's just three grand, babe,' he insists. 'We'll just cut something I want. Get a less good DJ for the afters.'

'Err, Zack, the fine is spread across all five couples,' says Malachi awkwardly. 'You basically just cost us all . . . Um—'

'Six hundred quid,' groans Whit.

Jackson and Bridget start yelling, and for a second I do wonder if Jackson is about to punch Zack.

But I can't quite believe it when Dolly joins in, muttering

about costs, as though we might not be next on the firing line. How can she be so calm?

'Settle down,' Lucas barks. Both Jackson and Zack plummet back down onto the bench in an instant. 'Let's get back on track, shall we?'

On the other side of Patrick, I hear Malachi whisper, 'Thanks for the help,' to Whit.

She smiles adoringly at him. 'I'll always be there to do your mental maths for you.'

God, I'm not sure what could be worse; almost certainly being imminently outed on national television, or having to sit between the fiancé you just cheated on and the most perfect couple in the world.

Karina rattles off everyone's current total wedding amounts, before confirming that there are more penalties to come.

I can barely listen. Fuck. *Fuck.*

'Are you okay?' Patrick asks, glancing down at my bouncing knees.

'Just stressed about the money,' I partly lie. I'm a coward. He's about to find out, and I can't tell him.

'There were two instances of sex in the villa over the last few days, caught by our cameras,' Lucas begins.

This is it.

'And they were by two different couples,' continues Karina, her eyebrows raised.

I'm about to throw up.

'The first couple was ...' Lucas begins. 'Bridget and Jackson.'

'Oh what!' Zack shouts. 'I was only having a little wank and you two were dick-deep.'

'Actually, we only did hands and mouth stuff. That doesn't count,' says Jackson, smugly.

'Guys, that definitely counts as sex,' Lina insists.

Bridget frowns. 'Does it, babe? I thought that was just foreplay.'

'If you're straight,' Dolly says, and I want to push her in the pool for speaking up. 'It's a very narrow view of sex if we only think of those acts as a precursor to penis in vagina sex.'

'She is right,' confirms Karina. 'And on *Wedded Bliss*, we consider all sex acts to have the same emotional weight.'

'And financial,' Lucas adds, with a wink to camera.

'You were doing stuff in the bed next to us?' grimaces Warren. 'Did I sleep through the whole thing?'

'Lucky for you,' mutters Lina.

'Come on, I'm sure you and Dolly were doing stuff too,' says Bridget.

'Negative! Nope. We are *very* good rule abiders, thank you very much.'

Well. One of you is, I think sourly.

'Wait, who is the other couple then?' asks Lina.

My stomach drops as all eyes turn to the Nguyens.

Please. *Please* don't read out my name.

Patrick takes my hand in his and I feel like I might throw up.

But then Karina looks down at her card, and . . . laughs?

'Whit and Malachi!' she announces, all the seriousness of a few seconds ago lost.

I gasp from shock that I didn't hear my own name. Did we . . . did we get away with it? I'm safe?

'Guilty,' Whit sing-songs, holding her hands up. 'We tried really hard.'

'Sorry, guys, but the firefighter outfit was too hot,' Malachi says.

'That's where you slunk off to!' laughs Warren. 'You *dogs*.'

'Hang on, you were just giving us a load of agg a minute ago,' grumbles Bridget.

While everyone deliberates whether this is fair, I look

over at Dolly. Somehow, she seems utterly calm like the surface of a lake. Did she not care about us getting found out? Or was she so confident we wouldn't that it never crossed her mind?

I wish I could feel the instant relief that some people say they feel, but my heart is still racing, my body drunk on adrenaline and fear. It's like I can't breathe enough air.

'Carys?' Patrick asks, and his words are muggy, distant.

That's when everything goes dark.

Chapter Twenty-Seven

Dolly

> **@generichandle:** Omg is Carys okay???
>
> **@prunetits:** Lmfaoooo imagine passing out because you heard people talking about sex, she is SO repressed
>
> **@generichandle:** @prunetits you can't just call people repressed!!!

I've never lived in London before. Or in a massive block of flats. Mum and I have always lived in our little terraced house. It's embarrassingly starstruck of me to think *wow we're so high up* but I do think that when I look out the window. I can see the big pointy building that Greenpeace kept trying to climb up a few years ago, and the curve of Wembley Stadium. Plus a lot more buildings that aren't remotely familiar to me.

'Welcome to the city.' Warren joins me at the window, arm slung over my shoulder.

'It's wild. It's *so* big and I feel like such a bumpkin looking at it.'

'You good?'

I feel Warren's eyes on me so I turn in his arms. 'Yeah. I am. Just getting used to it all.'

He kisses me on the forehead. We've got such an easy

intimacy that you could mistake us for an actual married couple. Which, yes, is the intention, but there's no one else here, and definitely no cameras in the apartments. It's just us. Just two best friends.

'Have you called your mum yet?'

I cringe. 'No.'

'And why's that?'

'I'm just . . . not ready. It's not you—'

'I didn't think it was,' he says, laughing. 'But you should talk to her.'

I'm not sure I have the bandwidth to call up Mum when this flare is barrelling towards me like a runaway train. I had hoped that I might escape the whole experiment without endometriosis reminding me it seeded its horrible little lesions all over my body, but no. I groan, clutching my pelvis with one hand and the cold flat of the window with the other.

Warren tucks his arm under one of mine for stability, ready to catch me if I drop. 'I got you,' he whispers as I press my sweaty forehead against the chilled glass.

The cramp passes. Such a small word for something that racks through my body with the aggression of an orgasm. Just the opposite, really. Totally fucking horrible.

'Nope. It's definitely coming.'

I had told Warren about my endometriosis during our warehouse dates. After all, I've been pretty open about it in my content. I hadn't told the show much about it or asked for accommodations. It's one of those disabilities that no one considers a disability because no one knows what disability really means. Anyway, production didn't kick up a fuss about me not mentioning it directly.

I hope that when I turn my work phone back on, I'll have messages and comments from people who've seen it. That is, provided the show doesn't edit it out.

Warren takes one look at my belly, which has swollen up hard and stiff like I'm suddenly eight months pregnant. 'Bedtime.'

'No, I need to power through. We've got the group dinner in a few hours.'

He looks at me like I'm an alien. 'Are you mad? You look like you almost splattered half of East London with your stomach contents.'

'Not sure my sick can pass through glass.'

'That's a relief. I was worried about the porcelain.'

I let Warren take me to the bedroom because I am starting to feel a little dizzy. I can argue all I want, but I know he's right. I need to rest.

I'll say this, the show didn't spare any expense on the huge king-size bed with a very comfortable mattress. Presumably because they want to get all the straight couples fucking (if they aren't already), but it has the added benefit of being the perfect sick day nest for me.

I pop painkillers and a cramp relaxer from my med kit into my hand and knock them back without water.

'That's a bit hardcore,' Warren says, passing me a glass to drink from anyway.

I down it in one go. 'Thanks. I'll have to get ready soon. I've powered through before.'

'Doesn't mean you should now,' he calls from the walk-in wardrobe where he's hanging up our clothes on wooden hangers. 'We've already had one person pass out on the show this week.'

Poor Carys. I got the distinct impression from the abject terror in her eyes that she thought our dalliances were about to be revealed.

Call me naive, but I was pretty confident that if the show knew about it, they'd have let us know before the Nguyens got there. It's not a good look to out your contestants, after all.

No wonder she passed out.

Luckily, we all managed to benefit from her 'migraine' situation as the show insisted we take a couple of days off filming while we made our way to our new homes. That meant a night in a hotel in Greece before they were confident we weren't all going to pass out on the plane. For the other couples, that meant a load of joyful shagging without the fear of racking up any fines.

I wonder if— No, let's not go there.

She sat in front of me on the flight home, had to walk past me a bunch of times, and never even looked at me. Not even a bitchy comment. It's really weird. I just hope she's alright.

Back on land, they took us to our apartments, but agreed that instead of filming a *we're arriving at our new apartment* segment as planned, they'd let us settle in and film some fake *welcome to our brand new apartment we definitely are just moving into now* content tomorrow so we can rest before the dinner party.

I'm sure the staff were glad for a break too. Reb looked so threadbare on the flight that I was tempted to ask if she was in a union.

Reality TV contestants' rights is a whole other thing. Signing them away is something we half agree to when we sign the contract. But maybe that's just me knowing what I was walking into. I've read the depositions and court cases for the various shows around the world. I was prepared for limited sleep, producer interference, no days off.

I don't think Carys was prepared for any of it.

I know that I could find her on Instagram and message her, but we agreed to keep away from each other. I think that includes checking in.

'We're being recorded for national television,' I continue,

blowing out a long slow breath with another twinging cramp. 'Be present or be forgotten. Come on, you know what I mean, though?'

I don't mention his sports injury, but he nods. He knows. You get sick, you might get left behind. That's just the way it is, even if I wish it wasn't.

'Fine, mad lady. I'll finish the unpacking and then shall we order lunch in?'

'God, yes. Have I told you that you're the perfect husband?'

'Not today!' he calls, as he walks out of the bedroom to grab another case.

I stare down at my belly, hard with inflammation. I think because I'm fat people are extra surprised when it manages to suddenly balloon out, like I'm pregnant on a *Sims* timeline of like three days. I'm just glad I got through the tiny dress and bikini sections before it hit.

Now I can just lie in bed and make phone calls about our wedding, eat chips and sleep it off. I may be plagued by a body that wants to grow tissue in all the wrong places just for kicks, but at least it's semi-regular about it.

Thank God for sweatpants with elasticated waists, and fancy trousers that are secretly sweatpants.

'I hope it's passed before I meet your parents. When are we doing that? Day after tomorrow?' I ask.

'I think so. Then yours.'

'Then fittings,' I sigh. Thankfully, I have my usual measurements on hand because I suspected this was going to happen, which means I can have something slinky that hugs my curves and makes every woman with a visible belly line realise she too can look hot as fuck showing it off.

I switch on the television, breakfast programming as background noise, the sort of thing I'd have on while flicking through my phone. I could be doing that – it's just in the other room, but I feel like if I touch it, Mum will know. She'll know and wonder why I haven't called.

I mean, maybe she won't because we didn't part on good terms. She thought this was a terrible idea, to put it mildly, and she'll know that Warren and I are together now. She'll have opinions. She *always* has opinions.

I mute the television. 'Sorry, I meant to ask how your call went before we got distracted. How are your family?'

Warren's love for his family is apparent on his face. 'Really good. I think Connor needs a new battery as the old one is not holding charge, so I need to help sort that out later. But yeah, everyone's good. Mum wants to know if you have a Jollof preference.'

'However she makes it, surely?'

'Correct answer. Keep that up, and you'll be fine.'

'I'm sure I can try harder than that.' I make a note to ask him for her favourite sweets or biscuits, so that we can take them and some flowers when we finally meet.

'If you're not going to call your mum today, I have one request,' he says.

'Go on.'

'I think let's lock the phones in the cases overnight. Or hand them over to production.'

I sit up a little too quickly. 'Absolutely not.'

'Dolly, your mum won't thank us for calling her late at night when we've had a few drinks and think it's suddenly a great idea to finally call her. You want to do it with a clear head. You know I'm right.'

'And I *dislike* that you're right, just so you know.'

'Noted.'

'But yes, fine. Can we lock them in the fridge or something? Freeze them into a block of ice?'

He laughs, and I realise how much I've grown to love that rumble. 'Do you struggle that much with impulse control?'

I snort. 'I try not to.'

Not that I've tried particularly hard over the last few weeks. In the same way my heart can recognise Warren's laugh anywhere, I feel like my body just always knows where Carys is. I swear I can sense her in the building, and I wonder if it's only a matter of time before we silently bump into each other. Will she ignore me then? What about when there's no one else there? Will we ever talk about what happened between us, or is that it forever?

I wish television could drown that feeling out too.

I open my show notebook that I've taken to using as a kind of bullet journal for keeping on track with our wedding plans. 'We should call up the florists. Thanks to the shaggers we're going to have to cut back on some of the grandiosity.'

'Do we even need flowers? We're getting married in a greenhouse.'

'Buttonholes,' I say, listing off on my fingers. 'My bouquet. Something for our mums. I don't want to scrimp on those if we can avoid it. We'll just go . . . lowkey.'

It turns out the shaggers cost us, collectively, *ten thousand pounds* from our wedding budget. That's two grand each, on top of the six hundred from Zack's wank fest. It's probably a good thing Carys fainted, or a huge fight would have broken out.

Somehow, I couldn't bring myself to be annoyed with Malachi and Whit when they're so in love. Probably because it would make me a hypocrite.

This leaves us with eighteen grand to do a television-ready wedding with, which is *a little tight* especially when our venue sucks up half of that.

There's a knock at the door, which Warren goes to answer. Unfortunately, it's not food but our handlers, Posh Louise and

Not So Posh John — I suspect he's actually very posh because it turns out basically everyone in television seems to be from some kind of inherited wealth, and you can see it in their nice clothes and lack of stress lines.

They arrive with cameras, which is a nuisance because I still look dreadful. I'm definitely leaking into my sweatpants already — that disconcerting squelchy feeling is like no other. The slinky robe they gave me for the Pulse Race Challenge is not thick enough to hide that, so I keep my back to the front door while Posh Louise silently hands us a golden envelope.

I hear the whirr of the cameras as they zoom in on us and the envelope, and take my time opening it so they get enough good footage.

I try not to think how rough I look. 'Oh wow,' I say, trying to seem enthusiastic. 'What's this?'

I turn it over in my hands. It's slightly too large, like everything on TV.

'Do you want to open it?' I ask Warren, batting my eyes to look romantic, but really it's so I don't start crying if I get a paper cut. Anything could push me over the edge today.

Warren slides out a card from inside the envelope. '"Couples." Wow they didn't even personalise this one,' he says, flipping it over.

'Come on,' I fake laugh, tugging at his arm because if I have to stand in this doorway much longer I will pass out, and I think there might be an investigation if multiple people faint.

'"Couples!"' he announces enthusiastically. '"Welcome to your first home together. Over the next week, you will need to work on deepening that connection you've established: emotionally, and physically."'

He turns to waggle his eyebrows at me, and I playfully slap him on the arm. I know this must play well, because Not So Posh John smiles.

'"We will send you compatibility exercises to complete so you can practise thoughtful communication and connection." Oh, that's all it says.'

'So you're just going to give us tasks randomly?' I ask.

'Sorry, can you say that again without referencing production?' asks the camera operator, who I don't recognise.

'Of course. What's your name, sorry? I'm not sure we've met yet.'

'Harry,' he says, moving his head briefly from the viewfinder so I can see his face.

'Thanks, Harry,' I say, composing myself and going again. 'So, this means we're going to get randomly given more challenges? That's exciting.'

'Yeah, seems cool. It doesn't say if we can win anything,' Warren says.

I place a considered hand on his wrist. 'Darling, it'll just be nice to do them together.'

Harry gives us the okay that we're done, and they all leave.

As I close the door, I realise they've gone to the room diagonally opposite from us. I wonder who is over there. I peer through the peephole with one eye.

My mind stutters, like I've missed a step, as Carys opens the door.

She looks beautiful. And so does Patrick. They wrap their arms around each other's backs as they read out loud, heads bowed together. They are the kind of picture-perfect couple this show was made for.

'What's all this then?' Warren asks, and I know that he knows full well I'm just spying and up to no good. 'Bed, missus,' he insists softly. 'I'll carry you if you don't get moving.'

'Fine. Fine,' I say as he follows me in, guiding me like a sheepdog.

Curling up under the plush duvet is so delightful that I immediately feel on the edge of sleep.

After a long nap, I manage a bubble bath and I sneak in my phone before we lock it down overnight.

Jas has texted me a few times asking for pics and the goss, congratulating herself on her heterosexual teachings that got me this far. There's nothing from Mum.

I try to resist going on my socials to see how high the numbers have crawled, but as we know, I'm not one for impulse control. I'm way over a million now. Warren's following has tripled and his comments are filled with thirsting girls. Thank goodness I'm not the jealous type.

It doesn't take me long to find Carys. Her Instagram is so normal, mostly just pictures of the farm or adverts announcing things happening at the farm and then an occasional dump of pictures of her doing things with four cookie cutter girls and their matching four husbands. I even scroll so far back that I find Mike who, admittedly, probably makes a good Niall.

I realise, with slight embarrassment, that I can't get out of the bath without help. When my endo flare gets really bad, it's like I can't use any of my core muscles as they're too inflamed or busy contracting.

Warren, the man that he is, doesn't bat an eye when I have to ask for help. This is the first time he's seen me naked, and I don't feel exposed or lusted after or unsafe. He just gathers me up in a big fluffy bath sheet, and tells me he's ordering sushi.

I have to do the classic lie down to dry because I'm too tired to do it properly yet.

The sushi arrives, and Warren brings me a little plate. 'Forgive me, I'm going to use my fingers.'

'I promise not to dob you into the entire nation of Japan.'

'Thank you.'

'Wife?'

'Yes, husband?'

'I know you well enough to know you're going to fight me if I try to stop you getting in the cab to dinner.'

'Too right,' I groan, closing my eyes as I eat a truly delicious bit of salmon nigiri. I swear, this stuff is healing.

I feel two taps on my wrist, and open my food-blissed-out eyes. 'That's the signal,' he says.

'For what?'

'For I've pushed it too far and we need to get out of there.'

'We won't need to use that,' I murmur, dipping an avocado maki roll in the soy sauce for a bit too long. I need the salt when I feel this shit.

'Dolly, with great respect, you can't see yourself. I'm your husband. It's my job to look out for you especially when you're not looking out for yourself, isn't it?' He has me there. 'Two taps, I'll keep the conversation going, then tell production you're unwell and we have to go. Easy.'

'Fine,' I concede, pretty sure I've told my mum the same thing at some time in the past. 'Did I tell you that you're the perfect husband?'

He laughs. 'I think we need to set a minimum reminder. Like, maybe four times a day?'

'Don't push it,' I say, feeding him a popped-out edamame covered in salt and chilli. He licks the salt off his lips, and I'm struck with a pang of sadness. I kind of wish I could love him, after all. 'But you are. Perfect, to me.'

Chapter Twenty-Eight

Dolly

**Bridget Evans, 26, Swansea, and
Jackson Smith, 25, Leeds**

BRIDGET	We had to do an intimacy challenge and it was pretty lush.
JACKSON	We had to stare into each other's eyes for ten minutes non-stop.
BRIDGET	Eye contact is sooooo important, babe.

In the end, I don't go for fake fancy trousers because the show drops off a present from a designer I've followed on socials for ages. It's a navy kimono-style dress with large draping sleeves, dramatic and beautiful all at once. I get Warren to take some photos for me to tag them on Instagram when I make my dramatic return, but all the makeup in the world can't conceal the slightly green tinge to my skin. I'm grateful the dress does give plenty of space for my endo belly, though.

Obviously we make it to dinner, because there's no way in hell I'm missing the communal dinner party. It tends to be an opportunity to air grievances, usually influenced by the production team. On the US version of the show, there's usually some arguments. On the Australian series, well, there were several simultaneous fist fights.

The show takes us out in individual cabs to a restaurant overlooking the Thames, all gently lit with orange and gold as the sun gets low in the sky. It's beautifully decorated, a kind of visual cornucopia with fake and real flowers everywhere. There's even a fountain. It's a lot but on camera it'll look incredible.

The ten of us are seated on one long table, our names written on white cards to guide us where to sit. Warren and I are in the middle, side by side, opposite Lina and Zack, with Zack directly across from me, which is less than ideal. If anyone is going to snap at him, it's going to be me thanks to my short temper exacerbated by my uterus's antics. Perhaps that's what production were hoping for. But then, not even Lina can really look at him for long. She keeps dropping her eyes whenever he talks.

And he doesn't fucking shut up.

'I just think,' he says, stuffing olives into his mouth and putting the nibbled stones right on the tablecloth, 'that maybe everyone was being a bit unkind about my indiscretion.'

'My man, if you stop bringing it up, we'd forget about it,' cringes Warren. 'Let it die!'

'If he wants the public to know he's a serial spaffer then go for it,' I mutter.

There's a pair of empty chairs opposite Malachi and Whit's setting, obviously for the Nguyens, who typically arrive right at the point we're arguing whether he should be known as the Weekly Wanker or the Compulsive Cock-wrangler.

'Well, sounds like we're off to a spirited start,' Karina says.

Lucas pulls out the chair for her and she sits down, and I note that none of the other men did that except Warren, who was covering that I really needed help moving about.

Whit and Malachi sitting opposite Lucas and Karina makes a special kind of sense. The future Mr and Mrs Vempati-Campbell are the clear winners and on track to make television history. It's clear production love them too.

Warren and I might be good actors, but there's nothing like *actual real deal* love on a show like this to win over the hearts and minds of the nation. It's a wonderful wild thing to see two people falling in love. Anyway, the couple who come in second tend to be the ones with the longer-lasting careers. Perhaps without the pressure of being The Winners, there's a little more freedom and a little less scrutiny? It's a trend no one understands and I'm not going to question it.

The waiting staff serve dim sum in huge bamboo steamers, stacked in one or two layers so as not to hide any faces for filming. The giant wafts of steam are scented with fresh herbs, prawns, a little spice.

'So, how is everyone getting along?' Lucas asks loudly down the table.

'It'd be easier if she'd put her knickers in the washing hamper,' Zack quips.

Poor Lina looks mortified.

I'm pretty sure the glass of wine in front of him is not actually his first drink of the day. I'm extremely tempted to kick him under the table. 'Maybe you shouldn't be airing your wife's dirty laundry on television,' I say, keeping my voice low.

'That's disrespectful, Zack,' agrees Warren. 'I'm really sorry, Lina.'

'Thank you,' she squeaks.

My death-glares must be obvious, because Carys briefly catches my eye. We said hello when everyone arrived, as is proper for when you're being filmed unless you're actively trying to start beef.

She looks different today. Gone is the cutesy retro look I'd got used to. Instead she wears a deep green silk dress that hugs her body, with an elegant Bardot neckline. The colour makes her fair skin pop and her hair glow. Honestly, it's more something out of my wardrobe than hers. *Sophisticated*, I suppose, is the word I'm looking for. Like someone's wife.

But I return her slightly worried look, glancing to Lina and back in question.

'I'm the messy one,' Whit says to move the conversation along.

'Yeah, I was really surprised. I thought surgeons have to be really neat and that,' Malachi says.

She shrugs. 'That's work brain. There's no space for work brain at home or I might start slicing.' She mimes her fingers into scissors and snips at Malachi, who giggles sweetly.

The conversation peters out after the normal back and forth of men leaving towels on the floor and toilet seats up (grim).

There's a short moment of quiet while we eat, but it's clear production are just waiting for us to get a little bit more wine into us. I notice one of the assistants give a signal to the Nguyens, reflected in one of the restaurant's massive windows.

I brace myself for what comes next.

'A major part of the apartments section of the experiment is intimacy,' begins Karina. 'Now, we know that some of you are ... let's just say, familiar with that already, but how are our other couples getting on?'

Lina stiffens as though she's expecting Zack to say something dreadful, and the last thing I want to hear about is whether Patrick and Carys have finally slept together, so I take the stupid option and speak up. 'Warren and I are working on building intimacy slowly. We obviously are dying for it—' I break here for us both to laugh and look at each other in the eyes with adoration. 'The physical desire is there for each of us, and we're exploring intimacy in different ways.'

'Can you tell us more about that?' Karina asks.

I go on a long spiel about sharing as a form of intimacy, checking in on our feelings, different kinds of touch – hinting very lightly at the sexual. It's something I rehearsed earlier, but I think it comes out sounding natural enough.

I finish just before somewhere in my belly gives a huge, painful tug. I pick up my napkin to dab at my lips and cover the quiet *fuuuuuuck* I hiss into it.

Warren slips a hand under the table, hovering above my thigh for me to take. I squeeze tightly, but his hands are the money-makers. I absolutely cannot fuck those up, so I drop it quickly.

'What about the rest of you?' Lucas asks.

'Well,' Zack begins, and I see everyone brace for disaster. 'I'm not really sure if we have that kind of compatibility.'

'So, you *have* done stuff then?' Bridget asks, leaning forward a little.

'Lina told me that she didn't think we had a spark,' he says tightly.

To my confusion, Lina whips her head round, eyebrows furrowed. 'That's—'

'I know you didn't mean to hurt my feelings, but it did set me back a little, especially when everyone knows you got proposals from Cobey and me and had to take a moment to choose.'

Is that what happened? I feel bad that I never asked Lina what the deal with her situation was, but I was mostly confused *why* she would go after this ding-dong. Still, my bullshit alarms are ringing full pelt.

'Oh, buddy, that's difficult,' says Jackson, a man who has never said *buddy* before in his life. 'And emasculating, I'm sure.' His lips purse slightly as he tries to hide his shit-eating grin.

'I didn't say that!' Zack backpedals quickly. 'I just ... it felt like just another occasion where maybe I'd been too nice upfront and made the relationship start off on the wrong foot. Like, was I too respectful of her?'

I'm quite positive I'm going to throw up, and for once it's

not entirely Zack's doing. The cramping deepens and I'm working to stay upright. There's nothing I can do. I'm going to have to try to walk to the bathroom to keep a sliver of dignity. And hope I don't throw up all over this nice visually intense restaurant.

I pat Warren on the knee twice, as agreed. His look, as I get up from the table, says he's registered my request that we exit soon. No one questions when I trot to the bathroom, and no one follows me.

Chapter Twenty-Nine

Carys

Lina Chen, 25, Glasgow, and Zack Allen, 31, Kent

ZACK	Our intimacy challenge was fun!
LINA	Um, yeah, we had some dice we had to roll and, well, whatever the dice said, you had to touch the other person there.
ZACK	I kept getting neck. Poor Leens must feel like she's marrying a vampire!
LINA	I suspect those dice were weighted.

This might actually be the worst dinner party of my entire life.

I'm only just about managing to follow what's happening; everyone's conversations meld into a barrage of sound, and masking is extra hard because I can barely hear anyone. My lip reading is pretty good, but not when people eat or drink.

I hear only some of what Zack spews out because I can't see him but I can tell by everyone's reactions that he's said something dreadful.

I glance over to Dolly, who is a useful human barometer for Zack's nonsense, only to see her getting up from the table. She walks slowly, steadily, but I can tell something is wrong. There's too much effort in the movement. She's stiff, not soft.

But Warren seems unconcerned and doesn't follow her.

It's not my place to worry. We agreed to keep our distance from each other. It's for our own good, and the good of my marriage.

I miss something else that's said, when all faces turn to us.

'Sorry, what was that?' I say nervously.

Lucas repeats himself, a little louder. 'And how are you and Patrick getting on, Carys?'

I feel uncomfortable that this man is asking me on national television, essentially, if I've slept with my partner, but that's what I apparently signed up for.

'We're taking it slow. One step at a time.'

Patrick slinks his arm round my shoulders, and I'm grateful for his physical support but his shirt is starched to high heavens and I can feel the scratch of it across my back. 'That's right,' he agrees.

We haven't slept together, obviously. I feel a bit strange about sex right now. After all, I keep sleeping with the wrong person. Kept. Past tense.

It's tricky. Being around her was just feeding the need for her. And it isn't a true need, it can't be. I *need* Patrick. I don't need Dolly, no matter how chemical our attraction is. I couldn't help but notice the way my breath hitched in my throat when I saw her sitting at the table in that midnight-blue dress with the deep V neck. That's where the thoughts need to end – admiration, not fantasising.

So I figured going cold turkey on sex in general might fix things, flush her out of my system while I grow closer to Patrick and build a whole new sense memory.

But as last night was our first time in our own place, I did initiate a make-out session with him. So far, all our kisses had been a little chaste, and I wanted him to know I'm into him. I needed to bring some more sexual energy into this flat, if this marriage is going to survive. I like sex, I think it's important, I just ... I need him to know it's coming, so to speak.

Poor choice of words, perhaps.

'Just like Warren and Dolly,' points out Lucas. 'I guess you guys are more alike than we thought.'

This comparison makes me want to sink into whatever hole Lina has fallen into. I reach for her hand under the table, and she squeezes back gently, but drops mine after a moment. What is going on with her? I'm really worried, and I can't work out what is going on with all the talking and noise and cutlery and eating.

There's another round of questions, this time about wedding planning logistics. I'm relieved that I need to wee because that means I can have a sensory break in the bathroom. I excuse myself politely, kissing Patrick on the cheek as I go, and I make my way to the loos on the other side of the restaurant.

The disabled bathroom is occupied from the flushing I hear through the door, but no one else is in the ladies', so I can sit in silence for a few minutes, feeling the rush in my brain slow. I'm glad there's no one else in here to use the hand dryer – often the worst sound in the entire world, even if it is useful to cover when you're doing a sneaky poo.

The strange thing is that Dolly isn't in here. When I wash my hands at the mirrored sink, I spy that all the stall doors are open. It's frustrating to be always on high alert for her, like my senses are always primed to find her.

As I step out of the women's bathroom, I hear a moan from the disabled loo. Not to be indelicate, but I would recognise that voice anywhere, even if the cadence of the moan is much more distressed than I've previously heard.

I knock on the door. 'Dolly?'

There's a muffled groan, generally not a good kind of sound. 'Dolly, are you alright?'

The thing about working on a city farm frequented by

schoolchildren is that someone is always having some kind of health emergency, and so I'm fighting all my training and instincts if I don't help her out. There might not be time to get someone else if this is serious.

And I'd rather embarrass us both than risk leaving her unwell in there.

The one thing I've learned about using disabled loos myself over the years to avoid the chorus of hand dryers on a bad day is that often the locks aren't that good and are liable to open, even with a RADAR key, *even* if you've locked it from the inside.

I test the handle, and a slight gap appears.

Propriety is out the window when someone is poorly, so I feebly knock as I open the door, just to create as much noise as possible so that she knows I'm coming in. 'I'm coming in,' I call.

There's no reply.

Dolly is on the floor, slumped over the toilet, her long frame folded over the seat.

The door bangs against the wall as I fling it fully open and push it closed behind me.

'Dolly?' I rush to her side and I am so relieved when she moves.

She makes a noise that isn't quite words. Her lovely new dress is slick to her back with sweat.

I try not to let my mind get carried away with the fact that this is a public toilet and she's touching so much gross stuff, because she's obviously not okay and that's more important.

'Dolly! You're sick?' I mean it more as a statement, but my voice goes all squeaky and it comes out very questiony right as Dolly yaks something up.

I have to spin round, plug my nose and blow out my cheeks so I don't accidentally breathe in the smell and gip. The last thing we need is me going too. That happened once at the farm. We don't speak of it.

She sits up, which is a relief, and wipes her mouth with a crumpled square of toilet paper. 'What gave it away?' she groans.

Oh my, she looks awful. Well, she still looks like Dolly underneath, but her face is grey, with deep purple blotches under her eyes. I'm not sure if she tried to wash off her makeup or just sweated it off, but it's almost all gone. There's a greenish tinge to her, vomit aside. Just a general swampy look.

I perch on my heels, trying to ignore the smell of vomit. 'Lean back a second,' I say, and she does without talking back. I close the lid and flush the loo, which removes that little problem for now. Just to be safe, I reopen the lid.

'Can a woman not vomit in private?' she growls. 'How did you even get in here?'

'Broke in,' I say, ignoring her growls.

This is the nice kind of restaurant where they have not just hand soap but hand cream, and soft tissues. I take a wad and fold it into cushiony squares to replace the gross bit of tissue in her hand, which I drop in the toilet. I run another under the cold tap, just enough to dampen the sheets.

'Sorry if it's a little cold,' I say, as I dab very gently at the back of Dolly's neck. I have to hold up the ends of her bob, and I try to ignore the strange mix of feelings that come with touching her again.

'How many times were you sick?'

She grumbles, eyes still closed. 'A few.'

'And when did it start?'

'Are you trying to first aid me?'

'Yes.'

She says a word I absolutely don't catch, and then adds, 'Five minutes ago.'

'Do you think you've got any more in the tank?'

'I hope not. We're already down to bile.' She slumps in deep exhaustion. 'Potentially.'

'Noted. I need to take your pulse. Is that okay?'

She mumbles something I think is a *yes*, and I slide my fingers along her neck, feeling the little burst of life under the skin. I try to focus, and count the beats. Her pulse is a bit fluttery, perhaps a tad too fast, but nothing worrying.

The last time I touched her here was with my mouth, and from the colour, I think I left a mark.

I notice her mic pack is on the floor, turned off. Why hasn't anyone come to check on her?

'Is it something you ate?' I ask.

'I doubt it.'

I try to make my voice as neutral as possible when I ask, 'Do you think you drank too much? Was it on an empty stomach?'

She looks up at me under heavy lids. 'If you go peer in my glass, you'll see it's as full as it was at the start of the night.'

'You've been fake toasting?'

'Real toasting. Fake sipping. I guess it goes along with the fake marriage.'

'I ... well, I'm going to guess you aren't pregnant?'

Dolly gives me a very hard look.

I can't help but huff a single note of laughter. 'Do you want me to get Warren?'

'He should be here any moment. We have an agreement. You can go.'

I linger because, well, things between us aren't exactly fine and dandy but also she looks like a rain-soaked Big Mac – once beautiful, now all kind of bloated and melting. That feels uncharitable to say, but she *really* does look dreadful. If I still actively hated her quite as much as I did earlier this week, I'd be enjoying it.

Now I just hate myself more.

'I'll keep an eye on you until then,' I say, my various instincts warring.

It's a good thing I do stay because another rush of vomit comes out of her. I stroke her back, relieved that this time my senses aren't quite so overcome because I was expecting it.

'Fuck, I hate being sick,' she growls.

'I think it's safe to let go of the toilet.'

Dolly recoils. 'That was a little overly intimate, wasn't it?'

I dampen some more tissues and tell her to sit back, which she does, leaning against the tiles with her eyes closed. Carefully, I clean her face. Tissues aren't the best and these are *fancy* but still, I don't want to irritate her skin. Her skin brightens as I wipe away the grime and sick, and I even clean the ends of her hair which might have got splattered.

I've never been this close to her before without us kissing or something more. It feels somehow even more intimate.

'You don't need to do this, you know,' Dolly murmurs.

'I know. We're on a truce, remember.'

Her eyes flutter open. 'You wanted to keep away from me. You should want to leave me sitting in my own sick.' Dolly's smile curls at the corner.

'It's no fun to beat someone who is already down,' I say, and she laughs softly.

'You're too much of a Girl Guide to leave me alone,' she whispers.

I get back up to inspect a wicker basket of supplies you'd find in a nice hotel, which I guess tells me a lot about how posh this restaurant is, along with pads and mini-deodorants. Way beyond my pay grade. I unwrap a disposable cup wrapped in plastic, fill it with water and hand it to her.

Dolly goes to knock it back, but I lower the cup from her lips. 'Slow sips.'

'Yes, boss.' I hate the little thrill that gives me. The thick way her voice makes the *s* sound almost like a *sh*. A whisper.

Her voice is different today, tarter. It's a tone I heard when we had sex, a familiar lilt that you sometimes hear at home in North Wales, but I just thought maybe that was ... well ... her sex voice. But it's here now – higher, sing-song, bunching over consonants.

I'm enough of a fake to know when someone has been changing their voice on purpose, but I wonder why she's been doing it.

I'm tempted to ask, but something rushes over her. Her jaw grits, and her body tightens up into a ball. As if in mimic, a balled fist slams onto her thigh.

'Dolly?' I want to grab her hand, I want to save her from this spasm of pain. 'What's going on, Dolly? Do I need to get an actual doctor?'

She shakes her head. 'Just the little red pouch from my handbag.'

I notice it finally, hanging on the peg on the back of the door across the room.

'That's a daft place to leave it,' I say as I hand it over.

'I didn't want it to go on the floor and get all gross,' she insists. 'Like me.'

The tiny sequinned bag is full of strips of pills. Unboxed of course because who needs identifying information or the leaflet about side effects? Not Dolly, apparently.

She snaps two little round pills out from one sheet, and a further two slightly larger ones from another, and necks them all back like they're mints. To my horror, she dry swallows them all.

'Dolly, please drink something – that was too disturbing,' I say, thrusting a refilled cup of water at her.

'Warren said the same.' She complies, but then says, 'The last few days, you'd have loved to see me choke.'

'I don't want you dead from dry pills lodged in your throat,' I insist. 'Just ... mildly inconvenienced.'

I can't help but laugh when she says, 'Oh yeah, just a small choking. A chokelet, if you may.'

'Well, you're in my care now, and it could ruin my first aid accreditation if I purposefully let you die on national television.'

She sips at the water. 'It *is* easier this way.'

'I'm sure that's what it says to do on the packet,' I say tartly. 'Now, what else do you need?'

'Nothing.'

'Should I get someone from production to get a medic?'

'Absolutely not.'

'Dolly—'

'I'm not making you stay!' she half-arsedly snaps at me. 'Warren was supposed to be here.'

'Well, he's not and I am, so get used to it.'

She groans. 'As much as I love our verbal sparring, can we leave it until I have stopped having contractions?'

I gasp, trying to wrap my head around this. 'But you—'

'Not pregnant, calm down,' she snaps, exasperated with me, and I feel a little foolish to have jumped right there. 'I've got endometriosis. The big cramps are like contractions.'

I want to say *fuck that's awful, I'm sorry*. But I still feel rather bitter from feeling stupid, so I snap back, 'Well, you can see how I misconstrued that, what with your using a term famously connected with giving birth.'

She doesn't give me anything back so I guess she really is too tired to argue with me. Why do I feel a bit disappointed?

I don't really know very much about endometriosis. That's not really something you talk about in first aid training; in fact you rarely get to assist people with chronic conditions. It's more likely you'd help someone giving birth unexpectedly. This whole situation has spun me out enough that for some reason I find myself muttering about the signs of labour in my ewes at the farm.

She raises a hand, heavy and slow. 'Carys, I know you Welsh people love chatting about your fucken sheep, but please shut up.'

'Fine. But we have to get you out of here.'

'No moving yet.'

'I'm stronger than I look. I can help.'

'Carys, I'm familiar with how strong you are from you going on about hauling your sheep, and,' she looks to my neck, and must notice my mic still attached, 'other things.'

The flush of heat runs up my skin. 'You said we needed to stop talking about sheep.'

There's a knock at the door and I leap up to answer it.

'Hey,' says Warren, as though he knew I'd be in here. 'Is Dolly okay?'

I shake my head. 'Pretty bad.'

'I'm glad you were here. You wouldn't believe how much production did not want to believe me that we needed to go home – and not film it either.'

'But they agreed?'

'In the end.'

'You're a good man,' I say, realising we haven't spoken much since we left the warehouse.

I suddenly feel a rush of guilt for what I've been doing with his fiancée. If they have a fake marriage, does he know what she and I have been doing? Why we fight?

He sighs, shaking his head. 'It was helped along by Zack decking Jackson for some reason.'

'No, what?' Dolly cries from the floor. 'Aw man, I missed it.'

I open the door wider so he can come in, and try to ignore the strange feeling in my stomach as I watch him gently wipe the damp hair from her forehead. They're so easy with each other.

'Yeah, Malachi had to grab Jackson before he got Zack,' Warren says, trying not to laugh. 'The guy would have been *obliterated*.'

'A real case of the worst person you know made a good point.'

'Anyway, there's a car for us. No cameras.'

Dolly looks up at the ceiling. 'Fuck's sake. I'm sorry.' It rushes out in one word, and I barely hear what he says to reassure her because he crouches down, and his voice is so low and deep at the best of times.

It's an intrusion to stay here, especially when he lifts her up, carrying her like a baby or a bride. This is what it's supposed to look like, isn't it? The man provides, the woman taken care of. It's all I ever wanted, right there.

Except, it's not even real. Not in the true romantic sense of the word, at least. Their love is all platonic. Maybe that's a real kind of love too? How do I make Patrick as happy as they are, when they're not even in love?

I realise that her things are still all over the place. 'Sorry, the bag touched the floor,' I say as I tuck it into her hands, but Dolly is already drifting off to sleep. Her face is tucked under Warren's chin.

'She'll be alright,' he says, and then he drops his voice to a whisper. It might be my overstimulated brain, but I swear he says, 'I'll look after her for us.'

I follow them out, unable to take my eyes off her until the two of them, combined into one figure, disappear out the front door.

I don't know how to process all this feeling in my chest. We need to keep apart from each other, that's what we said. A truce, not a friendship.

But I'm rattled. I didn't think Dolly Doherty needed anyone or anything. This whole time, it's been her coming to my aid when I've needed it, even when we were fighting. I guess this was just me paying back the favour, but why do I feel so strange?

I walk back to the dining table, to Patrick. Jackson and Zack are sequestered to separate ends of the table, seemingly guarded by Malachi and Patrick respectively, along with several members of production, while first aiders attend to them. There's a real shiner on Jackson's face. The Nguyens have gone already.

Bridget, Whit and Lina sit together by the big windows, far away from the men. 'You three alright?' I ask.

Whit gives me a look that can only be described as *please save me from the most awkward situation of my life*. 'It's been interesting!' she says, much too brightly.

Bridget has her head in her hands. 'God, I'm bloody mortified. Karina Nguyen had to hold me back. *Karina.*'

'From what?' I say, taking a seat.

'Walloping Zack. And like, I did egg it on. A bit. Well. Quite a bit. He was just being *such* a shit to Leens.'

Poor Lina is staring out the window, her eyes just as glassy.

'Lina?' I whisper, but she doesn't really respond. I know she's there, because her eyes flick over to me, her lips becoming a flat line. I don't think she wants to talk, so I just offer her my hand and she takes it.

'This might be the weirdest group dinner I've ever been to,' says Whit.

'Oh, do you not usually have celebrities witnessing a brawl?' Bridget drones.

'If the surgeons barny, it just always ends in an arm-wrestling match. Every single time.' Whit sighs, clearly missing the operating room. 'You and Dolly alright? You were gone a while.'

'Yeah. She was just a bit poorly.'

'Probably had too much to drink,' sniffs Bridget. 'I know we all did.'

I don't rush to correct her because it's not my business.

'Thanks for looking after her,' says Whit. 'She's special to me.'

I try to ignore the bit of my heart that says *me too*.

Transcript: Warren and Dolly family meetups

[Opening shot on a South London house in the sunshine, a ramp leading out from the front door. Warren steps up and knocks on the door. Dolly stands behind with a big bunch of flowers and a gift bag slung at her wrist. The door opens to reveal Warren's mum Joyce who squeals and pulls him down into a hug.

Cut to the living room table. Connor is seated at the table in his wheelchair, with Joyce and Peter, Warren's dad, and Dolly and Warren.]

DOLLY — It's a pleasure to meet you all. Thank you for welcoming me into your lovely home.

JOYCE — And you, darling girl. Thank you for looking after my son. He is a blessing and he needs someone to keep him in line.

WARREN — Hey!

DOLLY — *[laughing]* Oh, he does. These are for you – Warren said these biscuits are your favourites?

CONNOR — Did you get me any presents?

JOYCE — Connor! Behave, I beg.

DOLLY — I don't know, Connor ... Do you like video games?

[Cut to a similar scene at Dolly's house, with Warren, Dolly and Dolly's mum Moira, Dolly's Auntie Carol and cousin Jas around the kitchen table. A cake sits between them. The angle is much tighter as the terraced kitchen is small.]

MOIRA — Here now, Warren, you're the man here. You slice this up for us.

WARREN	*[laughs]* It's my pleasure, Moira.
CAROL	Ah well, he's an alright sort, isn't he? So, tell us about your wedding then?
DOLLY	Don't you want it to be a surprise?
JAS	We'll see it on telly anyway.

[Everyone laughs.]

DOLLY	You'll all come, won't you?
MOIRA	*[wiping a tear away]* I just wish I could be there when you pick your dress.
DOLLY	Oh, Mum.

[Dolly gets up to hug her mum.]

DOLLY	It'll be better this way. You can save your energy for the big day. We'll Zoom you in.

[A snippet of an interview with just Moira.]

MOIRA	That's the hardest bit, really. The missing out.

Chapter Thirty

Dolly

Transcript of a video from reality TV content creator @missgoss

Wow, what a wild episode! But I couldn't help but notice some editing shenanigans happening – using proper wine glasses means they can't hide from me! Do we think the show is trying to give Zack a more sympathetic edit than he deserves? Carys and Dolly disappearing over and over suggests Frankenscene to me!

Being back in Liverpool, just for the day, is like breathing fresh air. I suppose compared to the air quality in London, it is.

I finally called Mum, obviously. It was, well, a very short phone call in which I told her I was home, which she apparently already knew because production had been in touch about arranging to film Warren and me coming up to visit. Initially, production wanted her to come all the way down to London to meet Warren's family at the same time, but I said it was either we met my mum where she was at in a way that wouldn't nuke her energy levels for days or weeks, or none at all.

I want her there on the wedding day, and that's what we have to energy budget for.

Production didn't put up a fight. After all, they wanted the shot of my giant husband meeting my tiny Scouse mum.

Warren is polite, incredibly gentle and very deferential even when Mum is bossing him around no end. Even though he's physically massive, it feels like he *fits* as if he's been here a million times.

We get what we needed, and Mum even hammed things up for the camera without asking.

And now that the cameras are gone, I can tell The Talk is about to happen.

I get up to make us fresh cups of tea, so that I have something to do with my hands. A bollocking is imminent, I can feel it.

'Baby Jas, didn't you want Warren to go film something with you?' Mum suggests. Mum's never really got out of the habit of calling her 'Baby Jas' even though she's almost a legal adult and has been caring for my mum a lot the last few years.

Jas bats her eyes at Warren. 'Please? It'll get me so many followers.'

'Is this for school?' he asks, pretending to be serious.

'... Yes.'

'Don't listen to her,' I say. 'She's doing all the sciences so she can be a microbiologist.'

'Yeah, and *maybe* I want to use the platform to educate people about science and stuff.'

'And stuff? Dead convincing, there, Jas.'

'It's cool, I'll do it,' Warren says, getting up from the table and taking the dirty cake plates with him.

'He's on athletic rest!' I call after them. 'Be gentle with him.'

Jas bounces on the balls of her feet. 'I'll pick an easy one.'

They disappear into the back garden, leaving Mum and me finally alone. The saying 'you could cut the tension with a knife' was not designed with us in mind. It's so thick it strangles.

'He's nice,' she says. 'Good lad.'

'He is,' I say with a little too much pride. 'I like him a lot.'

She harrumphs but says nothing.

'Come on, Mum. Let's hear it.' I sigh. 'I know you weren't happy with me going on—'

'Why exactly are you doing this, Dolores?' Her uncharacteristic use of my full name is a shock to the system, and she fixes me with unimpressed eyes.

'I explained it all to you before. Influencing, it's just not stable enough as a long-term business. I needed to put some roots down into other industries. Make a name for myself. I can't go back to the kitchen, Mum. You know that.'

I wonder how much she and Auntie Carol have been talking about this in my absence. I want to ask her if she's been tuning in. What she thinks of everyone.

She stares at me over the steaming cup of tea. 'And he's fine with this all being a business arrangement, as you put it?'

'Yes.'

'And what if you're found out?'

I circle the handle of my cup with my finger. 'There's always a way to spin it. Like, we say we wanted to keep dating but had to get married for that to happen. Or that we realised late on there were differences we hadn't accounted for. People have been doing it for years. We wouldn't be the first couple from reality television to milk it for our collective gain.'

The problem with being something of a professional bullshitter is that there's always *one* person who can see right through you to your core, and unfortunately for me, that person happens to be my mother.

'I didn't raise a liar, Dolores.' She says it so flatly, looking right at me, that I think I might crumble.

'Mum?' I try to reach for her hand, but she moves hers, sitting back. I swear she looks at me like I am a stranger. After so many weeks away, I feel like I might be. 'Are you feeling alright?'

She scoffs. 'Oh, because I'm narked at you there must be something wrong with me? I'm grand, actually. Apart from being vexed by your personal and professional decisions, but what would I know? I'm only your mother.'

I feel the urge to explain myself, but how do you do that when the person who disagrees with your decisions is the person you did it all for? 'Mum—'

'Come on, Doll. I'm pissed off with you. Let me be annoyed about it.'

'I know you don't like what I do for work but—'

'I couldn't give a hoot what you do for your job, and if we had to survive on less, we'd manage it. We've always found a way to make do. I'm the mother in this house, it's supposed to be my burden.'

'Is that what you're upset about? That you're not in charge?' That's a bit over the line, even I can see that. 'I didn't mean—'

'I didn't *ask* you to do this,' she continues, and I really hear the anger in her voice. 'I would *never* have asked you to give up your life in this way.'

'It's not giving up my life,' I groan, trying to resist the teenager-ness that sets back in when I'm under this roof and being needled. 'He's a nice man.'

'I know he is. That part is not in doubt. But you two now have to get married and entwine your lives for years. Do you understand what that means?'

'Yes, I think so.' It comes out a little too haughty.

'You think? Shouldn't it be a little more than you think? Baby Jesus, save us. And if you think I can't lecture you because I divorced your dad when you were a pup, you've got another thing coming. I know more than anyone what can happen when you make a bad choice.'

I try not to sigh, but school my breathing. 'I know, Mum. That was so hard for you. But I need you to trust me that I'm going into this with someone I care about, who I trust. And I actually think the fact we don't love each other is a good thing. Fewer feelings to get hurt.'

She snorts. 'Don't say that too loudly around Jas. I think she's taken with the man. You'll encourage the girl.'

I look out the window to see her teaching him a dance move that takes him a few goes to get right. Jas is in her element, bossing him around, like every other woman in our family. 'A true Doherty there,' I murmur.

I think for a moment that the heat of the argument has dulled, but I'm wrong.

'What I'm hurt about,' Mum says, and my throat catches as she says *hurt*, 'is that you didn't ever present this as something for us to talk about. You went and applied without talking to me. You decided it might be a good idea. You decided that we needed the money, and let's be real, you were too chicken shit to talk to me about it because you felt guilty.'

'I didn't feel guilty,' I lie.

'No, you did. You felt guilty that you didn't ask in the first place, and you feel like it's some kind of moral duty to protect me from thinking about the hard things in life.'

God. I hate that she's right. 'I just want things to be easy for you. You've got so much on your plate—'

'Aye, but I thought we were a team?' It's so much worse now I can see the tears in her eyes. 'You've had to step up far earlier than I'd ever have asked for, and you have done it – most of the time – with grace. I'm so thankful for you.'

She takes my hand, and I realise that I'm shaking.

'If you'd brought this to me as an idea, we could have hashed it out. But you didn't tell me until it was a done deal. You took that choice from me, Dolly,' she says quietly.

Fuck. I did. I really did. How did I not notice this whole time that that was what she was obviously upset about? Mum's autonomy has been so decimated since she got sick, and I was just another in a long list of people who stomped all over her, making decisions for her.

'I love you, and there will come a time when you will have to make decisions for me about a lot of things,' she continues, her voice calm and steady. 'But now is not the time. And I don't think going on a reality show qualifies as power of attorney.'

'I'm sorry, Mum. I'm sorry I hurt you.'

'The hurt will pass, but I need you to understand that this has got to be my choice too. I've got to be part of the team. You can't be thinking you're the hero taking it all on – that just takes something else from me. It was bad enough when you gave up the kitchens for me.'

I sigh. 'We both know that the endo would have stopped me from being there sooner or later.'

'Another reason you shouldn't be taking all this on. Have you heard from your doctor about surgery yet?'

'Not yet.' I've been on the waiting list for over a year for a laparoscopy that will slice away all the endometriosis lesions in my body. And that's after years of gynaecologists who knew less than fuck all and told me just to get pregnant, or that passing-out levels of pain were normal. Then more years of trying different birth controls with doctors who kind of got it. I've spent so much of my twenties being curled around a toilet, just like the other night.

'Hmm,' Mum murmurs. She knows what a state the desperately underfunded NHS is in better than many. 'It is probably best you left the kitchens or you'd have punched one of the male chefs out for being a chauvinist pig,' she says with a laugh.

'Yeah, I would have. I miss it, you know? But when I get to make a new recipe for socials, it feels a little like that. I'm hoping that maybe the network will be interested in a food show I'll pitch to them.'

She gives me a knowing look. 'And I imagine you've got that pitch all prepared and ready to go for them?'

'Naturally.'

'That's my girl.' It's a relief to hear her call me that. 'Look, thank you for hearing my piece.'

'I'm sorry I wasn't listening hard enough this whole time. I thought you just didn't approve of the career and I got in my head about it, pushed you away until it felt more done.'

'You waggling your lovely little bum on television was never what I imagined, I'll admit,' she says with a laugh that I share. 'But you were never the girl I imagined. You've always been so much more than that.'

'Thanks, Mum.'

'Could you not have gone on that one with the host with all the camp outfits?'

'*The Traitors*?'

'That's the one.'

'I'm not sure I'm that good a liar.'

'Don't knock yourself. I just don't understand why you'd go on a show where they don't pair you with women. You've been telling me which girls you think are pretty since you could talk.'

'I can't have been that bad.'

'You came out the womb waving that pink, orange and white flag, girl.'

We both laugh because yeah, that's probably accurate. I resist the urge to correct her that the lesbian flag wasn't designed until 2018, but my teen bedroom was covered in posters of women, hung and admired in ways that the straight girls could never begin to understand.

'And I've always been so proud of that part of you. Proud to be your mum. You've always known exactly who you are, Doll. That's why I don't understand why you'd throw *that* Dolly away just because you think it might help me.' There's a tiny pause, barely more than an intake of breath, before she asks ever so lightly, 'Were there not any nice girls you met on the show?'

I can always sense the baited hook in front of me when it comes to Mum. 'Why?' I ask cautiously.

She chuckles to herself and sips her tea. 'I don't think that the production team understand what they have on their hands. I see how that little redhead girl looks at you.'

My stomach drops. 'Oh.'

I know I should feel scared that it might be obvious, that I should be panicking about the show outing me accidentally. But there's something particularly disarming about my mum seeing that the girl I can't stop kissing wants me.

Mum lowers her voice, reaches out her hand and takes mine. 'And I know you, so I know you're spending all your time trying not to look at her. That's why I don't understand.'

I glance at the door.

'You think he doesn't know?' she asks, and I shake my head. 'The man has two good eyes.'

'It doesn't matter. Carys and I squashed it.' Mum doesn't even look at me while she sips her tea. 'Warren and I are a team. I can't go risking that for a girl who had her queer awakening because of me.'

'Oh, she did, did she?' Mum snorts. 'Why am I not surprised something happened? You always were a little heartbreaker.'

'I am not.'

'I had half the girls from all the unis' LGBTQ+ societies milling round my front door when you were nineteen, Dolores. A few times I had to send Jas out to offer them tea and tissues.'

I swipe at her, my hand landing in the fluff of her big dressing gown she wears no matter the weather. 'You did not.'

'I did! I was running an unofficial branch of the Lesbian Line phone service for all the counselling I was doing. So what's she like then?'

'Getting married to a man, Mum,' I say pointedly.

She scoffs. 'I think we both know that doesn't mean anything in the grand scheme of things.'

'I think it means a lot this time,' I say, a little taken aback by how sad I feel about it. 'Plus she hates me.'

'Didn't old Willy Shakes say there's a thin line between love and hate?' She thinks for a moment. 'Oh, actually, maybe that was a Pretenders song.'

'My only love sprung from my only hate,' says Jas, dramatically swooning in the doorway. 'Juliet innit. We did that in year eleven.'

'Did you have fun using my husband for your algorithm?'

Warren reenacts the apple dance. Clearly he did.

'That's pretty much what *you're* doing, though,' Jas says. 'That's what Mum and Auntie Moira said.'

I round on Mum and I just know I have the biggest shit-eating smile on my face. 'Oh, is it?' There's nothing sweeter than catching your mum being a little bitch, especially when she's been occupying the high ground like an army general.

'Jaslyn Doherty the gob on you,' Mum groans. 'Is there no sanctity in this house?'

'So you *have* been watching,' I laugh.

'Look at her, smug as a creamed-up cat,' Mum says to Warren.

'Admit it, you were bitching about me,' I tease.

'Not just you. She thinks that Bridget is fake too,' Jas adds. 'No offence, Warren.'

He holds up his hands and sits back down at the table. 'None taken. Why don't you like Bridget, Moira?'

Mum wrinkles up her face. 'She just gives me a weird feeling. What is it you kids call it? The ick.'

'It's definitely not the ick,' sighs Jas.

'And she's highest on your shit list, over Jackson and Zack?' I gasp. 'Mother, you misogynist.'

'Oh, come now. They're just obvious. Why waste my breath on *obvious* arseholes?' She taps the tabletop with her finger. 'There's something funny about her. Just watch yourself, will you?'

I nod, even though I'm pretty certain Mum just hates her in the usual reality television way. 'Okay, I will.'

Mum gets up from the table, her arms shaking at the elbows. This has been a long day for her, and I know she's exhausted. 'Now, come on, future son-out-of-law,' she says, and Warren stands to attention, even if she has made it sound like he's a cowboy that's marrying into the family. 'I have lots of things in high places for you to reach for me.'

Transcript: Carys meets Patrick's family

[Awkward music plays over Carys, Patrick and his two parents sipping coffee together in an empty café.]

DAD	So, what do you do, Carys?
CARYS	I work on a city farm. That means a lot of—
MUM	A farm?
PATRICK	Not just any farm.
CARYS	Yes, like I was saying I do a lot of teaching as well as looking after the animals—
DAD	So you spend your day cleaning up after animals?
PATRICK	You could argue that's what my job is too, Dad.
MUM	It's a little more skilled, Patrick. Let's be realistic here. There is a wealth disparity that needs to be addressed.
PATRICK	That's not a conversation for this table.
DAD	I think it is, but fine. Whatever you want.
MUM	Have you heard from Peony recently?

Transcript: Patrick meets Carys's family

[Scene opens on Ang and Del walking down the corridor to Carys and Patrick's apartment. They knock on the door, and it's flung open with Carys leaping into their arms. The three girls come inside.]

DEL	Okay, wow, this is definitely a leg up from your house share.
CARYS	I love you for coming.
ANG	Do you not normally love us?
CARYS	Shush. Will you come meet Patrick?

[Montage of scenes of them saying hello. Patrick cooks in the kitchen while Carys pours the drinks. Together they lay out plates of pasta in a rich glistening red sauce, topped with parmesan.]

DEL	So, Patrick, do you think women should have jobs?
PATRICK	Err, yes?
ANG	And their own bank accounts?
PATRICK	Well, I think that we should have a joint account for some things but that Carys can keep as much of her money as she likes. We need to have a discussion but there's obviously a pay disparity—
DEL	And is that a problem for you?
PATRICK	No, I—
ANG	Patrick, are you attracted to my sister?
CARYS	Angharad!
PATRICK	*[visibly red]* Yes. Of course I am.
CARYS	You don't have to answer. My sisters are being impolite.

PATRICK   They just want to know that I'm being good
          to you.

[Ang and Del begin eating, and Ang's eyes close. Cut back to when their plates are clean.]

ANG   Patrick, it seems I have grown quite fond
          of you, especially if you keep making pasta
          like that.
DEL   Even if you are someone who looks in holes
          all day.
PATRICK   What holes?
DEL   More like *whose* holes.
CARYS   *[buries face in hands]* Please stop saying holes.

Chapter Thirty-One

Carys

Excerpt from podcast Rox' Docs, interview between Dawson Roxford and Cobey Worthing

ROX   So what's your *real* opinion about Zack then? Between friends?

COBEY   He's not good enough for Lina. I don't think I am either, but I wouldn't make her this sad. She looks so sad.

ROX   You know what would fix that? Surfing.

COBEY   Not sure even surfing could fix that, mate.

'And what do we think, ladies?' calls Karina, as I walk out in my dream wedding dress.

It's a modern take on a Regency wedding dress. The waistline has been dropped from directly under the breasts to the top of my waist and the sleeves end just at my elbows tied with little bows. The back closes with pearl buttons. I've seen this dress in pictures online for years, and I knew I wanted it. I can't quite believe that the show agreed to work with the designer and bring the dress to the fake filmset shop we're all sitting in, so that I could wear it.

It is perfect. I only wish I felt the same.

The room explodes with excitement, most of the noise

generated by my sisters. My mum didn't come. She and Dad promised to come to the wedding, but she seemed to think this was a bit of a pointless exercise when nothing was legal. Just like they often don't get me, to be honest. Normally I wouldn't mind but I'm in a room filled with mothers and daughters.

But my beloved sisters are here, whooping and hollering and crying all at once.

Whit gives a good 'Yeah, babe!'

'Do a spin!' calls Bridget, who has already chosen her slinky ice-white silk dress.

I acquiesce, and I feel like a princess, until I stop spinning.

The women who I am pretty sure actually do work for a bridal shop help me back to the changing room and make notes for my adjustments – everything always needs to be taken up, even if I'm planning to wear heels.

They leave me alone for a minute to put my normal clothes back on, and I take a second to try to breathe.

God, how did everything go so wrong so quickly?

First, there was that horrible meeting with Patrick's parents. I'm not sure they could have been *more* obvious that they don't like me, don't approve of what I do, and wish he was still with Peony. He tried to reassure me that they'll come round, but how am I supposed to win over people who clearly hated me before they met me? I've been trying that dance all my life, and I know precisely how far my skill extends. I can sway unsure, I can reassure confused. I cannot ever bring back pure dislike.

Second, I found out that Patrick had, in fact, texted Peony the minute he'd got his phone back to let her know that he was engaged. I don't know if she ever replied, but his parents took great pleasure (thankfully off camera) in letting Patrick (read: me) know that she was distraught about the whole situation.

'Carys?' calls Reb, her hand waggling the curtain. 'Are you alright? Do you need a hand?'

'Yes and no,' I sigh, pulling my dress over my head. 'Sorry, I just needed a moment.'

'Okay.' I hear her hover outside the cubicle. 'Are you crying?'

I put my fingertips to my cheek and find that I am, in fact, crying. 'Oh. Yeah.'

'Do you want me to get your sisters?'

'No. It's alright,' I say quickly.

If Ang and Del come in here, it'll all come out. I'm glad that they could come today, I really am. But I feel like my chest is a Pandora's jar (no, it wasn't a box) threatening to burst open with all the feelings I'm cramming in there.

Horrible imagery, really.

I have to mask for the camera and for all the other contestants, and that means my sisters too.

To be honest, everyone feels a little off today. Maybe it's just the presence of family. While Bridget is decidedly ecstatic, she has toned down quite how many swear words she uses, and chatters away with her mum in Welsh.

Whit sits upright with the posture of a ballerina.

Dolly, who looks much healthier than when I last saw her, claps along politely but sits alone. I wonder where her mum is. We haven't spoken yet today but I can't imagine her being fazed about being here solo. She's much more independent than me.

And Lina ... well, I can't work out what is going on with her. Her mother, a tiny and very enthusiastic Asian lady who kissed me on the cheeks when I said hello, seems to be putting on a good show, but I see the concern in her eyes when Lina is off camera. I tried to talk to Lina about the fight, but she brushed me off.

'The last thing I need is Mammy knowing my husband hit someone,' she sighed, and I really, really wanted to say *isn't that a bad sign* but then it was her turn to try on dresses.

And then there's me, wondering if Dolly has been right

all along about Patrick still being in love with his ex. I don't doubt that he's falling in love with me, because he's said it a few times. I have strong feelings for him too. But still the spectre of the other woman hangs over me.

The tears run harder now and I realise, in the detached way you might if you have cut yourself by accident at some point, that I'm really upset. 'Fuck's sake,' I mutter, looking for something to dry my eyes with, but there's only a row of fabric samples hanging from the hook and I really do not think they will take kindly to me using those as a hankie.

'Do you need a drink of water or something?' Reb asks, running through the list of things that she can feasibly do.

'A tissue, please,' I sniffle.

Reb slips back into the room with a box of tissues. 'They're well stocked in here. I guess people are always crying.'

I blow my nose so loudly it makes my ears pop.

'Go on, girl, get it out,' Reb says. 'I didn't think you had a sound like that in you.'

It makes me laugh, despite everything.

'Wedding jitters?' she asks, perching on the stool. 'It's very normal. It's a big decision.'

'Not just that,' I say, feeling my tongue loosen. Hell, if there's anyone I can tell, who might be able to help me out in this situation, it's Reb. Maybe she can find out what Patrick's been saying to his handler? Maybe she can help me find out about Peony?

Maybe she could help me call it off.

'Patrick's been texting his ex-girlfriend,' I tell her, and her eyes widen just a little.

'Ah. Shit.'

'Yeah.'

Reb sucks her teeth. 'And she's still around? Is he actively in a relationship with her? Have you seen her around the apartments?'

I frown slightly because none of these are things I'd even considered possible. Why does she think he's capable of that? 'No, he's not,' I insist.

'Okay, don't get freaked out,' she says, apparently seeing how freaked out I am. 'Just protocol. I have to ask you that in case it's, you know, a security issue.'

'I'm just *upset*.'

'Of course you are. Do you want to talk to the therapist about it? I can get you an appointment for later today, before we film the drinks tonight.'

'What—' My mouth goes dry. 'What if I didn't want to do it anymore?'

Her eyebrows meet. 'You mean, get married?'

I don't answer.

'That's what the altar is for,' she says, her voice taking on a firmer tone. 'If either of you decide that you don't want to take it any further, you can just stop at the vows and leave the relationship there. That's built into the show for you.'

Her words are straight out of the *Wedded Bliss* handbook.

'And if I didn't want to even go through with the wedding?' It comes out as a whisper.

Reb presses her lips together. 'Carys, there's a contract. The agreement is that you'd stay until the end, once you're engaged, unless the show decides to let you go. I ... I think it would be wise to stick things through,' she says slowly. 'For Patrick,' she adds hastily, though I have no idea how humiliating him at the altar would be in his best interests.

Something sinks in my stomach. It's clear that if I struggle now, the show is not here for me. They want that. That's what makes good television. I can't help but wonder if Lina has tried to have similar conversations with her handler.

I'm sad that it means Reb and I aren't real friends. I'm always misjudging that.

Still, we've got the rest of the day to film so I plaster on a brave smile. 'Sorry, I really don't want to leave. I just ... wanted ...' I shrug and can see the slightly silly face I'm pulling in the mirror, like oh gosh I'm so *random* aren't I. 'I guess I got carried away. And no, thank you for the offer, but I don't need to speak to a therapist. The good cry helped.'

'Sure,' Reb says, not meeting my eyes as she leaves.

I smooth out the fuzzed edges of my makeup with my little finger, and remember to slip my mask back on as I follow after her.

When I walk back into the dressing room, Dolly steps up onto the dais in a figure-hugging, off-the-shoulder cream dress in draped satin. She takes my breath away. Her slicked-back hair gives it a harder look, and I can imagine a vintage leather jacket draped over her shoulders. I imagine a different world where she stands waiting for me, clutching a bouquet in her hands. Her scarlet lips breaking into a smile as she sees me walking towards her.

I take the first seat I find, which happens to be right behind Whit's mum, a woman wrapped in a beautiful silk scarf and a cloud of heavenly perfume. 'God, she looks incredible,' Whit's mum says to her daughter, and she's right. She tilts her head closer to Whit. 'Where's her mum, though? Did she not want to be filmed?'

Whit says, 'Oh, Dolly's mum's disabled. She's very sick, and can't easily leave the house, so she's saving her energy for the proper wedding instead. They're very close, so I think she's missing her.' I feel my world crack in half.

'Poor girl. It's hard to be without your mother on a day like this.'

'Yeah. She's her main carer too, so I know she's been worrying the whole time. I think meeting Warren went well, at least. It's just hard.'

'I understand. Could they not Zoom her in?'

Whit shakes her head. 'Production got a bit weird about it.'

Whit's mum's posture stiffens. 'The wankers. Here, let me go take some good pictures of Dolly in her dress for her mum.'

Whit's mum gets up, and I see Whit spot me out of the corner of her eye, a flash of panic as she realises I might have overheard what I suspect is a secret.

It's not something Dolly trusted me with herself.

I get up and walk quickly to the bathroom.

Responsibilities. That's what Dolly had said, hadn't she? That was why she was here. It wasn't just wanting a good cover story for why we couldn't be together. She wasn't just rejecting me for her career; she was rejecting me for her mum. This whole time I just thought the worst of her, when she was trying to support her family.

I pushed her and I pushed her and I was so fucking set that *of course* she couldn't trust me with the truth of her family life. But Whit can't know her almost marriage is fake. It was smart of Dolly to give people only half the story.

I can barely look my mirror self in the eye. I take big gulps of the metallic too-warm tap water, and try not to cry again.

I've spent all this time trying to be a version of me that I don't even recognise. The only person who could break through and show me who I am is Dolly. She saw through all my masks; autistic and straight and all the other parts of me I was squashing down. She saw me. And I didn't take the time to see her.

God, I'm such a fucking idiot.

I've pushed her away.

I've ignored all the warning signs with Patrick, even though I adore him.

And now I'm crying in a bridal shop, realising I might have fucked up my life.

Chapter Thirty-Two

Dolly

Excerpt from podcast Rox' Docs, interview between Dawson Roxford and Cobey Worthing

ROX	If you could say one thing to Lina, what would it be? Cobey?
COBEY	Sorry, I have to go.
ROX	What? He's gone? Listeners, he's gone.

If there had been any doubts the show was running on a scant budget, the biggest sign should have been the joint stag and hen party that we couldn't even invite our friends to. Though, fuck knows who I'd invite at this point. Feels like all my friends are in this room with me.

And enemies, let's be real.

I know it's customary for the show to get us all loose on booze and bring in the singletons from the warehouse at some point, but I didn't think they'd do that *now* when we're about to get married. The showrunner chose violence, because I find myself on my hen do sipping on a very badly made margarita with Whit who is practically vibrating watching Malachi talk to Priya across the room.

'Come on, you're going to spill your frozen daiquiri.' I take it and set it on the bar top.

'No, don't take that from me. I need it.' Whit slurps the straw into her mouth, and takes a big hit. 'Oh tits, I've got sodding brain freeze.'

'Tongue to the roof of your mouth,' I tell her, as she rubs her forehead.

'This is the worst day ever,' she says thicky through a pressed tongue.

'You just tried on your wedding dress with your mum, and it's the worst day?'

Whit looks at me with sad eyes.

'Don't you dare feel guilty because mine wasn't there. We're not talking about that,' I say firmly.

'I said nothing.'

'You trust him,' I say, knowing I don't need to ask it as a question. 'He had a connection with Priya and hasn't seen her in real life before. He's just catching up with her. You've got to let it happen or it'll just be super weird and become A Thing.'

'You're right,' she moans, tongue still wedged. 'You're so calm. How are you so calm?'

I scan the room for Warren and find him on the couch talking to all three of the Hannahs and Niamh. It did give me a little thrill when their eyes nearly fell out of their skulls when they saw what he looks like in person, out of basketball kit. Sorry, girls, you can have him in a couple of years. He spies me looking, and blows me a kiss, which shatters their hearts. Oopsie.

'What will be will be,' I say.

I realise in my scanning that I've not seen Carys at all since we got here. Several of the men are on the other side of the cube-shaped bar from us – Patrick, Billy (who will forever be the teeth guy to me) and one of the other guys who I didn't even remember – with Bridget who is flirting up a storm.

Daniel, the guy who tried to guess my weight like a hog at the county fair, barely even said hello, and is over in the corner talking with Zack and Jackson about macros and weighing their shits or whatever red-pilled gym wankers talk about.

'You're looking for Carys?' Whit asks and I sense the hesitation in her voice.

'Why'd you say it like that?'

Whit licks her lip. 'The booze is making my mouth numb,' she says, but I'm pretty sure that's a lie.

A roving camera comes close, stopping at us, and I turn to wink down the lens, which I'm not supposed to do but fuck it.

'Yes, I was wondering where she is,' I say steadily. 'Lina too.'

'Do you think we should go look for them?'

'I think you need to finish your daiquiri, talk to a few other people and then swan over to Malachi to let them both know that you're actually cool with them talking.'

'But I'm not really,' she says glumly. 'I feel like a bad feminist.'

'Fake it, babe.' I give her a kiss on the cheek. 'I'll be right back.'

I do a quick circle round the room, but I don't find either women, so head to the toilets. If in doubt, you can always find someone hiding out in the ladies'.

What I didn't expect to find was Lina furiously making out against a sink with a blond man who is decidedly not Zack. They don't even notice me come in. Their microphone packs are turned off, strewn at their entwined feet.

My own secret bathroom liaison partner isn't in here with them. I could leave them to it, but I don't want the cameras to find them.

I close the door behind me, and they spring apart, lips rubbed red from kissing.

His eyes are the kind of bright blue that you only find in oversaturated teen movies. 'Cobey?'

He gulps. 'Hello.' It's clear he doesn't recognise me.

'You're not in trouble. It's Dolly.'

'Oh gosh!' He bounces a little, like he might want to give me a hug, but is still glued to Lina.

I don't blame him. I set my clutch bag down on the dry bit of sink top. 'So . . .'

'Please don't tell on us,' Cobey begs.

'I literally would not dream of it. This is actually really nice to see.'

Lina's cheeks are bright from all the frantic kissing, but so are her eyes. Finally, the old Lina is looking back at me. 'I made a terrible mistake.'

'Yes,' I agree. 'Now what?'

'I'm leaving. With Cobey. We're getting out of here.'

I raise my eyebrows. 'Before the altar?'

'I can't stand another second with Zack.' Her fists clench at her side. 'He's just such a . . . such a . . .'

'Cunt?' I offer.

'Raging haemorrhoid!' Lina yells. Creative, I'll give her that.

'I'll second that. Production are going to come down on you like a ton of bricks, you know that?'

'We'll weather it together,' Cobey says, and I'm glad that my instincts that he's a nice dude were right.

'Priya might be able to help you,' I say, remembering she's some kind of lawyer. 'Are you in touch already?'

She shakes her head, so I make her give me her phone so I can follow Priya's Instagram account from her own. It's quite bad that in the time I've had my phone, when I'm supposedly not working, I've hunted down everyone's socials. No surprise that I found Zack following some truly vile content creators.

'Next question, how are we going to get you out of here?' I pick up the mic packs, make sure they are off and wrap the loose wires around them.

'You don't think we can sneak out through the kitchen or something?' Lina asks.

'Not without them seeing.' I go into one of the stalls and wedge the two packs behind the toilet. 'You need time to go and clear out your flat with Zack. Do you have keys?'

'Yes, I do.'

'You've thought about this a lot,' Cobey says to me.

I wash my hands thoroughly because I've touched too much floor and toilet area for my liking. 'I'm always looking for an exit,' I say, a little too honestly.

I look past them to the window. We're on the ground floor, after all.

The latch is stiff, but the frosted glass slides with a little encouragement so there's just enough space for them to climb out.

'There. It'll be a wiggle, but you can do it.'

Cobey goes first, sliding through like he's going down a water slide. He lands with a healthy thud, but his face reappears ready for him to guide Lina through. She's so small that I have to give her a boost up onto the ledge.

The look she gives Cobey has love written all over it. There's no embarrassment or hesitation or fear or disconnection like her face has shown in turn over the last few days. This is the kind of love that'll keep her safe.

She's halfway through the window when she turns back to me. 'Thank you, for everything.'

'I just undid a window. You made the choice. Go, live happily.'

'Dolly,' she says, wariness in her voice. 'Just ... don't trust Bridget, okay?'

'What do you mean?' I ask.

'I—'

The bathroom door starts to open and Lina makes the

leap, gone before Bridget herself even notices as she just goes straight into the stall.

'You alright, babes?' she asks, mid-stream.

'Yeah,' I say, Lina's words still hanging over me. 'Just getting some fresh air.'

'Fresh is not what I'd call it.'

I take the opportunity to top up my lipstick, needing something to do with my hands. 'You seen Carys?'

The toilet flushes. 'She was outside earlier, I think? Probably doing an interview.' She washes her hands a little too quickly for my liking. 'You sure you're alright?'

'Just missing my mum,' I say, a little surprised when the truth slides out of my mouth.

She pats me on the shoulder. 'You'll see her at the wedding, right? Only a few days to go.'

'Yeah.' I give her a brave smile. 'I'm going to find Carys.'

Bridget snorts. 'I do not understand you two.'

'Why's that?' I say, even though I wish I hadn't.

'You just can't help yourselves. Always looking for each other, even though you hate each other. If one of you was a boy, I'd think you'd have a pash about it.'

She laughs at the absurdity of it and storms out the bathroom, and I cannot help but wonder if that was some low-grade accidental homophobia, or a warning.

I walk through the bar, saying hi to a few people as I pass, and make my way out to the front of the bar. There's no cameras out here, and Waify Liam, who walks past me back into the bar reeking of cigarettes, is the only production member I can see.

So where is Carys?

It takes me a few minutes to find her. She sits cross-legged across the road from the bar, on a bench that overlooks the river. She's alone.

'Bit cold out here,' I say, sitting down without asking her permission.

It's clear she's had a few to drink. Her face is flushed pink, almost red on the apples of her cheeks. 'I didn't notice.'

'Long day.'

'Long day,' she agrees.

I'm conscious that our conversation is still potentially being recorded out here, even if we're not actively being filmed.

'I'm sorry your mum couldn't be there today,' she says.

'Same to you,' I say, recalling her twin sisters cheering her on as she spun in her princess dress.

She scoffs. 'My mum thinks this whole thing is just another instance of me getting Carys'd away.'

'You mean carried?'

'No, that's just what she calls it. When I'm impulsive, or don't think things through.' She laughs, a loose sound that comes from a few too many shots. 'Mother knows best.'

'That's not very nice.'

'Not all of us can have kind mothers,' she says in an offhand way that breaks my fucking heart. 'She's not ... I mean—'

'I understand what you mean.'

I want to reach forward and take her hands, but I don't want to force her to look at me because that feels like top of the list of autism 101 no-nos. So does touching her without asking. There's so much I haven't asked her, haven't taken the time to ask. No wonder I keep finding her outside crying in the middle of the night.

'God, I'm so tired,' she sniffs. 'Everything is just *so* much all the time.'

'I can imagine,' I say, before adding, 'Me too.'

'And,' she sniffs, 'it takes so much energy to hate you.'

I laugh, despite myself. 'That almost sounds like a compliment.'

It gives me a little thrill when she laughs. 'Oh dear. Not again.'

We both laugh then and everything, for just a moment, feels normal. Like we haven't spent the last week breaking each other's hearts repeatedly. Like we're just two women on a dating show, talking on a bench at night about our upcoming weddings.

'I should have listened to you,' she says quietly. 'About Peony. They're still talking, I think.'

'Fuck, I'm sorry.'

She glances over at me.

'I mean it,' I insist. 'I'm sorry he's not being careful with your heart.'

'It's not his fault. It's not like I've been taking good care of it either,' she sighs.

We sit in silence for a moment, and I wish I still had my bad margarita. Or even a good one.

The sound of a throat clearing makes me turn around, and I see Posh Louise crossing the road to us. 'Hi, darlings. We're all done filming for the evening, so you guys can just have fun for the rest of the night. Can you hand over your mic packs?'

I unclip mine with ease, as Carys wriggles out of hers. I'm relieved to get rid of them. Maybe, for once, Carys and I can speak plainly.

'Thanks, Louise,' I say as she waves us goodnight.

We watch as cameras are packed up, and the team slowly disappear into their van. No one else leaves.

'Everyone else is having too much fun,' Carys says, reading my mind.

'Do you want to go back in?'

'Not on your life,' she laughs. Her skin is goosepimpling in the cold air.

'Okay, but we can't stay here either. You'll catch a cold for your wedding day. That seems like bad luck.'

'Will you walk me home?'

In another world, walking a girl I fancied home from the bar had a very different connotation.

'Not like that,' she says quickly. 'I'm just so tired I think I might get lost, and I don't really have the money for an Uber. Not until we get paid.'

I check the route and realise we're actually much closer to the flats than I thought – only a twenty-minute walk. I turn my phone to show her the route. 'That seem alright?'

She nods and gets up from the bench. 'I need to move.'

'Do you need to tell Patrick?' I ask, as I fire off a quick text to Warren.

Carys doesn't answer me. Woof, it must be bad.

We don't talk much, and instead I enjoy the quiet of London in the early hours of the morning. It's nice having a clock now, but it also means I'm very aware that it is 2 a.m., a time when I'm very rarely out of bed.

My shoes go from pinching to biting just as we get inside the building, and I kick them off when we are in the lobby. The porter looks completely unbothered. The things he must have seen.

Carys walks right over to the lift and presses the call button.

We step in, and I press the button for the twentieth floor. The familiar rise kicks in, but as we near the tenth floor, Carys suddenly leans forward and hits the emergency stop.

The lift grinds to a halt.

'Carys, what are you doing?' I gasp. I'm not afraid of lifts, but I've seen *Mission Impossible* enough times to have a healthy distrust of their mechanics.

'I want to talk,' she says. 'For the last time.'

Chapter Thirty-Three

Carys

I can't leave things unsaid.

Tomorrow, the whole cast has a last day off while we finalise things for our weddings. After that, everyone gets married. I might see her at the filmed reunion, but that'll be it. Dolly Doherty will walk out of my life forever.

'Could we not have done that in your flat? Or, you know, anywhere that's not a tiny, enclosed space that could fall at any moment,' Dolly says, pressing her palm against her collarbones. It's possibly the first time I've ever seen Dolly look so freaked out.

'I just needed to talk to you,' I insist.

'Okay, so talk.'

I take a deep breath. 'I've come to accept,' I begin, my voice shaky, 'that I like women.'

'Was it all the fucking that gave it away?' she laughs awkwardly. 'Sorry, it's the lift. I make jokes when I'm nervous.'

I almost feel bad about how much she's stressing out.

'Can I finish my coming out speech, please?' I say firmly. 'And then you can leave.'

She blows out a long breath. 'Go on. Talk to me, Cherry.'

My heart twists. 'I'm starting to accept that I like women and that's a lot for me,' I continue, conscious that I'm sliding into monotone monologue mode, but I'm too tired to modulate my speech. 'When I was a teenager, I kind of knew but I had to shove it away. I just didn't have space to think about it, because so much else was happening – finding out I was autistic right at the end of high school after years of struggling through, trying to understand all the complicated hierarchical rules of friendship groups and then uni too.'

'That sounds like a lot,' she says softly.

'It was. And being into women, whatever that meant, felt like bottom of the list in some respects, but also one of the most painful ones to look at straight on ... excuse the pun. Plus I knew I liked men so, you know, it didn't seem that relevant.'

I feel a little embarrassed admitting the last part to her specifically.

'That makes sense. Even when it's joyful there's the ...' She pauses as she searches for the words. 'Recognising how much is going to change for you. That separation from compulsory heterosexuality is hard, really hard. Of course you locked that away.'

'Yeah, Lina suggested that to me but I didn't really understand everything about it. I've been too scared to look it up.'

'Not to be your preachy gay elder,' Dolly says. 'But it's the idea our society just assumes every woman likes men and only men. And we can internalise that as our own truth, even if it's just something that the patriarchy is trying to sell us.'

I feel like my world is cracking open, for perhaps the twelfth time this week. There's a power in naming the Thing that you've been battling against. The silent malevolent force is less terrifying when you name it.

'Yes, that feels right,' I say, filing that away in my mind to look up online, and then process, later. I suppose it really did feel like that. 'I think it makes it more complicated that I do still like Patrick.'

'I bet. The community can rag on bisexuals, calling them

straight or just gay or cheaters or greedy, but youse don't have it easy.'

'I'm hardly beating the cheating allegations,' I sigh, and we both laugh. 'Anyway, I wanted to say thank you.'

'Thank me? Carys—'

'If it wasn't for you,' I steamroll ahead or I'll chicken out of what I want to say. 'If it wasn't for whatever this is . . . was, between us, I wouldn't have worked it out. Not for a long time, anyway. I'm still not really sure what to do with the information given the circumstances but I guess I accepted something about myself, even if it feels . . . I don't know, not relevant.'

'It can be relevant even if you're with Patrick. It's whatever you want it to be.'

'Yeah, so, despite everything, I think you deserve a thank you.'

She takes this in, watching me. God, I'm going to miss her just watching me.

'Carys, you don't need to thank me. I just—' She stops herself, glancing up at the ceiling. I wait, giving her the space. I hate it when people rush me, after all, but, more than that, the sooner we finish speaking, the sooner this is over. 'I see you, Carys. You've got a lot going on in that head of yours, so I'm glad that you worked it out and it has been . . . well, an experience to have been a part of that.'

I can't help but laugh at that. 'The Carys is a Bit Gay Experience.'

Dolly laughs and shakes her head. 'But that's the thing I can't help but admire about you.'

'What, that I'm repressed?'

'Shut up, I'm trying to be serious.' Dolly takes a breath. 'Since we met, I see how hard you're always working to be present or the "right" kind of person.' She adds the air quotes. 'I'm not sure it's even who you want to be, and no one else seems to notice the effort you're putting in all the time, or the dissonance. It's maddening to me, so I don't know how you manage.'

I feel seen in a way I never have before.

'I spend my life trying to make it unnoticeable,' I say, understanding how sad it might sound if someone else said it. 'You're the only one who foiled me.'

'The only one?' Her voice catches in her throat.

'The only one. I guess that's why it hurt so much when I thought you didn't want me.'

'I never said I didn't want you,' Dolly whispers. 'That's the whole problem.'

I step closer to her, even though I know I shouldn't. 'I know. I know the truth now. I heard Whit and her mother talking about your mum. That you're her carer. I know what the state of social care and welfare is for disabled people. So I know that you must be struggling, and that the protection isn't there long term. You needed the money for her, didn't you?'

Dolly sighs but she doesn't look angry. If anything, she seems relieved. 'I didn't tell you because—'

'I understand,' I cut her off. 'I'm the only one who could have put it all together. I could have got you thrown out.'

'But you didn't,' she says. 'And that's on me for not trusting you.'

'To be fair, for most of the time I was either trying to fight you or fuck you.'

We both laugh sadly.

'Can I tell you now?' Dolly says, and this feels like confession.

'Tell me.'

'Mum is my favourite person in the whole world, and I nearly fucked things up with her too – she's, err, kind of angry with me that I did this for her without asking.' She pauses now, to hold back tears. 'Which is fair, that was my fuck up. I just really want to protect her, which she finds maddening because she's the mum. She's so funny and brutal and honest. Just this absolute pillar of a person, she always was.'

'Sounds like someone else I know.'

'She ... well, she got sick when I was a teenager. Do you know what seizures are?' she says, in a rush of air.

'Yes, from my first aid training I know a bit. Not enough, admittedly.'

'Well, most people think of epilepsy when we talk about that, but that's just, like, one kind of seizure. You can have them for all kinds of reasons. My mum has this thing called Functional Neurological Disorder. When I was a teenager, she had a really bad fall at work and we thought it was *just* a fall, but it very quickly became clear it was not just a fall. Sometimes her legs wouldn't move right, or her hands would get stuck clenched up.'

'That sounds painful.'

'Yeah, it's shit for her. And she started having seizures, like the shaking kind mostly. It's really hard because there's still so much unknown about what it is, other than it being some kind of nerve communication problem, like the software on her computer-brain has gone wrong?' She pauses to laugh. 'Sorry, can you tell I know dick all about computers or neurology?'

'You're doing great,' I insist.

'Anyway, she's on a lot of meds for various things that she seems to *also* have alongside it. It's like every few years we'd spot something else was going on. So I guess she was just ... coping or trying to for too long, and it all went kaput.'

The fuzzing in my brain whispers that this feels a little too familiar. 'That must be really hard for her.'

Dolly looks a little surprised. 'You know, usually the first thing people say is "that's hard for you", meaning me, and that pisses me the hell off,' she says with anger. 'But it's hard for *her*. Sure, I help her with a lot of things, and I've worked from home for years so I could be there to help care for her, but I don't have to have the thing, you know?'

'Forgive me if this is an ignorant question,' I say, waiting for her to give me the go-ahead. 'Does she get any extra help, like someone to come in to help her other than you?'

'Well, there's my Auntie Carol and my cousin Jas. And me. At the moment, we've not had much luck getting her at-home care, but—' She bites down on her lip. 'Yeah, maybe in the future. It's a bit complicated. Plus, looking after her is my pride and joy. And it's also a doddle, most of the time. *She's* the one who has it tough.'

It all makes sense now. This version of Dolly I thought I knew, this conniving faker with a veneer of kindness, was completely wrong. 'I think you're allowed to say that it's hard for you too, because I imagine it's a lot of pressure.'

'Yeah, but what family isn't? We all have something,' Dolly says casually.

'Hmm, yeah,' I say, not wanting to add that that *something* was, for a long time, me. 'But you've been doing that while dealing with your own stuff.' I feel a bit stupid for the euphemism. It's like I can't get out of the habit of talking around things. 'Your endometriosis.'

'Like I said, we all have something,' she says, softer now. 'Have you told anyone else you're autistic?'

'Here? God, no.'

'Not even Patrick?'

I shake my head.

'Why, Carys? That . . . I don't want to presume what it's like for you, but telling me meant I could understand a bit more what was going on for you. Why haven't you told him?'

'Isn't it obvious? I'm scared of being the *something*,' I say, pointedly.

'Come on, he won't think that. He adores you.' I can hear the hesitation in her faux certainty. 'Sorry, I don't want to diminish your fears.'

'It's easier to lie,' I admit. 'I've been masking for so long that I don't know who Carys is half the time. In fact, if I'm honest, the most truthful I've felt is with you. How fucked up is that?'

We both laugh sad-laughs. 'We're both crazy,' sighs Dolly, and she takes one of my hands, then both. 'You know I stayed out all night.'

'After my meltdown,' I finish for her, unsure what to do with the swell of emotion cresting in my chest.

We stand together in the corner of the lift, heads bowed but not quite together given our height difference.

'Thank you for telling me about everything,' I say.

'I'm sorry I didn't until now.'

'It's a good way to leave it. With some final truths.'

'One hell of a goodbye,' she sighs. 'But an honest one, if this is where we're leaving it?'

'I think we have to. For Patrick and Warren and your mum, and for us.'

'Fuck, this is all so hard,' Dolly says, and I know she's thinking what I am – that it hurts more to say goodbye when the feelings are there. It's just circumstance, even if it's of our own making.

I look up into her beautiful eyes that swim with tears. My heart is breaking, but so is hers. It feels fair, that way, to both be falling apart under the weight of the realisation that this is the end for us.

'We're both liars, you and I. That's why we fit so well together.'

I reach up to kiss her, and she leans into it. It's sweet, soft.

A goodbye. We both know it is. I try to drink in every inch of her, every bit of her smell and taste. How do you form a memory of someone in the moment? How do you harness every last bit of them, knowing it'll be the final time?

There's no way we can be friends after this. We were never friends; we were always more than that to each other, and that's why we have to keep apart, if we're going to have a happy life.

Dolly has to protect her mother. I won't be the person who stands in the way of that, not any more. This whole time, I've been lying to myself that I've not been fighting for her in every barb and argument. I wanted her to notice me. Even irritation is attention. If her eyes were on me, she was still here. We were still *something*.

And now I know I have to let her go.

When our lips break apart, we stay in each other's arms. We have to break contact in increments.

My heart breaks further when Dolly whispers, 'I hope he's good enough for you.'

'I hope so too. I think he will be.'

'You really like him, don't you?'

My heart says *enough* but my mouth chooses, 'Yes.'

She pushes an unruly strand of my hair back behind my ears. 'Well then, tell him if he's not a good husband, I'll come drop kick him.'

I laugh but it's marred with a sob. 'I'm glad I won't have to tell Warren that.'

'Yeah. He's good. You were right when you said I don't deserve him.'

I don't know what to say. What is there even left to say?

The lift starts moving by itself, and soon we are rising back up to the flats we share with our fiancés.

My life with Patrick awaits. My future husband, the man I care so much for. I can see it now – our flat in London, us both bringing our work home in the form of bottle-feeding lambs, and surprise litters of kittens, and ancient dogs we say we're just fostering but will adopt. And the children we'll have, one day, with bright auburn hair and his laugh and my freckles.

And in embracing that, I have to say goodbye to the shadow version that exists, a future with Dolly. It's too painful to even picture beyond her waiting at the altar. But I take one last look at that image in my mind, and I say goodbye to that too.

Before the door opens, I kiss her again. Just once.

'Goodbye, Dolly.'

'Goodbye, Carys.'

We step out into the corridor like nothing ever happened, and walk to our front doors.

As my key enters the lock, I remember one final thing I want to tell her. 'Your fake accent is pretty good, by the way,' I say, giving her a smile.

Her voice drops, lower and thicker, Scouse through and through. 'You clocked that, huh? People prefer poshos, what can I say?'

I push open the door. 'Liars forever,' I promise.

'Liars forever.'

And with that, I close the door on Dolly Doherty.

Chapter Thirty-Four

Carys

Or at least, that's what I thought. There's a knock on the door, just as I closed it, and my heart thrills with possibility.

Has Dolly run back across, refusing to say goodbye? Is she going to choose me?

I fling the door open, my heart leaping out of my chest, and I see Dolly across the hall with her door open too.

There's no way she could have knocked on my door.

Instead, between us in the corridor, is Bridget. 'Evening, ladies,' she says. 'I'll make this quick.'

Dolly's eyes are wide with warning. Something is up here, she can tell.

'Hi, Bridge,' I say, slurring my words on purpose a bit. 'Dolly and I walked home together.'

'Cut the act, Carys,' she says firmly. 'There's been enough lying. I know you two are together.'

Dolly has gone completely white.

No, she can't know. She can't have seen. We've been so careful, haven't we?

'Together?' I say cutely, playing the fool on purpose. 'Yeah, we walked home.'

'No. You've been fucking this whole time,' Bridget snaps. 'Behind everyone's backs.'

I'm making her angry, but I can't give up. She has to understand. 'You— you've misunderstood,' I stammer.

Bridget looks at me, more sad than angry. 'No, I've not. I've seen how you two have looked at each other the whole time. How overnight you fell out, moved rooms and stopped being besties. The way you looked when you left the bathroom on the honeymoon. All of it. I've seen it, and I can't pretend like I haven't anymore. It's not right. And I don't buy that this is a fight over Patrick.'

'Please, don't tell him,' I beg. 'Please, Bridget. It's over now. Dolly and I have squashed it. Tell her, Dolly.'

'It's over now,' Dolly agrees, and it feels like a sucker punch to my chest.

'That may be the truth,' Bridget continues. 'But that doesn't change what I've come here to talk to you about. We're going to make a deal.'

My blood fizzes like melting sherbet. 'A deal?'

'You two are going to say no at the altar. Both of you. That way, neither of you get married.'

'And that puts you in second place behind Whit and Malachi,' Dolly finishes. 'You don't get the nest egg, but you might get the clout.'

'Lina and Zack are hardly competition. It's just you four.' She shrugs like this is nothing. 'I knew you were a game-player, Dolly. Too bad you spent all your energy cheating on your fiancé instead of using that brain to beat me.'

'And what if we say no?' Dolly's teeth are gritted.

'I tell production that you were sleeping together the whole time,' Bridget says calmly. 'I'm pretty sure the show doesn't take kindly to cheating. You'd all be ejected from the show, and the media would be informed, I'm sure.'

'You wouldn't,' I gasp. 'Bridget, you *can't* do that to me. I thought you were my friend.'

'You fucking scumbag,' Dolly hisses. 'You *worm*. Carys isn't even out. You want to do that to her? You want to take that from her? It should be her choice when she gets to tell people, if *ever*. You don't understand what you're doing.'

'I understand perfectly, and I don't want to out you,' Bridget says, like she's talking to two unruly children. 'So if you just agree to my deal, we won't have to even consider that.'

'Forgive me if I don't believe a jot of that,' Dolly spits. 'Lina warned me not to trust you, and I should have listened. You're a fucking snake.'

Bridget sighs like she's getting fed up of this. 'The fact is, girls, you two broke the rules. We should all have been fined for your finger-fucking or whatever *lesbians* get up to.' She says *lesbians* in the same way that I've heard that beautiful word weaponised my whole life; spat, with disdain. 'And I doubt that Warren and Patrick are all-in on this side project you've got going on.'

'I thought you were my friend,' I whimper, just as Dolly snarls, '*Fuck you.*'

'I think there's been quite enough of that for one series,' Bridget says, admiring her manicure. 'Now, do we have a deal?'

'I do not make it my business to make deals with homophobes,' Dolly rages.

'Stop calling me a homophobe. I'm not a fucking homophobe!' yells Bridget, and I think, deep down, she believes it. It's funny the things you can believe about yourself even in the face of glaring evidence. 'I just refuse to lose to you fakers! What Jackson and I have is actually real.'

'Please stop shouting, or someone is going to hear,' I beg, my hands shaking. 'Please, Bridget. You can't do this to us.'

'Carys.' She spins round to face me, and tries to take my hands in hers, but I step backwards away from her, stumbling into the wall.

'Don't touch me,' I snap. 'Don't fucking touch me. I can't believe you've done this.'

I burst into racking sobs, and sink to the floor, just as Patrick and Warren storm down the corridor.

'What the hell is going on?' Patrick says, wrapping his arms around me.

The worst part is that I can see all the fight go out of Dolly. 'We were just having a conversation,' she says.

'All's fair in love and television,' Bridget says, striding off down the corridor.

I barely register Patrick lifting me and guiding me back into the flat, tucking me in bed, because I can't stop hysterically crying. He keeps asking me what she said, but how can I even begin to tell him?

What the fuck am I supposed to do?

Chapter Thirty-Five

Dolly

Excerpt from podcast Rox's Docs, interview between Dawson Roxford and the Hannahs

ROX	Okay, girls, who do you think is the fakest?
HANNAH S.	Bridget!
HANNAH C.	OMG, Hannah, shut up.
ROX	You think she and Jackson could be *Wedded Bliss*'s Ottie and Seb, Hannah P.?
HANNAH S.	I'm Hannah S.
ROX	Sorry, Hannah S.
HANNAH S.	Actually . . . maybe I shouldn't speak about this without a lawyer present. Hang on, let me call Priya.

I've been trying to work out what to do for the last twenty-four hours, and I've come up with nothing.

Of course, I couldn't tell Warren what was really going on. I palmed him off with a drunken argument between Carys and Bridget, somewhat helped by the complete breakdown Carys had – though, well, I'm not sure if it was a meltdown or not. It seemed like one. Patrick beat me to picking her up, and I had to resist with every atom in my being. It would have made it worse.

I barely slept, my dreams always returning to Carys crumpled on the floor. And then all yesterday we were tied up doing last-minute wedding prep all the while my anxiety thrummed.

I know he knows something's up. He's smart; that's why we picked each other. But if I tell him what's going on, I've got to be honest with him about how stupid I've been throughout our entire fake relationship.

He would be in his right mind to say no at the altar.

I had hoped I'd have a good sleep before my wedding, but I slept in fits and starts.

I find myself scrolling Carys's Instagram again when I wake. I've not followed her. That feels too intrusive. It's so normal compared to my profile full of reposted content from other platforms of me cooking, outfits of the day, aspirational lifestyle content of a life I don't even live.

And then there's her, feeding animals. Shearing a sheep, somehow. Talking to children about animals. This feels like the most honest version of Carys, but it's still hidden behind a veil of not talking about her reality. There's nothing about meltdowns or overstimulation or anything else she experiences here. The only giveaway is all the autistic advice accounts she follows.

I end up reading through a bunch of them, feeling the urge to learn more about how she experiences the world, even though I won't be in her version.

After another burst of sleep, I check my phone one last time, and it's half four. The hair and makeup team will be here in the next hour to get us ready.

'Let's just get up,' Warren murmurs. He rolls over and slings an arm round my waist.

'Sorry, did I wake you?' I whisper.

'Mmm.' The sound rumbles through the mattress. 'I'm awake too.'

'Big day,' I whisper.

'Big day.' He rolls out of bed, stretching his broad back. 'I'm going to get us some food.'

I hear the coffee machine go in the kitchen, and I decide to have my shower, scrubbing away the stress of Bridget's threat. I'm going to have to talk to Warren about it this morning. I'm going to have to make a decision, but who do I protect? Carys, my mum, or Warren?

If I say no, Warren and I break up. Unless we agree to stay together, but that doesn't look so promising for brands.

If I say yes, Carys and I get outed.

I leave the shower wrapped in big fluffy white towels and a matching robe, moisturising my dry, tired skin with a hydrating mask that I hope won't bring me out in spots.

The hair and makeup team arrive soon after that, earlier than I anticipated, and get to work. By the end, I look like the bride I'm supposed to be. My hair is slicked back slightly, a bit of a flick at the bottom to give the look some edge. Red lipstick, of course, but the rest of the makeup is softer than my usual style.

I look like a bride.

The dress hangs on the back of the bedroom door, the shoes paired together underneath like a ghost's wearing the outfit already.

We need to get a move on soon. We need to be at the Barbican this morning but via the hotel our family are in to help everyone over. Production wanted the couples to spend the night apart in a hotel for tradition's sake, but we convinced them to give up those rooms to our family members so they didn't have to trek across London.

In the kitchen, Warren has set out a breakfast feast. There's bowls of strawberries, sliced peaches, crumbles of granola.

The yogurt and honey sit in their usual tubs, spoons at the side ready. From the oven, he takes out some pre-made pancakes he's heated up.

'I know they're not as good as my crêpes, but hopefully they'll suffice,' he says, placing a couple on each plate.

'This is wonderful,' I say, taking a seat. 'Thank you. Another good husband point.'

He huffs a little laugh to himself. 'As that might be,' he says, picking up his coffee and blowing the steam. 'Dolly, were you ever going to tell me that you are in love with Carys?'

I choke on the strawberry I'm eating, and he has to whack me hard between my shoulders before it goes down the wrong way.

'You good?' He looks somewhat terrified.

'Yeah, sorry. No eating while we talk about this,' I say, setting down my fork. I could deny it, I could try and hide. But where has that got me? Heartbroken with my neck on Bridget's guillotine. 'I think I was hoping I'd get over it.'

He nods. 'So you *are* in love with her?'

This is a question I hadn't even dared to ask myself, but I know the answer immediately. 'Yes,' I whisper. 'Oh shitting tits, I am in love with her.'

He sucks his teeth. 'Ouch. I'm so sorry.'

'Why are you sorry?'

'I've not had to watch someone I'm in love with falling for some other guy,' Warren points out.

'I *hoped* I'd get over it,' I say. 'For you. For us.'

'You could have told me,' he says without accusation. 'I'm sorry I didn't make the space for you to do so.'

'Well, I came out to you in the swimming pool. I should have told you the rest.'

'And she's in love with you too but doesn't know it yet?' He neatly slices up his pancake into triangles, like little slices of cake.

'I think she suspects, but she's better at lying to herself than I am.'

'That would be impressive if it wasn't so sad.'

'Ouch,' I say, wounded. 'Below the belt.'

'I'm just trying to ask questions about my fiancée's girlfriend. Speaking of below the belt . . .'

I flush with embarrassment. 'Yes, she and I have slept together. Twice. Sorry.'

'And that's what the fight with Bridget's about, huh?'

God, the relief. 'You nailed it.' I explain Bridget's plan to extort us, with the threat of outing Carys.

'And you,' he says.

'Yeah, but I don't really care. I've been out before. I can weather that storm,' I say. 'Hell, there's probably been a few lesbians from the Liverpool–Manchester scene tweeting about what a lay I am. I can play bisexual if I need to, I'll lie for us. It'll wash off me, though if I'm honest, I think it'll jeopardise some of our plans.'

'That's not what I'm worried about,' he says sincerely.

'Carys has never come out. This would rob her—' I can feel myself choking up. 'She deserves the chance to say it herself if she ever wants to, not that she ever has to. And Bridget is trying to rip that from her.'

Warren's eyes soften. 'You really do love her.'

'It's dreadful, isn't it?'

He takes my hand. 'Being in love is magical. Now, what are we going to do about this?'

'You don't have to do anything, Warren. I just need to work out what to say to Bridget. I was worried she'd caught me helping Cobey and Lina escape.'

'What? They escaped?'

'Yeah, right out the bathroom window. I suspect they're lying low right now.'

Warren chuckles to himself. 'That dog. Good for them.'

'I'm just glad she's away from Zack.'

'Wait, but why did you think Bridget was coming to you about that?'

Then my mind finally clears. 'Lina told me to be careful with her, but didn't tell me why.'

'Do you think she also knew what was going on between you and Carys?'

I think back to our conversation in the warehouse, when I thought Lina was trying to hint to me that she clocked me. 'Yeah, now you say it. But I don't think that was just it.'

I look at my phone. 'Is it too early to call someone?'

'I don't think you have to worry about being rude on your wedding day,' Warren says.

I open Instagram and see the little green circle that tells me she's online, and in a rush of daring, I video call Lina.

'Hey! Hello!'

'Sorry it's so early,' I say. 'I just needed to talk to you.'

'No, don't worry.' She and Cobey crowd into frame and I realise they are in an airport.

'Where are you two off to?' Warren says, wriggling his seat closer.

'Home to Scotland,' Lina says. 'We're going to see my mum, and go to the registry office today.'

'Wow, congratulations, guys!' Warren and I chorus in delight.

'We figured the show couldn't get too angry with us if we got legally married and offered them an exclusive on-camera interview,' Lina explains. 'And, well, this is the man I am going to spend the rest of my life with.'

Cobey kisses her on the cheek. 'Thanks for the bathroom assist. What did you want to ask?'

'Lina,' I say. 'You told me to beware Bridget?'

Her face pales. 'What's she done?'

I explain.

'Oh, that arsehole,' she growls. 'I'll kill her.'

'So, you also knew about Carys and I?'

'Well, I knew she was having a gay panic over you, yeah. I'm familiar with the signs. Is she alright?'

I shake my head. 'No. I'm scared for her.'

'Well, don't be. It's time to play Bridget at her own game. Look, I can text you the evidence after we get off the call, but she's a liar too.'

'What do you mean?' I say, my heart leaping with hope.

'It's a sham! She and Jackson were together on the outside before they came here. They faked it.'

'Holy fuck,' I gasp.

'Oh shit,' echoes Warren.

'The whole act of finding their soulmate or whatever – they knew each other and applied together and went no contact for months. She got a little cocky and told me after her proposal, after having too much show wine. I thought I needed a bit of leverage, just in case she remembered I knew and tried to get back at me. I went through her phone at the dinner party when Jackson and Zack were kicking off. Air dropped myself some of their texts.'

I am agog. 'Lina, you fucking genius.'

'Not just an airhead yogi,' she laughs, and I feel bad for pigeonholing her in my mind from the off.

We hang up, and she does indeed send screenshots and a screen recording of the message chains between Jackson and Bridget going back over a year. What a con. I'd be impressed if she wasn't also a total dickhead.

'Well. That's it. We don't need to worry. We'll just blackmail Bridget right back, and then we can all get married just as planned.' I nod along with all my words like one of those dashboard dogs. 'Should we send it as a text, or go to her room? I'm not sure if she and Jackson will have left for their wedding yet. Maybe a menacing phone call?'

But then, I look up at Warren and see that he's been watching me this whole time. 'Warren?'

'Go to her, Dolly,' Warren says, his voice so soft and kind and good. 'Don't let that love go, not without a fight.'

'Don't be ridiculous.'

'I'm not being ridiculous. I'm being honest.'

'No, we made an agreement,' I hold out, though fuck, I'm torn. I don't want to, but I'm not going to go back on this.

He takes my hand. 'Dolly, our agreement didn't count on one of us falling in the kind of love that people watching this show dream of. Plus, we are never going to win the nest egg.'

We both laugh, because of course we're not. Whit and Malachi have that completely tied up.

'But the brand deals – the couple power,' I insist.

'We're still friends, aren't we? We can still do that. I bet people would love if we have a divorcee-but-best-friends energy,' he says, and God, I know he's right. There's still a way we could play this that means we're not losing everything.

'I'm not sure I'm ready to be open. Does that make me a coward?' I ask.

'Do you really want to work with companies who wouldn't back you? I know pink-washing is a thing, but why are you boxing yourself in? Your mum would hate that for you.'

I know he's right. Mum has been, if I'm honest, a convenient excuse to some extent. Being out means I open myself up to trolling, maybe even death threats. It's not just losing money on platforms that might demonetise me for being gay.

'Love comes with sacrifices and compromise. Just depends on whether you think Carys is worth it,' he says.

I'm torn, drowning in guilt. But if I'm honest with myself,

I've been jeopardising our agreement since the first time I kissed Carys.

'Fuck, I'm sorry, Warren.'

'What for?'

'Putting you in this position. Our families—'

He puts his index finger over my lips, and all I can smell is the fancy hand cream he uses. 'Nope.'

'But—' I mumble.

'Negative. You probably do owe me a few apologies, and that's fine. Pay me back in cooking and collabs. But now you've got to go tell that girl you want to have her babies or whatever.'

'I can't do it,' I say, standing up from the table.

'You love her.'

'I do. I love her. But, the show?'

I know he understands what I mean. Am I outing her if I go speak to her? Is this going to play realistically into the fighting-over-Patrick dynamic the show has been airing, or will it all crumble down with me just showing up?

And even if I do manage to catch her before she walks down the aisle, what if she doesn't want me? When she so nakedly told me she wanted to leave the show with me, I told her no and I was only in it for the money. She really does like Patrick, I can admit that even though it riddles me with jealousy.

If she does want me back, what reason will she give for leaving Patrick? I don't want to force her to come out before she's ready either. It needs to be her choice, all of this does, but there's no time for her to comfortably make one without her ending the day legally married.

But I can't let her marry Patrick without fighting for her. This whole time, I've not fought for her because I was too scared about what would happen with Warren and my mum. I need to show her I'm in, if she is.

Liars forever, that's what she said?

I just don't know how to spin this.

'Contingency plan,' Warren announces, cutting through my thoughts. 'If it all goes south, slink back up to the Barbican, say you were running late, and we have a fun little cold feet storyline to play with.' He says all this as though this is so normal and fine, but then, this is how we've operated the whole time.

'But if she wants me back, you're alone,' I say.

To my surprise, he laughs and takes my hand. 'Dolly, do you know *how powerfully* getting left at the altar because you fell in love with a girl is going to play for me? I am going to make so much heartbroken but understanding, feminist, lesbian-ally ex-fiancé content. I'd get to be a single man with *hurt feelings* expressing them healthily.'

'Oh God, you'll be unstoppable,' I gasp. 'Think of all the women who could fix you.'

But still, I'm frozen. I can't quite move yet. There's too much running through my head about Mum, about Connor, about the whole reason we got into this mess.

Warren stands up, and tilts my head up from my chin. 'I know you're scared. But that promise to look out for each other? That still stands for me. You're family. It's you and me together, no matter what.'

I believe him. With every essence of my being, I believe him. What a joy to have found a soulmate of a different kind than this show offers.

'Oh God, I'm going to cry and ruin this horrible makeup,' I wail, throwing myself into his arms. 'I don't deserve you.'

'Nope. I'm exceptional.'

We break apart and I bite my lip as possibilities rush through me.

'Come on, we've got a wedding to stop,' he says.

'Fuck. I don't even know how to get to wherever the fuck that big house is. Surrey? Suffolk? Sussex? Why do they all sound the same?'

'I remember.' He takes out his phone and brings up the route options.

I take the phone from his hands. 'Shit, it'll take over an hour to even get out of London. And there's no train station nearby.'

A jingle of keys rings through the air, and I see him slinging them round his finger. 'I'll drive you.'

'What about the guests? They'll be getting ready.'

'I've told my mum there's a hold up. They'll go have a nicer pamper with your mum too. She'll be relieved,' he says with a laugh.

'Oh don't. She'll be devastated you're not her son-in-law.'

'She'll be glad you're being true to yourself, Dolly. You know that's all she wanted. Not the money or the glamorous wedding. She wanted you to be you.'

'See? She's going to be devvo that you're not in her house.'

'Eh, I'll marry her instead then.'

'I think Jas thinks she's next in line.'

'You lot can't get rid of me either way.' He takes my hand and kisses it. 'You were the best fake fiancée I could ever have hoped for.'

'Warren, I think you might be my best friend.'

'Come on, stop being a big wet and get your things.'

I run around the flat gathering up my things, and as I do I fire off a text to my mum.

Dolly

> Wedding to Warren might be off.
> I'm going to tell Carys I love her.

Mum

> Go ed, girl. Love you x

It's happening. I'm going to go tell Carys that I love her.

I'm ready.

Except, it's exactly that moment I realise I'm still in my towelling robe. 'Fuck, what do I wear?'

Warren appears from the bedroom holding my dress. 'It's a wedding day after all. May as well show up looking the part.'

Chapter Thirty-Six

Carys

Transcript of a video from Reality TV content creator @missgoss

Possible breaking news, Blissfuls. I just got wind that one of the final five couples cancelled their wedding venue. Do we have an elopement, a breakup, or a secret third thing on the cards?

I hated sleeping alone so much I made my sisters come share my king-size bed with me. It's not like it's the last night I'll spend in a bed on my own – Patrick and I are going to have to do long distance for a while yet.

If I say yes.

I wake up when the birds sing. Out in the countryside, the dawn chorus actually happens at dawn, rather than at night when there's less traffic like in the city. But, with the lull of sleep nipping at my heels and the exhaustion of the last few weeks deep in my bones, I fall back asleep, nestled between my sisters.

We wake to a knock at the door as the hair and makeup team arrive to get us prepped. They seem pretty narked that we're not showered yet, so I jump in while my sisters wash in their own room.

Our wedding ceremony starts at midday, so I have a while to eat a croissant and neck an espresso brought up by room service. The coffee is so strong I could stand a spoon in it, and it burns through my veins.

Probably not the best choice because I become deeply aware of the possibility I might need to fart, as the makeup lady does my brows.

My sisters come back in just as the hairdresser begins styling my long hair into soft waterfalling curls.

'Can we put some music on? Let's get in the mood,' Ang says.

'I did make a playlist for the occasion,' says Del.

Ang sighs, and sits down on the end of the bed. 'I am not listening to "2 Become 1" by the Spice Girls on repeat for three hours, no matter how much effort you put into adding it a million times.'

'Spoilsport. Caz, do you have something you want to listen to? Bride gets to be DJ.'

I pick up my phone to open my music app, and see a text from Bridget.

'Carys?' Ang asks.

'What?' I startle, knocking the hairdresser so that the hot curling iron burns the back of my ear. 'Ow fuck. Sorry! Oh shitting hell.'

The nice hairdresser gets a cool flannel and presses it against my ear.

'Why were you staring at your phone like that?' asks Del quietly.

I thrust the phone into her hand. 'Can you read it out for me? I can't handle it.'

Del clears her throat. '"Hi Carys. Deal's off. I won't speak a word. Go marry Patrick. Sorry for being such a cunt. Kiss kiss." Well, it's two xs but you know what I mean.'

'What was she being a cunt about?' Ang asks.

The biggest panic attack of my life crashes through my body

like a wave. I can't breathe. I can't breathe and I am about to claw out of my skin.

The hairdresser sensibly leaps out of the way and turns off the hot instruments at the wall. I hear Del usher her out the room for a break.

'Carys? It's okay, Carys,' Ang whispers as she kneels in front of me.

I shake as every bit of adrenaline that's been storing up in my body sets fire to itself at once. I feel like I could run up a wall, but in a bad way.

She's not going to out me.

'Fuck,' I manage to whisper as the feeling subsides.

'Carys, what happened? What did that text mean?' Ang whispers.

'Do I need to go punch this girl? I will! I'm ready to fight anyone!' shouts Del.

'Del, shush. Mum will hear.'

'Guys. I fell for Dolly.'

I burst into tears, and both Ang and Del pull me against them, so I feel a little like the Barbie they used to love so much they fought, but in a good way.

'Oh honey,' whispers Ang.

'She is very hot,' says Del, nodding sagely. I look up at her, wondering if that's something I've missed the whole time too. 'Oh, I don't like girls. I can admire a nice painting, you know?'

'I like her a *lot* more than a painting,' I cry.

'Where's this all coming from, Carys?' Ang asks. 'Sorry, I don't mean that I don't believe you, just what happened to make you realise?'

'On *Wedded Bliss* of all places,' murmurs Del.

And so I explain the ways that I've been masking, beyond what even they understand. Hiding myself, hiding my queerness (I'm pretty sure that's a word I can use?), as well as my autism. How so much of it is interlinked and that I've been hiding it from myself for so long that I forgot who I was, until Dolly reminded me.

'I just feel like maybe I've been contorting myself this whole time to get attention from men, and that's changed who I could be too. Like I masked all the way into a different straight girl. God, that sounds so pathetic.'

'No, it doesn't,' Del says seriously. 'This fucking culture constantly tells us that that's all that matters. Of course you'd get tangled up.'

'But I'm such a fraud.'

'Baby, male attention is the freest currency in the whole world,' Ang says, stroking my hair. 'When I feel a bit shit, I post a slightly titty pic, because I know the strange men who follow me online will tell me I'm beautiful. You're not a bad person for wanting that.'

'Caz, you've had it so fucking hard for so long that you need to give yourself a break for being human.' Del pushes a strand of hair away from my nose and it comes free slick with snot. To her credit, she barely reacts. 'I'm really proud of you for telling us. Do you have a word you like?'

I sniff. 'I think bisexual is right.'

'Well, you go at your own pace. I'm glad this Bridget dickhead didn't blow that for you.'

'There's just so much to unpack,' I whisper. 'Like how I dress.'

Ang tilts her head. 'What do you mean?'

'I am fed up of dresses!' I suddenly wail. 'I hate wearing tights because they always roll down. There are no tights on earth that are the right size!'

My sisters, bless them, nod along like I'm being entirely reasonable.

'And underwires? Why do I have to hoist my boobs up with

metal? And don't even get me started on shaving. There's so much shaving!'

I run out of things to be angry about and deflate suddenly like a sad whoopee cushion.

'You always were a shorts and t shirts and backwards baseball cap kinda kid. We just thought puberty changed you, or something,' Del says.

'I think,' I say slowly, trying to gather my thoughts as I speak, 'it's part of the masking, but I think I've been dressing for the men-attracting half of me, and maybe in doing that, I've lost the rest of me.'

My sisters nod like I'm talking sense. I can't tell if I am.

This part feels the hardest to explain. How once I probably did like the tea dresses, but I liked knowing I attracted men more. For once in my life, I'd gotten something about being a woman right. Vintage twee was a style that worked for me, and a mask of its own. It feels shameful to admit that it was all kind of fake.

'Have you considered whether you want to be ... or are even a girl?' Del offers gently.

'No,' I say quickly, but not because I'm brushing it away. 'Woman feels right. I just don't know who she is. I don't know what type of woman I want to be.'

'Well, femme isn't for everyone, babe,' Ang says. 'Maybe just for the really hardcore among us.'

Del picks up an eyelash curler. 'Like look at this fucking thing.'

'But designing my wardrobe to appeal to men? That feels unfeminist! I feel like I've failed somehow.'

'You need to quit it with this "failed" nonsense,' Del says. 'And look, I'm a feminist and am unfortunately exclusively attracted to men and I get it, it's complicated and weird, and it sounds even more complicated for you with all this on top.'

'We couldn't prise that baseball cap off your head when you were ten,' Ang observes. 'You yearn for the sportswear.'

I dab my eyes. 'I think maybe I just want to wear clothes that don't make my skin itch all the time. Maybe some shorts once in a while.'

Del pats my thigh. 'You can wear shorts, baby. If you want to take this bisexual awakening and live your best butch life as part of it, we will help you.'

Ang nods ferociously. 'You know we love a makey-makeover.'

I wonder if all straight people start to talk like they're judging *Drag Race* when someone comes out to them.

'I guess you can take my old clothes,' I say with a sniff.

'Oh no, baby, we don't want them at all,' Ang says with such a sweet smile.

'I don't know how Patrick will feel about it. He's only known feminine Carys,' I sigh, and I see my sisters pass one of those unknowing psychic twin glances they hate me mentioning but definitely is a real thing.

'So you *do* still like Patrick?' Ang says slowly.

'I do. I adore him.'

'You don't have to marry him, though,' Del says, 'if you're still working all this out.'

'It's on camera, Del. I would humiliate him if I said no up there. I don't want to end our relationship, so I'll just say yes so we can keep going.'

Another twin glance.

'Stop thinking things together,' I groan. 'I thought twins aren't supposed to be psychic.'

Ang shakes her head. 'Sorry. It's a habit.'

'Thanks for being so nice about all this,' I say quietly. 'I didn't know who to tell.'

'Have you spoken to Mum and Dad?' Ang asks, and the force of my reaction makes her add, 'Okay, that's a no.'

'Mum will just say I've got Carys'd away again.'

'Oh, I hate it when she says that. It's so fucking rude,' Del spits. 'I've told her off about it so many times.'

'You have?'

'Yes! It's infantalising.'

'And ableist,' Ang says, looking very uncomfortable. 'She doesn't like to think about that part, but I think they'd love to act like you're a girl who can't look after yourself half the time.'

'I've not done the best job,' I say. 'I was just crying about tights.'

'No, I'm dead serious,' Ang says, taking me by the shoulders like she's going to headbutt me. 'I am so proud of you and we would be proud of you no matter what you do, but the fact that you've been working and looking after yourself and teaching all those shitey wee kids about beef even though you've been carrying all this?'

'I don't want to call you strong because I don't think you should keep carrying it,' says Del, feeling out her words. 'But you *are*. You're so brave.'

There's a knock at the door, and there's Reb, headphone round her head. 'How are we getting on, ladies?'

None of us move, my sisters still crouched round me like protective lionesses.

'Erm. Yeah. Alright,' I say.

'Cool. You've got an hour, and then we'll take you down to the ceremony.' She hesitates at the doorway. 'Are you sure you're okay?'

I don't have the heart to tell her what I want to say, so I say, 'Just having a normal sisterly cuddle.'

'Nothing weird here,' Del affirms, even though frankly, it probably looks very weird that we're all wrapped up together on the floor.

'Okay!' says Reb briskly, as she walks out the door.

I go to get up, but my sisters are holding me down. It's the perfect squeeze machine – Temple Grandin's squeezer can't compete with two adult sisters.

'Are you sure-sure?' Del says. 'You can change your mind.'

'If Bridget gave us the okay, then Dolly and Warren will be getting married right now anyway. It's good. They get to look after their families together. That's all she wanted.' I feel my lip wobble slightly, and I bite at it to still the feeling.

My sisters relent, letting me get up.

'I guess I'll go and find the hair and makeup ladies we scared off,' says Del.

Chapter Thirty-Seven

Dolly

BREAKING: Exclusive interview with Lina Chen and Cobey Worthing on their unique *Wedded Bliss* journey

They say the true course of love never did run smooth, but today we have an exclusive interview with *Wedded Bliss*'s most unusual couple, Lina Chen and Corbey Worthing, reunited and eloping after Lina rejected Cobey's proposal ...

[continues below]

'Dolly, stop clock watching,' Warren says, not taking his eyes off the M25.

'We are literally racing to beat someone down the aisle. Time is of the essence,' I say, trying to sound light.

'You're stressing me. Find something to do or we'll never get there.'

We've been driving for about an hour, and so far, I've started and stopped about three podcasts, skipped through several albums, and turned Magic FM on and off.

My phone buzzes and I jump in my skin. I'm going to burst out this dress if I'm not careful – it was not designed to sit in for hours while on a mission.

It's a photo of Whit and Malachi, blowing a kiss. Underneath it reads, 'Wishing you both the best wedding'.

It's a bit shite that we aren't supposed to attend each other's weddings if there's no clash, which probably makes what I'm about to do even more taboo.

I turn my phone to show Warren.

'Dolly, I literally cannot look at that.'

'Sorry, I always forget the rules for cars. It's just Whit wishing us luck.'

His eyebrows shoot up. 'You haven't told her?'

'About our daring escapade? No.'

'Or any of it?'

'... No.'

Warren swipes away yet another call from Not So Posh John.

'Can I say something maybe a little harsh?'

'Of course.'

'No matter what happens, you need someone to talk to about this who isn't me. No hurt feelings, obviously, but you know.'

My stomach aches. 'I get it. It's complicated. Thank you for being honest about your needs while you're driving me to ... you know.'

He smiles. 'Perfect husband material, remember.'

'Oh, trust me, I know.'

Whit answers almost immediately, her black silk bonnet still covering her hair. 'What happened?'

'Why do you think something happened?'

'You're in a car and look stressed. Look, Malachi, doesn't Dolly have that stressed look she gets?'

Malachi squishes into the screen. 'She does, babe.'

'Thanks, guys,' I groan. 'Warren's here.'

I turn the camera to him. 'Affirmative.'

'Are you guys eloping?' Whit asks, her eyebrows meeting.

'Erm. No.'

It takes quite a long time to explain everything to her, and to their credit, Whit and Malachi stay silent. For a second I wonder if the signal has been lost.

'Wow. That's a lot,' Whit says eventually.

'I'm sorry I lied to you,' I say, feeling a lump catch in my throat.

Whit shakes her head hurriedly. 'Nope. I get it. It'll take a minute for me to adjust, but it doesn't change how I feel about you. I am a bit gutted I won't get to drop-kick Bridget until the reunion.'

'I think there might be a queue for that.'

'I did think you were really pressed by her for no reason. But I guess that's kind of a big reason. Did anyone else know?'

'Not officially, but this annoying thing keeps happening where it turns out I'm not actually mysterious and covert and people cottoned on.'

'I still think you're mysterious,' Whit reassures me.

'So you're in a wedding dress going to break up another wedding and if that doesn't work you'll go back to your own wedding and get married?' Malachi recounts.

'Yeah, pretty much. We've got the Conservatory booked for the whole day and night so there's time.'

My phone buzzes with another call from Posh Louise that I ignore. 'Production are looking for us.'

'What do you want us to say, just in case they call?' Whit asks.

'Just pretend you haven't heard from us and are busy with your own shtick.'

'Will do. Listen, Dolly, I can't imagine how things are going to go for you but you know we're always by your side, right?'

I bite my lip to stop myself from crying, which makes me think of how often I'd see Carys do the same. 'I love you.'

'Love you too. Go get your girl!'

'Have the best wedding ever. Send me all the pics. And most of all, make sure you win this.'

Whit cackles. 'Bridget and Jackson are toast, babe.'

Chapter Thirty-Eight

Carys

The next hour blurs in anxiety and excitement. Butterflies, not fireworks. More appropriate for a wedding, I suppose. My sisters leave me eventually to go sit in the rows of chairs, a kiss on each cheek as they leave.

I take one look at myself in the mirror and see a glimpse of a new me. A bit of the old me too. I vow to unpick this mask. I have to hope that Patrick is excited for an evolving Carys and will go on that journey with me.

If not, well, maybe I need to choose myself for once.

It's a weird thing to think when I'm standing outside the grand doors waiting to walk down the aisle to where Patrick will, hopefully, be waiting for me. But it's a strange comfort. I can choose me, and him.

The music swells – the traditional bridal march – and the doors open. The room is bright white at first, revealing marble columns, white wooden chairs with green ribbons on the back, a path of greenery and petals leading all the way up to where Patrick stands, a matching green sprig in his buttonhole.

He looks so beautiful.

I walk slowly, concentrating on the timing as the cameras watch me, recording this moment forever. How lucky we are that we will always be able to look back on this? My uni friends sit with their husbands behind my family, and all of Patrick's family including his siblings and their partners are here too. That fills me with hope; they might not approve of this, but they're here. I spy a couple that I don't immediately recognise until he turns. Victor. My driver from what feels like years ago, and his wife Shreya, who beams at me. I can't believe they came.

So many people who care about me are here.

This is the beginning of the rest of my life.

Patrick takes my hand as I reach him, and we stand facing each other. I take one last look at his face as an unmarried man, as though it might morph when the rings are put on. His lovely deep brown eyes, and those crow's feet that I will get to watch deepen over time. His lopsided smile and the lines. Yes, I could fall in love with him. It will come in time, I know it.

'Welcome, loved ones. We are gathered here today to join Carys Cadwallader and Patrick Stringer in holy matrimony,' the officiant, a nice lady called Jane, begins.

The show stipulates that we have to stick to the *Wedded Bliss* script, so she then adds, 'Our lovely couple have gone through a fantastic experiment to find wedded bliss, and we hope that today will be just the beginning of that.'

His smile broadens and so does mine, and soon we are giggling together.

'Now, before we continue, I need to ask if there are any witnesses among us who have an objection to this union?'

There's a heady silence and I hold my breath, wondering if, just if.

'Excellent,' says Jane, when no one speaks. 'I always hate that part.'

Suddenly the huge wooden door slams open, and there, panting and striding up the aisle, is a willowy woman I've never seen before, but I know exactly who she is.

'Peony?' gasps Patrick.

'I'm not too late, am I?' Peony asks, her voice clipped and

desperate. Her curly hair is perfectly styled, and she wears a dark green suit that I'm pretty sure was tailor made for her. I am awestruck by her Keira Knightley-esque beauty. No wonder Patrick was so in love with her. I think I might be a bit in love with her right now.

'I thought you were in Kenya?' Patrick asks, which surprises me because he's never mentioned she was working abroad.

In fact, he's never really mentioned her to me at all.

'I came back when I heard. I'm so sorry to do this,' she directs that last part to me and for some reason I say, 'Oh, it's alright.'

This seems to confuse everyone standing at the altar, including Jane.

'But I couldn't wait,' Peony continues, returning to the matter at hand. 'I couldn't leave it. I had to come tell you I love you.'

'Oh hurray!' cries Patrick's mother.

'Shut up,' hisses Del from across the aisle.

'Oh,' says Patrick, but I see it. I see the light in his eyes. 'Peony, I—'

'Please. Just give me five minutes. I need to say my piece. If you still want to marry ... err. Oh God, I'm so sorry, I don't know your name.'

'Carys,' I offer.

'Carys! Sorry. Yes, if you still want to marry Carys after that, I won't stop you.'

Patrick looks to me nervously and I do not have any idea what to do.

Do I say okay and let them speak? Do I say no? This is my wedding after all. What is the normal human reaction at this moment? I don't have a script for this.

I open my mouth, hoping that the right words will come out, when I hear 'Stop the wedding!'

And then there's Dolly, awkwardly running in through the

open doors, her movement restricted by her slinky dress. What is she doing here?

'Dolly?' I cry.

'Dolly!' chorus my sisters excitedly.

'Oh, hi, Dolly,' says Patrick cheerily. 'How was your wedding?'

'Non-existent,' she mutters, as she reaches us.

'You didn't?' I gasp.

'No. Not yet. I had something to do first,' she says to me.

'Oh, are you here to be maid of honour?' Patrick beams. 'How lovely! I didn't think that was allowed.'

Dolly's eyes move from me to Peony. 'Oh. Hello. Peony, I presume?'

'Yes, hello.' For some reason, Dolly and Peony shake hands. 'Sorry, were you the person I just overtook in the driveway?'

'Yes, but in your defence, you are wearing a much more sensible outfit to stop a wedding.'

Patrick looks very confused. 'You've come to stop the wedding, Dolly?'

Peony gulps. Dolly's eyes bore into me. She came? She really came.

He looks from Dolly to me. 'Carys?'

I can't speak.

'Carys, why has Dolly come to stop the wedding?'

'I—'

'This is a jolly strange coincidence,' Peony says awkwardly.

Finally, he looks at Dolly then back to me. That's when I see it, the moment of realisation in his eyes. It's a kind of heartbreak.

'Oh,' he says quietly. 'I see.'

'Can someone tell me what the hell is happening?' Jane says in the sweetest voice possible for someone who just said 'hell' during a wedding ceremony.

And that is when I run.

Chapter Thirty-Nine

Dolly

Well. I wasn't expecting to be the second interruption of the day, but this does make things marginally less awkward.

'So, you two—' Patrick stutters, still mentally catching up as Carys runaway-brides out the door.

'I'll explain later,' I tell him, conscious of the cameras that are on us. If we speak it out loud, I'm taking that coming out moment from Carys. I don't even know if she wants it, because she's run off.

'Excuse me,' I say to Patrick and Peony, and I take off running too.

When Warren suggested I wear this dress, I thought it was a cute idea because I hadn't anticipated *quite* so much athletic activity.

I spy Warren walking up the gravel to the front doors, having managed to park the car. 'What's going on?' he asks. I point in Carys's general direction, where she is fleeing across the stately home gardens. 'Oh shit.'

'Peony's here too,' I yell back as I struggle to turn a corner, taking it much too wide. I can't stop running or I'm going to fall right over. 'Fuck. The cameras, Warren.'

'I'll hold them off!' Warren hollers, and I hear doors slam, followed by a lot of angry muffled sounds.

'Fuuuuuuck,' I shout as I keep running.

Carys has slowed down somewhat, and I see her take off her nice white shoes (while still running, somehow?) and throw them angrily at the ground. A few ducks fly from the pond in fright. I slip out of mine, because I am absolutely going to break my neck if I run on grass in these slingbacks.

I manage to find a rhythm that allows me to run in this dress, not dissimilar from a maimed horse's gallop.

'Carys, please stop running, for God's sake!' I yell after the runaway meringue of a girl I've come to profess my undying love to.

'No!' she yells back.

'Okay, but I'm not going to stop running after you,' I tell her, biting out each word.

I start to gain on her, but it's so much effort to take a single gallop that I'm going to exhaust myself quickly.

'Oh fuck this.' I ball up the dress in my hands and find the seam along the left leg. 'I'm so sorry,' I tell the dress as I tear open the seam, making a slit that runs all the way up to mid-thigh. If it wasn't ragged as hell, it would look quite good.

It means I can now sprint at full pelt like we're on a *Traitors* mission to steal keys and betray people or whatever the fuck they do on that show Mum thinks I should have gone on.

I've never been a runner, but there's something about the adrenaline of this moment that turns me into what feels like a sprinter who's broken a ton of world records, though I know I'm probably slowly jogging after her. I really hope the cameras aren't seeing this, for the sake of my own dignity.

'Carys,' I plead, but she keeps going. I'm not even sure she knows why she's running at this point.

We're going uphill. She heads straight towards some big marble columny building thing that overlooks the lake. I have no idea what you'd even call it. I don't have oxygen left for thinking.

I am relieved when she stops just inside it, grabbing hold of one of the pillars as she catches her breath.

'Please,' I gasp as I manage to catch up with her. 'Don't. Move.'

She pants hard, clutching at her side. 'I'm not going anywhere.' She bends in half, like a Barbie someone is trying to make sit down. 'I have a stitch.'

I can't tell if this is supposed to be a complaint or an accusation, but I just try to breathe deeply like YouTube exercise instructors say to do when you feel like you're going to die.

'What . . . what are you doing here?' she pants out. 'Why is Warren here? Didn't you get married?'

I hold up one finger to try to get her to stop asking me more questions. 'I came to stop you marrying Patrick. Warren drove.' I take another deep breath. 'And no, he noticed I had a bad case of the—'

I stop myself. I can't make a joke right now.

Carys looks at me like I'm an utterly mad person and honestly, I might look pretty batshit in my bare feet and torn-up dress and wild hair.

But this is it. This is my one chance to tell her I love her.

'Carys, I love you,' I say, making my voice steady. 'I've loved you since that day in the middle of traffic. I've loved you this whole time, even when you're being a little bitch. Especially then, in fact.' I can't help but laugh. 'I think you might be the most interesting person I've ever met, maybe also the weirdest, and together I think we have some bizarre kind of magic that makes me run across stately homes to get you.'

Her mouth falls open but no words come out.

There's a crash, and we both look across the gardens to see the camera crew pouring out of the front door, and several of the production team try to grab hold of Warren, but he's so massive and lithe he nimbly gets away.

I look back to her. 'I'm so sorry, I didn't want to pressure you. And you don't need to come out. You don't need to do anything. We can pretend we're just best friends, old school style, if that's what you want.'

Her scared eyes look back to me.

'But I think you are the future I need. I've thought this whole time that I knew what I wanted, needed, what my mum needed. But I never stopped to think about whether that was true. And that's why I kept getting so annoyed about you coming in and screwing up all my plans. You made me stop and *think*.'

'How rude of me,' she laughs breathily.

'I'm sorry it took me so long, but I'm here now. You're my world, Carys. What do you think?' I say, wanting to ask her a million more questions but I know that she just needs the one.

The cameras are approaching, I can tell. We are running out of time, and I worry that this small window that Peony and I forced through is closing.

'Dolly,' she begins. 'You've made me realise so much about myself. And now it's time for me to be honest.'

Her words are a little stilted, and I see with horror that she's still wearing the show microphone. They can hear everything she says.

The stable door is open and the horse has bolted because no matter what happens, my speech to Carys has been recorded by the show. There'll be no backup of Warren and me marrying later, if this all goes truly tits up. It'll be out there, that this happened. Everyone will know when this airs. There's no way they'll leave it out.

It's a weird kind of peace that comes over me. I guess the relief of letting go of a lie you were imprisoning yourself with. Yes, I'm a lesbian and now the world knows.

But that doesn't have to happen to her.

'Carys, you don't have to say anything,' I insist, cutting her off. 'You don't have to say anything. Not for me. Choose *yourself*. This doesn't have to be your moment.'

I look behind us, and I see a cameraman approaching us. The wedding party is running across the grass to us too – Warren, Patrick, Peony, their families, and for some reason the officiant who is absolutely having the worst day of her life. Reb stands in the middle of the lawn by the lake watching us, silent.

'Carys—'

I want her to run away. I want to free her from this moment, even if it means she won't pick me. The last thing I want is for her to be forced into this.

'Please—'

'I am choosing myself,' she says. And there, I see the small smile growing on her lips. 'It's time. I want to be honest about who I am.'

'Are you sure?' I whisper, even though I know it's quite possible she might be about to be honest about what's happened between us and still say she doesn't want to be with me.

'I'm bisexual. And I'm autistic,' she says, and I hear some surprised murmuring from the team behind us. 'I'm both, and I've always been both and I'm done hiding all the more complicated parts of me just for everyone else's comfort. I'm done being palatable.'

I'm so proud of her. She's lit with the golden sunlight that streams down from above, like she's on fire. An angel on earth.

I am so fucking proud to know her.

There's movement behind me and Carys raises a hand. 'I'm not done.'

She turns back to me, and I can't help the thrill of hope in my chest.

'I choose myself,' she repeats. 'But also I want to choose you. Dolly, you've shown me exactly who I can be. You've seen the real me, the worst parts, the scary parts, and you've not been afraid. Well, perhaps a little.'

I laugh and it's a happy, sobbing sound. 'Just a bit. I never knew how fast you were. You made me do cardio; terrifying.'

I step forward, one moment at a time on painful feet that I barely notice because I'm radiating with joy.

'For a long time, I thought compatibility was just being identical, but I understand now that it's not just that. It's about understanding each other, trusting each other. I don't always understand you, but I want to, so much.'

A sob lodges in my throat.

'I love you, Dolly Doherty,' she whispers, just for me. 'You're my golden Goddess. You're the kindest person I've ever known, and will go to every length to protect your people. You're the woman who can see through every wall I try to hide behind. And I want to show you it all, forever. Nobody is going to love anyone like we love each other. We might be liars, but we can be something much more to each other. I think, together, we could make a perfect team. You feel like a home to me, Dolly. Will you be my home?'

'Always,' I promise.

And then, she throws herself into my arms.

Our kiss is a promise, and just for us, even if I know it's being filmed. I don't care. She is all I've ever wanted, and I can't believe that I now have her.

My girl. My home.

When we break apart, Carys has a mischievous look on her face. 'Shall we ... get married while we're here?'

I almost drop her. 'You want to—?'

'Sorry, your mum isn't here. That was silly.'

'Oh, she is!' shouts Warren, waving his phone. 'Her Uber's pulling up in ten minutes.'

'Iesu Grist,' Carys gasps. 'How much was that?'

'Warren, you didn't,' I cry.

'Moira insisted,' he says. 'I'll go get everyone back inside.' And with that he sprints off, corralling confused family and friends.

That's when I realise Patrick and Peony are also here, standing by the cameras.

'I think,' I say, putting Carys down carefully, 'that you have some things to talk about first.'

Chapter Forty

Carys

My heart is still racing from all the ill-advised running and declarations and kissing I've done in the last few minutes.

I can't believe what's happened, what's happening.

My sisters stand behind the cameraman dancing and laughing and are so full of the joy that I feel within my own heart.

But there's one last thing I need to do.

'Hi,' I say to Patrick and Peony as I walk over. 'Sorry, what a way to meet for the first time.'

'Well, it's kind of my fault,' Peony says, offering her hand for me to shake. I take it because, well, why not shake hands with your future ex-fiancé's ex-girlfriend-slash-future fiancée. 'I rather fucked up your wedding. But it seems like maybe it was for the best?'

I look at Patrick, and I can see the hurt and confusion there, muddled among the relief. 'Can I borrow your boyfriend for a moment?' I ask Peony, who flushes a little at the word, but it feels right to be honest about the situation. 'I promise I won't try to marry him again.'

To my relief, they both share a smile. 'That would be quite a pickle,' chortles Peony.

Patrick and I walk back over to the folly, and we sit on the parapet together, away from everyone else.

Well, except the cameras. But our entire romantic relationship has been on film; why not the end too?

'You heard all that, huh?' I say.

'Most of it, yeah,' he replies. 'It ... explains a lot.'

'Which bit?'

'All of it really. I knew ... well, not that you weren't happy, but that there was a part of you I couldn't access, perhaps.'

I squirm a little. 'I didn't realise it was so obvious.'

'I think only under those circumstances, the pressure cooker of it all. I'm sorry that you couldn't—'

'No, Patrick,' I insist. 'It's not your fault. We're just two strangers who thought they fell in love with each other.'

His mouth flattens. 'I think you're right. Despite all that, I loved getting to know you, Carys.'

'Patrick?'

'Yes.'

'Let's not get married. I adore you, I really do. And I know that I could fall in love with you if we stayed together.'

'I feel that too.'

'But we both have people here who we are *already* in love with, people we want to spend our lives with.' Patrick and I turn to where Peony and Dolly wait anxiously. 'I know she's really important to you.'

'She is,' he whispers. 'And I screwed it up so awfully. That's why I came on the show, to try again, I suppose. I'm so sorry I wasn't honest about that.'

'We both had a lot going on. You got your do-over. Do you want to use our wedding? It's going spare.'

'I couldn't.'

'You *should*.'

'I haven't asked her.'

'So ask her!' shouts Dolly, her hands cupped around her mouth.

We both look over, and Peony doesn't blush, doesn't hide away. She waits for him to notice that that's what she's here for.

'I should ask her,' he whispers, not taking his eyes from her for a second.

I pat him on the shoulder and slip off my engagement ring. I place it in the palm of his hand. 'Go ask her.'

He does. Patrick gets down on one knee holding out the ring to her, and I think about that moment in the city farm where he did the same to me.

She accepts, because of course she does. The ring even fits her, like it's magic.

I realise, as he stands and they kiss, that their suits match. Like it was supposed to be this way all along.

Needless to say, the rest of the Stringer family look particularly pleased that he is marrying Peony and not me. We all trudge back to the venue, where our collective guests sit in their pews as before.

This time, I take position as Patrick's best woman.

It's not strange; it feels right. We barely notice the cameras as they share vows they make up on the spot, but feel so real.

In the front row, next to my family, Warren, Dolly's mum, Cousin Jas and Auntie Carol, sits Dolly.

My Dolly.

'And I now pronounce you man and wife. You may kiss the bride,' Jane declares, still rather confused about the whole affair, and everyone cheers when they kiss.

'Now,' Peony says to me, as they break apart, 'your turn.'

'Oh no,' mutters Jane. 'There's protocol. You've already had one wedding.'

'It's alright,' I say. 'This was perfect.'

'No, actually, I would quite like to marry you,' says Dolly, standing up. 'You did ask, and I didn't get the chance to say yes, so this is me saying yes, with my mother as my witness.'

'But I don't know what the rules are. If we can't, that's fine!' I say to Jane.

'I think you should,' insists Patrick.

'Do you need a witness? I'll witness,' peeps Moira.

'Me too,' says my mum, which nearly knocks me out. I had been too scared to look their way, but they're here still, aren't they. My parents may not always understand me, but they showed up. They stayed.

'I don't think it's a legally binding ceremony, is it?' adds Del.

'Well, you can't get married in here,' insists Jane, a little awkwardly. 'You only paid for one ceremony, I'm afraid.'

'What about outside?' I ask. 'On the lawns?'

'You can't get married without a celebrant. Or on the lawn. Legally.'

'Oh, come on, Jane,' groans Ang. 'Help us out here.'

To my surprise, Reb stands up from the back of the room. 'Actually, I'm ordained. I could marry you.'

'Reb!' I gasp. 'You would?'

'I'd love to.'

I understand this is an apology for everything she couldn't do, everything she didn't understand at the time, and I forgive her.

'It wouldn't be legal,' sighs Jane.

'We'll do that after,' Dolly insists. 'We've done everything else the wrong way round. Why not this?'

I step down off the altar and take her by the hand, and together we all go out onto the lawns, families and friends together.

Reb leads the way.

My uni friends and their husbands look, let's just say, quite baffled but then we've not been close for a while. Perhaps they're realising that now. Either way, I wouldn't be here if it wasn't for them, in a way. They walk, in their couples, out with us.

Warren wheels Moira in her wheelchair with practised hands, though the poor man has to bend over quite far to reach the handles.

Ang and Del animatedly talk to my parents, in what I suspect is a quick run-down of not just the events of the last few weeks, but why exactly their daughter is marrying a woman despite going on a heterosexual dating show.

Jas takes Dolly's phone and calls Whit and Malachi so they can watch, and Whit manages to add Lina in too.

Victor and Shreya follow along, like they've always been part of this world of mine.

Everyone carries stacks of chairs, or flowers ripped from the altar. Even Jane helps, even though she makes sure to tut enough that we know she doesn't approve.

Our love is surrounded by love.

In the middle of the lawn, I marry my nemesis, my liar, the woman who helped me see who I really am and, importantly, wasn't afraid of that Carys.

It turns out that Victor is right. My wife is someone who challenges me, who sees who I really am.

Under the protection of my Goddess of Wrath, I can be anyone. I can be *me*.

Maybe it's silly to not think about the future, the long distance, the things we are giving up, but I don't care.

I don't care, because I'm free.

I found freedom in Dolly Doherty's heart, and I plan to live here forever.

Epilogue, Six Months Later

Dolly

> **@mirivanilli:** Leonard's fave couple is Dolly and Carys obvs, @saraaaa agrees bc he always makes biscuits on us when they're on screen
>
> **@ShreyaSpeaks:** It's so strange seeing myself on screen, but what a joy to be there to cheer on love!
>
> **@BabyJas:** No guys I'm not spilling the tea, you have to tune in with the rest of us. But yes Warren and I have some more content coming up lol.

If I'm honest, I was a little afraid of the reunion episode. Back when I was still with Warren, I had this whole plan of how we'd talk about our relationship. I pretty much knew, beat for beat, what highlight clips they'd show of our relationship timeline.

In fact, what I imagined is very like the reel of Whit and Malachi's best bits we all watch together in the studio, along with the live audience filled with fans, family and, apparently, the Hannahs, as the Nguyens orchestrate the whole affair.

'Let's hear it for our incredible season one winners!' Karina cries.

We all knew they'd win. We were discouraged from

checking social media in the apartments, but realistically production couldn't stop us, and I'd seen the glowing adoration for them across not just TikTok and Instagram, but Facebook too. The nest egg was theirs, quite rightly. They ended up being the only couple who really did things the *Wedded Bliss* way.

I shouldn't have been afraid. Beside me, my wife (I will never get over saying that) squeezes my hand.

'She is just the most wonderful, kind partner, and I'm so thankful that I left this show with her,' Malachi swoons, still as in love with her as the day they met.

It's funny, a few people have asked me if you really can fall in love in just a few weeks and I think, for most people, the answer is no. But Whit and Malachi are proof that love at first sight, while rare, is real.

'And we have a surprise to share,' Whit says. I naturally know what's coming as she stands, turns sideways and essentially mic drops her baby bump to the camera.

'We're pregnant!' they chorus, as the studio goes wild. Even me, and I knew the second she got those lines on the pee-covered stick.

Karina bursts into happy tears. 'Our first *Wedded Bliss* UK baby!'

Baby Vempati-Campbell was a bit of a surprise, but the parents-to-be rolled with it. I know there's never an ideal time for surgeons to take maternity leave, but if anyone can handle the competitive nature of the operating theatre, it's Whit. She survived *Wedded Bliss*, after all. Malachi's kept on his orthodontist job and put his long-term plan of firefighting on the back burner until the baby is a little older, but he's still training. I guess his dream job pales in comparison to his dream wife.

Bridget and Jackson get a much frostier welcome. We've had to say hello to them a few times at various events, but they know they blew it with everyone here. Once news of Bridget's blackmail spread through the various reality TV ex-castmate WhatsApp groups, they were pretty much ostracised.

'Your first year has been a bit of a challenge, hasn't it,' offers Lucas generously.

Jackson snorts. 'We got slandered on social media because people *think* for some reason that we were together before the show, but the thing is people can fake things. Deep fakes, isn't that what it's called? We're the actual victims here, aren't we, Bridge?'

'There's definitely two Deep Fakes here,' mutters Whit, which earns some *ooos* from the audience.

'Um,' murmurs Bridget, as the screen behind them shows screenshots of their text messages going back prior to the show. 'Yeah.'

Carys is stiff beside me, and I put my arm around her. It was worse for her – Bridget was supposed to be her friend. Bridget has tried to speak to her a few times, reaching out to make up via text and stuff, but I'm proud to say Carys has stood her ground and ignored her. You don't come back from threatening to out someone, even if you didn't really think that's what you were doing.

'We take that kind of allegation very seriously on *Wedded Bliss*,' Lucas says sternly. 'But we're glad to see that you're still wedded, if not that blissfully?'

About three people in the audience clap. Malachi coughs.

Karina nudges Lucas in the side. 'All marriages have their ups and downs, and we hope that you are able to find a good place again. Thank you for joining us, Bridget and Jackson.'

Was it worth it, ding-dongs? All that blackmail for this little screentime?

'Speaking of ups and downs, what a rollercoaster it is to see Lina and Cobey together!' Lucas cries as the cameras pan to the couple looking both very tanned and trim.

'Our runaway bride!' says Karina, clapping her hands together.

'Cobey, the thing we need to know – how is the surf school going?' Lucas asks and the audience laughs knowingly. Cobey has become something of a meme, but from what Lina tells me, that's just spread the word about the business.

After their elopement to Scotland, and the many interviews on the media circuit that seemed to keep the big bods at Sunset Motions happy, Lina moved down to Cornwall to be with Cobey, combining their Pilates and surf school businesses into a very cool wellness venture for stressed-out city women.

'All the better for having this incredible woman and business partner with me.' Cobey kisses his wife, and the audience whoops with delight.

'Though, of course, your ex-fiancé Zack was left surprised by your disappearance at the joint stag and hen party. He couldn't make it today, but is there anything you'd like to say to him?' Karina asks.

'Nothing to him, no,' Lina says. She looks straight down the lens of a camera. 'But to other women, even if you like someone, if you don't like the things they say, the things they do, you can leave. That can be enough.'

'Wise words,' Karina agrees, as the audience applauds and nods and a few people tear up.

I'm glad Zack didn't show up. I heard through the grapevine that he was invited and was giving it all gob about 'starting shit', but I think he knew this would have been a bloodbath. Perhaps he's got more sense than I give him credit for.

'And now, we turn to the shock of the season. Two break-ups, two marriages and one singleton, but somehow not in the combination that any of us expected,' Karina announces. 'First, let's welcome Patrick and Peony!'

Peony had been kept off-screen for the first bit of filming, as she wasn't known to the audience. This is her grand entrance, in the same glorious green suit, twinned by Patrick who escorts her to an empty sofa.

'Golly, it's a bit strange being on camera, isn't it?' she laughs, charming an audience who could have been totally set against her. But with the melodic chime of her laugh, everyone is enrapt.

The Nguyens explain Peony and Patrick's backstory, showing photos on the screen of the couple through the years. It's quite sweet, really.

'I think people might be surprised to hear that we didn't move in together immediately,' Patrick admits.

'Though, I *was* still in Kenya,' laughs Peony.

'Hell of a commute!' adds Patrick. It's rehearsed, but it works. They're a comedy duo of awkward brunettes.

'We just wanted to get it right this time,' Peony insists.

A couple of months ago, Peony finished her secondment and moved back to Newcastle, and Patrick joined her up there. They've got this beautiful house with a big garden they're going to fill with wonky animals and elfin children. Carys has been up there twice already as she was insistent about helping them unpack, and we'll go again together later this year. Turns out, Peony is an eager cook, so I've promised to teach her some of my skills when I'm up.

And now, it's our turn.

'With Patrick marrying Peony, Carys was left alone. But in a first for *Wedded Bliss*, Carys and Dolly ended up in our first ever same-gender couple! Let's see how that played out.'

So it turns out the whole time I was paranoid about cameras, I needn't have been. There weren't hidden cameras, for once, because the show had about ten quid left by the time they'd furnished the warehouse and apartments. Reb let slip that there were security cameras in important places, but that mysteriously, footage from several cameras had been deleted for some reason definitely not by her nope no way. She's a good egg but I wish she'd get a new job.

Still, the show did manage to pick up quite a lot of our lingering looks and, in the context of us falling in love, the editors managed to stitch together a pretty solid timeline of our relationship. It ends with shaky camera footage racing through a garden to find us kissing at the folly.

We were both frightened about what would happen next, but after a lot of terse discussions, the show decided that if they made Patrick and Peony an official *Wedded Bliss* couple, they had to recognise us too. In the end, the queer community came out in force and voted us into second place, the only part of my plan that remained the same.

'Now, we've never had a romance like this before,' says Lucas. 'And we had Lina escape out of a window!'

'Plenty has been said on social media about your relationship,' says Karina carefully, and boy, she's not kidding. My followers' count has had more ups and downs than Alton Towers, losing a bunch of homophobes and gaining all the gays of the UK. Somehow, I seem to have kept pretty much all of my beloved Nigella-wanting middle-aged men contingent.

'What do you want to say about your first year so far?' she finishes.

'I love her,' I say, which weirdly gets a lot of applause, but then how often do you see women say they love each other romantically on television, even now? 'She's very supportive, even when she's having a tough time. And she's had a pretty tough time from some of youse.'

Carys nudges me. She always worries when I go protective bulldog mode.

'It's been tricky,' she says diplomatically. 'But it's been really lovely connecting with the autistic community, and the queer community finally. There's hard stuff but I've felt the support too.'

'People need to quit with the *bisexuals are always cheaters thing*, though,' Whit says, sitting up a little straighter.

'But she did cheat on Patrick, so maybe that's deserved,' snips Bridget.

I am about to leap over and beat her with my shoe, seemingly along with most of the audience who boo Bridget.

'I made mistakes. We all did,' Carys says. To Patrick's credit, he even nods here. 'I've been working on myself in therapy and, it's no excuse, but—' She takes a breath. 'My entire understanding of self was warped. You don't know how to make a good decision when that's what you're working with. What's a moral compass when you don't know which way North is?'

'I'm glad I got to be one of your mistakes, though,' I insist, and the audience takes the bait and cheers, drowning Bridget's protestations.

'Give it a rest, Bridget,' snaps Lina, which might be the most surprising moment of the night. 'Patrick forgave her, didn't you?'

Patrick startles as he realises he's being addressed. 'Oh yes!'

'Focus on your own flop of a marriage,' Lina says, and Bridget storms out, slowly followed by Jackson, trying to keep his composure.

I love gobby Lina. She's found so much more confidence now she's bossing around children and adults into impossible shapes on land and sea.

'Can I just say,' Carys begins, her voice wobbling, 'I think everyone expects me to be a spokesperson on autism and bisexuality, and I'm not ready for that. The people who do stand up and give advice are amazing and have helped me so, so much. But I'm not sure that's really me, or who I want to be either. I need to focus on understanding myself.'

I'm really proud of her for resisting that too. I think she felt some pressure, inadvertently, from me talking a lot about my endometriosis online. I even met with hospitals in Merseyside, a few MPs and some charities to talk about the chronic underfunding and constant misunderstanding people with endometriosis get. But that's because it's something I want to do, not something I was pushed into.

Plus, endometriosis might rule my body with creepy little lesions, but it's not as central to self as autism is for Carys. There's historical hysterical stigma, but also I'm a gobby shite, so it's way easier for me.

'Just leave her alone with her goats, is what we're saying,' I add.

Saying all that, I've seen her unfold, more and more, over the past few months. That Carys I used to see glimpses of comes out all the time, and she's been working hard on her own boundaries. I've been listening and learning about how best to support her.

I don't think she'll be able to drop all of her mask always and forever, but part of my job is to create a safe place where she doesn't need to, and help her recover when she has had to mask. Guided by her, of course.

The fiddly little tea dresses remain, for now, but she's started experimenting a bit more with her fashion, how she presents herself. I got a jumpscare a few months ago when I found her in one of my old plaid shirts and jeans, but she looked so happy. I didn't even know Carys knew where to buy jeans.

But it all builds up to a new Carys, or rather, the Carys she wants to be.

It took a few months, but Carys got a job working on a city farm in Liverpool where she's pretty much running the educational side of things. I've seen her light up when she goes to work, and even though autism means it drains her battery quicker than it would an allistic person, she loves it.

She got a flat, near to Mum's house, and I'm splitting time between the two for now, while we work out what our family setup is going to look like long term. Hopefully a house big enough for us all, with a ground floor bedroom and bathroom for Mum.

'Well, we at *Wedded Bliss* are extremely proud to stand with the queer community, and are pleased to say we are nominated for several inclusivity awards!' says Karina gleefully, because well, of course they have. I'm not really sure they earned it given everything, but there we go.

'Dolly,' begins Lucas and I know what's coming. 'Would you like to respond to accusations that your relationship with Warren was faked?'

I have this answer pre-prepared. 'I'd say excuse me, have you looked at him? No one can resist his charm.' It's what Carys calls my fairy answer — there's no lies, but no truths about me either.

The audience falls for it, cheering and wolf whistling and generally throwing themselves at Warren's size 14 feet.

'Wow, we've got some Warren fans in tonight!' cries Karina.

The camera focuses on his face, and Warren laughs, looks right down the lens and says, 'Hello.'

The audience goes wild again, even though he's just right there.

'You and Dolly have gone from success to success with your content online, including your series *Teaching My Ex to Cook* and *Teaching My Ex Basketball*,' Lucas says, clearly reading the series titles off the teleprompter.

'The response has been mad. Like these guys,' he laughs, thumbing at the audience who take the cue to scream their desire at him again. God, he's good, and he *loves* it. I wasn't wrong about him doing well post-breakup, and he was bang on correct about the heartbroken lover playing perfectly for him. The man was getting panties mailed to his management's office!

I would say we've been incredibly lucky, but really *I* have been incredibly lucky, not only that we've done so well, but that we're still peas in a pod. Travelling around Mum's care isn't always easy, so he comes up to Liverpool on his days off to film and be bossed around.

'It's been so amazing, and we can film content around my games schedule, as I'm back playing for the London Phoenixes – come see us play, people!' The screen behind Warren shows footage from some of their last games, of a sweaty, toned Warren running around and looking godly. 'And, I think it's alright for me to share that Dolly and I are in talks to bring our concepts to *other* screens, if you know what I mean.'

There's quite a lot of excitement in the audience, which is great news, because our cooking show has already been greenlit. It's wild that we still get to follow our dreams as friends.

'Has it been hard, working with the woman you thought you'd marry?' Lucas asks, clutching a hand over his heart.

Warren adopts what Carys calls his heartbreaker face. It reminds me of boyband music videos when they're trying to be a bit deep and sad. 'It was hard, to begin with. But I still have Dolly as my very best friend, and that love I had for her has morphed to the most wonderful platonic relationship we could ever have dreamed of. She's my work-wife!'

I blow him a kiss as the audience goes gooey for him. Oh, he's getting a few numbers tonight.

'I think I'll be ready to open my heart to someone else soon,' he adds, just to seal the deal. Squeals of excitement echo through the room, and I spy Priya in the audience sit up a little straighter.

Filming flies by, but I'm so unfazed by it now. Anything is comparatively easy now I'm fully clothed; no one expects me to wear bikinis or fishnet bodysuits any more. Or at least, I hope.

Lucas looks straight into the camera, ready to close out the episode. 'We hope that you'll join us ... for season two! That's right, *Wedded Bliss* is coming back. Will it be as chaotic as season one?'

I wonder if we'll get to speak to any of the next generation of Blissfuls before they get in, not that I have much advice to give other than don't go in if you're a lesbian. Or well, maybe they'll get lucky and fall in love like I did. Can lightning strike twice?

'Half of me hopes so, and half hopes not. Perhaps less wife-swapping this time?' laughs Karina, and I can't help but join in.

It's been a weird experience, and not one I'd repeat, except if I hadn't gone through all that pain, anxiety and performance, I'd never have met my wife. Silver linings, in every turd cloud.

I turn to my beautiful Carys, my world, and kiss her on the cheek. After this, we can do all our favourite things – lying down, eating takeaway in bed and watching the same TV shows over and over. My favourite thing of all is just being with her.

That's true bliss, really.

ACKNOWLEDGEMENTS

Writing this book was a feat, in a year of major transition where I released three books, wrote two, bought a house and moved into it, and lowkey broke my brain, alongside about twelve other major life decisions that left me all crumply like an old autumn leaf. I basically got through it all thanks to many of the people listed here, and lots more.

First thanks go to my agent Abi Fellows who is always at the end of a text to discuss bisexual and lesbian reality television chaos, and who will have been my enthusiastic champion for nearly seven years (!!) by the time *Reality Check* is out.

Making the jump to a new publisher is always scary, but I've been welcomed with open arms. Thank you to Molly Crawford for your incredible enthusiasm for this book when it was just ideas on a page and for bringing me into the Simon & Schuster family. We will never not find twelve tangents to talk about and I love that about us.

Everyone else at Simon & Schuster I've worked with have been absolute angels: Misha, Sabah, Harriett, Kate, Katie, and the legend that is SJV. Thank you for giving my chaotic stories and self a home.

I'm blessed to have lots of pals who've supported me in writing this book, and particularly through a bad batch of seizures alongside it. I am too terrified to list everyone because then I'll miss people (yes, I know, it's a copout). But some special thanks go to Lola, Ash, Darran, Katherine, Faridah, Bea, Beth, Laura, Griff, Zohra, Tazmyn and Debbie for pepping or helping me exactly when I needed it. The Murder Cat Gang (Jade, Greg, Lucy, Steffie, Tim, Stacey, Adam, Mollie, Sammy and Lilith) deserve a lot of thanks, too.

I'm very thankful to have friends who are equally as obsessed with dissecting reality television as I am, who helped me think about *Wedded Bliss* as a show. Thanks to all the members of Casa Amor (with three rs) aka Ash (and Molly the gender-affirming dog), Anika, Elle, Emer, Jade, Megan, Meghan, Nikky, Ravena and Steffie for signing on for our six-nights-a-week discussions. Thanks also to Mollie, Bea, Fiona, Fubar and Robin for other various chats and recommendations.

A few other assorted but important thanks: Thank you to Hari Connor and TJ Alexander who went briefly mad with me on Bluesky trying to work out what to call the 'big columny thing' aka something that looks like the Temple of Apollo at Stourhead. Thank you to Lucy Saxon who heard me talking about this book and suggested the idea for the next book – next burrito's on me.

I owe so much to Elle McNicoll, my April-release-mate, romcom scholar and fellow autistic high priest, for reminding me why I do this, every time I have a little wobble. It's probably time for another debrief over tea.

As ever, my friend-family Alice and Lauren King who keep me going with silly drinks and BBQs and also telling us to buy the house that we now live in. Lewisburg forever.

Thank you to my sister Julie and brother-in-law James for driving me round basically every bookshop in Massachusetts. I wrote a chunk of this at their house, hanging with my niblings after school, and honestly it is a delight to create stories about love and acceptance and being your true self surrounded by family. Thank you to the rest of my family for generally putting up with the chaos and many books (my own and otherwise).

I always say thank you to Nerys for being my constant writing companion, but much of this book was written curled up with Suki and Ammy too. Biccies all round.

Throughout it all, my incredible partner Tim kept me going, ensured the words kept coming on days I wanted them to, and helped me rest when I needed it. One particular day, he literally picked me up, washed my hair and taped up my sore limbs for me, because I couldn't. I write disabled love stories because I am lucky enough to experience it every single day. Thank you for being my home.

FURTHER READING

I've been a scholar of reality television (or unscripted entertainment programming) my whole life, for better or worse. Writing about one of my biggest special interests was *always* on the cards, and I'm so thankful I got to.

To beef out my knowledge of the systems, history and design of the various shows I know and love, I did quite a lot of research.

Here are a few things I particularly enjoyed – as one might expect, many dive into the darker sides of reality television so please check the content warnings where relevant.

- *Out of the Pods* podcast with Deepti Vempati and Natalie Lee
- *Unreal: A Critical History of Reality TV* podcast with Pandora Sykes and Sirin Kale
- Ashley Norton's entire *Bachelor Nation* series on YouTube, but especially her episode on *Bachelor in Paradise*
- *The Unreal World* Substack by Leigh Alexander and her various works on reality television and narrative design
- *Cue the Sun! The Invention of Reality TV* by Emily Nussbaum

- *Bachelor Nation* by Amy Kaufman
- *Edge of Reality* by Jacques Peretti

Additionally, writing Carys' experiences of compulsory heterosexuality was bolstered by the incredible *Thank You For Calling the Lesbian Line* by Elizabeth Lovatt.